THE CONFIDENT HOPE

Also by E. C. Jackson

A Gateway to Hope
A Living Hope
The Certain Hope
Pajama Party: The Story

THE CONFIDENT HOPE

a novel

E. C. Jackson

ISBN: 978-1-7329592-2-4

Editing: amberbarryeditor.com and angela.trent@sbcglobal.net
Cover design: FormattingExperts.com
Typesetting: FormattingExperts.com
Book blurb: angela.trent@sbcglobal.net

The Write Way – A Real Slice of Life: https://ecjacksonauthor.com
Author Page: facebook.com/ecjacksonauthor

Acknowledgments

My fifth book, book four of the hope-themed series, is finally completed.

The scripture *"against all hope, Abraham in hope believed"* sustained me the entire time.

My family and friends supported me with prayers and encouragement during the two-year process. A huge thank you goes to my editors, book formatter and book cover designer.

I thank God for surrounding me with people who care about me and my books.

Whenever we pray, we always give thanks for you to God, the Father of our Lord Yeshua the Messiah. For we have heard of your trust in the Messiah Yeshua and of the love you have for all God's people. Both spring from the confident hope that you will receive what is stored up for you in heaven. You heard of this earlier in the message about the truth. This Good News has made its presence felt among you, just as it is also being fruitful and multiplying throughout the world in the same way as it has among you since the day you heard and understood the grace of God as it really is.

Colossians 1:3-6
Complete Jewish Bible (CJB)

Chapter One

Motes reflected in the sunlight that beamed through an eastern bedroom window. Background noise filtered past closed doors. Turning over in bed onto her stomach, Pamela Hayes yanked a beige satin comforter off the floor with one hand. That same hand then tossed a navy-blue neck pillow upon the bed. Footsteps on the other side of the door grabbed her attention.

Mom's on her Saturday-morning prowl. Five, four, three, two, one ...

Anna Hayes's head poked inside her daughter's bedroom. Hallway lighting bathed her trim figure in artificial brightness. "Morning, babe. Touching base before I go." Her warm gaze surveyed the tousled bed. "From the tangled cover, it looks like you had a rough night."

With a hand covering her yawn, Pamela shook her head and turned onto her side. "Just my normal Friday night tug-of-war. It's my preferred method of winding down."

Anna's soft laugh sounded like music. "Any special plans today?"

Leaning on her elbow, Pamela rested her face on spread fingers as she gazed at her mother. Forty-eight-year-old Anna wore desert-green ankle boots, cropped white pants, and an oversized olive-green sweater. A brown suede bag hung over her shoulder.

"You look like a dream, Mom. If I didn't know otherwise, I'd think you were going out with someone special."

Laughter flitted through slightly parted lips. "I'm late. Give me a quick rundown on your activities for today."

Oh boy. I had hoped she wouldn't ask. Better mention my afternoon expedition last.

"Shopping for a spring wardrobe around noon. My jeans are tatty. And then, shooting the rapids."

The door opened wider as Anna grasped the doorknob. "Water rafting somewhere near South Town?"

"Oklahoma City. The spring season begins today. It's safe, Mom. Stop frowning."

"I'm sure they take safety precautions. But promise to be extra careful. I can do without mental pictures of my twenty-five-year-old daughter drowning."

Pamela flopped onto her back. "Yes, ma'am."

"Thank you. I love surrender whenever I hear it." Anna checked her watch. "I'll be out late. Don't hesitate to call if you need me."

After those parting words, her mother floated out of the house. Her all-day Saturday excursions had begun late last year. A seeming whim had developed into a lengthy pattern.

After the front door lock clicked, a sleepy Pamela hid her head beneath the sheets and immediately fell back to sleep.

* * *

Fully dressed, Pamela sat at the kitchen table picking single oats out of her favorite cereal bowl. She had eaten breakfast from the same dish since high school.

She snapped the milk carton closed. As she stuffed a heaping spoonful of cereal into her mouth, the doorbell rang. Her eyebrows arched. Who visited people unannounced at nine thirty-six on a Saturday morning? Her brother Skylar and his wife Melinda used their key when they visited. Was Anna expecting a package she hadn't mentioned to Pamela?

As Pamela reached the front door, she put one eye up to the peephole. "Ack. Ack. Ack. Ahem." She patted her chest, swallowing the stuck food. Mark Simon, wearing a hoodie and with his hands stuffed inside jean pockets, faced away from the door. He glanced at his car, then at his shoes. When a tremor shook his body, he perused the cloudless sky until concentrating on his feet again.

Pamela knew Mark seldom visited anybody's house, especially on weekends. He saved his free time for an abominable woman. But today, something had gotten the Saturday late-sleeper out of bed before noon—and over to her house. Pamela bet it wasn't because of a sudden, unshakeable desire to visit his friend.

She blew air through pursed lips and wrapped her arms around her body. *Here we go. Lights. Camera. Action.*

She unlocked and opened the door, leaning on the doorframe. "Welcome. I'm surprised to see you. Glad you stopped by."

2

"Is your mother home? We can grab breakfast out if she is." Hooded eyelids hid his pupils.

From his demeanor, Pamela knew this wasn't a "let me cool off a moment" visit. Mark required sympathetic ears.

Pamela could tell her lazy morning was quickly going to morph into a difficult afternoon—and possibly an unsettled evening. Golden toasted oats soaked in her milk-filled bowl. Her visions of shopping for a new spring wardrobe evaporated. Water rafting waved goodbye.

Mark rang Pamela's doorbell whenever his life turned upside down. On those days, he remembered his go-to sounding board. Eleven years of friendship. Might as well invite her pal indoors and forget about her heartbreak when he says how much he loves Jessica.

"You missed Mom by two hours. Lately she spends Saturdays with friends." Mark glanced everywhere except at her face.

She hadn't seen him anguished before. Angry, numerous times; distraught, not once.

"Ooh, casual clothes. You haven't worn a hoodie and sneakers since college." She stole another look. Gucci sneakers.

Hands stuffed inside his pockets, Mark shrugged. "We only see each other on our afternoon lunch dates during the week. Then, I'm always in business attire." Head held back, his vacant gaze touched her heart. Tears pooled in the corners of each of Mark's eyes.

Pamela couldn't stay detached when friends cried for help. She could tell that Jessica Hubbard had either cheated on Mark or said goodbye. The writing had been on the wall three years earlier, on the day the couple met. Yet just this past Thursday, Mark had told Pamela he'd purchased an engagement ring for Jessica. Did Jessica reject Mark's marriage proposal? If she had, he should consider himself lucky to have avoided a disastrous marriage.

She waved him in with a finger. "Come in. Stay awhile." She thought about her now-soggy cereal. "Eat breakfast with me. I was eating when the doorbell rang."

When he stepped inside, she locked the door and headed down the hall. They had small talk as they made their way to the kitchen.

He trailed her steps into the room, frowning at the oversized bowl. "Your bowl looks overloaded. Your cereal almost spilled on the table."

"Join me for breakfast," Pamela said, searching for ways to lift Mark's spirit.

3

The silent man still looked everywhere except at her. Shoulders drooping, his shiny gaze finally captured hers.

From his obvious distress, Pamela realized the romance had ended. Jessica must have done the dumping.

Oh, Mark. I'm sorry she called it off instead of you.

"Want anything to eat?" she asked as he turned away.

"No, thanks." Leaning on the counter, he pointed at her bowl. "Still habit-driven. You're eating the same things for breakfast from the same bowl and wearing your hair in a ponytail like you did in your teens." Mark grinned when she glanced at him. "That's not criticism. Just an honest observation. Please, eat."

"Mom sets our clocks by my actions." She glanced at the milk carton, cereal box, and honey. Tidy, tidy. Everything must occupy a designated place.

Pamela returned the milk carton to the refrigerator and the cereal box and honey to the pantry.

"Grab a seat while I finish eating."

She scooped up a spoonful of mushy cereal. The texture was awful. Her body shuddered as she stared at the spoon.

"I'm unfit company this morning," Mark said with a sigh. "My loyal friend deserves better."

Pamela could tell Mark would stay until her mother arrived home. She plopped her full spoon into the bowl. A distraught Mark was interrupting her plans once again.

She shoved the milk-logged mess aside.

"I'm here when you need me," she said. "What happened?"

He slumped on the stool. "Only if you continue eating. I interrupted your breakfast."

"Hold on while I fix myself a fresh bowl. Take a seat at the table. I'll be right back."

Pamela felt his gaze follow her movements until she joined him at the table.

"I'll get to the crux of the problem." Head lowered, he poured his heart out while she ate.

Leaning back into the chair, he fished a ring from his pocket. Last week, Mark had shown Pamela a picture of an engagement ring over lunch as he talked about planning to propose to Jessica. The 18-karat, rose gold morganite ring with pavé diamonds had mesmerized Pamela. How much money had he

4

wasted on this unaccepted bribe to marry him?

Tears welled in his eyes. He kissed the stone then slid the ring across the table.

"Do with this bauble whatever you please," he said. "Last night the ungrateful cheater dismissed me and my gift. She's getting married next month."

"No, thank you. Disposing of the ring is your call." The stone glistened as she placed the ring into his palm and closed his hand. "Sell it in your father's pawn shop."

Mark should have been thanking God for liberation. He had allowed Jessica to use him. He should have seen this coming when the couple first met. Jessica had exposed her uncaring, contemptible, and unapologetic nature three years ago. How could he be shocked now?

At any rate, he should be happy his prison guard had set him free.

Mark had fallen in love with a narcissist instead of with his trusted friend. Choking back tears, Pamela reached across the table. She grasped Mark's hand and squeezed tight.

Chapter Two

Spring. One Year Later.

Elm branches performed rhythmic dances on the four corners of the entrance to West Gate subdivision. Bald cypress trees lined the road. Each day, the tree-lined, suburban street welcomed its residents back home. Two competing home styles, Spanish and modern, dominated the block. The large houses and fenced backyards promoted familial lifestyles.

Pamela gazed along the landscape until the black BMW pulled into a drive-way in a cul-de-sac. She studied Mark when he gave the punchline to a not-so-funny joke. His confident grin matched her excitement.

Chin high, shoulders back, his gaze surveyed the property line.

"Home sweet home."

His bride gnawed her bottom lip. She could feel a gentle breeze rifle her pixie curls.

He gripped her hand and placed it over his heart.

"You're a lifesaver, love. Last spring, a bruised man turned up on your doorstep. You took him in, held his hand, and turned his life around." His direct gaze searched her face until he kissed her fingers. "I want you by my side night and day. You're owed a debt I can't repay. But I'll live my life trying."

Heat flushed Pamela's body. Her heartbeat accelerated. The man she treasured gazed at her with love-filled eyes. Her rose, matte-polished fingernails pinched her thigh. Nope. Wide awake. Home at last.

Pamela faced the house the couple had fallen in love with at first sight. She and Mark had clasped hands before the real estate agent had turned into the driveway.

Three weeks were spent renovating the place. After the work concluded, her sister-in-law, Melinda, asked her interior decorator friend to stage the perfect dwelling. Mark lived in his condo until it sold. He moved into their house two weeks before the wedding. Although Pamela didn't move in at the time, she had brought over her belongings a few days before the wedding so they would be in place after the honeymoon.

Now she focused on the house she had adored at first sight. A sculptured landscape framed the couple's forever home. Several eastern redbud trees designated their property line on the east side. Manicured shrubs divided land on the west lawn. Natural slate tiles created the walkway. Rattan furniture and a wooden swing outfitted the spacious porch.

Her fingers clasped together. She sat in the car in front of her cherished house with her love match. Dreams really did come true. They had for her. She treasured spending their honeymoon in the Turks and Caicos, but Dorothy in *The Wizard of Oz* had nailed it: There is no place like home, especially one filled with love.

"Our home called to us in the Caribbean," Pamela said. "Except for church, nothing can blast me outside this house before Monday. Consider me a weekend couch potato." Rubbing her upper arms, she studied Mark. "We made it home. So now answer my question. You know which one I mean, so don't pretend otherwise."

"I'm a straightforward man who hates speculation. So, please ask me again." His wiggling lips stifled laughter.

"Stop laughing and answer my number one question since we married."

"Nah, I think you have a tie on five." His grin revealed teeth an orthodontist might advertise. "You asked multiple questions on our two-week vacation. So please, enlighten me."

Vacation? It was more than just a vacation; it was their honeymoon. Pamela pulled a loose thread on her blouse. Her voice dropped an octave lower. "The threshold. Will I walk across on my own? Or will my strong husband carry his bride inside? I vote you carry me inside."

"To keep them guessing is my number one ploy. Why should anyone show their hand too soon? Someone said yearning heightens anticipation."

"I dislike smokescreens coming from men wearing smirky grins. Let's bring a little unity into this conversation."

"Oh, Pamela, lighten up," Mark said. "Don't you like surprises?"

"Yeah. About as much as you enjoy playing guessing games."

A delicate floral fragrance wafted from the flowers in her lap. She fingered the yellow-rose bouquet. Mark had made two surprise stops on the way home from the airport: Toomey's Gourmet Steakburgers and Flowers for Every Occasion.

Her lips brushed a petal. "Of course, my present is excluded from my indictment against you. Thank you much."

Having stowed his sunglasses into the sunglass holder above the dashboard, he kissed her, slowly pulling back. "Glad to hear it. The trunk and back seat are loaded with stuff. Let's take this show inside. It'll take several trips to get everything."

The newlyweds exited the vehicle together. They stopped at the car's rear.

Mark pulled her close.

Pamela leaned into the quick kiss.

He handed her the overnight case. "I'll bring in the heavy stuff. Carry this bag and your flowers inside first."

A slammed door ripped the air. Heels clicked on brick steps.

Pamela's glance across the shrubbery almost stopped her heart.

She recognized the jean-clad, high-heeled woman. Her husband's old girlfriend, Jessica Prentis, marched down the walkway of the house next door to their home. Strained features and deliberate steps depicted a mission-minded woman.

This can't be happening. Not on the first day home from our honeymoon. Does she live close by?

Pamela's hand tightened around the suitcase handle.

Luggage and boxes were piled on the ground, in the car trunk, and in the rear seat. Mark examined their accumulated stash. "Too many boxes. We shopped more than I thought."

"Your ex-girlfriend is standing in the driveway next door. Wonder who she's visiting."

Mark's shrewd gaze appraised the scene. He appeared irritated, not surprised. "Forget her. Take this load inside. I'll bring in the rest of our gear." His voice softened. "Why don't you grab the food bags and set the food out. I won't take long."

Pamela rejected the request before his mouth closed. Hide from a possible conflict? Habitual retreat was a proven failure.

She stole another glance across the property line.

With her back turned toward them, the woman faced the garage.

Back at the car's passenger side, Pamela retrieved the copper vase filled with flowers. Fighting tears, she sniffed the blooms. The unexpected gift's appeal vanished. Eyes half closed, she inched up the walkway, hoping not to trip on level ground.

"I'll come back out to grab the food bags," she said.

Carrying three hefty suitcases, he kept in step beside her.

"You go on inside," he said. "I'll get the food in a minute, and you can set it out for us."

Pamela's involuntarily glance over her shoulder showed that Jessica hadn't moved. She occupied the same spot.

"She isn't an inanimate object," Pamela said. "Why doesn't she move?"

"Her movements don't concern us." Grinning, he nudged Pamela's temple with his head. "Go on. Take your load inside. Rest until I bring in the food. Four more trips, tops."

No one had dropped Jessica off. Jessica's footsteps started at the house before Pamela saw her walking. Where was she headed? The driveway and curb were empty. No vehicles were parked in either place.

Pamela's trembling legs felt like they were about to give out.

Remain calm.

Perhaps her old rival was visiting a family member or friend. Pamela sneaked a quick peek next door. Jessica pointed a device at the garage door and tapped her foot until it raised.

Pamela's knees buckled. Panic seemed justified. *Mark's old girlfriend lives next door.*

Now Jessica's sudden appearance seemed more curious than ever. No sane person walked outside their house to open their garage door.

A spiteful woman sending a message might take irrational measures.

Pamela slowly stepped onto the porch. Breathing deeply, she faced her neighbor's house. Mark had always claimed he never saw or spoke to Jessica once they broke up. Did he buy a house next door to Jessica on purpose? But how did he know she lived next door if they hadn't talked?

He had lied. Pure and simple. The worst part was Pamela's belief in him. *I could be wrong. Most people are when hurt feelings dominate their thoughts.*

Her agitated ideas roved all over the place while her breaths released in small gasps.

"I think she lives next door."

The talkative man turned unusually quiet. Either he didn't hear her, or he was pretending that he hadn't. Mark hustled to the car for more gear.

Mark had insisted they buy this house even though they couldn't afford it. He went into hock with his parents for the hefty down payment. Today's shenanigans put the unwise decision into perspective. He still loved a woman that had dumped him to marry another man.

More luggage was deposited on the porch. "Why are you still outside instead of inside the house?" Mark asked. He held out food bags Pamela ignored. "Jessica just wants attention. Why supply her with what she's after?"

He set Toomey's sacks on a glider, following her gaze past the lawn. Jessica glanced across the street, then entered the garage. He nodded at the front door. "Show's over. Please go inside."

"Go inside and miss the second act? No. You're making multiple trips. Get moving."

He retreated to the car, carrying back numerous boxes.

A vehicle started. Jessica backed a purple Jeep into the driveway. She stopped and tooted the horn.

Jessica's derisive gaze studied their faces. The woman's contempt turned mischievous. With a load balanced on one hand, Mark made that twiddling finger wave he often did. Laughing, Jessica extended her hand out the window. She mimicked the greeting. Mark's habit, which Pamela normally found endearing, incensed her in that moment. She closed her eyes then reopened them as Mark gave a cynical smile that matched their neighbor's sardonic grin.

Mark doesn't seem surprised to see her. He lived at our house for two weeks before our wedding. I don't know what to think. Has he been secretly seeing a married woman?

Pamela remembered the advice of people who warned her not to marry Mark. Sunlight reflecting off her wedding ring ensemble caught her attention. Too late for course changes. Her fate had been sealed two weeks before.

Pamela made both arms relax by her side. She disliked confrontations but stood her ground each time conflict rose. She had developed that habit during her freshman year in high school. She wasn't going to break it now.

Mark piled boxes on a bench and moved closer, wrapping an arm around her waist.

Jessica flipped hair off her face. She sat in the car, staring at them. A mocking grin replaced speculative features. "Hello, neighbors," she shouted. "I see the newlyweds found their way home. Those in the know said you took a week-long trip. Were you lost?" Her gaze never left her old boyfriend's face.

10

"It's difficult to leave paradise. We loved the Turks and Caicos. Extending our honeymoon was a no-brainer."

The ex-couple volleyed the conversation ball back and forth. Each second felt like a time bomb ticking within Pamela's heart. It was past time to learn her husband's explanation.

If Mark had deceived Pamela, their marriage was a sham.

Her legs were planted wide. Her body shook.

Don't explode. Wait until you go inside the house you once considered your home. Calm! Down! Let this mockery—if that's what it is—play out.

Soundless wisps of air escaped her closed lips. Anger anchored her feet to the porch.

When the conversation lulled, Mark repeated to Jessica the ridiculous joke he had told Pamela when they pulled up to the house.

Pamela's heart sank. She wouldn't fall apart or run and hide. Her husband's deceit degraded their home into a battlefield.

She knocked his arm from around her waist, set the flowers on a teak wood side table, and unlocked the front door. The answered threshold question sparked a tear avalanche. She walked alone into their forever home. Tears rolled down her cheeks as she crossed the entrance.

* * *

The copper vase filled with twelve yellow roses clanged on the nearest table. The overnight case plonked on the floor. Her gaze darted around the room. The house fulfilled their expectations, yet right now it failed to soothe her achy spirit. Their home lost its value after her faith in Mark had collapsed outdoors.

Her gaze was drawn to the mantelpiece over the fireplace.

On their wedding day, she had stopped by the house and set up an after-honeymoon surprise before driving on to the church. The threshold question had served a hidden purpose. Carrying her inside the house would slant Mark's body toward the fireplace so his post-wedding gift could become the focal point. Would the insufferable man notice her tribute?

Viewing her labor of love added tears to her eyes. How could she be so blind about his true intentions!

Her arms wrapped around her body as teardrops soaked her collar. Their fairytale wedding and storybook honeymoon had meant nothing special to Mark. Her trust in Mark had died on the porch. Last year a broken man had

11

arrived on her doorstep unannounced. Pamela had had to basically rearrange her life to breathe life into his existence. The ingrate should've been left outside last spring.

A loud crash penetrated through the walls. She scurried to the window and slid one slat of the blinds higher, peeking through its gap. Mark righted boxes that had tumbled off the bench. Jessica observed him from her spot beside the Jeep. Half their belongings still lay by the car. Undisturbed by her absence, Mark and Jessica's mating game intensified. His head tilted to the side, Mark wore a wide grin, and Jessica appeared mesmerized by their conversation. Maybe Pamela should've remained outside after all.

But Pamela refused to babysit another adult. Like she had refused to whine when Mark casted her friendship aside after his and Jessica's first date. For almost three years, except for their biweekly lunches, she had only seen him when he cried on her shoulder over Jessica. Honorable men didn't require an overseer to honor their wedding vows. Fingers flexing at her side, Pamela watched the scene unfold. Jessica sauntered toward their house. Mark trekked down the steps, meeting her halfway. They met beside billowing redbud trees.

Too bad Pamela couldn't read lips. However, their gestures provided ample information. Jessica indicated Pamela and Mark's house. Stroking his arm, she angled closer. Mark also pointed toward their house, then he pushed the woman away.

A finger jabbed his chest.

Laughing, he swatted her hand.

A four-door white sedan slowed in front of their house. The vehicle turned into a driveway across the street. The man remained seated inside the car. Would a concerned neighbor consider the quarrel serious enough to involve the police?

Were other neighbors watching the exchange? A woman peered out of a window at the same house across the street. Unwilling to become a side attraction in their circus, Pamela left the window.

Noise erupted outside the front door. Pamela executed a perfect eyeroll, trotted into the closest bathroom, and booted the door closed. She preferred lying across her bed while she worried, but at least the inadequate cooling-off spot included a door lock.

The mosaic floor tile that took a week to install netted her attention.

For four weeks, I went in and out of this house. Did Jessica stay hidden to spring a trap today?

12

"Hey, love. Where are you?" Mark called. "I'll be done in a jiffy."

Did he truly expect pleasant conversation when he had just spent fifteen minutes chatting with Jessica?

He made several trips outside the house and back inside, calling her name after the last trip. Had he brought in one item at a time to have an excuse to be outside longer?

"Where are you? Everything's inside. Food bags are on the kitchen island."

Her foot tapped the floor as he halted at each room, opening and closing doors.

The guest bathroom was his last stop.

The walnut doorknob turned. Rapid knocks pounded the door.

"The luggage is in the master bedroom. I put boxes and crates inside the laundry room."

Mark's knuckles rapped the door before cracking.

It was another grating habit of his that she ignored.

The doorknob turned again.

Did he believe the lock would magically unlock itself?

"Good thing we stopped by Toomey's for burgers and fries."

His light tone and small talk vexed her. He had betrayed her. She wanted contrition. Nothing less.

Mark's fingers beat a pattern upon door panels. "Coming out anytime soon?"

Pamela's closed eyes held back tears. "Leave me alone." Her voice broke. "Ahem. I'm not ready to speak with you."

Not now. Maybe not ever. Magic wands and suave words can't fix duplicity.

"Don't let that obnoxious woman separate us. Listen. I will always talk with you. Remember that."

Copycat. He was mimicking her mother's favorite catchphrase "remember that."

She balanced her hip on the tub's edge while combing her fingers through her hair. Curls sprung back into place.

What were her choices? She couldn't stay inside the bathroom all day. Could she do anything to stop the pain she was feeling?

Cell phone in hand, Pamela speed-dialed Anna, but she then canceled the call before the phone rang. Anna had advised her daughter not to say "I do" without knowing what she was agreeing to. Her mother had suggested that she wait a year before getting married. Pamela had blown off the advice and set a wedding date for four months after Mark proposed.

The moment Pastor Paul pronounced the couple husband and wife absorbed her mind.

Her happy marriage with Mark was tanking on the first day the couple arrived home from their honeymoon.

Deceptive men wrecked lives. Pure and simple. She was a tool so he could appear to be reputable, nothing more.

What would the Simons say when they heard about their son's treachery? Whenever Mark bamboozled others, his mother always asked, "Did he respond to provocation? What did they do to him?"

Somehow both parents would flip Pamela into the villain if she told them what he'd done.

But she had to remember that their relationship consisted of two people: Pamela and Mark. Other people's opinions and ideas didn't matter. She needed to focus on the man she had begged the Father for. The old friend who had been in love with a morally corrupt woman.

Mark still hadn't said "I love you" to Pamela. In her heart, Pamela imagined he did love her. Time might make his feelings known.

Pamela thought back to the moment Mark proposed at an exclusive restaurant's opening night. The friends had eaten countless meals together, but never dinner.

Mesmerized by After Hours' authentic Italian cuisine and topnotch service in a romantic atmosphere, Mark had reminisced about their early days and subsequent years together. Plus, he had nodded every time she spoke. She could tell his mind was only on Pamela. He had criticized his relationship with Jessica, supplying additional facts about their time together.

The conversation had flowed unhindered until his quizzical gaze sought hers.

Her heartrate had accelerated at his searing look. It marked the first time she had witnessed that expression. His dialogue then filled with halting words as he tugged on his collar.

Stroking her wrist, Mark had smiled. "I ... enjoy your company ... and trust your loyalty more than ever. If you ... if ... you marry me, I ... promise you ... we'll live a happy family life."

Pamela had heard, "We'll raise adorable children and enjoy a wonderful life. I'll always love you."

Now she realized he had meant, "We'll have friendship, children, and sexual fulfillment."

14

His stammered words had endeared him to her heart. In hindsight, his broken dialogue hadn't expressed nervousness. Today she understood he had been speaking to himself as well as her. The stutter allowed his brain to process what his mouth spoke. Enamored with gut feelings, Mark had ad-libbed a sudden idea. He had accepted that marriage to his best friend would make him happy.

The proposal left an indelible imprint upon her mind. While stroking her hand, he had said, "You are my lifelong companion. I adored you the moment I saw you walking through the hallway."

The first day at Calvin Gibson High School had terrified Pamela. In the cafeteria, some guys stood behind her in a food line, and Mark's friend ridiculed her size. She could still see a crooked finger pointing at her.

"There's another fatty who should eat salads and not take up space at the pizza counter."

Kids laughed at the put-down.

Pamela cried.

That day, she cursed not having superpowers to disappear—until she noticed one boy stayed silent. The junior who twiddled his fingers when they passed each other in the hall smiled at Pamela. Ignoring his friends, the upperclassman placed her plate on his tray, led the way to the cashier, and paid for their meals. Those kind acts launched their biweekly lunch dates until he graduated and thereafter.

For eight months after his relationship with Jessica ended, Mark had pretended Jessica's defection meant nothing. On the rebound, he must have sought safe haven. Pamela's adoration provided a barrier against his ex-girlfriend's rejection.

Pamela realized that her husband hadn't duped her. She had duped herself.

She should have seen what happened outside coming. Instead, she had acted brain-dead and not as an independent woman.

The rattling doorknob snagged her attention. "If you refuse to talk with me, then at least listen while I explain what happened."

Pamela didn't respond.

"Your silence says it all," Mark said. "I'll back off. Take whatever space you need before our discussion."

Footsteps retreated down the hallway.

Pamela had cultivated a relationship with Mark since ninth grade. Yet the heartbreaker had pursued every girl except the one who adored him.

Until meeting Pamela, he had never shared his hopes and dreams with anyone. How could he date other women but trust only Pamela with everything valuable? She had invested eleven years on hopes and dreams. And then he proposed four months ago.

Pamela Hayes had won over her cherished friend. A man who never loved her back. Teardrops trickled down her face. God's answered prayer had plunked her into an inescapable predicament. The locked bathroom made her feel caged.

She carefully cracked the door and quickly peeked to see an empty living room. Unprepared for any confrontation, she fled.

I'm slinking out, but I won't crawl back in.

Chapter Three

On the sidewalk in front of her house, Pamela slowed her steps to a more sedate pace. Confident people didn't wring their hands and talk to themselves in public places.

Mauve curtains moved at the house window across the street. Either that person had too much spare time or held a vested interest in their neighbors' activities. She kept walking, but a second glance over her shoulder didn't show anyone watching her.

Walking briskly, she quickly passed by Jessica's house. Why cause potential battle opportunities?

Could she have responded any differently than she had? Should she have gone inside once she recognized Jessica as a neighbor? Perhaps her shock in that moment had eroded any wisdom.

I've lost hope regarding my marriage.

Cell phone in hand, she called Anna.

Thank God today is Friday. Please be alone so we can talk. I need good advice from a seasoned listener.

* * *

Her mother sounded breathless when she answered. Pamela fought back tears. "Mom, I'm on my way to the park from my house. Could you pick me up at the tennis court so we can talk?" Moisture on her face tingled from the gentle breeze.

"The square is at least two miles away from your house. I'm on your side of town. Meet me at the pet store four blocks down the road in fifteen minutes."

Pamela's shoulders lifted. Life looked brighter since leaving the house.

She struggled to keep a tearless voice. "Thanks for saving questions for when we're together."

"Of course. On my way. Take care, babe."

"Thank you. I better hang up before I cry. Drive safely. And don't rush."

Trudging along, she shoved the cell phone into her pocket. Was she right to walk away without telling Mark? After their engagement, the couple had listed their top ten ingredients for a successful marriage. One weekend, while cuddled in Mark's arms on his living room floor, Pamela penned their ten-point agreement while he watched.

1. Never leave the house in anger. Don't allow a wedge to build between us.

2. Hear each other out before reaching conclusions. Be willing to listen.

3. Admit when you're wrong without being asked. Apologize without finding fault.

4. Reach a consensus before going to bed. Sleep within the same bedroom.

5. Keep Sundays open for one another. Extended family gatherings are permissible.

6. Celebrate all milestones when crossed. Daily thank the Father for His faithfulness.

7. Esteem each other higher than ourselves. Support one another in every endeavor.

8. Remember both sets of relatives. Keep familial ties alive.

9. Raise our children within a God-conscious home. Build on a firm foundation.

10. Pray and read scripture together weekly. Nurture His presence in our home.

Pamela had fled in anger within thirty minutes of arriving home from their honeymoon. Plus, she hadn't listened to his explanation. Two strikes tarnished her commitment on the first day back. But why hang around? He couldn't transform having Jessica as a neighbor into an asset. A rational defense for his deceit didn't exist.

Was he still in love with that despicable woman? It was too late for Mark to show remorse at any rate.

Anger fed a rebellious spirit in Pamela. She started to think that a separation could allow both partners to regroup and use caution.

Thank God for mothers like hers. Her husband had let this travesty develop. Did he possess any regard for his so-called best friend?

Mark had played the field in high school and college. Yet he had sunk like an anchor tossed into an ocean over an unprincipled woman. He and Jessica had met at his father's pawn shop two years after he graduated from Shiatown University. A computer science degree landed him Techno Plus's chief information officer position. Even then, he worked considerable hours at the family stores without compensation.

His then-girlfriend had regularly visited both store locations with useless pawn items. While the other clerks sent the woman packing, Mark secretly purchased whatever crap she peddled. Their quasi-business association developed into a three-year tumultuous liaison. The ungrateful woman used Mark and his resources to hobnob with influential people, then she dumped Mark and married another man six weeks later.

Mark had repeatedly forgiven Jessica's self-absorption and her disrespect for him. Only her engagement pushed their relationship beyond restoration. His obsession with an acid-tongued woman had never added up to Pamela. Jessica's caustic barbs removed paint from walls. Whenever Pamela met the couple in public places, she said hi and moved along.

Everyone figured Jessica had dated Mark until a wealthy prospect materialized. Some people branded Jessica's husband a likable man. Yet he had married an egotistical woman. Perhaps using bad judgment in choosing a wife didn't disqualify him from being a decent person.

Her thoughts returned to Mark. He obviously had known where Jessica lived before Pamela and Mark bought the house. Was he still in love with Jessica? How could she have missed that fact if he was? Pamela had acted like a schoolgirl once Mark proposed. Her agreement to marry him could be against her own self-interest.

After today's events, she now realized that Mark still loved Jessica and bought their house to keep her near. Her husband had always handled adversity in self-pity mode. He never cared about who he had to hurt to have his way. After Jessica dumped Mark, his self-esteem suffered a blow. His excessive ego used Pamela's support to rebuild his self-assurance.

In three years, Jessica had dismantled his self-confidence. Mark had folded instead of accepting that Jessica had never loved him, and he failed to learn the correct lesson from his mistake. Pamela thought Mark's comeback spirit had reignited.

Her steps slowed. Did she believe the gibberish occupying her brain? She did today, if not tomorrow.

Anna's blue sedan was parked in the pet store's lot. Pamela jogged fifty feet to the vehicle. Her mother's presence offered safety and compassion. She slid into secure open arms, slobbering over her mom's neck. Tears flowed until she coughed and sputtered.

Her concerned mother dabbed tissues over her daughter's wet face.

Pamela's cheek lay on the headrest. Her eyes teared up as she stared ahead. "You were right. I never should've married Mark."

Her mother's empathy unleashed another teary round.

Anna patted her daughter's trembling shoulder. "No man or situation warrants a breakdown. You can't move forward while stuck in neutral."

"I know. It's just that ... this is all so brand new. My life crumbled because I insisted on having my own way."

"One mistake doesn't constitute a life sentence. Miscalculations can occur with anyone. *And* they can get corrected." Anna smoothed loose hair strands from Pamela's forehead. "Explain what happened without emotional embellishment. Give facts as you understand them."

* * *

Mark departed his vigil at the window when a door clanged shut. The sound implied his stubborn bride had left the bathroom and was now ready for conversation. Her speedy withdrawal from the clash had ruined the united front he'd planned for when they met up with Jessica. Now they were against each other instead of opposing Jessica.

The skirmish he had had outside with Jessica replayed in his thoughts. Emboldened by Pamela's sudden departure from the porch, the ex-girlfriend had claimed a bogus victory, declaring war on his family after Pamela went inside.

The confrontation with Jessica was nothing like he'd imagined. She was not the same woman who had ditched him. Fine forehead lines and shadows underneath her eyes suggested marriage had taken a huge toll on her. Their foolish conversation revealed her mental state had also been affected. Despite her earlier boldness, Jessica resembled a sunken ship. Smugness no longer underlined each feature.

The ex-couple had talked as she stood beside her Jeep, and Mark stood on his porch. After he carelessly knocked boxes off the bench, it was like

20

a magnet drew him and Jessica into his driveway.

She stroked his arm, leaning closer.

He pushed her body aside. "Thanks for turning me down. An exceptional lady said yes. My forever partner nursed me back to full health. I don't play mind games with my life these days."

"Comparing milk toast to me?" Jessica sneered. "Admit you settled for second best."

"Even you don't believe those insults. Since high school, men stood in line to date a woman who loved me. Pamela and I will grow well together. We'll raise our children within a loving home."

Her finger poked his chest. "You're criticizing me? Really? *I* rejected *you*. You bought the house next door. Neighbors told us the new owners, *the Simons*, were on their honeymoon. Friends revealed you had gotten married. Workers at the pawn shop confirmed your week-long extension."

Laughing, Mark pushed her hand away. "Get to the crux, if you possess news worth conveying."

"Listen well. Seeing me surprised your wife. She didn't know I lived next door to her dream house."

"Yes. Our forever home."

"Dream on. I didn't know you were getting married and moving in next door. Your marriage only happened because Victor and I spent five weeks touring Europe and weren't home. Pamela would've dumped you before the wedding if she had realized I lived next door."

"I don't keep tabs on your whereabouts." His head jerked to her house. "How would I know you lived over there?"

"Because my sister said she told you Victor and I bought a house in West Gate subdivision before we married."

Mark tracked a man who spied on them from a passing car. The vehicle turned into a driveway across the street.

He turned back to glare at his sworn enemy.

"Your bride could've dated just about any man she wanted to," Jessica said. "Men surrounded her wherever she went." She paused, eyeing the older man studying them from across the street. "Get ready. I want you back more than your wife desires to keep you."

Mark turned his back on Jessica and retreated to his car to carry more luggage to the porch. The Prentises' vacation explained her absence before today's sneak attack. He had known that Jessica and Victor lived somewhere within West Gate

21

subdivision, but he didn't know they were next door to his house.

Mark figured he hadn't seen her around the neighborhood because she'd decided to remain lowkey and not further disrupt his life. But, clearly, she hadn't waved a white flag after all.

The sullen woman aimed to sabotage his marriage. A decent person would've just stayed inside or waved and moved along. The narcissist brought the fight outside.

The kicker was her expectation that he would sneak behind his bride's back. That assumption peeved him more than dumping him after he proposed marriage. Fools risked their marriage on seasoned cheaters. Those wedding vows she vilified shifted Mark's allegiance to his wife.

He desired to live inside a love-filled home. His lifelong friend obliged his preferences in most situations they faced together. Would she believe he had only known Jessica lived somewhere in the neighborhood and not next door to their house? How far would she bend to maintain peace within their home? The self-conscious girl he first met in high school no longer existed. God had molded Pamela Hayes into a confident lady.

Years ago, he had observed a cutie peering into classrooms. He followed the scared rabbit up the stairwell. On reaching the top floor, she retraced her steps to the main level and entered the first classroom she had passed. The room teemed with boisterous students acting out. The fright on her face affected him.

A freshman. Better keep an eye on her.

His favorite person now bore no resemblance to her younger self.

Four months earlier, Mark had chosen his perfect spouse. Pamela's loyalty proved boundless. Her love eclipsed any hardships the couple might face.

Would longtime favor overcome harsh realities?

Mutual respect and high regard dominated their relationship. He flourished under her confidence in him.

Jessica Hubbard, no, Prentis, deserved rejection. Mark wouldn't take her back even if she divorced Victor and gave a social media proclamation that she loved Mark. His wife embodied both his present and their future. At his bachelor party, friends had commended his wise choice in his future wife. Family members concurred with his brilliant selection during the wedding reception.

Mark had preened under accolades until an uncle burst his bubble while eating cake. "You overcame the bloodsucker quicker than we expected. We're glad you asked Pam to marry you after you got dumped. She is a remarkable lady."

It was mere gossip that Jessica had rejected him. Mark prided himself on keeping personal business private. Only Pamela had heard a fuller version of what had happened the night he and Jessica broke up. No one else would safeguard his stupidity.

Riled by the comment, he let it go. And then, an aunt said, "You married a jewel whether or not you recognize the fact." A younger cousin added, "Tread softly. Winning Pam as a bride is easier than keeping her as your wife, unless you change certain habits. Don't look surprised," she said when Mark glared at her. "You like having your own way. When have you ever compromised with anybody?"

Never fond of barbed comments, he cast the remark aside.

Stay focused on this moment. Your bride left her hiding spot in the bathroom. Engage her before she goes into hiding again.

Scattered suitcases occupied the spot where he had dropped them after being rebuffed. He maneuvered around the clutter, clearing a route to the door.

This house and his wife proved he had overcome rejection, rebounding on higher ground. In a year's time, Mark had made significant changes in his life. The sacrifice of accepting money from his parents had secured the substantial down payment. His folks had forked over an enormous loan to make the mortgage payments affordable. He felt like he'd sold his soul by accepting favors from his parents. They exonerated the money he owed them as a wedding present. But in their eyes, the bill could never be repaid. He would deal with their hostage taking later.

Regardless of Jessica's shenanigans today or in the future, the newlyweds would dwell in their forever home.

A brash interloper couldn't undermine what God ordained.

Mark plodded down the hallway. "Pamela? Are you ready to talk?"

The guest bathroom door stood ajar. He strolled through the living room and into the kitchen. Opening the front door, he looked outside. Retracing his steps, he searched each room, plus the garage.

His stomach muscles knotted. He combed every room inside the empty house. *Pam has to be here. Where did she hide?* He repeated the process twice, indoors and outdoors.

Minutes later, a puzzled man sank onto the sofa. He felt the truth rush through him. His wife had left him. Pamela had walked away.

The couple's ten-point promise agreement honoring their marriage hadn't fazed her.

Mark's lifeline had discarded him without saying goodbye. Shoulders rising, he leaned forward. Perhaps she just needed to regroup for a bit. He prayed to God that was the explanation.

The barb Jessica had given him outside suddenly hit home. *"I want you back more than your wife desires to keep you."*

His cousin's sarcastic comment invaded his thoughts. *"Winning Pam as a bride is easier than keeping her."*

His chin rested on his chest. Two hits in one day.

First, Jessica believed his buying the house invited an affair. Had Pamela also assumed he purchased their place for that express purpose?

If so, both women were wrong. His integrity didn't go to the highest bidder.

Rotating hunched shoulders, he grabbed his cell phone and called his wife. When the call went to voicemail, he dialed his mother-in-law. There was no need to leave messages neither woman would return.

Pamela had left her car parked outside Anna's house across town after the wedding. Had Pamela walked somewhere? More than likely, a family member had picked her up.

Mark grabbed his car keys off the mantel, studying the fireplace. A portrait-size montage showcased his life from infancy until his bachelor party. Every award he ever received graced the mantelpiece. Two-inch votive candles were placed in silver holders with flower sprigs twined around each one.

Pamela had obviously gone to a lot of trouble to create this magnificent display for him. He hadn't noticed it when he was bringing in their gear.

He slapped his forehead. Now the threshold questions Pamela kept asking him made sense. If Mark had entered the house at an angle, the mantel would've been the focal point. Why hadn't he said, yes, I will, and done so? Instead of pleasing his bride, Mark had chatted with a calculating woman that desired to take him down.

Mark, too, had broken a rule on their agreement list.

Admit when you're wrong without being asked. Apologize without finding fault.

He had not asked Pamela to forgive him for not telling her Jessica lived in the neighborhood. But he had fumed about Pamela's lack of cooperation. He let an adolescent-level mood swing waste the vital time required to salvage their marriage.

Dressed in blue jeans and a Bianchi's T-shirt, Anna's and Pamela's server stood beside the table. "Dessert? Our apple pie à la mode tastes fabulous."

"No, thank you. I'm stuffed and still eating," Anna said. "My daughter needs a doggie bag. She's scarcely eaten a bite."

Pamela glanced around the restaurant. Customers had come in and left since the duo arrived. A new crowd queued inside the lobby.

"I'm starving, but I just don't feel like eating anything. This has never happened before. Bianchi's is my pig-out restaurant." She poked at the kaiser roll with her fork. "I love the cheese garlic bread."

"Me too." Anna washed a hefty chunk down with cherry limeade. "Continue your story. This tale sounds better than the novel I began yesterday."

Spontaneous laughter gushed from Pamela. She was encouraged by her mother's perky humor. Life proved far from being over until thoughts of Mark brought more tears.

"I don't know how you can stand to hear all this again. I ignored your warning not to marry Mark too soon."

Teardrops escaped the eyes she dabbed.

"Love's a potent motive for ditching reason." Anna set aside her fork in thought, then picked it back up. "That same love is a rational motivation to give marriage another shot. These days are early. My beloved mother always says, 'Toughen up the rump. Life goes on.'"

"You mean it simply feels like I'm dying. But either way, the pain remains the same." She massaged her forehead, staring ahead. "Grandmother only says that in dire situations like this one. She advised you to ditch Dad and take the money."

Green specks dotted her mother's light-brown irises as her body shook with laughter. "That's the woman who raised me. She said, 'When people want to leave you, sweep them out the door.' I asked, 'How do I dismiss a twenty-one-year marriage?' Ditched for another women eight years older than me. Those facts bruised my ego."

Pamela remembered those days well. Her father's selfish decisions had disrupted three lives, mainly Anna's. Steven seldom considered any person other than himself. Throughout the divorce, Grandmother kept her daughter grounded.

"Did the advice seem impractical at the time?"

A dreamy look replaced Anna's keen gaze. "Mother ticked off every bit of advice she'd given over the years. Trust God for direction and everything else you need. Listen to wise counsel and make good decisions. Time heals all wounds, even the ones that mimic dying."

Laughing, Anna picked up her glass.

"The lack of sympathy ticked me off." Anna continued. "Nevertheless, her sound guidance provided strength during difficult circumstances. Our matriarch is a special lady."

"Grandmother said, 'The Father protects His children within each storm.' I feel like an abandoned child. All alone." Pamela's chin lowered. "Present company is excluded. You always drop everything anytime I call. My problem is that I did this to myself. That simple fact is disheartening."

"Mother speaks truthful words I finally trust. Successful lives are lived from God's perspective. But we want what we want when we want it. Your father taught me one important lesson: Some people believe their own lies. Remember that."

"Dad isn't a liar, Mom. Although he failed you as a husband, he's a good man in many respects."

"He lied to me and probably deceives himself with those selective memories he lives by. Truth stands on a firm foundation. You recognize Steven's positive qualities. How about your husband's?"

Pamela's earlier diatribe to herself on the walk to the pet store came to her mind.

... Mark still loved Jessica and bought their house to keep her near. Her husband had always handled adversity in self-pity mode. He never cared about who he had to hurt to have his way. After Jessica dumped Mark, his self-esteem suffered a blow. His excessive ego used her support to rebuild his self-assurance.

Geez. Ugly thoughts.

"Mark is nothing like my father. My husband epitomizes kindness. Dad seldom does."

"Random kind acts don't make someone a nice person. Like Steven's, Mark's compassion serves dual purposes. He likes himself better when helping people. Self-interest oftentimes benefits others."

"I ... do you think ..." Pamela's shoulders drooped. "Including me? Does his friendship with me make Mark feel better about himself?"

"Especially you. Spending time with you builds his confidence. I never doubted Mark likes you. He does."

"Likes. Not loves. Even though he never said he did, I thought he loved me."

26

"Emotions are tricky business. Like I said, individuals want what we want when we want it. The outcome of love may come in time. These are early days in your marriage."

"You keep saying that, Mom."

"Truth bears repeating. Your husband asked you to marry him because he envisioned a successful marriage." Anna scooted her chair closer to her daughter when Pamela grimaced. "The concept is simple. Knowledge acted upon is wisdom. Choose wisely."

"Your words aren't adding up. If I love him and he wants to love me ... where did I go wrong?"

"Marrying conflicted people produces complications. Still, what's done is done. Forward motion serves your purpose better than regret. Love is a commitment to another person." Anna squeezed Pamela's hand. "You left your home to regroup. Learn to resolve your marriage difficulties without taking flight."

"I couldn't have a rational discussion with Mark until I cooled down. He lashes out when he's angry, and then he berates the other person. He does that same thing even if he instigated the problem. I knew I had to leave before I said something I might regret." Her hand brushed her forehead. "Plus, I couldn't think straight inside that house. I needed to talk to you first. We speak the same language."

Laughing, Anna stacked saucers on plates. "Sometimes we ride the same wavelength. And you haven't sniffled in several minutes. No more tears?"

Giggles escaped Pamela's lips. "Are there any more left to cry?"

"Fresh batches can replenish fast. Now, give me your going-forward plans."

Pamela twiddled her thumbs. "I'm out of ideas," she finally said.

Anna leaned forward then sat back. "Out of ideas about your life or how to handle your husband?"

"Mom, I changed my routine when Mark started dating Jessica. And then, I changed them again once they broke up."

"Which routines did you change? And why?" Anna asked.

"I didn't attend any events that centered on either Mark or his parents. I couldn't chance running into Jessica. Although I accepted Mark's extended family's invitations."

"Why didn't you cut them off as well?"

"Jessica hated Mark's relatives. She wouldn't attend their celebrations even if she had been invited." She hesitated, looking down. "Mark took up all

27

of my spare time after Jessica broke off their relationship."

"Keep talking," Anna said when Pamela glanced at her.

"The problem is, I don't know what my plans are. After Jessica booted him, Mark consumed my life. I gradually rearranged my usual activities to accommodate him. The only thing I kept doing was my monthly card game. Because we hung out together all the time, I imagined we dated before he proposed. Now I realize Mark only saw me as a friend."

"He allowed his need to take advantage of a trusted friendship. All of your attention helped him heal. He respects your friendship."

Pamela's fingers drummed the table. "I didn't expect this scenario with Jessica. What should I do?"

"Go home, so your spouse can stop driving around in circles."

Eyes squinted, Pamela stared out the tinted window. "You saw him?"

"Mark has circled the parking lot six times. Good thing this parking lot was full when we arrived, and we parked behind the building across the street. It was better for us to talk in private and without any interruptions."

Pamela glanced outside again. "He's checked the parking lot six consecutive times?"

"Intermittently. I imagine he checks out your other haunts in between cycles."

"I better go. Although ... I—I'm not in any hurry." She rose, pushing her chair underneath the table. "Thanks for spending time with me. You always help keep me sane."

Anna picked up the check. "For a person uneager to go, you jumped up fast enough."

"I left home to cool off. Their chitchat riled me. The more I listened, the angrier I became. I might've blown if I'd stayed within earshot."

"You don't know why Mark chose to buy your home. Can you conduct a decent conversation when you get back?"

"Yes, ma'am. I learned my lesson the first time around." She laughed, then gave a deep sigh. "Thank you. You're a lifesaver. I'll remember to think before I act."

They headed to the cashier and waited behind five customers to pay the check.

After they left the counter, Anna opened the exit door. "Master what is in your control. Remember that."

Chapter Four

Mark pulled up outside Anna's house, taking another chance Pamela went to her mother's home.

On this trip, his mother-in-law's car replaced his wife's vehicle. Making a U-turn, he headed home. "Please be at home. Don't leave me."

How had his life spiraled out of control in one afternoon?

A little over a year ago, Mark's world had caved in around him. The woman he had dated for three years disrespected a special gift. Jessica was the first woman Mark had seriously dated. She possessed a lure that attracted him the first day he watched her stroll into his father's pawn shop. He found her whimsical nature impossible to resist.

Little by little, she wormed her way into his heart. He wanted to tame her capricious spirit and release the wonderful woman he imagined she was. He ignored family and friends who told him to replace her with a stable woman. None of the advice-givers understood the deep affection he and Jessica shared.

One day before Mark purchased the ring, he showed his final selection to Pamela. He knew he'd selected the perfect ring after tears filled her eyes.

Mark took the day off from work on the evening he proposed. He spent the time turning his condo into a romantic haven, sent flowers to her job, and prepared a six-course meal for their dinner.

He could see the happiness on her face when she stepped inside his condo. She gave him a lingering kiss and thanked him for the flowers. After Jessica raved about the meal, Mark proposed and held out the engagement ring. Jessica had initially ogled the engagement ring as her face glowed. Pride filled his heart until her gaze met his. His girlfriend took the ring from him and chucked it across the table.

Bull's-eye. The present he went into debt to purchase hit his nose and bounced underneath the breakfast bar.

Jessica's amusement at his expense chilled his blood.

She brushed her fingers across her lips but failed to stifle giggles. "Well that was a totally unexpected outcome. Incredible dinner, though. You cooked my favorite pasta dish." Her eyes sparkled with humor. She daintily dabbed her mouth with a napkin. "But really, the meal and token make my decision harder. Accept my regret and congratulate me. I'm getting married next month."

Mark forced himself to shut his gaping mouth. He repeatedly told himself to keep his dignity. Regret? The woman appeared overjoyed with herself. Mark thought they were in a relationship, but Jessica had only been using him for fun.

He silently watched her grab her purse off the sofa and open the front door. His reaction to her dismissal surprised him. For the first time since he had met Jessica, he withdrew his emotions from the scene.

Turning around, she stared at him. "Don't act shocked. Long-term relationships require two invested partners. We will connect again. Until then, I won't risk being denied my trip down the aisle. Victor isn't a forgiving man."

After mocking him with his preferred twiddle-finger greeting, she left.

Mark slumped against the table as all coherent thoughts vanished.

The door reopened. Jessica poked her head inside. "Marry Pam. We can have an affair if you marry her. She'll accept whatever crumbs you give her." She cast an amused gaze upon the breakfast bar. "Exchange the ring for a cheaper version. Your *friend* will accept whatever offer you make her, even my engagement ring, if you marry her."

She stepped aside, leaning on the door. A calculated stare examined his face. "I prefer you talking. Perk up. I'll be back after I whip Victor into shape."

Mark's brain cleared before the door snapped shut. He couldn't believe his own stupidity. Jessica was a demanding, narcissist. How could he have thought she would make a good wife?

Now, as he drove to his new home on autopilot, he realized his insight hadn't improved since those shame-filled years. Even worse, he had humiliated his wife by talking to the enemy.

He continually called Pamela on his way home. Each call went to voicemail.

Be at home. Let me explain how this situation got offtrack. You are part of the life I crave.

He had planned to tell Pamela today that Jessica lived in the neighborhood. After all that had happened, though, he realized he should have told her before they bought the house.

While being held captive by a devious woman for three years, he had at least learned two important lessons.

Number one: Engage in relationships he could cultivate with pride.

Number two: Invest his life in people who returned his love.

With Jessica, he had courted disaster for far too long.

Could he repair this humongous breach with the one person who added substance to his life? All his relatives loved her. Pamela had attended their picnics, graduations, and social affairs for years. After he met Jessica, Pamela continued to socialize with his extended relatives but shunned his immediate family's events. Mark had missed her supportive face in the crowd, especially when Jessica was another no-show. After the breakup with Jessica, Pamela began attending his and his parents' celebrations again. Now he understood she had stopped coming to avoid seeing Jessica. His ex-girlfriend had refused to attend his extended family's get-togethers even before they'd stopped inviting them to come.

As he neared the house, he saw no vehicle in the driveway. He banged a closed fist on the steering wheel. He hoped she had parked inside the garage.

Leaving his vehicle at the curb, he hurried inside the house. The place appeared empty. Even if Pamela had left home again, she'd come back. Fluffed pillows replaced the flattened ones where Mark had lounged on the sofa. A sweet aroma led him to the fireplace.

The life tribute was replaced by a berry-scented candle. She wouldn't light a candle and leave the house while it burned. The guest bathroom door opened when he turned the knob. He entered the kitchen. Their two food bags sat on the island where he'd placed them. An empty plate and glass were in the dishwasher.

Neither Pamela nor her luggage occupied the master suite. He found her suitcases stacked inside a guest bedroom down the hall. Rule four of their marriage agreement taunted him.

Reach a consensus before going to bed. Sleep within the same bedroom.

Standing beside the bed in the master suite, he tossed keys upon the nightstand.

Somewhere, his wife was listening as he searched the house for her.

Pamela was lounging on the sofa when Mark walked into the family room. She was eating ice cream and reading a book, and she didn't look up when he entered.

Mark sat beside her, touching her hand. "Where did you go? I hit all your

31

favorite places. Were you with your mother or someone else?"

"Mom." Her lips moved without an upwards glance. "If you want the burger and fries, warm them up in the microwave. Try thirty seconds first."

"I'll eat later. You worried me." He reached for the book, then dropped his hand onto his lap. "Our talk is overdue. I didn't know if you were coming back."

Inquisitive eyes gazed at him. Laying the paperback aside, she heaped ice cream on a spoon. "Where else would I go? I live here."

"Remember our successful-marriage agreement? Never leave the house in anger. And it's impolite to walk out and not say where you're going." An excruciating pain rippled his temple. Eyes closed, he massaged the spot. "We should let each other know where we are. Why didn't you tell me you were leaving?"

"Why didn't you tell me Jessica lived next door? I feel deceived."

Mark glanced across the room. The anticipated conversation hit a dead zone. Pamela wasn't in the mood to placate his wounded ego. What did she and her mother discuss?

"This house suited us and our future family." He paused when Pamela laughed. "I didn't want you changing your mind about the place. I realized Jessica lived somewhere in the neighborhood, but I didn't know it was next door."

"The first visit marked the perfect time to tell me what you knew. Okay. So Jessica lived somewhere in the subdivision. But I like this house. I would've moved here regardless of our neighbors."

"You say that now. Your pat answers are as bad as my hindsight."

"Only because I lacked the opportunity to say them then."

Mark knew they must deal with Jessica's stunt before morning. The vengeful woman had set them up to fail on their first day home.

He shifted closer. "I had valid reasons for not telling you. Although my motives appear pointless on second thought."

"So explain yourself. Why did you deceive me?" Pamela slipped an ice-cream filled spoon into her mouth.

"That remark sounded snarky. How about us engaging in a serious discussion? Spouting words at each other won't help."

"My vocabulary matched my husband's delusion."

Delusion? Mark didn't expect the disrespect and low blow.

Pamela's half smile didn't reach her eyes. "Please explain why you deceived the one person who has always stood by you. I have always taken your side despite endless pain."

Mark shifted positions. She was right. It was his fault the couple was at odds.

"I understand your justified anger and doubt about my honesty. I should have told you that Jessica lived somewhere in the neighborhood before we agreed to buy this house. I ... listen. The right moment never came before the house closing and wedding." He hesitated when her lips pursed. "Please keep an open mind while I explain."

"No one can explain the unexplainable. But give it your best shot."

Mark pulled at his collar as his temples pounded. "Too much time had transpired. I planned to tell you on our honeymoon. But ..."

"Your inability to find the perfect setting plays like a broken record. I am an adult. You blindfolded me then led me down the path."

Mark couldn't defend actions that defied logic. He should have been honest. A trusted friend genuinely loved him. Despite contrition for hurting her, only time would diminish pain. His soul felt branded with remorse.

"I betrayed the trust you always showed me. My entire approach was off-center from the beginning. Having high hopes is my downfall. I wanted us to experience the family vision in my heart."

He hesitated as Pamela's eyes closed.

"Before we saw this place, you were lukewarm regarding every house," he continued.

"Without even seeing a for sale sign in the yard, we both knew this would be our home when the agent rounded the corner. I was hopeful for the dream, so I rolled with it."

Squinted eyes stared at him. "For four months?"

"Momentum took off in the wrong direction. In the Turks and Caicos, I decided to confess at home. Jessica's appearance pre-empted my confession."

Bubbly laughter erupted from Pamela's lips.

He winced, touching his head. Skin pulsated beneath his fingers.

Leaning forward, her concerned gaze searched his face. "Are you okay? Tell me the truth."

Mark spoke through clenched teeth. "You don't believe me. Your distrust hurts more than I thought possible."

Pamela sighed and glanced away. "We renovated this house for three weeks. You moved in two weeks before our wedding. Where was Jessica hiding? I might believe your account if Jessica had made an appearance before today."

"She explained her and her husband's absence after you went inside. They returned home last week from a five-week tour in Europe."

"Overseas, huh? How convenient." Lifeless eyes stared at him. Yawning, she covered her mouth. "I'm tired. Give me those highlights tomorrow."

He pushed up his sleeves, studying his wife. "This problem requires resolution now. I want to hold you in my arms tonight."

Pamela sucked in a deep breath. "Enough nonsense. Sleeping in the same bedroom with you tonight won't happen."

She had never shaken her head so much to oppose anything he'd said. That reaction proved he must smooth the wrinkles in their relationship tonight. Mark had come closer to apologizing than he ever had before. Plus, he offered an explanation.

"Be reasonable," he said. "Your disliking what I say doesn't mean I'm making things up."

Pamela ate the last scoop of ice cream, placing the empty bowl on the table.

Mark grasped her hands in his. "Jessica's sudden appearance caught us off guard. I ... I wanted to kill two birds with one stone. For over a month, we viewed multiple houses. You fell in love with this house."

"The other bird?"

"Last year, I explained Jessica expects an affair. I figured a glimpse of our happy marriage from time to time might dissuade her."

"Can you hear yourself? You married me so you wouldn't sleep with a married woman?" Pamela sighed through her fingers. "My goodness. The problem's worse than I imagined."

"You misunderstood my comment. My wife isn't a buffer against an old girlfriend. Our marriage is the real deal. I wanted Jessica bombarded with our reality. She wounded me, but I recovered. I want us to build the perfect life together. Take this house. You and I loved our forever home on first sight."

"Keep explaining. But make it quick."

"At first, her sudden appearance threw me off-balance. I never contemplated the Prentises as neighbors. Although appalled, I wanted us to present a united front."

Pamela rose and peered down at him.

He hesitated as she stood over him, but then he continued, "I last talked to

34

Jessica on the night she ditched me. I wanted my wife by my side when we eventually met again. I expected that Jessica recognizing our solid commitment would lessen her desire to cause trouble."

Picking up her book and bowl from the table, Pamela headed toward the door.

Scurrying across the floor, Mark stepped in between her and the doorway. "Do you believe I would've told you if I understood that woman lived next door or across the street?"

"I do. But it doesn't matter whether I believe you." She studied him with sad eyes. "Where Jessica lives isn't the only issue here." She stared at the floor. "Um. I need a break."

His feet shuffled while his life suspended in midair. The words he never expected to hear resonated throughout his body. Was the marriage ending before beginning?

"From this conversation or from me?" His own dull voice sounded far away.

"At the moment, both. I don't hate you. I just don't like you right now." She glided around him. "And don't ever block my exit route again."

Excruciating pressure throbbed inside his brain.

She studied Mark's face. "Why did you grab your head?"

"Do you have a pain reliever?"

"Look in the bathroom closet."

Pamela left the room, tidied the kitchen, then shut the guest bedroom door.

Mark sat on the bed in the master suite holding two caplets until the door to the guest bedroom clicked. Walking slowly down the hall, he entered the kitchen. At the farmhouse sink, he swallowed the pills and popped both meals into the microwave. Hunger surged in his body despite the devastation he was feeling. Usually his wife was a reasonable woman. Tonight, she wouldn't accept his sensible defense. Someone had turned her against him. Pamela claimed she had seen her mother. Were Ace and Melinda present? Although they were friendly, none of Pamela's family liked Mark.

His brother-in-law and sister-in-law were popular in high school. Popular himself, Mark flew beneath Ace's radar. On Pamela's first day in high school, he protected the scared freshman from a friend who bullied her in the cafeteria. Mark ate lunch with Pamela for the first time that day. But before the period ended, her brother descended on the lunchroom, spoiling for a fight. Someone had told him a guy had bullied his little sister in the cafeteria. Pamela saw the senior enter the room and head straight to the boy who had disrespected her. She rushed over to deflect the thrashing Ace threatened to give. After Pamela intervened, Ace let him walk away. The frightened boy switched schools the next day.

What advice had Ace and Melinda dished out to Pamela? Certainly nothing beneficial for him. Ace blew hot or cold on a whim. At least Pamela's mother maintained a fair mind, even though she had never sanctioned their marriage.

Throughout Mark's life, trusting his gut feelings had brought him unlimited success. An unplanned proposal to his treasured friend while eating dinner out had proved a first-class decision. Until arriving home from their honeymoon, he'd been happier than he'd ever been in his life.

Deciding to date Jessica was the one time he hadn't listened to his inner voice. He should not have ignored the warning.

* * *

Pamela unpacked her sleepwear and lay across the bed, crossing her ankles. Her Bible sat open on the nightstand. Her whole world had turned upside down that day. Mark wanted her to forgive him and forget that it happened; as if she couldn't forgive him and still remember what had happened.

Forget the unforgettable. How could anyone accomplish such an impossible feat?

Pamela hadn't seen the Jessica train coming. The inescapable collision caught her unawares and collapsed her marital bliss.

Sliding off the bed, she wandered around the room, piddling with decorations. At the window, her sightless eyes gazed into a silent night. West Gate subdivision's family-oriented neighborhood delighted on many fronts. Each evening when decorating the house, she'd heard children playing in backyards. Now their outside play would give her constant reminders that her loveless house had become a no-child zone. Pamela's ideal home incorporated love, godly conversation, and family commitment. Her husband's dishonesty placed the couple on uneven terrain.

She understood the heartbreak of marriage inequality firsthand. Little ones deserved to dwell within a loving home and a stable atmosphere. Her childhood home was infused with both comfort and indignity. Whereas Anna provided warmth and constant protection, Steven added conflict and tension. That time of her childhood had become the not-so-good old days.

Her father turned their house into a battlefield, erupting whenever his spouse stood her ground. Pamela's older brother, Skylar, who most people called Ace, seldom stayed home. Pamela refused to abandon their mother to her fate. Cozy mysteries and jigsaw puzzles became her favorite pastimes.

One day, her father ranted and raved all evening. He threw their dinner into the garbage disposal. After he left the house, her mother packed their things and stored the suitcases inside the laundry room. The next morning, they went across the river to her grandmother's house in a neighboring city.

Martha Frierson opened the door sporting a magnetic grin. Beckoning them into the house, she surveyed their luggage scattered along the porch. "Your morning visit whetted my appetite. Get comfortable while I cook our feast."

Pamela's grandmother whipped up a scrumptious meal with a yummy breakfast dessert while she reminisced about the good times the family had had with her husband before his death. The lively conversation around the table made Pamela forget they had run away from home.

Finished eating, Grandmother spoke in soft tones. "You kids wait in the living room while your mother and I talk."

The teenagers left the kitchen, then listened at the door. Pamela never forgot the conversation that changed their lives.

Martha placed her chair beside her daughter's. "Turning my family away isn't easy, but I can't let you stay here. Steven should leave the house, and not you guys. Anna, you have biblical reasons to end the farce. If you're done cleaning up his messes, call Timothy Simms and begin divorce proceedings. But don't leave your home again. Always start the way you intend to finish: in control of your life." She sighed. "I miss your father's wisdom in such times, although I know he would agree with me if he was alive."

"Dad always advised me to stand my ground. The kids and I will talk on the drive home. I feel better now than before we came. I desire healthy relationships and see a different pathway for our future. We will enjoy our lives."

Chairs scraped the tile floor. Pamela and Skylar hurried into the living room.

Pamela and Skylar were playing a card game when the women appeared in the doorway.

"We're leaving," Anna said, smiling. "I'll explain on the drive home."

Grandmother hugged them on the porch. "Taking a strong stance now will serve you better than a swift retreat. Think about long-term strategies.

What actions will best secure your futures and well-being? The Father will bring you safely through it all. I promise. We hold on to the faith we profess because He who promised is faithful. Call me when you guys reach the house."

An unfamiliar peace enveloped each of them as they took the scenic route home. Grandmother's advice worked wonders for everyone. From that day forward, they viewed their family dynamics from different perspectives.

Their peaceful life accelerated until it screeched to a halt four years later. While playing a board game at the dining room table, her father dropped the divorce bomb one Saturday afternoon.

Steven cleared his throat, capturing everyone's attention. "This marriage is over, Anna. Yesterday, I filed for divorce."

Pink streaks appeared on her mother's face and neck. She stared at Steven with startled eyes, then glanced away.

Pamela's shaky hands covered her face.

Skylar took up the gauntlet and allowed their stunned mother some space to regroup.

"Why did you waste our afternoon with a family get-together? You could've phoned in your newsbreak."

Their pale mother spoke in a dull voice. "You've been removing your belongings for several days. Care to elaborate on why now?"

Her father's face tightened. His arms crossed on his chest.

"Do I know her?" Anna began. "Or is this a new woman?"

"You see Pam standing there. Just take out an ad in the paper and tell everyone my business." Glancing at Pamela, Steven hesitated. "Valerie Tillerson." Steven eyed his son when Skylar laughed. "Val understands my needs more than your mother does." His scathing look included his children. "More than anyone in this room does."

Skylar grunted. "Mom worked endless hours putting you through medical school. What does this new woman bring to the table?" His brow cleared as if a light bulb had turned on. "Ah, yes. Connections. You want the medical director's job."

Steven uncrossed his arms. The pencil he held snapped in his fingers. "Your mother hasn't worked outside this house in fourteen years."

Breathing easier, Pamela jumped into the fray. "Mom quit the day job and slaved at home."

Both men stood together. Mother stepped in front of son. After placing a game piece into a container, she faced her husband. Satisfaction edged her grin.

"You won't disrupt peace within our home any longer," she said. "Pack your bags. I want every item that belongs to you gone today. Make it count. You're not coming back."

"Mom!" Skylar grinned when their mother winked at him.

Steven's cold eyes raked Anna. An ugly laugh spewed from his throat. "Prepare for a court battle."

"I made my own arrangements once our son graduated high school. Leave your attorney's number on the table." She paused. "Valerie Tillerson. Now everyone will see you for the pathetic man you always were."

Pamela cringed, but Steven just staggered backwards. His Adam's apple bobbed up and down. He gaped at Anna until she walked into the kitchen and shut the door.

Skylar loped up the stairs, then he looked back down at Pamela. "Come on. We'll help him pack."

Anna had broken into tears after her husband had left the house, despite her strong demeanor while standing up to him.

Not me. I won't fall apart.

Pamela believed Mark was unaware that Jessica shared the property line. However, had her husband strategized a scheme to stay married to Pamela and keep Jessica close by?

Was he playing a game to keep both women active in his life without committing a physical sin?

Grandmother's wise words to Anna came to mind.

Don't leave your home again. Always start the way you intend to finish: in control of your life.

If Mark was unaware of his true feelings, then he'd better pay attention to his actions.

Pamela had never played games with her life.

Chapter Five

Birds chirping outside the window woke up Pamela bright and early. Her anger had waned overnight. Saturday morning presented an ideal day to start afresh. She wanted a successful marriage with her longtime love.

Jessica and her husband were still her neighbors. That fact wouldn't change unless the Prentises moved away. But Pamela knew she would've chosen this house even if she had known Mark's old girlfriend lived next door. The messy part was his deception. Unable to alter reality, she must proceed the way she might've had she known.

Her husband's dishonesty proved she couldn't trust him with her heart. Yet she still loved him. Despite his withholding of affection for twelve years, Pamela had remained loyal in hopes of one day marrying the man she loved. Why give up their intimate and legal relationship? Could she bridge the gap he'd made? Given time, she would secure Mark's love.

This morning's goal was to eradicate yesterday's bad beginning. Breakfast was a start. But not in bed. Let him walk into the kitchen.

* * *

Tossing off the quilt, Mark sat up in bed. Self-pity had departed during the night. Did Pamela rest well without him beside her for the first time in two weeks? He had fallen asleep after one o'clock, wishing his wife a restful sleep. He lay on what she had claimed as her side of their bed. He had wanted to feel near her, even though a chasm separated them.

Anyone would feel attacked when they thought they'd been betrayed, so he didn't blame Pamela for her reaction. His and Pamela's friendship had thrived on mutual convictions that his dishonesty had now destroyed. Mark must win back her confidence and keep her trust.

Their vows at the altar provided the proper incentive to persevere. His wife was the most significant individual in his life. If he went down, it would be fighting.

Thirty minutes later, he peered into the kitchen from outside the doorway.

Pamela cracked three eggs into a skillet, adding cooked sausage, grated cheese, and diced vegetables. She lightly stirred the ingredients with a spatula.

Deep breaths steadied his labored breathing. Stuffing his hands into his pockets, a soundless sigh escaped his parted lips. Pamela never ate three eggs for breakfast. Was his wife serving up reconciliation? How could Mark turn one meal into sharing their life together? Since yesterday, he had dealt with bottomless questions and limited answers. This weekend appeared up for grabs like everything else in his existence.

Perhaps she had forgiven him overnight. Sometimes the compromise bug defied logic. Standing behind her, Mark wrapped his arms around her waist, pulling her close to him. He loved the subtle fresh scents she wore.

"Good morning, love." His lips brushed her cheeks, and then air.

Pamela evaded the lingering kiss.

She dropped eggshells into the garbage disposal. Then she swiped her brow with a paper towel and threw it into the trash can. "Thank God for weekends. Except for church, I'm vegetating today and tomorrow. This upcoming week has a loaded schedule."

If Pamela remained at home this weekend, so would Mark. His limited knowledge regarding her career shamed him. He knew his wife baked delectable treats in her own commercial kitchen, but he didn't know many details.

"Loaded with baking or something else?" he asked.

"Baking. Mom and Mellie filled my regular orders while we were on the honeymoon. Four large contracts are due beginning Tuesday."

It was strange that she had never offered any details about her business before. He wanted to keep her talking to learn more.

"Give me a complete rundown about the pending orders." He crept closer.

Pamela squinted at him. "I'm surprised you asked. You haven't shown an interest in my business before today. You always interrupted me whenever I tried to tell you."

Mark's jaw slacked as shame pierced his mind. He couldn't think of one word in his defense.

"Here's the scaled-down version," she said. "Tuesday is for the library's cupcake fundraiser in Tulsa County, neighboring cities, and towns within a 40-mile radius. Plus, Hamilton Junior College will serve cookies to juniors, seniors, and their parents that same evening. Thursday is the multi-church mission tart and peanut cluster campaign. Community centers are hosting a meet-and-greet cookie bonanza on Saturday." Her eyebrows wiggled. "Mmm. I can almost taste the goodness."

Mark stepped aside after Pamela rejected his second kiss. He dropped onto the nearest stool. He'd forget reviving the Jessica discussion anytime soon. He knew he should follow Pamela's lead to the conversation's obvious conclusion. With small talk, his wife redefined their present relationship.

Still, the information she shared with him activated his business-passion heart. Mark leaned forward. "Those four major clients will reach more potential customers. How many orders do you have for what items?"

Pamela crunched on carrot chips. "Excuse me." Fingers covered her mouth until she sipped water. "Three hundred one-pound bags of peanut clusters, four hundred tarts shaped in biblical themes, seven hundred fifty book genre-specific cupcakes, three thousand cookies, plus my regular restaurant and shop orders. I'll spend the week baking nonstop. Timeless Pastries's clientele rises weekly."

"Impressive work. I'm proud of you."

Two years ago, Steven Hayes had set up his daughter with a commercial kitchen in a one-story building somewhere in the industrial center. Mark didn't know the exact location. He did know she supplied baked goods for restaurants and fundraisers in South Town and neighboring cities.

His wife knew specific details about his job because she asked questions about everything concerning him. Mark felt like a useless friend.

Pamela clapped. "More success is on the horizon." She set a porcelain food platter on the trivet. "Breakfast is ready. Take a seat at the table."

"Besides the upcoming week's large order, fill me in on your clientele. Who are your steady clients?"

Mark understood the glance she cast on him. Was it too late to take an active interest in her career?

"Why didn't you ever tell me about it?" he prodded.

Her mouth hung open as she stared at him. "I forgot our drinks," she said, then she turned away. Removing an orange juice carafe from the refrigerator, she filled their glasses and chose the chair across the table from him. "You never asked about my job or why I love it. And then, you changed the subject whenever I mentioned baking." Eyes lowered, she prayed a silent grace, then placed a small omelet onto a toasted roll.

42

Mark took a sip of his juice, staring at her. Like she had said earlier, he'd always interrupted her when she tried to tell him. There wasn't a way to right that wrong.

"You really enjoy toiling in a kitchen all day?" he asked.

"Yes, sir." She wiped her mouth with a napkin. "Satisfaction to the nth degree."

"What makes you love the work so much?"

"For starters, I control the environment. I mostly work alone, but Mom and Mellie will help me this week on Monday and Tuesday. K.C. will help all week."

Mark's hand trembled. Food fell off his fork. "Hodges? Ace's friend?"

"I know. Most people react the same way. He's a superb baker." She reached for another napkin. "He blocked off five days to get us over the hump next week. After this job, he is officially off bake detail. He has other obligations. Thank God for his support. He's a huge help."

She paused, glanced at Mark, and then continued. "Next week we have four other fundraisers to plan for. Mom and Mellie will work on those."

Unknown to Mark, Pamela led a whole other life. And K.C. Hodges, man about town, baked. Did he make house calls? Mark sipped juice while his brain demanded answers. His wife hadn't revealed her clientele when he asked, but he would insist on information about the baker.

He leaned against the back cushion. "Hodges has assisted you before?"

"Many times. Before Dad bought my current building, I used K.C.'s house whenever necessary. He designed a professional kitchen any chef would adore."

Hodge's house. Grown women disgraced themselves chasing behind him. Mark pushed his plate aside. "How did you learn that he baked?"

"He told me. K.C. got me out of a jam. Five years ago, I overextended on my first fundraisers."

Whether intentional or not, Mark had a hard time wringing critical facts from his wife. She spouted scanty answers then resumed eating. Reticence always piqued his interest.

"Tell me about the time you spent with Hodges. You supplied the edited version. Elaborate more."

Pamela's bright eyes widened. Now he had her full attention.

"You provided the beginning and the end," he said. "Enlighten me on the missing middle part."

"And you accused me of sounding snarky yesterday."' Pamela continued eating.

"Excuse my tone. Please, love. Bring me up to speed."

She put her fork aside. "Timeless Pastries debuted its fundraiser service one spring. Our selling point had been a four-day turnaround. Instead, I should've guaranteed a two-week deadline from the date we acknowledge their order had been received. I was unprepared for the response. Four organizations booked fundraisers on the same day."

"The launch proved successful. Did your company deliver on its promise?"

"K.C. saved Timeless Pastries' reputation. Still, it would've worked without his help, if Mom and Mellie had been available. Skylar, Mellie, and Mom were going to be out of town, so Skylar asked his friend to bail me out."

"This is the first time I've heard the story. You left me out of the loop. Why?"

"For real, Mark? We just discussed your noninvolvement in my work. K.C. is Skylar's best bud. Five years ago, his help kept Timeless Pastries afloat, upgrading its service level. I owe the man an unpayable debt."

"That may be a bit much. So what's the deal with your relationship with Hodges?"

Happiness highlighted each feature of her face. "I'm on watch for a wife for K.C. The right woman is out there. Somewhere." Picking up her glass, Pamela giggled.

Mark hadn't heard that sound from those lips since high school.

She set the drink aside. "I'll find her. And then maybe I can stamp 'paid in full' on the debt."

Mark wanted to hear the baker's version of the odd-pair relationship. He had met Hodges on the same day he met Ace. Something about Pamela's explanation seemed askew. Skepticism took over Mark's thoughts as he dismissed his wife's sketchy account.

Pamela sighed, looking at Mark. "Fundraisers require extra hands on deck when handling more than one at a time. Except for this week, Mom and Mellie help with them all."

The doorbell rang. "Who could that be?" Pamela asked. "Are you expecting anyone this morning?"

Shaking his head, Mark walked a few steps behind Pamela. She'd just voiced his unspoken question for her.

Approaching the door together, they both reached for the doorknob.

Pamela opened the door. The couple Mark least wanted to see stood before them.

Pressed lips eclipsed the woman's usual winsome smile.

The man's surfer boy appearance hid a mercurial personality.

* * *

"Mellie, Skylar. What a surprise." Scooting back, Pamela opened the door wider. "Come in, family."

Melinda spoke.

Ace's flinty eyes speared Mark.

Great! Their unexpected company included a disgruntled brother and sister-in-law.

Pamela often accepted advice from her mother and brother. It appeared that the tag team had hustled over bright and early the very next day after Pamela's talk with Mrs. Hayes. They had come to convince his wife to divorce him. They didn't know whether Pamela and he had reached an agreement. He and his wife should have an objective discussion about Jessica before they listened to another person's viewpoint.

Pamela opened the door wider. "Please visit with us awhile."

Melinda's head shook. "We can't stay long enough to come inside." She touched her sister-in-law's forearm. "That must've been some honeymoon. Ace didn't extend our nuptial retreat."

Pamela hugged her, giving her brother a thumbs up. "Thanks for telling us about the Turks and Caicos. It was amazing. We should all go together next time."

"Sounds like a plan," said Melinda. "The children are at my parents' house. We just dropped by to welcome you guys home after having breakfast with your mother. Can you believe we shared a meal on a Saturday? Mom proved in top form this morning. She kept me laughing."

"Yesterday, I dined with Mom," said Pamela. "Fun stuff. I laughed a lot, too, and then, I immediately went home."

Pamela studied her brother through squinted eyes.

Ace's distinctive jawline became more defined.

Were the three of them passing secret codes? Melinda appeared in tune with their verbal and nonverbal communication. Once again, Mark was the odd man out.

Fantastic! What else could go wrong? Mark returned the other man's

45

grim gaze. *Leave. Let us work out our difficulties alone.*

His blue eyes twinkling in bright sunlight, Ace chuckled to himself.

Stepping backwards, Mark eyed the couple. "Glad you stopped by."

Melinda glanced at him. "Eat dinner with us soon. The kiddies miss you guys."

"We should go," Ace said. He glanced at his sister. "Walk us to the car."

Ace glared at Mark then headed off the porch.

Melinda fell into step beside her husband.

Trooping behind them, Pamela glanced at Mark and ambled after the couple.

Hands stuffed inside his pockets, Mark studied their procession down the driveway.

Details concerning his wife's absence yesterday took shape. He figured that during the meal with her mother, Pamela had sought motherly advice. Perhaps his mother-in-law hadn't advocated for her daughter's divorce. Yet she had Ace and Melinda over for breakfast on a day she usually kept for herself. Perhaps she had made an exception to unfold the Jessica situation with her son and fill-in daughter.

Movement across the street captured his gaze. An older couple observed the trio from their front porch. Yesterday, the man had scrutinized his and Jessica's discussion while sitting in a white sedan parked in the driveway.

Mark closed the door and headed to a side window. He refused to entertain neighbors with his follies.

If Ace insisted that his wife leave him, would she walk away?

Their shared breakfast had indicated she'd decided not to bolt. Of course, the Jessica uproar merely slumbered. He knew his wife would eventually bring it up.

A major confrontation brewed.

* * *

Pamela leaned on the car once the front door closed. "I guess you guys heard that Mark's old girlfriend lives next door. I wept all over Mom at Bianchi's, and she still made me laugh."

"Humor is our mother's favorite weapon," Skylar said. His face muscles tightened. "She artfully lowers the boom on fine points amid laughter. That's wisdom gained since her own shipwrecked marriage."

As Melinda gasped, she unzipped her purse. "Tone down the rhetoric, Ace.

Don't make this situation worse than it is."

Pamela dabbed her eyelids on tissues her sister-in-law dug from her purse.

"Shipwrecked marriage? Are you dooming my relationship with Mark?" Tears filled her eyes. "My goodness, Skylar, have a heart. I do have feelings."

A heavy groan escaped her brother's lips. "Which is why I didn't beat down your spouse on his porch. I almost decked the dimwit when the door opened."

His wife patted his arm. "Your frustration has showed all morning. We came by to support your sister through this chaos."

Skylar studied Pamela as he chucked a knuckle beneath her chin. "You've always loved Mark. We came over to encourage you, not to derail your marriage."

Pamela immediately hugged him while Melinda stroked both their shoulders.

Pamela still valued her brother's opinion. He was tenacious and could be dogmatic, but he held several nonnegotiable principles. Her brother didn't make knee-jerk reactions, and he prayed about everything. Skylar believed in family and spent time nurturing relationships with his in-laws as well as with the Hayeses.

Skylar strove to obey God. Pure and simple. That was the real reason Mark remained unscathed. Her brother's life changed for the better after that time Anna had packed their bags and drove the family to her mother's house. Grandmother's godly influence reaped dividends in her grandson's life.

"My thoughts were chaotic when I fell asleep last night," she said. "Bird tweets shifted my mood when my eyes opened this morning. I woke up determined to save my marriage."

Melinda rested the back of her head on Skylar's chest. "You chose the best of two options. Yet somehow you seem unsure. What else happened this morning?"

"Mark blew into the kitchen without a care. He probably did have concerns regarding the Jessica conflict, but he kissed me. Based on that, one would think our marriage is on track."

Melinda nodded. "It's a man thing. Ace believes his kisses can move mountains."

"Wishful thinking," Pamela said, laughing. "I don't want Mark to grovel at my feet, but some attrition should be evident. At least a little bit. Do you agree?"

"Yeah, I do," Melinda said. "Forgiven transgressions aren't forgotten overnight. Due to their severity, you may never forget some of those offenses."

"Mark wants us to discuss the Jessica situation while brushing off my feelings. It matters that he didn't tell me Jessica lived in the neighborhood."

"You forgive your husband the same way you forgave Dad," said Skylar. "You let love overcome his faults. Forgiveness lessens pain daily until you no longer feel the sting."

"I agree," Melinda said. "In my experience, remembering the good times de-escalates stress." She touched Pamela's shoulder. "Are you really okay? This predicament is hard, even on your family. It can't be simple for you."

"The outcome isn't easy to take, but the mistake is mine. My mind boggles at the countless errors I made concerning Mark."

"Nothing that happened yesterday or this morning should have surprised you," Skylar said. "When has the man apologized for his faults?"

Pamela shrugged. "First he has to admit he made a mistake. I'm working on him."

"If you couldn't snuff out his selfishness in twelve years, why would you think you could manage an overnight revamp?"

Pamela rolled her eyes at Skylar. "I accept that Mark is in like with me and not in love. But why did he ask me to marry him?"

Her brother's head jerked toward the property line. "He wanted to erase the mess he made with the woman walking out of the house next door."

Dressed in midcalf boots, jeans, T-shirt, and a cowboy hat, Jessica opened the garage door from the driveway.

"Ignore her," Melinda said. "Mark didn't realize he's still vulnerable where that conceited woman is concerned."

"Why not?" Pamela asked. "He's an astute guy, not an idiot."

Skylar gave his best "that's debatable" expression. "No one likes having problems, but adversity handled correctly helps us grow. Mark uses multiple buffers to feel safe in numerous areas. Personal growth demands a person's complete cooperation."

"You're a fountain of information today," Pamela said. "Why were you missing in action before now?"

"You cut communication with us for four days after Mellie critiqued your engagement."

"Skylar—"

"Mom and Grandmother played the heavy with you. They warned you several times against marrying Mark too soon. You disregarded their advice, but you didn't break off your communication with either of them."

Shaking her head, Melinda nudged her husband. "We don't dislike Mark. But Ace was upset when Mark ignored your desire for romance and made you his best friend."

Melinda stared at the neighboring house when the garage door lowered—with Jessica on the inside of the garage. "That woman is unstable, but not a physical threat. Ignore her antics."

"That's a difficult assignment when the person demands attention. She loves being noticed."

"Don't give her that satisfaction," Melinda said. "Just ignore her absurdities."

Pamela nodded. "Continue what you were saying, please."

"Listen, I jumped the gun and married Ace our junior year in college. I cut short my education to support our family. Your brother insisted I finish my degree after he graduated from medical school. Three children and nine years later, we're a happy and well-grounded family. Rocky starts don't necessarily mean a divorce."

Ace wrapped an arm around his wife's waist.

Melinda cooed and snuggled closer, rubbing her cheek on his chest.

Their unity and affection encouraged Pamela's spirit. The couple anticipated longevity in their marriage.

"Cheer up, Sis. Like Mom said earlier, your husband abhors appearing reckless. Plus, he truly likes you. Mark plays to win. I guarantee that your relationship with Mark is his top priority."

"But not for the right reasons. He wouldn't want people saying his marriage failed."

"Take your opportunities wherever you find them," Skylar said. "We all have our strengths and weaknesses. One day, maybe Mark won't care what other people think about him."

It was hard for Pamela to accept Mark's faults, especially with Jessica's nearness. It irritated Pamela that Mark had fallen in love with a dreadful woman instead of with her.

"Mark is still in like with me after twelve years of my dedication to the relationship." She paused. "At least most of his family loves me."

Skylar kissed her forehead then walked around the car to the driver's side.

"He likes you better than any other person alive. Either build on that reality or walk away from the marriage. The choice belongs to you."

"We'll talk more later," Melinda said as she stepped into the car.

The couple waved at Pamela when the vehicle turned onto the road.

Pamela lingered on the steps until the car rounded the corner. She knew there was no way to delay the inevitable discussion. Even if he didn't say so, she knew her husband would want to discuss the Jessica issue this morning.

She looked across the lawn again to the closed garage door. Where was the husband? The man probably required constant breaks from his wife. Jessica was his problem.

Pamela took a deep breath, hesitated, then opened the front door.

Chapter Six

Mark met Pamela on the other side of the front door when she re-entered the house.

She acted as if he wasn't standing there and swept past him.

"Jessica's at it again," she said. "She opened the garage door from outside the house, then she lowered it from inside the garage."

Mark trailed her steps across the floor while holding her purse and sunglasses.

"That woman's behavior doesn't concern us. Yesterday her foolish actions disrupted our plans. Even through this mess, one fact remains clear: You're a godsend. I appreciate your kindness."

Pamela stopped in front of the fireplace, staring at Mark. A lit cinnamon apple candle fragranced the entire house. She loved fruity scents and had stocked a two-month supply before the wedding.

"Over the years you failed to recognize even one kind act. Which good deed earned your regard today?"

"I married a precious woman who treated me like a special friend for twelve years. Your thoughtfulness exceeds bounds. Can you stand still a moment?" he said as Pamela moved away. He waited until she faced him. "Take these last two days for instance. Yesterday, you didn't walk out on our marriage. This morning, you cooked us a deluxe breakfast. Just now, you didn't leave with Melinda and Ace."

Her blank expression hurt Mark more than a verbal attack would have. His silent lips parted. At a loss for words, he simply looked at his wife.

"Are you finished talking?" Pamela asked.

"Thank you for the post-wedding tribute. You managed to put together a showcase of my life just hours before our ceremony took place." He inhaled a deep breath when Pamela didn't speak. "It required true diligence and perseverance to worm those photos and awards from Mother's clutches." He reached his hand out to her, then he dropped it to his side. "Each considerate act conveyed your genuine affection."

His water-filled eyes studied the floor. "May we talk outside of this house? Our marriage requires an honest discussion as soon as possible. Preferably away from here. I disappointed you at home. I prefer discussing what happened yesterday someplace else."

Pamela took her purse and sunglasses from his grasp and snuffed out the candle.

Opening the front door, she stepped onto the porch, then pivoted around. "Where to, master negotiator? Did you choose a destination for us?"

"Wish that title was accurate." His head tilted to the side. "Since Ace and Melinda cut our breakfast short, how about we go somewhere for brunch? I cleaned up the kitchen while you were outside."

When Pamela nodded, he locked the door and followed her down the walkway.

The man who'd prided himself on overcoming adversities was out of ideas.

* * *

Mark made a left turn out of West Gate subdivision. "Bianchi's? Have you eaten there recently?"

"I ate there yesterday with Mom. It popped with people."

Mark glanced at Pamela. "I drove past it several times. Where did your mother park?"

"The lot was full when we arrived. Mom parked behind the office complex across the street."

Pamela noted her husband's double blink. The bland action signaled that information was filed inside his mind safe. Mark always blinked in rapid succession after hearing what he considered to be valuable information. Next time he would conduct a broader search by driving around the entire neighborhood instead of spotlighting one location.

Why didn't he know her habits as well as she knew his? She knew why. Because he hadn't cared enough to pay attention to anything beyond the superficial. Pamela wished she had had those realizations sooner and not remained friends with him.

Unable to rewind the clock of her life, she pressed forward. "Bootsies serves the best homecooked meals. We haven't eaten there in four weeks."

"Bootsies it is," Mark said.

On the drive through lightly traveled streets, her husband chatted about their high school years. The chatty tone prevailed as the vehicle maneuvered to a nearby neighborhood. Whenever traffic permitted, Mark grabbed Pamela's hand and squeezed her fingers.

The windshield received her rapt attention. She added a comment now and then but couldn't lift the responsibility to apologize and explain his deception off his shoulders. She knew he was just using chitchat to avoid what he really wanted to say.

Quit stalling. Make whatever you want to say easier on both of us.

Mark reminisced about their college years while they ate smothered chicken, roasted potatoes, and salad.

Fed up with the stall tactics, Pamela almost demanded he end the pretense of making amends for his mistake and take her home before they finished eating.

* * *

Mark held the door open for his wife as the couple exited the restaurant. The targeted discussion he'd left home to accomplish hadn't occurred. His resolve to explain his thinking had cooled before the car had pulled from the curb outside their house. An in-depth Jessica discussion was vital to save his marriage. But both the couple's home and the restaurant proved too claustrophobic to broach the topic. Both places served as constant reminders that he had dishonored their engagement.

Neutral ground might supply the proper setting. He'd always planned to visit some hiking trails but had never gone. They weren't appropriate for his friends and previous dates. Pamela had probably frequented the trails since their opening day.

He glanced at her solemn expression, then quickly turned away. "Pam, will you join me in fulfilling a wish?"

"Sounds promising," she said. "What do you have in mind?"

"Let me surprise you. Perhaps you've been there before, but you won't guess the location."

When Pamela nodded, he released the breath he held and tucked his wife into the car. Once inside the vehicle, Mark headed across the river and parked outside The Amazing Facts Trail at Shiatown University.

Pamela's head nodded as she laughed. "Right on both counts. I walk here several times a month but never took you for a trail walker. Thank God we're wearing sneakers and casual clothes."

Only a few seniors traipsed on the boardwalk as they arrived. The couple held hands and began their trek on the trail. The three-point-four-mile oblong track blended a scenic landscape with various fun facts about cities in their area. Marble plaques included information about the region's short-lived gold rush that occurred in the late eighteen hundreds.

Fifteen minutes on the trail led hikers inside of a walk-through greenhouse showcasing exotic plants and flowers. The trail then went across cobblestones over a pond into a forty-foot-tall birdcage filled with fruit trees and a ten-foot waterfall.

Thus far, words still stuck in Mark's throat with each attempt to speak. Pamela switched topics as Mark began to stutter.

Even without her lighthearted nature on display, his wife had chatted with Mark all morning. Did she long to forgive him but lacked adequate motive to do so? He could no longer pretend everything was okay. Yesterday happened. They had both realized their one-sided relationship collapsed outside their home.

Although the couple still held hands, she went unusually quiet ten minutes after the walk began. It seemed her patience had worn thin.

The trail's halfway spot led to a conversation area. An authentic alabaster table in the clearing's middle drew Mark's attention. Beautiful maple trees shimmered in the gentle breeze and shaded the whole area on three sides. Gorgeous butterflies flew everywhere they looked.

The mounted tension had produced a now-or-never moment. He couldn't protect himself from possible rejection from his wife without giving her a sincere explanation. Mark had never attempted an open self-evaluation in front of another person. Now he understood how hopeless people felt and why they honestly humbled themselves.

Squeezing her fingers, he pointed at two secluded seats in the quiet alcove.

* * *

After the couple sat down in the conversation area, Pamela's heart broke as Mark crept toward whatever he wanted to say. Constant shoulder rolls and darted glances around the boardwalk reflected his anxiety.

True repentance might've prompted her sympathy for Mark. So far, she surmised his nervousness derived from an unease about apologizing. Her husband had little experience with heartfelt regret.

Still, watching him sweat curbed Pamela's impatience. Perhaps successful marriages required a selflessness she didn't possess. But this was his show and not her own. She could reprimand herself tomorrow.

Mark wrapped an arm around her shoulder. "I may ramble a bit, but hear me out."

He searched her face as if he sought agreement.

Pamela nodded, hoping he would follow through this time.

He cleared his throat with a cough. "I won't forget our wedding day. Every second of the ceremony and reception is engraved on my heart." He shook his head and studied his fingers before he stole a peek at Pamela. "You were a beautiful bride. My anticipation increased as you came down the aisle. And then I broke into a cold sweat just before you reached me."

Mark stared straight ahead for several seconds, then he faced Pamela. "Relentless images of the last night I saw Jessica assaulted my mind. When the vision evaporated, I was gazing into my best friend's eyes. The ... most important person in my life ... chose to marry me. I had never ... been happier ... in my life."

His halting speech indicated that Mark spoke to himself as well as to Pamela. Just like he did the night he proposed.

Pulling on his collar, he continued speaking in a deadpan voice. "Before repeating our vows, I thanked God for saving me from a sure disaster. He protected me from marrying the wrong woman." Bemused eyes studied Pamela. "In the past, I'd considered myself a Christian. That deception shattered during our marriage instructions."

Mark brushed his lips across her temple when her eyes closed for several seconds. "You and Pastor Paul thought I rededicated my life to Jesus when we prayed. But really, I was accepting Jesus as my savior for the first time in my life."

Pamela's fingers touched her parted lips. "Seriously? Weren't you raised in church?"

"Not really. I figured attending Vacation Bible School gave me a relationship with God."

"A lot of people who attend church are benchwarmers and not believers," Pamela added.

"I suppose living to please myself should've given me a clue. You think?"

"Um. Kinda, sorta. That, and your preferred lifestyle."

"How so?" he asked, staring at her for the first time since they'd sat down.

"You indulged in obvious sin. You didn't live a God-centered existence."

After a long sigh, Mark squeezed the bridge of his nose. "You didn't marry a pathetic man. Your husband is an active learner. Don't give up on me." He paused.

Did Mark want her to make a comment? All Pamela wanted to do was believe his explanation.

With a deep sigh, Mark continued speaking. "Our honeymoon highlighted life at its fullest. I held a woman in my arms who cared about my welfare. I didn't know you loved me until you told me the night I proposed."

That remark seemed like a stretch of the truth, but maybe it wasn't. "I'm surprised you never guessed my hidden secret. Everyone else did."

"I have a lot to learn about my wife. For the first time, last night I understood how cruelly I've treated you."

"I accept the blame for letting you mistreat me," Pamela said.

"What I'm about to say is the truth and not an excuse." He took a deep breath. "Low self-esteem has dictated my behavior since my elementary school days. I lived in day care and after-school programs until I was old enough to stay at home alone. My folks provided material goods without making time for me."

"Your parents love you. Since we met in high school, I saw their fondness for you deepen as time wore on. Once their affection matures, they will prize you more than they honor themselves. Those changes will come with age as they do for everyone."

"My mother and father aren't emotionless toward me. However, they never gave up anything they wanted to do to spend time with me. I'm an only child because my parents dreaded having more children. They both claimed that kids are too time-consuming. I wasn't allowed to be."

Mark's revelation about his childhood released unwelcome memories for Pamela. Anna had always made herself available for Pamela and Skylar. As for Steven, daily interactions with his children spared him from being an absentee father. Because her father had maintained communication with his children after the divorce, five years ago he discovered he not only loved his offspring, but he liked them as well. The Simon family had dwelled within an unhealthy home, yet both parents clearly loved their son. Pamela wouldn't have guessed that Mark had felt unloved.

How did she chart the proper course after Mark's explanation? She wouldn't accept the status quo, nor could she reject a broken man. Especially when she still loved him.

Swallowing hard, Mark continued. "Seeking approval, I learned to sell myself to everyone I met. My subterfuge usually worked. Yet Jessica remained underwhelmed by my brilliance. Three years later, I still hadn't won her over. She threw my engagement ring at me and laughed."

Surprised by this admission, Pamela studied Mark's face. She didn't understand her special friend as well as she'd imagined. Now she understood Mark's fascination with his ex-girlfriend. He sought continual approval from other people. Some folks branded him as self-centered. But his self-promotion resulted from his need for acceptance. He'd survived an unhappy childhood, so now approval made her husband feel appreciated.

No wonder he had protected Pamela in the cafeteria years ago. Mark knew firsthand the importance teenagers placed on belonging. Her mother had nailed it once again. His self-interest had benefitted Pamela that day.

She studied the man whose thoughts appeared to be far away. Mark resembled a man who was trying to come to terms with his life.

I can't make the telling easier for him. Internal conflict resolution is a private undertaking.

Her husband grasped for the correct words while exposing his soul. He'd never had difficulty opening up to Pamela before. Or so she'd thought. Now she realized he'd been holding back as he shared additional information about Jessica walking away. For the first time, she understood he had previously only told her snippets of information.

"Jessica and I were equally matched in the experience department. On our honeymoon, I couldn't offer you the innocence you presented to me. You began dating on your sixteenth birthday, yet you saved a special gift for your husband. I considered sex without marriage okay until our wedding night."

Dropping her hands, Mark stood, then he sat back down, tugging his collar. Sweat beaded on his forehead. "I convinced you to extend our honeymoon because I wanted my bliss to last forever. Our time in the Turks and Caicos gave me pure joy."

Eyes closed, he paused, grabbing her hands. His tear-filled eyes opened. "This isn't a calculated attempt to keep you with me. I recognized my deep affection the moment I thought I'd lost you."

Pamela's head had bobbed along as he spoke. Now she leaned away from Mark.

"I love you, Pam. I can show you that my words are true better than I can tell you that they are." Mark refused to release her hands when she tugged against his grip. "Give me the chance to prove we share a treasured bond."

Pamela's body tingled from head to toe. Her dream man had finally said, "I love you, Pam." The emotion in his eyes conveyed deep affection. She glanced away before finally looking up to search Mark's face. "How do you convey deep emotion after twelve years of standing on the sideline of my life? You didn't care about my business or any aspect concerning me that didn't involve you."

"Please don't think that. I cared. I always have."

"Then you had a strange way of showing it. I blame myself as much as I blame you."

"Watch me value you higher than I regard myself," Mark said. "I'm ready to become an active participant in each facet of your existence." He lightly touched her face and stroked her lips with his thumb. "Guess what?"

"I can't feed myself false hope. Tell me whatever it is you want to say."

His chin rested on his chest. "If you wanted to hurt me, that remark did." He grabbed her hands. "Listen, this morning I discovered you live a life I never knew about. You're an engaging woman with diverse pursuits. Trust me that I will celebrate them all."

Her body tensed as she sat upright. Somehow his assertion didn't assuage the pain of what Pamela had accepted as Mark's friendship.

Compromise wherever you can to save your marriage.

Pamela closed her eyes, thinking of all the reasons she had fallen in love with Mark. He'd made her feel special when no one except her family had. Something about his spirit had pulled her in.

She opened her eyes and smiled at him. "That's a tall order. Consider me your number one cheerleader and pupil."

His head jerked back. "What else is left to discover? You know me well enough. You've always taken the time it took to learn about your friend."

"I thought so too," she admitted. "But over these last two days, I've realized I haven't done enough."

Mark grabbed her hands and kissed her knuckles. And then, he gazed into her eyes. "Will learning intimate details about me drive you away?"

"Commitment works both ways. My mind says you only think you know me. We'll see."

Pamela's tinkling laughter bubbled forth as she rose.

Mark stood and smoothed down his clothes. He appeared unsure of what to do next until he gazed at her. "I love you. Watch while I earn your loving respect in return."

He maintained a steady discussion on child-rearing while the couple finished walking the trail.

His ideas would raise well-rounded children. Evidently, he'd gathered valuable insight while growing up. Over the years he learned what it took to have good parenting skills.

Because of her own disrupted childhood, Pamela had developed a few crucial concepts of her own. She wanted to raise her children within a love-filled home. Yet she had agreed to marry Mark without a love declaration. He proposed, and she accepted. It suddenly felt like raising little ones would be more difficult than it had ever seemed before.

* * *

Later that night while her husband slept, Pamela slid off the bed and tiptoed into the family room.

Before going to bed that night, she hadn't received enough alone time to critique her day. Mark had glued himself to her side for the entire afternoon and evening.

His actions had appeared natural, and his speech had sounded sincere. The attention supplied the connection she'd always craved.

But a small voice in her head rejected the sudden change. All afternoon and evening he had treated her like a man in love.

Maybe he had fallen in love with her in the Turks and Caicos. Perhaps a deeper affection had steadily increased since their school days.

Her husband wasn't a profuse liar, but he also didn't always speak simple truth. Did he stage a heartfelt declaration to save his marriage? That would be great if Mark truly loved her—and disastrous if he only wanted to keep their marriage intact.

Several times that day, Mark had asked about the play she would attend next weekend. Friends had planned a ladies' night out last month. A neighboring city featured weekly author book readings, plus four plays per year. She and Mark had attended a few together. He had glowered when she said he couldn't go this time. Just like how he'd scowled when she had nixed his tagging along to her monthly spades game before they married. Her favorite card game was the lone activity she hadn't given up for Mark.

His shadowing her steps everywhere would soon wear thin. No person could make up for lost time. People must begin where they ended and build on what they had.

A shuffling noise sounded in the hallway. Moments later Mark studied her from the doorway.

"Are you okay?" he asked in a raspy voice.

Pamela rose and met him at the door. "I just slipped from bed for a moment to think. I was on my way back."

As he scooped her into his arms, he kissed her brow.

With her eyes closed, she lay her head on his shoulder.

After a lingering kiss on her cheek, Mark carried his bride back inside their bedroom suite.

* * *

Early the next morning, Mark held a plate filled with buttermilk pancakes, honey, Canadian bacon, and fried eggs beneath Pamela's nose. His hand shook when her stomach gurgled.

Her eyelids fluttered. "Mmm. This is either a vivid dream or my husband cooked a delightful meal." Her fluttering eyelids popped open. "My breakfast in bed looks scrumptious. Ah!" she said, smiling at him. "You even included parsley sprigs. I love your plate presentation." Pamela patted the empty space beside her. "Joining me for breakfast? Where's your plate?"

Mark felt his shoulders relaxed at her acceptance. After a sleepless night, she had vacated their bed while he slept. In the Turks and Caicos, his wife had fallen asleep early, only awakening when the birds began chirping. At home, he wanted Pamela to sleep as peacefully as she had while on their honeymoon.

He set her plate next to his on the cart. The covers on his side of the bed lay smoothed into place.

Pamela propped herself up in bed. "What time is it? Church service begins at ten."

"Eight thirty."

Her back pressed against the headboard, Pamela slid over, chewing Canadian bacon.

"What's the word this morning, other than my husband is a thoughtful man?"

"He's also a fantastic cook. Good thing we went grocery shopping yesterday. With everything that's happened this weekend, I forgot eating food is a daily requirement."

Giggles abounded. In the past, Mark had either ignored or overlooked Pamela's playful spirit. Adverse circumstances never stopped the Hayes family from being happy. Even Ace would catch the humor bug.

Unlike his brother-in-law, when Mark was presented with a problem, he sequestered himself away from human company until the problem no longer existed. Hanging out with Pamela after getting ditched by Jessica was the lone exception. Normally he conquered his foes in private. Time spent with Pamela had hastened his recovery period from Jessica's rejection.

He ogled his wife. She was beautiful even after sleeping. "What's on the agenda for today?"

"Church, and then I'm coming straight home." Pamela giggled. "Stop laughing. This is a couch potato day for me. Do you have any plans?"

"Staying home with you. Although I might drop in at the office and take a preview before the real deal tomorrow."

"Sounds reasonable. Give me a full report when you come home." She eyed him. "We should've discussed this topic before today, but will we attend my church or yours?" She hesitated when Mark popped a fork filled with pancakes into his mouth. "We took our marriage instructions at my church. After they ended, you stopped coming to church with me on Sundays."

Mark sipped juice and scattered food across his plate.

Pamela pushed her plate aside. "We can alternate between our churches if you like."

He finally looked at her. He'd stayed away from church because the messages prompted unwanted introspection. Before then, he hadn't attended any church in many years. He knew it was best to admit the truth up front. "The last time I went to the one church in my neighborhood was in junior high. I'm happy to attend church with you. I enjoyed the family atmosphere of In His Word Temple. It's puzzling that your mother, father, and your stepmother all still attend the same church."

"As you know, my father is an obstinate man," Pamela said. "After the divorce, Dad and Valerie remained inflexible about anything concerning Mom. They are the ones who sinned. She didn't." Her lips pursed together. "They lacked remorse and sympathy about breaking up our family. Mom's resolve to control her life proved stronger than their disdain for her." Smiling, she shrugged.

"How about you and Ace? Did you let your father know you wanted him to leave the church?"

"We sure did. I think our opinion made Dad more determined to stay. Skylar and I supported Mom's decision not to leave. But I almost left the church. It bothered me that Pastor Paul never weighed in. As the church's overseer he should have asked my father and stepmother to go."

"Anna Hayes is the real deal. She didn't need his help. Five years ago, when Mother was in rehab after falling down the stairs, your mother encouraged her with regular visits. Mrs. Hayes disrupted her regular routine and visited my mother four days per week. Without being asked, she traveled back and forth to rehab for a woman she met after the fall occurred. Your mom still sends Mother uplifting notes."

"And each time, your mom responds with a lunch invitation. They get along well for two women with only their offspring in common."

"Their association proves opposites do attract." K.C. Hodges entered his mind. "That reminds me. What hours will you and your helpers work this week?"

After she chewed the last bite of pancake, Pamela wiped her mouth on a napkin. "Breakfast tasted awesome. Looking forward to a repeat meal real soon. Hint, hint."

She tapped a finger on her cheek when Mark didn't comment. He repeated his question.

"Six until five for me. Mom, Mellie, and K.C. will work from eight till four. I'll run by the shop today for an hour or so while you're at work. Tomorrow we can get a jumpstart on baking if I prepare the dry ingredients today."

Keep Sundays open for one another. Extended family gatherings are permissible.

For a person who wanted to stay in this weekend she spent a lot of time away from home yesterday and now today. It was Mark who had suggested their brunch date and walking the trail, but Pamela had manufactured tasks that kept them out of the house and busy until evening. Now she wants to spend time at work.

Admit when you're wrong without being asked. Apologize without finding fault.

False blame benefitted no one. Mark had broken the honesty agreement by withholding information about Jessica living in their subdivision. Pamela had followed where his deceit led.

"I don't comprehend your logic," he said. "That's the wrong schedule for a self-proclaimed weekend couch potato. We're supposed to keep Sundays open for each other."

Pamela laughed. "Did I mishear you say that you were going into the office?"

"You heard me," Mark said. He couldn't refute her reasoning. On his feet, he placed his glass on the cart and rolled the cart toward the door. He turned around and faced Pamela before he left the room.

His wife sat in the same spot, watching him. Her features tightened when Mark remained silent. She slid off the bed.

"It's amazing how plans sometimes don't come together. I better get dressed."

Pamela walked into the bathroom and shut the door.

Mark had just squandered another chance to make amends for his two sets of rules for their household. He couldn't always please himself. He had to compromise with Pamela.

* * *

Once at the church, the couple exited the car together. Mark clasped Pamela's hand, whispering love declarations in her ear. Laughing when she blushed, he kissed her cheek as they trekked across the parking lot.

"Your face has the cutest pinkish hue. What can I do to make the shade more pronounced?"

Pamela's body tingled to her feet. She swung their hands in time with Mark's conversation.

She relished the heady love emotion being with her husband brought.

I'm ecstatic, Lord. Please don't let my bubble burst a second time.

Church members swarmed the couple once Pamela and Mark stepped through the door. Gushing congratulations, people surrounded them inside the entrance hall. Today she was receiving more goodwill from her church family than she had heard in twenty-six years.

Mark shook all offered hands along the way to the sanctuary. "I forgot how friendly these folks are," he whispered. "I hope the welcome sentiments last."

"Leopards can't change their spots." Her cheek touched his upper arm. "Does that phrase work here?"

Excited voices blasted through the air before Mark could answer. Laughter abounded behind the couple.

He glanced over his shoulder. "Should've known. The baker arrived with a bevy of women. Never thought I'd see football groupies in God's house."

Pamela nudged him with her elbow. "Shush. Don't cause unnecessary problems. Everybody here knows K.C. He grew up in this church."

The crowd parted for the man dressed in black denim jeans, a white polo shirt, and a gray blazer. After dispatching his fans, he stopped beside Pamela, kissing her on the cheek. "Welcome back. Glad you're home." After K.C. waved at a group of people who called his name, he grabbed her hand and squeezed her fingers. "I knew you would choose to stay at the church where your mother attended." With a wide grin, he offered Mark his other hand. "Here's my official welcome."

Mark's arm remained locked around Pamela's waist. His other hand remained in his pocket. "That kiss is a provocative greeting to another man's wife. I hear you bake." Grinning, he shook his head. "What other tricks do you perform?" After kissing his wife's temple, Mark reached out a hand.

K.C. dropped his arm to his side, flashing a broad grin that instantly vanished. "Too many stunts to recount. But playing dead still isn't one. It's your turn if you choose to cause trouble."

"In the future, greet my wife with words and not your lips."

Pamela sucked in her cheeks to keep quiet. Mark seldom provoked others, yet he had just baited her family friend. Generations of Hayeses and Hodgeses had grown up together.

K.C.'s jaw muscles pulsated. He studied the parking lot through the glass before he turned to Pamela. "My grandparents just drove up from Edmund, so I'm going to go greet them now."

Pamela clapped her hands. "Tell Nana and Gramps hello for me."

K.C. nodded. "Can we discuss business later?"

Her words ran together when Mark's lips parted. "Call me any time. I'll visit Nana and Gramps this week."

"Later this afternoon works for me." K.C. nodded at Mark before he walked away.

Pamela glanced at her husband, who glared at K.C.'s back. "That was rude of you. What were you thinking? That man is a family friend."

"And a cool adversary," Mark said. "He's still up for any disagreement at any time. Can't he stand down?" Mark opened the sanctuary's door. "You go in first."

Chapter Seven

At five o'clock, Pamela locked the shop's door for the day. She left the kitchen in tiptop condition. Three helpful hours were spent shopping for wet ingredients, stocking the cooler, and prepping for the cooking spree that week. Dry components were transferred from stock to counter and frozen items from freezer to refrigerator. She disinfected the prep area and baking utensils, and laid out aprons, disposable gloves, and caps.

After Pamela finished working, she backed the car out of the gravel parking lot while wondering if Mark had left work. The long day, filled with highs and lows, neared its end. After church, the couple had eaten a meal with her father and stepmother. Steven and Valerie were at odds with each other. Their bickering made it hard for anyone to enjoy the delectable food.

On the drive home, Mark had suggested they limit visits to both sets of parents except for Anna. Pamela had given a quick no. Mark had ignored the Simons' calls since he gave his parents a guilty verdict while he and Pamela walked the trails at Shiatown University. Pamela knew her husband must forgive his folks in order to release the pain.

On reaching home, she parked the car in the driveway and walked around the block. Her stroll allotted Jessica ample confrontation time. Their neighbor appeared to be otherwise occupied. Soon Pamela regretted her careless whim but took another trek through the neighborhood. Upon her return home, she drove the car into the garage.

Why invite trouble their neighbor would've happily provided?

Finished courting conflicts, she cooked her husband a fabulous meal.

* * *

Before dawn the next morning, Pamela backed the car out of the garage as a sturdy-built man with close-cropped hair exited a four-door sedan in the Prentises' driveway. She couldn't make out his features, yet she saw the hand wave before he went inside his house. His commanding demeanor appeared friendly. The purposeful gait depicted self-confidence. Despite the historic Mark exception, Pamela was an excellent character judge. She could tell Jessica had married a no-nonsense, take-charge man.

Still thinking about Jessica's husband, Pamela parked on the lot in front of Timeless Pastries.

Two years earlier, in a rare show of familial pride, her father had helped set her up in business. The twenty-two-hundred-square-foot building housed a commercial kitchen in the rear. An office, restroom, and a combination sitting room and dining area dominated the rear east wall. The huge space in the front portion of the building remained unused.

In the kitchen, she switched on instrumental music, donned a wraparound apron, and moved fruit mixtures and tart shells from the freezer to the cooler for Tuesday's baking. Then she transferred rolled cookie dough and freezer bags full of batter from the refrigerator to the preparation area.

Someone tapped on a side window ninety minutes later. When Pamela opened the steel door, Anna and Melinda stood there. Her mother was holding two thermal bags.

"Morning, family," Pamela greeted. "What's in the bags, Mom?"

"I cooked dinner for you and Mellie last night. I'll put both bags into the cooler."

"Thanks, Mom. I'll get a chance to rest this evening." Melinda said.

Pamela nodded. "That was very sweet of you. And today I'm ready to bake after my two-week honeymoon."

"Good. You have a busy two weeks coming up," Anna said.

Before they stepped inside the building, another car pulled into the parking lot.

"He's bearing gifts," Melinda noted.

The women waited at the door for K.C. to reach them.

"Breakfast." Pamela clapped her hands and stepped aside.

"Santa came early this year," K.C. said.

He placed a warm box embossed with The Sandwich Factory into Pamela's hands.

Lifting the lid, she peeked inside. "Sausage rolls! Thanks! I'll make a lunch run around noon. Tacos?"

"Tacos work for me." Melinda set paper plates and napkins on the table and quickly unwrapped a sausage roll. "This spicy wrap tastes delish. I'll tell

Ace we need to make a visit."

Grabbing one from the box, Anna indicated the front of the building. "I was thinking about how you can develop your unused space. Serve light meals on weekdays. Lunch from ten until two are the perfect hours."

"Seriously?" Pamela asked, craning her neck to peer past the kitchen.

"Serve desserts, deli sandwiches, salads, and homemade potato chips," Melinda added. "This business park has a lot of light and medium industry. The workers need nourishing meals for lunch."

"Don't forget about the tech and financial firms in the area. Plus the community and the technical colleges," said Anna.

Melinda nodded. "And countless private businesses too. You have a centralized location in the business park. Providing lunch will also advertise your fundraisers."

"I think you guys are on point," K.C. said. "Pam could then sell pastries and candy from eight to four."

Pamela bounced on the chair in excitement. "How long have you guys been discussing my business without telling me?"

"Mom and I discussed those possibilities while you honeymooned," Melinda said. "K.C. just agrees with excellent suggestions."

Pamela's heart fluttered as she digested their advice. Serving food and selling baked goods to walk-in customers had seized her mind on the first day her father had bought the place. After a year of fervent wishing, she had put her dream onto the back burner. Business expansion entailed too much work for one person to undertake.

She removed another sausage roll from the box. "I can't afford to hire workers. Permanent part-time employees require consistent pay. I mean, they're great suggestions but too much work for one person. Unless ... you guys are offering yourselves as volunteers."

"Consider us the think tank. Hire employees," her mother said, laughing. "Build momentum. Implement a twelve-month plan."

Melinda dabbed a napkin across her mouth. "Also, you can sell your products online. Your technology-proficient husband can set you up in style. Strange that he never set up a website for your business."

Mark never considered any aspect of her job. He just ate the goodies Pamela brought to lunch. Even after Jessica left Mark, he still appeared oblivious that his friend worked for herself. Selling her baked goods online must wait until she could hire an affordable expert to set up her website.

Perhaps selling baked goods and candy during weekdays had been doable all along. Could she add services that wouldn't require permanent outside help?

"I hear suggestions that will require a lot of work. I had considered some of those ideas when Dad bought the building but thought the projects were overwhelming."

"Don't get into a rush," Anna said. "You have time to research and execute the best plans."

Pamela nodded. "I'll pray about it for a while."

When a flute composition rang from the counter's alarm clock, she switched it off and rolled up her sleeves.

"It's eight o'clock. Let's light up the kitchen."

* * *

Ten minutes away from Timeless Pastries and situated on ten acres, Techno Plus occupied the business park's southernmost tip and overlooked Horseshoe Lake. This whole area housed the city's commercial district. Four miles away, the Ellis Bridge linked South Town to its neighboring city, Shiatown, where most of South Town's workforce lived.

Bright and early at seven o'clock, Mark had held a meeting with his staffers. Now he and his administrative assistant, Lavine Tibbs, headed upstairs for a mandatory meeting for the entire building.

With his mind focused on the Pamela and K.C. baking escapade, he endured simultaneous claps after each sentence the CEO uttered. He wanted the CEO to get to the crux so Mark could leave and check on his wife.

An hour later, the CFO took over the microphone. Mark zoned out until he heard a faraway voice call his name.

"Give us your take, Mark. Our email initiative will save the company four hundred thousand over three years."

As the CIO, Mark set guidelines and administered Techno Plus's overall technology goal. His crusades freed his staff members from needless tasks that wasted their department's manpower and the company's resources. Mark began the unexpected discussion by critiquing bankrupted companies who'd abandoned quality customer service to save pennies and ended up losing millions.

The operations department had advocated for one change that would decimate businesses with an older client base: switching patrons to paperless bills without their written or verbal consent. Two changes would displease

68

younger customers: adding a surcharge for online payments and limiting telephone payments to one payment per month.

Numerous factors might prompt consumers that had other choices into procuring comparable services elsewhere. And if too many did so, Techno Plus would go bankrupt.

Mark explained how lowered customer satisfaction would cost them forty-seven million over four years. The company had built its reputation on cutting-edge technology and market savvy. Now Techno Plus was treading water due to having copied stale policies instead of setting poignant trends.

After the meeting ended, the board treasurer and secretary requested to have lunch with Mark the next week. It appeared both board members recognized his business acumen during Mark's unplanned presentation.

After the women walked away, Lavine and Mark chatted by the snack table. His administrative assistant held the unique distinction of being the first employee hired at the company twenty-five years ago. The dynamo fashioned her own job description, embraced new skills, and retained old-school aggregating concepts. Plus, Lavine and her husband, Stan, were personal friends of the Techno Plus founder and board chairman.

"You tell them, boss." Lavine bit into a brownie. "Your wife owns a bakery. Shouldn't she cater our events instead of The Ultimate Doughnut Holes?"

"Pamela doesn't operate a retail facility. She may need more space to branch out further."

He didn't want to admit to Lavine that he'd never seen Pamela's building to even know if she could handle more business. His outrageous oversight would be rectified that day. He would learn more about her business than any other person ever could.

He lifted a black business card featuring pastries and candies from his shirt pocket. That morning he had grabbed a stack off his wife's nightstand.

Mark handed Lavine the information. "Pertinent details are on the back."

Lavine scanned the front side of the business card then gazed at Mark. "So your wife operates wholesale, selling baked goods and candy to restaurants and eateries." She flipped the card over. "Fundraisers! I could use that service for my sorority."

"You and Stan know a network of influencers. Keep me posted if anyone is interested in receiving more information."

"Gladly. Pam can cater our events at Techno Plus without a retail outlet. Does her business have an online presence? If so, I'll push the website on social media."

His unprecedented failures as a close friend mounted.

"Great idea!" he said. "Expect relevant material this weekend. Techno Plus will make Timeless Pastries's presence known."

"May I have those business cards?" Lavine accepted the business cards Mark handed to her and stashed them into her purse. "Thank you. Bring more in tomorrow." She paused, studying Mark. "You never told me K.C. Hodges is Pam's old boyfriend. I haven't had a chance to ask you about their relationship. At the wedding, Stan said some people had bet those two might get married."

Mark flinched as if a searing iron had branded his skin. He started to speak then paused, thinking of a ruse to stay quiet.

No wonder Pamela had appeared dreamy-eyed at breakfast on Saturday when she mentioned Hodges. Mark had figured she'd given him the short version of the so-called friendship; and she had indeed.

"Do Stan's friends know either of them?" Mark asked.

"I don't think so. He's our only national celebrity, so he gets a lot of attention around here. His dating Ace's sister had fostered hope among his fans." Gray flecks glittered in her eyes. "But you won her hand. Congratulations. Well done."

Pamela had dated Hodges without his knowledge.

Heat surged through his neck in such a rush his ears sizzled.

When were they together?

How long did the connection last?

Why hadn't Pamela told him she was dating Hodges?

His family and so-called friends were worthless. Everybody had probably known about her romance with the football star.

How did a liaison between those two escape Mark's notice?

Pamela had shrouded him in darkness on purpose.

He realized he'd been fuming for who knows how long. He gazed at the woman staring at him with keen insight. Widening his stance, Mark looked directly at Lavine. "My beautiful wife had plenty of dates aside from K.C."

Lavine nodded. "Maybe K.C.'s eager fans misjudged the relationship."

Perhaps their guess had been an accurate deduction. Pamela had lived another life Mark hadn't known about. His negligence as a friend had run deeper than he'd imagined. The neglectful friend wouldn't become an absentee husband. Mark planned to play active roles in her business and personal life.

Whatever concerned his wife deserved his attention.

Being angry with himself was meaningless unless he changed the shameful way he'd treated Pamela. He did wonder what else had happened without his knowledge.

A discreet cough reminded Mark of his administrative assistant's presence.

Her thoughtful gaze engaged her boss as he pulled himself together.

Mark dropped a napkin into the trash can. "I'm leaving early. Please reschedule the two o'clock appointment with eService's manager until ten tomorrow."

"Consider it done," Lavine said. "I wish Stan and I could have stayed after the wedding ceremony to meet your bride. We had weekend guests and had to get home."

Her warm smile encouraged Mark's heart. He must change the dynamics of his relationship with Pamela.

His wife knew details about his job, family, and friends. To his discredit Mark had only thought about Pamela while preparing for their lunch dates. He had even treated her carelessly as she supported him after Jessica walked away and during their engagement. The one-way friendship was over. Marriage provided him the chance to secure an unbreakable bond.

Before leaving the building, he walked into his office and grabbed his laptop and briefcase.

Had Pamela's and Hodges' social engagements amounted to little more than outings between friends? Had onlookers turned a friendship into a romantic tale? Perhaps the gossip had hit the target after all. Busybodies insisted truth existed within each rumor. Mark had been too occupied with Jessica to notice anyone else.

Even at the office, he often heard Hodges' name. Because they lived in a fairly small city, playing a professional sport for seven years had turned him into a household name. The baker had officially retired from playing football last month. Gibson High School had hired him as their head football coach. Just that morning, in the elevator, the security guard had told Mark the full story after highlighting Hodges' entire pro career. Pamela had never told him about any of it.

Mark hesitated while looking out the window. The sun shone outside despite his dark thoughts.

He set the laptop on the credenza and closed the blinds. Picking up the laptop again, he left the office, waved at his administrative assistant, and headed to the elevator.

Melinda placed sixteen pans that each held twenty-four cupcakes into four double ovens, giggling when her stomach gurgled.

"I heard that," K.C. said. "Doesn't your husband feed you at home?"

"He cooked dinner yesterday, and then you provided my breakfast this morning."

Pamela sauntered into the room after rolling two racks filled with seven hundred fifty cupcakes into the cooler. She pulled on a pair of gloves at the cookie prep table and began slicing cookie dough for her regular client orders.

Melinda clocked her progress. "We're ahead of schedule. When are you making the taco run?" she asked.

"You're hungry? It's too early to eat lunch. I was thinking around twelve."

"That's too long to wait. We ate breakfast at seven thirty. I'm starving now. I think the constant arm movements, bending over, stooping down, and reaching over my head for almost four hours is plenty of exercise for one morning. I'm ready to rest and eat a meal."

"Me too," said Anna. "I'll be ready to sit down and eat in thirty minutes." Blowing a wisp of hair off her forehead, Anna repositioned her hair cap, then washed her hands in the sink. She nudged K.C.'s back with her elbow as she strolled pass him. "How about you? Hungry?"

"I'm always ready for a meal. I only get tired of chewing. I should've brought more than ten sausage rolls. I'll bring fourteen bacon and egg biscuits in the morning."

Pamela layered ninety-six cookies on four trays, then she set the trays on a rack that held twenty trays of baked cookies and several trays of unbaked cookies waiting to go into the oven.

She shed her gloves into the trash. "Okay, avid eaters. I'll tidy up and leave pronto."

* * *

Food trucks queued in strategic spots on multiple streets in the manufacturing district. Mark drove to the core of the business center, parking in a gravel lot. Good thing he'd remembered his wife's general location information and spotted her parked car outside the building. Pamela's commercial kitchen looked like a vacant building. Except for the four cars parked outside, the nondescript building appeared to be empty. Yet the building occupied an ideal location in the hub of the industrial park.

As he got out of the vehicle, Mark grinned at his surroundings. It was the perfect location for what he had in mind. Her father had selected an admirable spot. Holding multiple food bags, he knocked on the shop's window, then stood in front of the steel door.

Mark watched as a shadow appeared in a small side window. An excited voiced sounded through the door.

"It's Mark! My husband's here!" He heard his wife say.

Pamela unlocked the door and threw her arms around Mark's neck. "You stopped by. Welcome to my kitchen."

Mark felt like a first-class heel. His wife's elation with one visit highlighted how much she'd wanted his involvement in something dear to her heart.

"This visit is long overdue," he said. Kissing her lips, Mark held up multiple lunch sacks. "I come bearing gifts for lunch."

"And right on time," she said, backing up. "I was just leaving to make a taco run."

The restaurant's name wasn't printed on the bag. Pamela tried to peek inside the closest one, but Mark held the sack out of her reach.

"No peeking. Be surprised along with everyone else. Pam ..." he said. Then he hesitated. "Thank you for accepting my peace offering. I had to hunt for this building when I should've known the address. Am I your only friend who has never visited the place?"

The tears Mark saw pooling in her eyes didn't spill over.

Nodding, Pamela called over her shoulder to the people bustling inside the open kitchen. "Hey guys, food. Take a well-deserved rest."

She beamed at Mark and pointed across the room. "The breakroom is through that door. Follow me."

Trailing behind his wife, Mark surveyed the building. The stainless-steel kitchen was a baker's dream. The area contained multiple double ovens, a walk-in cooler, and a separate side-by-side refrigerator and freezer. Several closed doors indicated more than one pantry. Floor-to-ceiling cabinets lined one wall. Steven had spared no expense in the kitchen's execution.

Time to take the commercial kitchen to the next level: a retail bakery.

Mark followed Pamela into an open-concept space. The breakroom was a combination social area and dining room. On one side, a round table seated eight people. Upper and lower cupboards covered an entire wall. A microwave occupied the counter beside the refrigerator. There was plenty of counter space, plus a small island sat in front of the sink.

Across the room, two sofas, several comfy chairs, four decorative tables, and two bookcases created a social atmosphere. A thirty-two-inch television topped an entertainment center. Mark visualized the workers eating tasty meals and taking comfortable breaks away from baking.

K.C. entered the breakroom and stood off to the side, leaning on a wall. *Time to hire permanent employees.*

Anna removed the food bags from his hands. "Hello, son-in-law. I hope you brought enough food to join us."

"Yes, ma'am. Lunch and cleanup duty are my contributions for the day. He placed his laptop and briefcase on an end table. I'll do a little work after you guys finish eating lunch. I might have time to watch television until we're ready to clean up the place."

"Work and relaxation," Melinda said. "You came prepared." She peered inside each bag. "Soup, sandwiches, and salad. This is a lot like what we were talking about earlier."

"What do you mean?" Mark sat at the table, but his peripheral vision kept tabs on Hodges. Thus far, the man hung behind the others, refusing to join them.

Pamela grabbed Mark's hand and sat on the seat beside him. "These two were busy planning for the future while we were on our honeymoon. They suggested I should serve deli sandwiches, salads, and homemade potato chips on weekdays from ten to two."

Joy lit his wife's eyes as she squeezed his fingers. "And since I'd be here anyway, K.C. thinks I should sell pastries and candy weekdays from eight to four. We would remain closed on weekends."

"Sounds like a good plan," Mark said. He left the room and stood in the center of the kitchen to survey the building. At the breakroom door, he stole another glance around the area.

He couldn't stop grinning when he reclaimed the seat beside his wife.

Pamela's enthusiastic gaze made Mark glad he had come.

"Don't keep me guessing," she said. "Do you approve of my little kitchen?"

"Your setup is far from little. You could've rented this place out on evenings and weekends for extra money."

"You think so?" Pamela said, looking around the room. "I don't have a real commercial kitchen. At least, not professional enough to rent it out."

"Even with my limited experience I know your setup is top-notch." Mark hesitated to collect his thoughts. Hodges' presence threw him off his game. "You have a workable plan, but it comes with a hefty workload. It's too much labor for one person. But hire employees and go for it. Score another win."

The love on Pamela's face almost stole Mark's breath. It was as if the two of them were alone in the room.

"Oh, Mark. Do you truly think so?"

"I do. Let me know how I can help."

When Melinda cleared her throat, Pamela glanced at the others.

"My husband is on board *and* offering me his assistance."

K.C. chuckled. "He will continue to support you as long as I'm working here. I'll take this call in the car." His cell phone in hand, K.C. gathered his lunch and headed outside.

Mark scooted back the chair and headed toward the breakroom door, then he grinned over his shoulder. "This is his last week to get my wife by herself. Where's the restroom, ladies?"

Anna pointed toward the restroom's direction. "Turn right and hook a left at the corner."

"Please give me a rundown on each idea and operation when I get back," he said.

Mark stood at the window and watched Hodges eat lunch inside his car. So much for the phone call. Why did the man attack Mark and then leave? Hodges relied on the one-two punch.

* * *

A silent Pamela sipped water, trying to make sense of what had just happened.

Two off-kilter comments proved inappropriate for the occasion. Neither Mark nor K.C. had mentioned each other after they had clashed at church. Before their latest confrontation, Pamela had suspected both men regretted yesterday's questionable behavior.

Why, Mark? Why are you helping me now?

Somehow K.C. played a role in her husband's sudden desire to be of assistance.

Deal with the problem at hand without speculation. The truth will be revealed sooner or later.

When the restroom door clanged shut, Pamela studied her mother and sister-in-law. "That conversation didn't go well. I feel like I missed an important message."

Melinda's brow wrinkled. "When the air crackles then snaps, it's an overload of male testosterone."

"Is your husband aware you and K.C. once dated?" Anna untied her apron and sat across from her daughter-in-law. "Either Mark knows or he's the jealous type."

Pamela shook her head. "No. Mark and I never discussed who I dated."

"I agree with Mom," Melinda said. "He knows."

"Mark lacked interest in who I dated. None of my date's names surfaced in any of our conversations. Although yesterday, he and K.C. had a small spat at church."

Anna and Melinda shared glances.

"What happened?" Anna asked.

"Mark took offense when K.C. clasped my hand and kissed my cheek. And then K.C. showed his disapproval of my husband's reaction."

"Along with kissing you and holding your hand yesterday, K.C.'s comment today was improper," Anna said. "Your spouse's feelings take precedence over any other person's. Remember that."

"Their run-in yesterday caught me unawares," Pamela said. "I didn't know how to react and figured they both would cool off."

"That's an understandable summation," Anna said. "But do not sweep rudeness under the rug. Deal with problems as they arise."

Melinda nodded. "And now there's this idiocy on top of the Jessica-living-next-door issue. Hang in there. Ace knows his friend better than we do. I'll tell him about everything tonight and get his opinion."

The women switched topics when Mark walked into the room. They filled him in on Timeless Pastries' current menus, fundraisers, and regular clientele.

Chapter Eight

"I like your M.O., sis. Thanks for paying us on the first day we work." Melinda placed the envelope into her handbag as she winked at Mark. "Your wife is the only employer I know who pays early." Her wide glance took in everyone. "Remember my London trip with friends? This check tops off that vacation fund. Though Ace forbids me to travel out of the country without him."

Mark glanced at Pamela then back at Melinda. "Are you serious?"

Melinda gave Mark a solemn nod.

"Then your husband is concerned about your welfare," he said.

Pamela shook her head. "No, sir. Skylar likes to have control."

Anna laughed as she zipped her purse. "Did my son really use the word 'forbid'?"

"I'm afraid he did. And Ace didn't like my reply."

"I can only imagine," Anna said. "I thought you planned to go to England this spring. Are you still going then?"

"I'm going in late April. I keep getting new hurdles to jump over with Ace."

"That sounds like Skylar. Name them," Pamela said.

"Well, thankfully, I've jumped over them now." Melinda nodded at Anna "You took care of the reputable babysitter requirement. Mom and Dad agreed to pay the hotel fee and airline fare. My sister-in-law just topped off my cash issue."

K.C. chuckled. "Why marry a doctor if you can't spend money like a doctor's wife?"

"My thoughts exactly," Melinda agreed. "Run that logic by your friend. Now he says I can't travel out of the states without a family member going with me—because he doesn't think I have one who will be available to go. But he insists we take the children to Florida for two weeks in June, and our parents and grandparents to Arizona for one week in August."

"Can he join you on the trip?" Pamela asked.

"I was about to ask the same question," Mark said. "Your husband wants to keep you safe."

"Ace is trying to keep me at home. And he isn't welcome on my women-only trip. None of my friends are taking their spouses along."

"You guys will figure it out before April," Anna said. "Take a solo vacation with Skylar once you return home from Europe. I'll keep my grandchildren. For now, I'll see you tomorrow."

Melinda hugged her mother-in-law. "Thanks for sending me home with tonight's dinner. Goodbye, everyone."

"See you tomorrow," the others chorused.

Anna hugged her daughter. "A delightful day, Pam. And Mark, unless you stop by here tomorrow, I'll see you at church. Bye, K.C."

Mark glanced at the silent man staring at him. "My tentative plan is a repeat performance of today," he said to Anna. "If that scenario doesn't pan out, count on seeing me at church on Sunday."

Pamela stepped outside the building. "Thanks, guys. As always, your assistance is greatly appreciated."

Ready for a night's rest, the team headed for their cars.

Snug within Mark's supportive arms, Pamela waved at her workers until the last vehicle drove off the lot.

Despite still wearing his business attire, her husband had given a creditable effort along with the work crew. The spotless building glistened. An unidentified reticence kept her from gushing over Mark's performance. He'd gratified and disappointed Pamela since he'd arrived.

After the initial clash, Mark and K.C. had ignored each other the rest of the day. During cleanup, her husband clamped his mouth shut. He loved people and normally engaged in lively debates and discussions. Dialogue was his forte.

Back inside the building, Pamela grabbed her purse and the thermal pack and perused the room.

Switching off lights, Mark touched her elbow before she stepped outside.

"Who does your accounting?" he asked.

"I do. My business is too small to hire an accountant."

"Timeless Pastries employs people who get paid real money. And certain tax requirements must be met. Are you handling all of that?"

"Mom, Mellie, and K.C. aren't actual employees. They're volunteers."

78

"You do give them monetary compensation for their work."

"Oh no. Did I do something illegal?"

Her jaw dropped as she set the thermal pack containing their dinner on the ground and locked the door.

"No worries," Mark said. "Techno Plus provides accounting services for businesses large or small. You're booked this week and the next with fundrais-ers. I'll start the ball rolling on your behalf. Can you attend an appointment in two weeks?"

"Yes. Any day except on Monday or Tuesday. Make it around noon."

After she retrieved the thermal pack, Mark hooked Pamela's arm and walked her to her car. "Hire a full-time baker. You'll need two part-time cashiers. My cousins are looking for supplemental income because teenagers bring added expenses."

"Emily and Tina? They told me they wanted part-time employment at our reception. But not with Mr. Simon. They said their uncle is a crabby boss."

"Father does have his pigheaded moments, along with maintaining long-term employees. Evidently, he's doing something right."

Pamela's fingers tapped her lips. "Um ... a single mother at my church is an outstanding baker. Maybe we can figure some things out. I'll contact everyone when it becomes necessary."

"That's progress," Mark said. "And my assistant made a superb suggestion earlier. Timeless Pastries will have a website by this weekend."

Her husband was full of surprises today: accounting concepts, hiring prac-tices, and establishing an online presence. What a sea of change overnight. Where was the real Mark Simon hiding?

At Pamela's car, Mark held open the car door for her to enter the vehicle. "I'll make a stop by the cleaners and head right home," he said. "Can't wait to taste what your mother prepared for our dinner."

Once she slid inside, he gave her a quick kiss, watched her fasten the seatbelt, then shut the car door.

My husband opened the car door for me and tucked me safely inside. Someone stole my spouse.

Pamela waved at Mark after he reached his car. "Bye-bye. See you soon."

Before her car reached the corner, she received a call from Skylar. Pamela switched on Bluetooth.

"Hey, sis. Mellie just told me about the Mark and K.C. square off in your breakroom."

Pamela turned off her music. "Even if you were present, you might've doubted what you witnessed."

"I never doubt what I see," Skylar said. "In case your husband recently learned you dated K.C., bring him up to speed later. You probably should've told him before today."

How would Mark have found out about who she had dated? If he had, why would he suddenly care about a man she dated three years ago? He had cut her off the one time she had attempted to tell him about K.C. Mark had refused to listen then, and Pamela rejected divulging her past life now. There would be no point.

She shook her head even though her brother failed to see the action. "I did try to tell him before my first date with K.C. He changed the subject then, and I won't drudge up old news now because some person spread gossip. Besides, most people never knew we dated."

"Perhaps the right someone did and told your husband. He refused to listen the first time you tried to tell him. Forgive Mark. Tell your husband now and move on."

"I have forgiven Mark. It doesn't do any good to dwell on the past. We're better off focusing on the future."

Skylar grunted. "Forget that he refused to listen before you had the first date with K.C. You can't make him pay now for his past mistakes. Set the record straight this evening. Doing nothing always escalates problems further than they ever need to go."

Pamela turned on her blinker and pulled into the right lane. She made a turn at the corner.

"I refuse to answer questions before they're asked." She laughed when her brother groaned. "If he asks me, I'll tell him. Deal?"

"Listen. Start fresh this evening. Forget about Mark's unwillingness to listen when you tried to tell him about K.C. Remember that he proposed marriage and you accepted. Forget about Jessica living next door. Remember how much you fancy your home. Deciding against separation means beginning where you are. Only forward movement brings success."

"Mark justified his betrayal concerning the ex-girlfriend. I accepted his excuse. Skylar, I still don't understand why he withheld significant facts."

"Try viewing the situation from Mark's perspective. He probably wanted to rub your happiness in Jessica's face. Somewhat like, look what you missed, even though he was ecstatic that she had."

Her brother's summation fell flat. "You mean Mark likes having his cake and eating it too? But once he eats the cake, there's nothing left."

"What?" Skylar asked. "Do I need to pay you a visit?"

"So you don't like my reasoning, huh? Well, at least you know what I mean."

"No. I don't. And I kind of suspect neither do you."

"You are so funny. Enjoy the marvelous meal Mom cooked for dinner. Thanks for calling. Love you much."

"Love you more," Skylar said. "And remember, it isn't too late to tell your husband tonight."

She shook her head again when her brother hung up. His phone call reminded her of old times. He still ran interference for Pamela.

Skylar had been a sensational running back in high school and college and still approached life with proactive tunnel vision. He and his buddy K.C. made a formidable pair for eight years on the playing field. K.C. created holes his friend charged through at will.

K.C., an offensive lineman, had chosen professional football as a career.

Instead of declaring for the draft, Skylar had attended medical school. After years of hard work and dedication, he followed in their cardiologist grandfather's footsteps of opening his own private practice.

He normally gave sound advice and made good decisions.

At home, Pamela parked inside the garage, strolled into the kitchen, and placed Anna's thermal bag on the counter. Autopilot led her to the bedroom. Lifting her Bible off the nightstand, she fell onto the bed, moaning. Exhaustion oozed from every pore. Tiredness accelerated as she rested. She was too tired to eat, think, or read scripture. Inertia led her to sleep.

* * *

A tickle on her cheek made Pamela bore deeper into the mattress. Her lips twitched. Something that felt like feathers brushed her face again.

Her eyes popped open and focused on Mark's smiling face. "Wake up, sleeping beauty. I'm home."

She sat upright in one fluid motion and patted her hair into place. "Oh. Sorry. I took a nap. I only intended to rest a little before you came home."

"You left the house at five thirty this morning and left work at five. Rest is justified."

"How sweet. My husband remembered my early schedule." Pamela slid off the bed. "I'll freshen up and meet you in the kitchen."

While washing her face in the vanity bowl, she glanced at Mark, who hovered in the bathroom doorway.

"Mother called," he said. "We have an open dinner invitation for any evening we choose. I explained your two-week heavy workload."

"I look forward to seeing them." She kissed his cheek as she headed toward the door. "Set up something for Sunday. Are they usually free on Sundays?"

Mark followed her to the bedroom door. "Who knows. No visits are possible with my folks for the foreseeable future. I don't want to see them."

Pamela swung around to face him. "Why not? They're your people. We can always make time for your parents. I will for Mom."

"Anna is a certified mother. The Simons are mother and father in title only." Mark urged her through the bedroom door, propelling his wife into the kitchen. "I am starving and wish I'd stopped by Toomey's on the drive home."

Pamela removed a casserole dish and a medium-sized bowl from the thermal pack.

"I forgot your mother supplied our dinner. Glad I didn't stop by Toomey's."

"Mom made pot roasts, potato casseroles, and side salads for two households. She told Mellie and me to pop dinner into the oven, shower, and then enjoy our families. Pretty terrific mother, huh?"

Pamela thought about Mark's parents, Celeste and Ed. *Maybe I shouldn't have praised my mom.*

"Wonder what Mom's doing tonight. She's acting cagey lately," Pamela said.

Mark nodded. "It's hardly a new pastime. Your mother began charting her own course before I showed up on your doorstep last spring. Do you think she's hiding a man somewhere away from the family?"

"I don't know." Pamela nibbled her bottom lip. "Mom evades all of my questions whenever I broach the subject. Why won't she own having a man in her life if there is one hanging around? Why turn dating someone into a covert operation?"

"I think she has a serious relationship with a man she loves. This may sound like a big leap, but expect a quick wedding after an introduction from your mother."

"Uh-uh. Mom won't contemplate marriage without first consulting me and Skylar."

"Wishful thinking. I bet that your mother has been dating someone before this past year given how she's been acting. Trust me. Nuptials are pending. Signs are posted everywhere for anyone who cares to take a close look."

Pamela liked teasing Anna about marrying a special guy without believing that would happen. Still, her lovable, trustworthy mother merited a perfect love match. Her children worried about her marrying another indifferent man.

Pamela scowled at her husband. Now she couldn't dislodge visions of her mother dating some man behind her and Skylar's backs. Her lips pursed, she shoved the casserole dish into the oven and thrust the salad bowl into the refrigerator.

"Hope you're wrong," she said, rolling up her sleeves. "Mom falling in love, if that's what's going on, should be a family thing. Dad made Mom's life miserable. We want to celebrate her dating the right man along with her."

"Of course you do. You'll get an invite to the wedding. Listen," Mark said when Pamela pouted. "For whatever reasons she may have, your mother is going solo on this trip. This may sound harsh, but she doesn't need her children's permission to remarry."

Pamela rolled her eyes at Mark. "I refuse to stress over speculations." She pulled a portion of her blouse away from her body. "I feel gritty. I'm going to shower while this cooks. Expect dinner in thirty minutes."

* * *

Throughout the meal, Mark searched for ways to discuss Hodges while his wife asked questions about her husband's day.

Later in the family room, Pamela fell asleep before Mark could broach the subject.

She dozed in his arms as he brushed fleeting kisses on her forehead. His wife looked so innocent while asleep, yet she harbored verified secrets. Lavine Tibbs was an excellent news source who only repeated valid information.

Pamela didn't move when Mark lightly tapped her arm. He then decided not to nudge her again. Somehow, waking his wife up to an interrogation seemed like a terrible idea. Her alarm clock pinged at four thirty on weekday mornings; she needed her rest.

But images of Hodges dating Pamela assaulted Mark's mind as he studied her peaceful posture. The football player and his wife had been an item at some point in the not-so-distant past. He wanted and deserved immediate answers.

He softly shook her body that lay within his arms. "Pam, may we talk about a matter that has bothered me all day?"

When Pamela snuggled closer but failed to wake up, Mark reminded himself again about his wife's early morning and hectic workday. Their vital K.C. talk must wait until another evening. However, he and his wife couldn't blend their lives while another man flirted with his wife. Jessica's war on the couple's marriage paled against a charming suitor camouflaged as a family friend.

It sounded like people had considered Hodges and Pamela a perfect match. What had derailed their relationship? Groupies? His schedule? Living in separate cities six months a year? Or did the relationship end because Pamela loved Mark? If so, why did she date a man she might've married? Were they exclusive to each other, or did they simultaneously see other people? From the little he knew about her social life, his wife had seldom dated the same man twice. How long had the ex-football star escorted Mark's bride around town?

Mark felt that Pamela had failed him. A confession of the romance should've preceded her accepting Mark's proposal. When he finally got the chance to ask her, she'd probably say, "That happened years ago. No one cares about stale news. Pure and simple."

Of course, Pamela could have dated whomever she wanted to. But it hurt him that football fans knew, yet he, the man who counted most, did not.

Flashbacks seared his brain. Maybe he had heard the rumor. Jessica had gossiped about seeing Pamela and Hodges together twice. She'd spotted the pair eating dinner with Melinda and Ace and at the airport. On both instances, Mark had just assumed they were friends.

His brain exploded with a new speculation: Had she spent time at Hodges' apartment on the west coast during football season?

Chuckling to himself, Mark breathed easier. Over the years, she'd never missed a single lunch date with Mark. Pamela was always in South Town on Tuesdays and Thursdays. Then his newly found composure died a sudden death. What about the weekends?

His ears crackled with escalating anger.

His wife's docile face lay on Mark's chest.

As he gazed at her, he knew their present and future relationship must feature coordinated lifestyles: like having honest discussions, supporting each other when needed, and building a quality relationship. When Jessica walked away, Pamela had given Mark her full support. She'd changed her routines to fit his schedule until she thought he had fully recovered from the shock.

Perplexed over the next step he should take, Mark concentrated on his new channel-surfing hobby.

* * *

The next morning, Pamela rolled out the bed, still tired after sleeping for eight hours. Mark invaded her mind on the drive to Timeless Pastries. His jealous behavior yesterday still stumped her. He had seemed peaceful enough last night. And she had slept within his arms while he watched television.

The conversation with her brother played through Pamela's thoughts the rest of the way to work.

"Go away, Skylar. I don't need your insight in my head this morning."

She turned on the radio and sang along with a popular song.

At the shop, she switched on lights throughout the building. Standing in the front portion, she envisioned a dine-in area. The room held space for around twenty tables and a small banquet hall. She didn't have a clue how to hire employees, provide health insurance, or any legalities that pertained to business ownership. Thank God for Techno Plus and her husband's executive position there. Could she afford their service on Timeless Pastries' earnings? Her mother had recommended spending a year planning her next moves before adding lunch and selling candy and baked goods. Mark estimated the retail establishment was achievable much sooner. At least selling sweets on weekdays seemed like the uncomplicated part.

How much money would renovations cost? Would her father loan improvement funds if she signed a promissory note?

Pamela mused over that idea until a flute melody ripped the silence.

And it made her realize she had just lost thirty minutes of prep time.

"Buckle down, woman," she told herself. "It's work time. No more daydreaming for now."

* * *

Back-to-back problems surfaced after Mark's ten o'clock appointment ended. Negative thoughts concerning Hodges working closely with his wife intruded on his day. Knowing Hodges' history with women and his wife's trusting personality worried Mark. He'd heard about the man's escapades since middle school.

Mark stared at the computer screen, noting his overflowing inbox. Authority carried immense responsibility with it. Despite the planned one-week honeymoon in the Turks and Caicos, he'd scheduled a two-week vacation from work beforehand. Leaving work early again today might send middle management an inappropriate message.

As he thought about middle management, he realized that perhaps his forte was corporate administration rather than IT oversight. He thrived on formulating strategies that shaped a company's culture margin. Throughout the day, he resisted urges to micromanage departments requiring IT's direct participation.

Casting thoughts about his wife and K.C. aside, he concentrated on IT's agenda.

* * *

"K.C.'s inside his car. The engine is started. He's pulling out of the parking lot. See, he's gone." Pamela glanced at Anna. "It's safe to go and leave me to my own devices. But now I have a question for you. Who'll guard my honor over the next few days? You and Mellie are off work until Monday."

Anna's side-splitting laugh cut through the tension. "Do you think I distrust you?" she asked.

"Yes. I do. You're still here." Pamela retrieved her car keys when they dropped onto the ground. Blowing off loose gravel, she twirled the key ring on her finger. "For the record, I won't cheat on my husband."

Anna laughed, smiled, then laughed again. "No one doubts your exemplary conduct. I stayed behind to talk to you. You finally see Mark's quirks and human weaknesses. You don't trust him. Forget about your rah-rah spirit to make your marriage work. Jessica's living next door devasted you. You felt used. While your husband was here yesterday, you watched him nonstop."

"It sounds like you're blaming the person who got deceived. I'm the same person I always was. I didn't change."

"Neither did Mark. That you both interact on a higher level is encouraging."

Pamela brushed away tears. "Okay, I made a character-assessment mistake. But innocent people aren't guilty. I did nothing wrong."

"Consider your part in this confusion," Anna said. "You misread plainly posted signs. I recognize you've now adopted a different strategy: Get along at all costs to maintain peace with Mark." Anna hesitated, rifling her fingers through her hair. "Ignoring the Jessica incident will backfire. Resolve issues with your husband through honest dialogue and mercy. If not, one day your true feelings will erupt in an inappropriate manner. Forgive Mark and maintain your values."

Forgiving Mark was a priority Pamela hadn't achieved. Mistrust and compassion fought for domination.

"No one can make up for lost time," Anna said. "And do not strategize for problems that may never occur."

Pamela leaned on the vehicle. "What do you mean?"

"Live an even-keeled life by balancing optimism with sober thinking." Anna paused, smiling. "Babe, learn from your mistakes. Wisdom is knowledge used correctly."

"I think Mark's deception is keeping me from being happy. I'm going about my day, and then I remember Mark's deceit." Tears sprang into her eyes.

Anna moved closer to Pamela. "When do those thoughts occur?"

"It varies, but they come up often. At first, Mark pretended nothing significant took place. But I don't like his business-as-usual approach."

"Mark doesn't want to lose you. Yesterday we ate lunch with a different man. Real change takes time and hard work from you both if you want to make your marriage work."

"I ... I just didn't foresee my happiness ending this way."

"Your life together is a beginning. Consider God's word before making decisions. Don't rationalize your behavior or Mark's." Anna's thumb brushed teardrops off Pamela's damp cheeks. "Are you okay?"

"Yes, ma'am. And on my way home. Thanks for staying behind and talking to me. Knowing you love me helps me to forget that Mark used me in the past."

"You know I'm always here for you." Anna glanced at her watch then hugged Pamela. "I'm eating out tonight with friends. Gotta run." She scooted into her car. The engine immediately started.

Anna Hayes leaving now must mean she had dinner plans with a special person. Someone she truly wanted to see. Mark had nailed it. Before he proposed, Anna had only spent her Saturdays away from home. When Pamela got engaged, her mother dedicated her evenings and Sundays to these friends her children hadn't met.

"A date?" Pamela asked. "Are you seeing someone? Tell me who he is. Does Skylar know his name?"

"Get in your car so I can go."

Someone's in a hurry to leave. Opening the car door, Pamela slid inside her vehicle.

"Drive safe," Anna mouthed when her daughter started the engine.

The pair drove off the parking lot, one vehicle behind the other. As always, the younger woman proceeded first.

Chapter Nine

All day Mark had fixed problems that wouldn't have happened if Techno Plus had had sound business practices. His growing frustrations with the company fueled his desire for a major career change. He wanted to leave his job at Techno Plus by the year's end.

That evening, Mark left work two hours later than he had hoped. But because he finally knew what he wanted regarding work, his workday ended on a positive note.

He knew he wanted to help his wife fulfill her Timeless Pastries dreams In recent days Pamela's shop had consumed his thoughts and unearthed forgotten memories. During his formative years and beyond, Mark had watched Ed turn a mediocre pawn shop into a thriving enterprise. These days, Enough for Everyone occupied two prime locations: South Town and Shiatown. Mark's grandfather would've escaped yearly bankruptcy scares had he adopted his son's business stratagems.

His grandparents resided in a retirement community across the river in Shiatown. Eight years ago, his mother's parents had moved to Tacoma, Washington, with their eldest daughter's family. On the third Sunday of each month, the senior Parkers talked with their grandchildren on a conference call. During Pamela and Mark's honeymoon, his wife got inducted into the Parker family's lovefest network. His family-oriented spouse appreciated the connection.

The saying "no one is ever too old to learn" included him. At twenty-eight-years-old, he was still taking tests he should've conquered years ago. Now Mark understood that healthy family bonds were an essential component of triumphant lives. The unfulfilled existence he'd endured with his parents no longer counted. Jessica had slipped into his life and bankrupted his un-grounded soul. Now Mark had a strong foundation he could build his life upon.

He pulled out of the parking lot and raced home. Time stood still as he neared his neighborhood. It was like getting a fresh start on a tiresome day.

Exiting the main street, his shoulder muscles relaxed. West Gate subdivision lay ahead. His heart lightened as the car rounded the corner into the cul-de-sac.

He spotted Jessica watering her lawn at the property line.

Well, well. Chuckling, Mark pulled his vehicle into his driveway.

His hand dropped from the garage opener attached to the sun visor. Parking the car in the driveway, he shoved the device into his jacket pocket. What fresh threats would the provocateur make today?

Exiting the vehicle, he opened the door to the back seat to retrieve his briefcase and laptop.

He wondered where Pamela might be inside the house. And then he realized he shouldn't talk to a woman if he had to sneak behind his wife's back to do it.

Mark had just congratulated himself on the drive home for tracking the correct pathway for his life. Now he flirted with another disastrous move.

"Hey, neighbor. Where's the missus hiding?" Jessica asked.

Laptop and briefcase in hand, Mark's head dipped in a dismissive nod as he strolled to the walkway. The sound of water fizzed in the air. How long could the shrew keep up the friendly tone?

She turned off the hose. "Wait, so we can talk," she said in a cajoling voice. "On Friday I didn't have the chance to congratulate your wife."

Mrs. Prentis wanted another confrontation more than Mark did. Should he stop and grant her wish? His steps hastened to the walkway. Had either of them gained wisdom since Friday?

"I'm talking to you, Mark," she said.

Mark's neck craned toward the house. Hopefully Pamela was either reading a book in the family room or cooking their dinner in the kitchen. Lord, let her be somewhere in the back of the house.

His steps slowed. "At church we received enough congratulations to last us a lifetime."

A crack sounded as the water hose nozzle hit the decorative bricks around the neighbor's lawn.

"Hold up anyway," Jessica said. "We need to talk. Now. Don't ignore me."

"If you wish." Mark veered around, trying to hide his satisfaction. He needed this talk for self-vindication. "Although you disrespected my marriage last Friday, your apology is accepted."

The transparent woman designed her next move before his eyes. Today he noticed blatant changes he'd missed four days ago. Her appearance and mannerism seemed at odds with the woman he'd dated. Plus, she dressed less trendy these days. In fact, her demeanor bordered on regret. Yet Friday's cockiness waited in the wings.

None of Mark's friends had seen Jessica after the couple had broken up. How did marriage with Victor fare? Perhaps she hadn't yet whipped her husband into shape.

Jessica peeked across the street then hurried over the lawn.

Curtains moved at the house across the road. Unlike Saturday, the older couple didn't sit on the porch. This time a shadow surveyed them from an upstairs windowpane.

Touching his arm, Jessica peered across the road again.

"Yes. You're being surveilled," Mark confirmed. "Across the street, upstairs window. Who lives over there?"

"My husband's parents. His mother is a gossipy old biddy. The father is just as bad. Forget about those two. I have."

"Then stop peeking over your shoulder like a scared rabbit. Tell me what you want to say."

Mark barely contained his smile when Jessica bit her lip instead of lashing out. Her body quivered. Was she trying to contain her anger?

"Listen," she said, then she took a deep breath. "Forget what I said on Friday." She smiled up at him. "Truce?"

Her hand fell to her side when Mark ignored the offered handshake.

The historic moment notched itself into Mark's memory. Earlier, Jessica had bitten her lip, now she wrung her hands.

Entwining her fingers, she glanced across the street again.

Interesting. People who are afraid of getting caught should behave themselves. When Pamela darted across his mind, Mark refocused on Jessica. What concerned the woman about her in-laws? Unless she had told her husband about her and Mark's association, Victor's parents wouldn't link them together. But clearly, they did. People weren't that nosey without a cause.

"I apologize," Jessica said. "You and the spouse caught me off guard on Friday. I behaved poorly. It's just ... look. I ... erred when I accepted Victor's proposal." She touched Mark's arm then dropped her hand. "I miss your singlemindedness regarding my welfare. You cared about me, Mark. I want

91

that back. I want YOU back."

Mark snorted before he could stop himself. He couldn't imagine living a lifetime with a tortured woman. What if his children turned out anything like her? No chance of that happening with Pamela. Just like her grandmothers and mother, his wife would provide an excellent example their children could follow.

"That offer is no longer valid. I'm a happily married man."

Fire lit her eyes. "Do you and Pam share this magical connection? I don't think so. Sure, she's a pretty little thing. If you wanted conventional weak tea, you could've married her years ago." She hesitated, sidling closer. "You and I connected in every way possible. Some men contribute enthusiasm or heart. You supplied both. I still remember our romps together."

Shame engulfed him. "My wife and I share genuine intimacy. We make love. We don't just have sex."

"You've lost your self-respect. I expected more substance from a married man. So, Pam's in the driver's seat."

The forceful, loud tone prompted Mark to step back. For once, the woman forgot to look over her shoulder at her in-laws' house.

"My wife's compass is perfect. Pam steers us on the proper route. We've always enjoyed the same pursuits. Our marriage is our number one priority."

Jessica's jaw dropped until she belted out a laugh. "Oh, really. Then thank me for pointing you in the right direction."

"I acknowledge you removed the blinders, but I charted the perfect course." It was time to brag on Pamela in a way Jessica would understand. "My present task is reminding K.C. Hodges that his friend's sister lost her free-agent status. Pam signed an irrevocable contract with me. Cheating isn't allowed on either side."

Jessica studied Mark. "The football player? Is your wife his number one fan?"

Movement across the street snagged his attention. No longer peeking out the window, Jessica's mother-in-law sat in a rocking chair outside.

Mark took a deep breath before he answered. "Pam attended every game he played in high school and college. Her brother was the star running back. By the way, your mother-in-law is talking on the phone and staring at us from the front porch. She's probably giving her son a play-by-play."

Venom oozed from Jessica's body. Mark started to bait her further but walked away.

He felt her calculated gaze follow him into the house.

His adrenaline surging, he could barely wait to see his wife.

* * *

Pamela met Mark inside the front door. She gave him a long look before speaking.

"Dinner's ready. You're later than usual. Hard day at the office?"

"It was a long day but not a particularly hard one." Mark switched his briefcase into the other hand. "Obstacles pounded IT from all sides. I expected to help you close shop earlier, but other duties called."

"Those everyday tasks will keep our house three steps ahead of foreclosure."

Pamela removed the briefcase and laptop from his hand and took them into the den.

She laid them both on the desk.

Would Mark mention his discussion outside with Jessica? Whatever had transpired between the two, his ex-girlfriend had retreated in bad spirits. Jessica stomping across her lawn was not the usual image she projected.

Do I admit what I witnessed or wait until I'm told? What if Mark doesn't tell me?

From the den door she saw Mark enter the kitchen.

He was lifting the casserole cover from the dish when Pamela walked inside the room.

"Something smells delicious. Lasagna. When did you have time to fix such a meal? I figured you left work at five."

"Mom again. She set up Mellie and me with complete dinners. Toasted bread sticks and seasoned summer vegetables are keeping warm in the oven." She eyed him. "Mom admitted to having a dinner engagement before she left."

"I told you a stepfather is on the horizon. My prediction will pan out real soon."

Pamela finished setting the table.

"So says my over-dramatic husband."

Turning around, he kissed her cheek. "Cheer up, love. Give me a minute to shower and change. Where do you want to go this evening?"

"Nowhere. Unless we're visiting your parents." She paused until he reached the doorway, all the while shaking his head. "Can't we at least make a short trip?"

"Not tonight. I'll set up something later."

"Ugh! Why wait? We don't need an appointment to visit your folks."

"How well do you know those people?" he asked.

Her husband left the kitchen without waiting for her reply.

* * *

Mark revealed his plans for Timeless Pastries while the couple ate dinner. A business analysis meeting had been set up with a new account advisor at Techno Plus.

Pamela would have preferred to hear news about his latest Jessica interaction.

After they finished eating, her husband cleaned the kitchen while Pamela kept him company from the table.

After Mark tidied the kitchen, he sat beside Pamela and stared at her until she wondered what was wrong.

He grinned as his head tilted to the side. "Stop looking surprised. You've worn that same expression since I began straightening up. Your husband is helpful around the house." Mark hesitated when Pamela remained silent. "Let's discuss an important matter. In here? Or in the family room?"

Is it about K.C. or Jessica? Maybe both. Pamela's lips pursed. Here we go. "Right here," she said. "I'm getting a vibe that this is a vital discussion and you're up to something."

"I'm wounded, love. What gave my wanting something from you away?"

"You tidied the kitchen and sat beside me. You usually just watch me work. But go on. Don't switch topics now. What do you want?"

"Carte blanche to set up any future appointments for you regarding Timeless Pastries. That's all."

Her mouth hung open, and then she smiled. Whew! "I think that's plenty enough for starters." She eyed him. "Who do you want to make appointments with?"

Mark chuckled. "Influencers to market your business for starters."

"Influencers for starters? Okay. Win me over. Paint me a scene I can agree with."

Her husband proposed a daunting online and local campaign for her goods. Their talk reminded her of conversations they'd shared in high school and college. Mark still possessed a heart for business. Well-informed opinions heightened Pamela's interest in branching out. Her husband covered the business spectrum: aesthetics, regulations, postal delivery, and management.

94

Plus he gave his father credit for teaching him what he knew. Ed had ensured his son understood solid business concepts firsthand.

She listened until Mark paused to catch a breath. "You still love holding business discussions. And I still enjoy playing your eager pupil. For now, I'm on board with some of your suggestions. But Mark, please remember Timeless Pastries is a local establishment. I'm not sure how far out I'm willing to go."

He slid his chair closer to hers and grabbed her hands. "I'll trim my wish list just for you. But don't let fear deter your progress. Branching out is a positive thing that business owners should embrace."

"Well, it definitely is positive to you. What's the next step?" she asked.

Mark clapped his hands. "Those words represent real progress. Let's start by bringing your business into the twenty-first century. Shiatown has a topnotch worldwide advertising firm. I play racquetball with the owner."

My husband aims to improve my business, and I'm delighted by his support. I won't complain.

"I will consider your ideas. So keep it simple."

Despite his easy-going approach, Mark eagle-eyed Pamela while he explained his ideas. He analyzed each word of her reply. Her husband loved constant dialogue and having lively debates. Despite that, she could tell something was troubling Mark. Yet she refused to introduce unnecessary topics into their conversation.

When Pamela pulled her hands from his grasp, Mark leaned back in the chair until it dangled on two legs.

"Enough about my business," she said with her gaze fixed on the pantry. "Tell me about your hectic workday."

"Why are you looking across the room? I'm over here."

Pamela coughed into her hand. "I breathe easier when chairs rest on four legs."

"Sorry." Mark set the chair upright. "Work was work. There were too many unfinished projects without substantial headway for any of them."

"What do you mean?" she asked.

"Techno Plus executed an electronic bill conversion this month for four major clients. We transferred their automatic pay customers from paper statements with an opt-out option in an email."

"So four major companies eliminated paper statements without their customers' expressed consent. Is that legal?"

"Yes, but it's still the wrong move to make. Some folks rely on monthly statements to budget their money."

"Most people won't see the opt-out option either. Who reads unsolicited emails these days? Besides, some individuals change their email addresses on a regular basis."

"Those scheduled payments will draft their checking accounts this Friday. The campaign will unleash a call-in avalanche that could've been avoided. Customer satisfaction will suffer a preventable hit."

"Did you voice your concern to the appropriate parties?"

"Of course. I spoke up with the suggestion that we at least mail follow-up letters after the initial emails went out. Operations and eServices rejected that advice. IT stood alone once again."

"I'll make you a plaque for your desk that says, 'The CIO who stands alone always has it right. Next time, listen to him!' "

She continued speaking after her husband finished laughing. "Don't they recognize you've been right each time?"

"No. The company is never hit as hard as I predict."

"Because you typically have a backup plan. Going forward, let those departments solve their problems on their own."

"That's easier said than done for a man who despises failure. Even if he isn't a direct part of the problem."

Mark stood and pulled Pamela to her feet. "Enough about work. When you talk to your mother, tell her she made two terrific meals and makes the best potato casserole and lasagna I've ever eaten. Speaking of Mrs. Hayes, she and Melinda are off duty until Monday, right? Is Hodges discarding his apron for good on Friday?"

"Uh-huh. Guess who Gibson High hired as the new football coach? Pre-season training starts in June."

"I got that update yesterday. Does that mean you'll work alone after your mother and Mellie help you next week?"

"I can handle my regular clientele by myself. It's the fundraisers and meet and greets that are difficult for one person."

"Hiring permanent workers is our next step," he said. They walked into the family room. "Are there any mysteries on television tonight?"

"Whodunits. British-style. My favorite kind."

As Pamela cuddled in Mark's arms on the sofa, she struggled with memories of his old girlfriend. Was Mark consumed with thoughts of her brother's closest ally?

* * *

On Wednesday, Mark knocked on the shop's door before noon, carrying Toomey's sacks.

A surprised Pamela opened the door and called to the back of the building. "Break time, K.C. Someone brought our lunch today."

As if he was on a mission, K.C. skirted around the moving couple and headed toward the door. He faced Pamela when she called his name. "I have an errand to run. I'll pick up something to eat on the way."

Pamela removed a food sack from Mark's hand and waved it at her helper.

"These steak burgers smell delicious. Take some food with you." Still shaking the bag at K.C., Pamela walked backwards behind Mark as he headed to the breakroom. "No? We'll eat without you this time."

Flashing a wide grin, K.C. stared at her for a few seconds. "I have a prior engagement I can't break. Maybe next time."

Mark doubled back to the open space. "Give me your order for tomorrow before you leave." He looked from Hodges to Pamela, and then back at the man walking toward the door. "How about pizza?" he asked.

K.C. instantly spun around. "Bring food for your wife if you stop by tomorrow. I'm eating meals with friends all week." He winked at Pamela. "Be back in an hour. Enjoy lunch."

"Tell her I said hi," Pamela said. "Whoever she is. Care to give me a little hint?"

K.C. chuckled as he opened the outside door. "You're an incorrigible woman. See you in a bit."

Before leaving, he nodded at Mark.

Pamela locked the door behind her old friend. "Do you think K.C. found a wife without my help?"

"The man getting married would be progress at any rate."

Then he can stop hitting on my wife. Mark barely kept himself from speaking out loud.

Inside the breakroom, he rubbed his hands together. "I have a slew of business ideas. Take a seat while I roll out possible scenarios. Your bakery—"

"Commercial kitchen," Pamela said, taking a seat at the table. "I don't run a full-scale outfit."

"Mere semantics, love. Leave further licensing and regulations to me. Whether you go big, small, or hover somewhere in the middle, I've come up with some suggestions based on your wish list. Here are the options and probable costs of upscaling from what you now have."

Overnight, Mark had figured out how to transform her small company into a full-scale operation. Laborious ideas restructured Timeless Pastries into a café, banquet hall, and catering service. He hoped his over-the-top enthusiasm would encourage her to consider his recommendations.

"Well, you've taken a lot of liberties with my dreams," Pamela said.

* * *

On Friday at four thirty sharp, Pamela locked the shop door, waved goodbye to K.C., and sped home. All day, she had envisioned taking a lavender-scented bubble bath. Those images kept her energy pumping throughout the day.

Exhaustion overtook her on the drive home. Pamela dreaded going into a messy house. Before she got married, she had tidied her bedroom and cleaned her mother's spotless house every Saturday. Despite being overly efficient in many arenas, Mark appeared not to mind living inside a cluttered house—which Pamela decluttered each evening. She shook her head as she drove the car into the garage.

* * *

Refreshed from her bath, Pamela stretched across the bed. Her cell phone rang.

"Hi, Grandmother. ... I'm exhausted. Lying across the bed doing nothing. ... I haven't made any plans and Mark hasn't mentioned having any. ... Great idea. I love it. ... Yes, ma'am. Can't wait to see you. ... Thanks for inviting Mark's parents and grandparents to our family luncheon. ... I'll call his mother when we hang up. Bye-bye. See you Sunday."

Pamela speed-dialed her mother-in-law, left a voicemail, texted her grandmother's address, and hopped off the bed to get started on dinner.

Moments later, she peered into the refrigerator. "Leftovers. Food tastes best the second time around."

Pamela picked up her vibrating cell phone from the kitchen island and read the text.

The Simons are coming. We can't wait to see you guys this Sunday.

"Fast work, Mrs. Simon."

Rejuvenated, Pamela heated up yesterday's leftover meal.

The front door closed with a click.

Pamela trailed Mark's footsteps into the den and lingered in the doorway.

"Hello, husband. Do you want to hear good news or excellent news first?"

Mark laid his briefcase on the desk. "Kiss me while I decide."

Pamela smacked his lips with hers. "Why do you park in the driveway instead of inside the garage?"

Mark gathered her into his arms. "Does that question have anything to do with your good or excellent news reports?"

"No sidetracks. Why do you leave your car parked in the driveway? You're the one who wanted a two-car garage."

"I enjoy walking through the front door," he said. "Tell me the good news first. Excellent news might overwhelm me."

"Grandmother invited our entire family over for lunch on Sunday. She said to prepare to eat a culinary feast."

Mark unwrapped his arm from around Pamela's waist and ushered her through the den door.

"Good news is right," he said. "Mrs. Frierson is an exceptional cook. No breakfast for me that morning so I can save room."

"No food, huh? Not even a fruit salad?"

Shaking his head, Mark sat at the kitchen table. "I'm ready. Hit me with your excellent news."

Pamela laughed. "Hold on to your chair. A genuine family reunion is underway. Grandmother's invitation included your parents and grandparents and Mellie's parents and grandparents."

"That's not going to happen," Mark said. He leaned against the chair cushion. "Tell your grandmother the other Simons can't come."

Pamela blinked at Mark. *Lord, give me patience.*

"Too late," she said. "I've already invited your parents and grandparents. Your mother responded saying they'll be there. All the Simons are coming."

Mark's eyes narrowed as he stared at her. "The Simons aren't the loving family you want us to be. Stop trying to make us something we're not."

"Our objectives are the same. You love your folks." Pamela paused. *Admit when you could be wrong even when you don't think you are.* "Forgive me, Mark. I should've told you first."

"No. You should have asked me if I wanted them to come." Mark's cheeks pulsated. He squeezed the bridge of his nose. "No worries. We'll get through this."

Pamela massaged his shoulders then kissed his cheek. "Of course we will.

They're your people."

"I guess DNA counts for something." When she moved away, Mark rose then sat back down. "Dinner ready?"

"Yeah. Heat-ups make the best meals." Pamela removed their dinner from the oven and set the casserole dish on the table. "Let's eat," she said, sitting down.

Whew! I made a narrow escape from getting in the middle of Mark and his parents. He needs an attitude adjustment.

Smiling at her husband, she smoothed a hand across her hair.

* * *

Birds chirping outside of Pamela's bedroom window woke her up to bright sunlight. She'd been getting up so early during the week, these were the first tweets she'd heard since last weekend.

The landline rang as she turned over in bed. She reached for the phone on the nightstand.

The grumpy man beside her raised on an elbow. "Who's calling us at eight on a Saturday morning?"

"Your mother," she said, picking up the phone receiver. "Hi, Mrs. Simon. You're up early. Is everything all right? ... Good. Can't wait to visit with you guys tomorrow. ... This evening?" Pamela glanced at Mark, who shook his head. "I have tickets for a play tonight in Shiatown. Your son is finetuning the Timeless Pastries website for me. ... Yes. Several people suggested I add baked goods and lunch. ... Ah. Thank you. I appreciate your support and endorsement. ... Okay, I'll tell him you called. See you all at Grandmother's house tomorrow."

Pamela rolled her eyes at Mark. Her husband had suffered through a lousy home life growing up, but he moved out of his parents' house seven years ago. The Simons exhibited selfish love, but they both loved Mark. Pamela believed that adult children should overlook their parents' deficits and be grateful to even have parents.

"Since you declined your mother's dinner invitation, what's on your agenda this evening?"

"I prefer spending my off day with my wife."

"And me with you. But tonight, I do have the play. I bought a ticket and can't flake out on a promise made to friends."

"Yeah. Right." Mark pushed back the cover. "I'll finish the setup for the

Timeless Pastries website today. Lavine expects a link this weekend. Look to receive multiple orders from Techno Plus."

"Mark, we came home last Friday. You've talked to your mother once since then. You haven't stopped by either pawn shop. Are you ignoring your parents' calls?"

Mark glanced at her. "Of course not. I text them back each time they call. Starting next week, I will pay biweekly visits to both store locations."

"And stop answering their calls with text messages. Mrs. Simon probably called on the landline because she wanted me to know she called you. Call your folks before your father makes a call."

Pamela left the bed and walked across the room. She studied Mark, who leaned against the headboard piddling with his cell phone.

"You should visit your parents this evening," she suggested.

Pamela glanced away when Mark shook his head while still piddling with his cell phone.

"I'll be busy setting up your website," he said without looking at her.

"Can you at least call your mother, Mark?"

"I'll see them tomorrow at your grandmother's luncheon." He grinned at her. "Are you serving me breakfast in bed?"

"That was my original plan."

"Good. The perks of married life. Don't forget the fresh-squeezed orange juice."

"Men who ignore their mothers don't deserve the extra labor."

Pamela closed the bathroom door behind her.

Chapter Ten

Finished with his top job of the weekend, Mark checked his watch. Five thirty. Setup of the Timeless Pastries website had filled his afternoon. The house was silent. Had his wife left home without a heads up that she was leaving?

He trudged down the hallway as Pamela left the master suite. She dazzled in a champagne midcalf dress and nude slingback heels. Loose curls framed her face from an upswept hairdo. The peach eye shadow emphasized her almond-shaped eyes.

Her lips smacked his cheek with a light kiss. "I was just looking for you to say goodbye."

His body relaxed. "Glad you didn't leave without telling me."

Her keys jingled as she switched them from hand to hand.

Why does Pamela suddenly look shy? Stop it. Don't search for trouble that isn't there. She's just going to a play with friends in Shiatown.

"Coming home after the play or going somewhere else?" he asked.

"I'm not sure. We may grab a bite to eat afterwards. If not, I'm homeward bound."

"Why would you go out to eat after attending a dinner theater?"

Pamela giggled. "To resume our chitchat. We can't talk once the performance begins."

Mark followed her to the laundry room when she headed that way. What could he say to make her want to come straight home?

"I sent website invitations to our email contacts and asked them to invite their friends to view it, too."

"Already? I won't meet with the new account advisor until next Monday to accept Timeless Pastries online orders and customer service requests."

"The contract signing is a formality. The website and Techno Plus are ready to accept Timeless Pastries' online orders, payments, and provide your patrons with customer service."

Pamela's eyes twinkled for the first time since the couple had arrived home from their honeymoon. Hopefully, just having an active website made her happy.

"We've had the website's first three visitors," he said. "One was Melinda."

"Mellie and two other folks already checked it out?" Pamela squeaked. "Then she probably knows the other folks and told them about it. I'll call her in the car." She paused in thought. "Two actual visitors I may not know." She hugged his neck. "Wow, Mark. Just wow."

He hesitated when Pamela giggled again. Her sheer joy pulled him into the excitement with her. He wanted his wife to see her website before she left home.

"This is the first evening we'll be apart since our wedding."

Pamela raised the garage door. "I've neglected my friends lately and must make amends. You hung out with your pals on a regular basis before we got married."

Mark stood beside the open door when Pamela slid inside the car.

"We arrived home from our honeymoon last week. We need to settle into being a married couple."

"It's only been one week? A lot has happened since then." She started the engine. "Last Friday seems like a lifetime away. Goodbye, Mark."

Mark closed the car door. "Drive safe."

Pamela nodded while she backed the vehicle into the driveway.

The garage door lowered while he watched.

His wife didn't comment about the couple settling into married life. They must form new habits together.

Stepping inside the laundry room, Mark leaned against the door he closed.

* * *

As Pamela drove into the garage, a light came on and the door to the laundry room opened. Her husband stood in the doorway. She saw the pleasure in Mark's eyes before she reached him.

"Over dinner, we all checked out the website," she said. "I love it. Everyone raved about the professional job during our meal. And Mom bragged on her son-in-law's skills on my drive home."

Mark squeezed her body in a tight hug when she kissed his cheek.

"I heard the garage door lift from the bedroom, so I came on down. Did you enjoy the play?"

"It was terrific. I just gave Mom a glowing report." Pamela scooted inside the laundry room. "Since I know you'd love it, too, I purchased two tickets for us for next Saturday." She eyed him. "Please confirm that I didn't waste money."

"I haven't made previous plans. I keep my options open in case my wife desires a date night."

"Aw, thank you much. Please remember we can't have a date night on weekdays. All orders received online will be filled by me. My friends said they made a few."

"It's already taking off," Mark said. "There are orders from people we know and from strangers."

"Friends and relatives no doubt. The increased volume will pile on more work for me, but I'll give the new process a valiant try."

"You should hire permanent workers."

"And pay them with—"

"We'll brainstorm ideas tomorrow." Mark reached out his hand. "Ready for bed?"

Pamela backed up. "I need to unwind a little first. I'll read a book in the family room. Are you headed to bed? Goodnight," she said when he nodded.

Sadness entered Mark's eyes. "Goodnight sounds much better than the goodbye I heard earlier."

Pamela felt his gaze on her back as she stepped into the family room.

Sometimes it seemed like the long-term friends had lost the easy camaraderie they'd once shared.

* * *

Sunday after church, the couple swung hands until K.C. stopped beside them. He glanced at Mark. "Hey, man. Good to see you." A smile softened the face he turned to Pamela. "My grandparents are leaving town this afternoon. They want to thank you again for the pie you dropped off on Thursday."

"Great! I love those folks." Pamela separated her hand from Mark's and winked at him. "I must say goodbye to my surrogate grandparents. I'll just be a few minutes."

With K.C. trailing in her dust, she scurried across the parking lot to a beige luxury sedan. A small group of relatives stood around the vehicle, hugging one another. Pamela embraced each family member, mingled a few minutes with K.C.'s sisters and cousins, then hotfooted back to her husband.

Mark had watched the group's interactions from the exact spot where Pamela had left him. What had her scowling husband been looking for?

He evaded Pamela's attempt to hold his hand. "I forgot the Hayeses and Hodgeses are long-time family friends. It seems that hugs and touchy stuff are natural for both families."

Pamela clamped her lips together. His accusatory tone stopped her from having empathy for his bruised ego. The man who had stewed about her prior relationship with K.C. still hadn't revealed his latest conversation with Jessica.

"Wonder what Grandmother is serving us for lunch," she finally said, linking her arm through his. "Glad your folks and grandparents can join us for lunch with the short notice they were given."

"Don't remind me," he said. "Next time, warn me before issuing my parents invitations that include me."

I'm trying, Lord, but he isn't making my cooperation easy.

"Would you have agreed to their coming if I'd asked your permission?"

"No. I finally accept the light association they established years ago. It's too late to break a twenty-eight-year habit."

"Simplify your life by letting your parents off the hook. As my granny loves to say, we must live in forgiveness to skip landing into regret. She probably learned that lesson from raising my father."

Mark nodded. "Your father was probably a difficult child."

"I'm sure he was," Pamela agreed, happy to change the subject. She didn't want Mark to say negative things about the Hodges family. They were all decent people, unlike his ex-girlfriend. Besides, Jessica Prentis was the problem, not K.C. She lived next door and might appear at any moment. Pamela had caught glimpses of her coming and going.

She wondered where the husband hid. Except for his early Monday morning appearance and Jessica's accosting Mark last Tuesday, their neighbors remained low-key. The old Jessica had invented reasons to get attention.

Pamela smiled at Mark when he held the door open for her. His lips brushed her brow before he clasped her hands in his. She remembered the many times he had shown her affection after he'd hurt her feelings. Maybe he apologized to people in an obscure way.

* * *

That evening, Mark rejected one bad conversation starter after the other. He didn't know where to begin. He lost hope his wife would confess her past romantic relationship with Hodges. For seven days, she had ignored every dangled carrot. Emotional honesty might be her quicksand, but not his. Mark searched for an innocuous way to ask about her dating Hodges behind his back.

He shifted his position on the couch when Pamela's voice sifted through his thoughts.

"I don't think you're watching this movie. You seem preoccupied with something else."

Nodding, Mark stared straight ahead. "You're right. Too busy thinking private thoughts."

Pamela snapped off the television. "Care to tell me what's wrong besides work exhaustion?"

He might as well plunge in with that lead-in.

"How long did the affair with Hodges last?" Mark studied her expression.

Pamela gave him a squinty-eyed stare. "Affair? Seriously, Mark?"

His knuckles cracked. "Affair was the wrong word. You know what I mean."

"I dated K.C. for a brief period three years ago. Anyway, that's stale news. Pure and simple."

He'd almost gotten her statement right.

Mark never wanted a mental picture of Pamela kissing any man. He knew it was a terrible double standard, but it was also an accurate evaluation of his feelings.

He halted grinding his teeth. "The inconsistencies within our relationship astound me. I divulged details about who I dated and every pertinent facet concerning my life."

"So did I," Pamela said. "Long ago I tried telling you about who I dated and giving you Timeless Pastries reports. But you always disengaged and began a new conversation whenever I discussed my dates or business."

"That's a flimsy excuse for hearing secondhand that my wife dated Mr. Baking Wizard. My administrative assistant told me on Monday morning after a very important meeting."

"Then why are you asking me about what happened on the following Sunday? You're seven days too late to get an explanation. Besides, you knew I dated without the official news reports. What's significant about my dating him?"

"Hodges' name would've captured my attention in a flash."

"No, sir. It didn't," Pamela said, scooting away from Mark. "I told you my brother's friend asked me out. You began a discussion about yourself. Telling me your mother's friend's daughter invited you to dinner. Of course, the dialogue segued to your 'life love,' the current Mrs. Prentis." Pamela paused when Mark glared at her. "If you're angry at the reference, blame yourself. You chose the pet name 'life love.' "

"Don't criticize me for foolish comments I made almost four years ago. My relationship with Jessica was in the infant stage."

"Exactly. Why dwell on old news?"

"Because I had a right to know you dated Hodges before we got married." A snort stopped his grinding teeth. "Secrets destroy relationships."

Pamela stood, then sat back down. "Are you certain you want to lodge that argument? We bought a house next door to your 'life love.' "

"My problem is you dated a well-known womanizer."

"Don't believe written or verbalized gossip. K.C.'s a gentleman and a respectful friend."

"Did he kiss you?"

"Mark! We dated. Okay?"

Rubbing his forehead, Mark assessed Pamela's reaction. "Here's the problem. I didn't think you seriously dated anyone."

"It was only for six months, and K.C. lived in another city the whole time I hardly saw him."

Tense neck muscles reminded Mark of his one and only migraine. Heat flushed his body as his knuckles flexed. When Pamela had said her brother's friend had asked her out she was probably asking for advice. He hadn't listened. How many times had he failed her as a friend? Still, she should've confessed her dates with Hodges before the wedding.

"A half year?" he asked. "We ate lunch around fifty times while you and he dated. You didn't think it noteworthy to tell me you were an item with a man I knew?"

The book she'd been reading closed. Her squinted eyes stared at him.

Calm down. Don't box her in. Mark reconsidered their former relationship He'd been a failure as a friend.

He cleared his throat and managed a crooked grin. "How did the relationship transform from friendship to dating?"

Pamela's facial expression softened. Mark recognized that as the exact moment his wife decided to give him answers.

"There isn't a simple answer to give you. One day we thought maybe ... It doesn't matter when we began dating. We're better friends than lovers. Uh, bad word choice."

"Point taken," he said while feeling that his wife had left out details. "But someone initiated the romance. Who? You or Hodges?"

Her gaze held his as she slowly rose. "It just happened. Let it go."

"In other words, I should ask Hodges instead of asking my wife?"

"If you do—" A light pink glow flushed her cheeks.

Mark's head tilted to the side. "What's the outcome if I ask him what you won't reveal?"

"K.C. will think our relationship is dysfunctional."

"Then answer my question. Otherwise, I'll confront Hodges." Mark focused on wall sconces above Pamela's head. "Why did you hide the relationship from me?"

"You didn't believe me the first time. Why should I belabor the point?"

"Look. Jessica living in the neighborhood doesn't match you hiding that you dated Hodges from me."

"Your convoluted, outrageous indignation doesn't move me, Mark. You're not flipping the table on me." She backed up a few steps. "What concerns you about my dating K.C.?"

"The man didn't deserve a woman of your caliber."

Pamela headed for the door. "That remark doesn't make your offensive comments any better."

Mark hurried across the floor to forestall her bolt from the room. Then he recalled her command not to ever block her exit.

His feet shuffled underneath him. "Why didn't you tell me about Hodges before we got married?"

"How many times are you going to ask me that question? Look, our dates fizzled within six months. Why should I revive the conversation three years after the fact?"

"You don't get it," Mark said. "Who people date is information they normally share with friends."

"Again, I did try to tell you. How would you have responded if you'd listened to me?"

Mark's shoulders slumped. How would he have reacted had he known Pamela contemplated dating a man every member of her family liked? Someone she might marry.

"I would've advised you to ignore the whim. That God had the perfect man for you."

"Did you ever see you and me as a couple back then?" Pamela asked. Her voice was barely above a whisper. Tears welled in her eyes because she already knew the answer.

At the time, Mark hadn't seen himself as the perfect fit for any woman other than the one that had consumed his life. He'd been obsessed with Jessica Hubbard.

Pamela appeared to read his mind. She shook her head and turned away.

Did Mark go too far this time to bridge the gap? Pamela loved him. Surely she wouldn't give up on their marriage without a fight.

He sidled closer to her. "Today, all the major players in our lives got together inside one house. Our families had a wonderful time. Don't ruin what we shared earlier because I brought up Hodges tonight."

* * *

Memories of her parents' tit-for-tat clashes kept Pamela silent. Her father had said things that hurt her mother for months after the arguments ended. She glanced away then stared at him. Mark never mentioned the most recent time he'd spoken to Jessica in the driveway. His trickery before the wedding stole her right to choose a different house. And now, he still hid secrets from her. Who was he to question her choices? Jessica had treated Mark like he was a nuisance. K.C. had treated Pamela with respect.

"Good night. I'm over this conversation."

Pamela stepped into the hallway and kept walking until she entered the laundry room. Too bad she wasn't immature enough to slam doors. His slanderous words insulted her sense of fair play.

Someone initiated the romance. Who? You or Hodges?

As if his knowing the answer would introduce meaningful dialogue. The relationship had just happened. K.C. had lost patience with his groupies, and Pamela had lost hope Mark would ever love her. The dinner invitation came on the night her heart had broken.

Her friend, Tori, had texted that Jessica might have moved in with Mark. Tori saw her exiting his condo on several early mornings for an entire month.

There hadn't been a climactic moment between Pamela and K.C. They both had pursued a relationship for the wrong reasons, although time spent together had solidified their friendship. Up until then, K.C. had just been her brother's friend. Yet empathy for each other stretched the romance for five unnecessary months. They'd known the truth after a few dates: They respected each other as trusted friends, but friends were all they would be.

Skylar had also played some hardball tactics to break them up. Especially when he and Melinda caught a playoff game on the West Coast. Pamela had flown out three days earlier to tour San Francisco.

In her hotel room, while K.C. practiced, her brother cautioned, "Lose the game face. K.C. is the wrong man for you. You both want different things from life. End the relationship. Heartbreak is a ridiculous reason to wreck two lives."

Pamela agreed with her brother's assessment but refused to snub a man trying to redirect his life.

"I won't walk away from K.C. while he's vulnerable to rejection. He deserves better than that."

Skylar peered out the window before he faced his sister. "Do yourself and my best friend a favor. End the dating relationship on this trip. You both can thank me later."

Pamela sorted clothes to wash while taking deep breaths. Why hadn't Mark asked her about the relationship with K.C. as soon as he'd heard about it? But she knew the answer before contemplating the question. Mark clammed up whenever he felt threatened.

Summing up their dating story would've taken five minutes if Mark had broached the topic without allegations. Just last week he had spoken to Jessica without telling Pamela about the conversation. And yet he wanted to know about her having dated K.C. when it was almost four years ago.

Her husband had a different set of behavior rules for himself than he had for everyone else. He had misinterpreted K.C.'s cheek kiss and made a big deal out of nothing. And then K.C. overreacted to Mark's unease and made a defensive move. Her husband must trust her love, and her friend must respect her marriage.

And adults shouldn't withhold information while demanding answers. What did Mark and Jessica discuss in the driveway? She should've asked him right as he'd come inside the house. Too much time had passed to inquire now.

If only he had been honest about that conversation, she would've been more likely to share information about her relationship with K.C.

* * *

Later that night, Pamela slid into bed inside a darkened room. With deft movements, she pulled a quilt over her body and settled on her side of the bed. Mark lay close to the center of the mattress. Even so, at least twelve inches separated the couple.

Once she lay still, Mark turned on a light that spotlighted the couple. He propped on his elbow, looming over Pamela. His lopsided grin wavered until he nudged her with his knee.

"Earlier, we ended our discussions on opposite sides. Care to give it another try? I want to."

Behind her straight face, Pamela's inner self smiled. "I prefer not going to sleep at odds with you."

She gazed at the ceiling. *It's your show. Direct the conversation wherever you wish.*

Mark cleared his throat several times. "Let's start at the beginning. A Sunday ago, you took Hodges' kiss in stride. I wondered why you didn't find his touch intrusive, but I let it go." He hesitated, glanced away, then took a deep breath. His gaze caressed her face. "His touching you irked me. On the very next day, my administrative assistant told me that you and Hodges had once dated. I overreacted. I hate thinking of you being around other men."

"My dating life consisted of a few light kisses. I seldom dated any man twice."

"Which is why your dating Hodges bothers me. You dated him for six months. Who initiated the first date?"

He should first bring her up to speed concerning Jessica, and she would reciprocate with K.C. information. Mark's unreasonable stance regarding K.C. was nonsense when he had chosen an atrocious woman over her. Thanks to Mark continuously doubling down on K.C., her angst increased each time she remembered Jessica lived next door. And his jealous behavior sparked Pamela's justified irritation. Pure and simple.

Play nice, even if your husband doesn't. Answer his questions and move on.

She blew air through her lips to steady her voice. "K.C. called me from Atlanta after he kicked a housekeeper out of his room. He'd flirted with her earlier and found the woman in his bed after a training session. Similar scenes had played out in the past. K.C. had grown tired of his singles lifestyle. Skylar and Mellie had welcomed their third child two months earlier. Most of his

111

closest friends were happily married with children. He longed for stability and his own family. That night he reflected on his life and called me."

"So ... when Hodges considered a permanent relationship, he thought of you."

Someone finally had. Gritting her teeth, she nodded. "That same evening, a friend told me she'd seen Jessica leave your condo on consecutive mornings for a month. He called right after I'd read that text. I gave up on you ever loving me." Pamela fingered the quilt. "Romance just seemed like a workable solution for us."

"What were Ace's and Melinda's views?" Mark asked. "Your brother and his wife usually weigh in on every aspect of your life."

"Skylar went ballistic on his friend. Mellie didn't speak to K.C. for weeks."

Mark chuckled. "That's the Ace and Melinda I've always known." His finger stroked her cheek. "How did the relationship end? Was the breakup mutual?"

"Skylar continually voiced his concerns while he, Mellie, and I were out of town for a playoff game. I talked to K.C. when he picked me up for dinner. We both realized we were better as friends. Now I'm looking for the perfect wife for him." Looking away, she cleared her throat. "Um ... is there anything you care to share with me?"

Pamela kept her features expressionless while Mark studied her face.

His fingers halted as he stroked her cheek. "You know I talked to Jessica outside again the other day." He chuckled when she nodded. "You've been patient for a person waiting on a full report. In a way, your patience puts my accusations in a pitiful light."

"I understand your wanting clarity about K.C. and me."

"That's because I love you, Pam," he said. "But here's the lowdown on our neighbor. According to her, I bring enthusiasm and heart into relationships."

"Jessica laid the flattery on thick, huh? Does she want you back that badly?"

"Flattery? The woman's dead-on. I aim to please."

"Right. What other claims did she make?"

He dimmed the light and snuggled close to Pamela. "She partially apologized for what happened on Friday. Said we caught her off guard. She also said she should've rejected her husband's marriage proposal. And I fawn over you too much." Mark laughed.

Pamela's eyebrows rose. "Fawn. Curious word choice. Hers or yours?"

"My own. Jessica labeled you as the driver in our relationship. It's a true statement," he said when Pamela's brows wrinkled. "My wife is leading us in the proper direction." He paused. "She also said she wants me back. I'm sure only because I treated her like a queen." Pain entered his eyes.

Pamela wrapped her arms around his neck. "Too late. You're mine."

"Forever, love." He kissed her lips then pulled away. "Victor's parents are the ones who live across the street."

"What? So the man was monitoring your conversation with his daughter-in-law. Do they know about you and Jessica?"

"She didn't say, and I didn't ask." His voice lowered. "I told her about your time with Hodges."

Pamela broke her hold and slid away from Mark. "Before telling *me* you knew? Why did you blab my personal business to your ex?"

"Jessica never understood why I value you. She didn't comprehend your unique distinction. Now, she does."

"So, adding that I dated a pro football player to my list of accomplishments validates my worth?"

"It will for some folks, especially for social climbers. Mrs. Prentis is included." He lay back on his pillow. "Ready to go to sleep?"

"Yeah. This conversation is over. Next time, keep my business to yourself."

Pamela curled onto her side in the opposite direction and scooted as close to the edge as possible. Tears threatened to fill her eyes, but she blinked them back, refusing to let them fall.

Chapter Eleven

The next day Pamela parked in front of Victor's parents' house. She darted from the car, carrying a vase filled with Shasta daisies. The blue note card on the gift read, *From Your Neighbors, The Simons, Pam & Mark.* She left the arrangement in plain sight on the porch. The gift idea had hit her while driving past The Flowerpot.

She drove into her garage wondering where the younger Prentises were hiding out. It was strange that Jessica now seemed to be avoiding a confrontation with her. The woman had always sought head-on collisions with Pamela whenever possible.

She was certain that Jessica didn't work. How did Victor make the couple's living?

* * *

One Saturday night while driving home, Pamela switched on Bluetooth when her cell phone pealed. "Hi, honey," she said without checking the caller ID. "What's up?"

"You're out late. I expected to find my wife home when I got here. Doesn't the card game end at ten? Where are you?"

Pamela was happy Mark couldn't see her head shake.

"I'm still in Shiatown but on my way to the Ellis Bridge. We chitchatted a little after playing the last hand. Are you in a good mood?" she asked, laughing.

"Why do I need to be in a good mood? What's going on?"

"I accepted a lunch invitation for us with my father for tomorrow. We haven't spent time with him since last month. Valerie too."

"You always tag Valerie on. You don't have to," Mark said. "Not loving your stepmother is permissible."

"I like Valerie more these days, though I can't totally forget how my stepmother disrespected my mother."

"It's understandable that you don't embrace Valerie under the circumstances."

"Anyway, did you enjoy your racquetball game?"

Pamela listened while Mark gave her the highlights of the match. She was two miles from their home when he finished.

"Don't forget," she said. "We're having lunch tomorrow after church with Dad. And Valerie."

Laughing, the couple hung up the phone.

Pamela liked to keep things light just for the sake of having fun. And she hoped things would stay light with Mark when the next problem arrived.

* * *

Early Sunday afternoon, the front door opened before Pamela and Mark reached her father's porch. Valerie and Steven greeted them inside the doorway. Her subdued father appeared more relaxed than he had been on their last visit, yet Valerie's dark-brown eyes looked unusually cloudy.

Steven talked about that morning's sermon as the couples strolled past the dining room.

Pamela peered into the room and silently clapped while she walked behind them. She preferred eating in nondescript kitchens over stuffy dining rooms.

She waved at the empty room they passed by and nudged Mark.

"Yay. We don't have to eat in their dining room today."

"Behave yourself," he mouthed back.

The couple led their guests into the kitchen, where food lined the island buffet-style.

Steven seated his wife at the table and set a steaming plate of food in front of her before he fixed his own. Pamela and Mark waited until he finished, and then they took turns piling food onto their plates.

Pamela had never seen her father and Valerie show each other affection. The caring action of her father fixing Valerie's plate pleased her. She would hate for him to have a second failed marriage even though he'd sabotaged the first one.

And then she almost choked while sipping water: Steven bowed his head and said grace.

He lifted his fork then laid the utensil across his plate. "The buzz is on about the Timeless Pastries website. Get any orders?"

"Too many for me to fill by myself. Didn't foresee the order flood."

Steven eyed her. "Was that a complaint?"

"Dad, the onslaught is both good and bad. K.C. can't help. Football training at Gibson High begins next month. Mom and Mellie are real troopers, but they both have lives outside of Timeless Pastries. And your son can't bake."

"Speaking of Ace ... I stopped by your brother's house yesterday."

"Humph. You don't visit Mark and me."

"You and Mark visit me. Ace and Mellie need to take lessons."

Pamela rubbed knuckles on her chest then blew on her balled fist. "We'll give them pointers. Won't we, honey?"

Mark laughed. "Sometimes my wife toots her own horn."

"Only when no one else will toot it for me." She washed the last shrimp on her plate down with her lemonade. "Mom suggested a twelve-month business plan before I branch out."

"Give us your agenda. Where you are and where you're headed. What's the timeline?"

Pamela pointed at the grinning man who sat beside her. "Mark ..."

Her husband pushed his plate aside and unveiled a thirty-day plan.

Steven scribbled notes on a napkin.

Pamela scooted her chair closer to Valerie. "Are you feeling okay?" she asked.

"Just a little under the weather. Steven insisted I check in with my doctor last month. I'm feeling better than I have in weeks. Thanks for—"

"It's a sound business plan," Steven butted in. "I'm on board. Have an architect draw up blueprints."

Pamela smiled at Valerie, then faced her father. "Mom said—"

"Anna slow walks through life. Don't accept her advice regarding your business."

"Mom offered a valid suggestion. I agree with her opinion." Pamela glared at him.

Steven stared back at her. "What about your father's views? Or does your mother's counsel trump everyone else's?"

Her opinions will always win with me.

Valerie tapped the table. "Take advice from Steven and Mark. Make the final decisions for yourself."

"Trust me," Mark said. "My wife has a voice she isn't afraid to use."

Steven gazed at his wife. "Dear, are you up to assisting your stepdaughter

116

on this venture?"

"Oh, yes," Valerie said. "Our collaboration is nine years overdue. I never spend time alone with my stepdaughter."

Mark wrapped an arm around his wife's shoulder. "Prepare yourself for a real treat, Valerie. Pamela is an amazing woman."

* * *

Mark designated himself Timeless Pastries' project coordinator. Once he and Pamela arrived home, he called his father. Ed maintained vast business resources throughout the county. Numerous people owed him favors. He called in debts from five surrounding cities.

Pamela sought tasks to keep busy at home while her husband worked on her behalf. Mark had stored keepsakes in the smallest bedroom closet. Unpacked items in those boxes deserved a permanent home. She turned on an overhead light. A violin case was wrapped in a paisley blanket inside one of the boxes tucked away in a corner. He had won awards playing violin in high school and college. She hadn't heard him play in years.

Pamela turned off the light and closed the closet door.

Maybe unpacking her husband's personal items was a bad idea.

* * *

Later that evening, Pamela pushed a serving tray into the den, brushing Mark's paperwork aside.

He blinked several times until he focused on her. "What time is it?"

"Late. Clear that stuff away and eat a meal with me. You work at Techno Plus. Don't take on another full-time job."

Mark leaned against the chair cushion. "I found my calling. My future doesn't lie with Techno Plus."

"IT doesn't work for you these days?"

"I enjoy shaping a company's future."

Not Timeless Pastries' future. Revamp your father's pawn shops.

She smiled at him. "That's because you watched your father turn a mom-and-pop shop into a sustainable business. Technology was a hobby. Business has always flowed through your veins."

Pamela placed their food and drinks on the desk and sat beside him.

"What's wrong?" she asked when Mark stared at her.

"You voiced those exact words while hugging me at my college graduation."

117

He winked at her and smiled. "Thanks for sitting beside me, love. Being close to you matters to me."

"I like eating our meals together. And the den is cozier than the kitchen."

Mark pushed his plate aside. "Sometimes you look at me with an expression I can't identify. Don't ever give up on us. Bring back the woman who thought her friend a special man." Clasping both her hands, he squeezed her fingers, then kissed her palms. "Let me back inside my treasured spot within your heart."

It seemed she wasn't the only one having difficulty letting the past go. The couple had to live for today and not yesterday or tomorrow. Yet Mark's recognition of their problems did help.

Her shoulders relaxed. "We're okay. These are our early days."

* * *

One Friday evening, a loud crash and screams woke Pamela from a nap. She yawned and patted the empty spot beside her.

Her gaze flew to the window. No sunlight. It was dark outside.

"Mark! Where are you?" Her feet tripped her up as she jumped off the bed.

Her eyes adjusted to the darkness as she dashed down the hallway.

The noise had sounded from outside the house. But where?

Turning on the outdoor light, Pamela stood on the deck, squinting into the backyard.

She rushed to the front of the house, turned on the porch light, and opened the front door.

Mark's car was parked in the driveway. The driver door stood open.

Her bare feet slid across the slate tile as she scurried across the walkway. Pamela peered into the vehicle's empty front seat.

She swung around and looked up and down the road until a door slammed across the street. Mr. Prentis rushed down the steps and toward his son's house. Standing on the top step, his wife talked into a cell phone. Neighbors on the east side of the Prentises' house hurried across the lawn. Other neighbors stood on their porches.

Then Pamela realized the screams sounded like a female.

The commotion centered on the Prentises' house. Voices sounded inside the garage.

She peered across the lawn as silhouettes appeared in the neighbor's driveway.

A bedraggled Jessica clung to Mark's arm as he led her outside the building

Pamela went inside her house and closed the door. She lit a candle and sat on a chair in the living room, waiting for her husband to come home.

The disheveled man entered the house minutes later. His jacket was draped over an arm. His tie was askew.

Pamela watched him from her cross-legged position on the chair.

Mark placed his laptop and briefcase on an end table and sat in the chair beside his wife when he saw her. "A top-shelf bracket broke in their garage Multiple shelves came down. It sounded like an explosion. I heard Jessica scream as I drove up, so I went over there."

"I went outside as the show ended. Sounds like your ex-girlfriend sprang a trap."

His thoughtful eyes stared ahead. "Her panic seemed real. However, I have exceeded my drama quota for the evening. Her father-in-law took over. Is dinner in the refrigerator?"

"Yes, sir. Warm up the purple container in the microwave. Did you accomplish your goals at work?"

"And then some." He stood and reached out a hand. "Care to watch me eat?"

Pamela grasped his fingers. "Of course. I want a detailed account of your workday and Jessica's latest drama."

* * *

Days later more activity next door drew Pamela's attention. She slowed the car as she pulled into her driveway. The casually dressed Prentises stowed luggage into a cab's trunk. It was usual-enough activity for most people, but she had pegged the husband as the type of person who parked in long-term parking at the airport.

That evening over dinner, she told Mark what she had seen.

"Did you come home at the normal time?" He continued when she nodded. "I think Victor sent us a message that he curbed his wife's nonsense. It seems he wanted us to know they were leaving town. Someone in the Prentis household was whipped into shape."

"Their vacation is our oasis. Hope they take more," Pamela said.

"Likewise." Mark followed his wife into the family room. "Do you want to work a puzzle together?"

"A jigsaw puzzle? Really? I'll grab a box with a thousand pieces. Next I'll have you reading romance novels."

"That's unlikely," Mark said. "But I will try my hand at a jigsaw puzzle."

Pamela laughed. "You'll come around. Just watch and see."

* * *

April breezed in and whiffed out in a blur of activities as the shop underwent a massive renovation.

Melinda took her solo trip to England.

Anna was busy babysitting her grandchildren.

Frozen batter, cookie dough, tart shells, and fruit mixtures saved Pamela's hide again.

Despite having scores of construction workers underfoot, Timeless Pastries continued operations with limited aggravations. Pamela watched Mark's vision spring to life thirty days after her father and Valerie decided to fund the operation. Steven's monetary contribution and Ed's business contacts secured an amazing team. Continuous work and dedication breathed life into her renovated shop. The transformation proved enormous. A paved and striped parking lot anchored a marquee sign. They added hand-etched store hours on a signpost.

Now Timeless Pastries had been sectioned into a retail bakery, a banquet hall, and a dine-in area set in a posh European-style eatery. The dining room housed fifteen various-sized tables strategically strewn across the space. The banquet hall facilities could seat one hundred people at circular and rectangle tables.

On Saturdays, a locked door would bar the dine-in area and retail bakery from the banquet hall. An outside entrance had been installed on the north wall and would allow visitors to reach banquet gatherings from the parking lot.

Future employees would enjoy an employee area that included the kitchen, office, breakroom, and restrooms.

Steven had upgraded Timeless Pastries from just a commercial kitchen to an enviable retail bakery. His benevolence stumped Anna. Granny praised her son's generous and caring nature. However, Grandmother contended that unrepented guilt supplied perks for other people every time.

One afternoon, Steven and Valerie dropped by the shop unannounced. Her father trooped through the building, opening doors, closing drawers, and peeking into cabinets.

Valerie took a seat in the dine-in area. For weeks, her health had steadily improved. Although they would never be friends, Pamela accepted a relationship with her stepmother. She stopped cringing every time she looked at Valerie.

Steven sat beside his wife after he completed his inspection. "I had trouble envisioning a retail bakery inside a European café setting, but you pulled it off."

"Thanks, Dad. That's a wonderful compliment coming from a seasoned traveler." Pamela pulled a notepad from her pocket and sat beside him. She passed it to him. "Read this."

After he finished reading, Steven glanced at her before he extended the notepad to his wife.

Valerie read the message then handed the notepad back to Pamela. "You want to repay Steven? I'm learning gratefulness is your character. Pure and simple, as you like to say."

Steven beamed as if the compliment had been directed toward him. "Repayment isn't necessary. This bakery is a gift, though a new marriage makes giving you the building outright a risky venture. I will deed the building to you in time. Keep a firm hand on your business."

What!?

She laid the notepad on the table as her hand shook.

"Why?" Pamela asked. "You think Mark might steal the business from me?"

"Well, I wouldn't have thought he would move my daughter next door to his ex-girlfriend, but he did. Who knows what else the man will do."

Pamela gnawed a fingernail. "Who told you about that? Only a few people know."

"Folks who have your best interest at heart," Steven said, standing. "Your grandparents."

"Granny and Granddad? Who told *them* where Jessica lives?"

"Her husband's parents did. They attend the same church as your grandparents and live across the street from you. Did you know they're related to your neighbor?"

Pamela nodded. "Jessica told Mark weeks ago."

His eyebrow rose. "Are those two friendly?"

"No, sir. She accosted Mark one evening in our driveway."

"You heard the conversation, or did you believe his account?"

Pamela sighed. "My husband told me."

Please don't give me opposition. I'm finally dealing with what happened.

"Pam ..." Steven hesitated. "Learn from your mistakes. Protect yourself from whatever Mark might do." He glanced at his wife. "Valerie knows Victor's sister quite well," he added when his wife stood beside him.

"We met years ago when I attended a military prayer breakfast." Valerie retrieved her purse from the table. "Her family lives in Houston. Her parents bought a condo there as well."

"Sometimes they spy on us. His parents must know Mark dated Jessica before she married their son."

"Dated? Your husband and Jessica practically lived together."

"Who told you that?" Pamela asked.

Steven glanced at his watch. "We're headed to lunch at the country club. Is Monday your open house?"

You didn't answer my question. "Uh-huh. I'm beyond nervous thinking about it."

Valerie tucked her hand around Steven's forearm. "Reserve this table for me on Monday at one. I'll bring over friends for dessert on your grand-opening day."

More surprises from her stepmother. "Oh. Thank you. Seeing a friendly face will calm my nerves."

Pamela walked Steven and Valerie to the door. Since renovations began, Valerie had tried to make amends for her part in breaking up Pamela's parents' marriage. But Pamela felt that friendship with her stepmother seemed disloyal to Anna. She didn't want to condone Steven's mistreatment of her mother in any way.

* * *

The month ended with Timeless Pastries serving baked goods and candy weekdays from eight to four. Daily assistance from Anna and Melinda allowed Pamela to run the counter and keep the showcases filled with mouthwatering treats.

All temporary hands waited on deck to help with the shop's increased business, but permanent hands were required.

Her retail customers took up precious baking time. Plus, having new customers increased the requests for fundraisers and meet and greets. Her success proved to be too much too soon. The good old days of baking without daily customer contact called to Pamela. She wanted more business without the demands of running a retail establishment.

* * *

One Saturday afternoon Mark drove a rental truck loaded with baked goods and lunch items into the medical center's parking lot. Valerie had organized a weeklong fundraiser for the medical center using Timeless Pastries' baked goods and some lunch items created especially for this event. The funds would provide walkers, crutches, wheelchairs, and hospital beds to any patient that required assistance. That day's catered lunch was the medical center's official thank you to the participants.

With this fundraiser and lunch, Timeless Pastries received free advertisement and monetary compensation, and it all would help launch the planned addition of soon serving lunch. Pamela had decided to test the waters before telling her family she may disregard the twelve-month plan to serve food.

The fundraiser proved beneficial for the patients and for Pamela. She beamed as attendees made repeat trips to the dessert table.

After the last official pledge tally had been given, the medical center's cleaning staff began clearing off the serving tables.

"Let's work opposite sides of the room," Mark said. "We'll meet up at your father's table."

Before long, Pamela and Mark sidled beside the table where Steven and Valerie were gathered.

"Goodbye, Dad." Pamela kissed his cheek and hugged him. She smiled at Valerie. "See you all at church tomorrow."

Mark shook their hands. "Mr. Hayes, Valerie, it was an awesome turnout. I'm pleased the fundraiser exceeded the goal."

A matronly dressed woman sitting next to Valerie passed Pamela a business card.

"Our auxiliary club will host a fundraiser next month. We're advocating higher standards at nursing home facilities. Please do for us what you did for your stepmother's campaign."

Pamela read the card then extended it to Mark. "My husband set up this event. He'll call you."

Mark glanced at the card then held out his hand. "Mark Simon. I'll contact you Monday."

"Heidi Hampton," the woman said. "I worked on a few political campaigns with your mother. Celeste and Ed are elusive these days. How are they doing?"

"Just great. I'll pass on your regards. Please excuse us. My wife got up at three o'clock this morning."

The couple headed toward the door and grabbed their gear on the way outside. Several people stopped them on the way.

"Marvelous menu," said a man still eating a slice of apple pie.

"Hope you decide to serve lunch," said the lady standing beside him. "Your café is close to my job. See you on Monday for dessert."

"Thank you," Pamela said. "I look forward to seeing you there."

She smiled and waved to each person they passed as Mark moved them swiftly to the truck.

She covered her mouth when she yawned. "Using disposable serving pans, bowls, and trays works wonders. We only have to cart away two sacks."

"It's been a great day all around. You are an effective salesperson. Your love for what you do is better than having marketing skills."

"Think so?" She beamed an uneven grin. "I bake better than I mingle. Cook, too. I never entertained the idea of catering full meals until this event."

Mark's eyebrows arched. "I asked you to open a café, banquet hall, and catering service."

"And I agreed to add a retail bakery and to maybe serve lunch on weekdays."

"You can hire staff and serve lunch now. Please trust my judgment on this one."

Mark opened the truck door on the passenger side.

Pamela climbed onto the seat.

"I'm too tired to think, much less dream about the future. Everyone will get my praise report later." Pamela giggled softly. "I'm exhausted. Thank God Mom, Grandmother, and Granny showed up at the shop at seven o'clock to help me cook." Yawning, she slumped on the seat. "Wake me up once we reach the shop."

He started the engine. "You've worked nonstop since leaving home at four. Good thing you finished baking yesterday. I'll drop you off at home

124

before I stop by the shop and return the truck."

"You've stayed by my side all day. I can ride with you."

"I fell asleep on the couch after we reached the building. Go home and rest. I'll bring dinner home." He nudged her knee. "Love those Toomey's steak burgers."

"How about a mystery movie marathon tonight?"

She fell asleep before he answered.

* * *

On Monday, Pamela drove into the garage as movement on the street caught her attention. The Prentises exited a cab that pulled into their driveway. Her prayers for them to stay away longer had failed.

She lowered the garage door. "Too bad I can't say 'welcome back.' "

Chapter Twelve

Pamela snacked on popcorn in the family room. Her legs dangled over one side of the chair.

Mark studied her body from the doorway with his head tilted to the side. "Won't sitting sideways put a crick in your neck?"

She wiggled her fingers at him. "Hi, hubby. Dinner is simmering in the slow cooker."

He leaned on the chair, staring at her. "You're mighty engrossed in that book. Did you read the Timeless Pastries plan I gave you?"

The book shook when she laughed. "You mean the nineteen-page report or the instructions on the last page?"

"I designed the report to soften the list of instructions at the end." He gazed at her.

Closing the book, she stared at him. "The list on the last page is fine. The preceding nineteen-page lecture repulsed me. Just joking," she added, laughing. Pamela followed him to the couch and knelt beside him. "You did an excellent job removing the stingers from tasks I detest." Touching his arm, she smiled. "I have good news."

His jaw dropped. "You've already made headway on the list?"

"Uh-hum. Someone was busy this morning." Pamela batted her eyelashes at him. "Do you want the long-winded or short-and-sweet version?"

Laughter rocked his body. "You read my twenty-page report."

"Okay, I'll give you the long version of my decisions. Well...you had hits and misses. I disregarded directives nine through thirteen. No food as of yet. Catering is out. Customers will furnish their own food and dessert in the banquet hall. We may cater banquet hall meals when we open up the café for lunch. *If* we ever do. I've still given myself twelve months to think about it."

"Why should clients bring in food Timeless Pastries can provide? The four meals you provided at the medical center received raves."

"Cooking food for the fundraiser was a one-off thing. Mom and my grandmothers began helping me cook at seven o'clock that morning. We don't employ cooks, which is why we can't serve lunch. I can hire extra workers to help with the bake side because my three grandparents furnished funds and won't accept repayment."

"Other possibilities exist to open the café side. A second mortgage is one."

"And risk losing our forever home? No thank you. We've won battles in this place."

He tried to kiss her.

She evaded his lips.

Mark released her. "What about the other points on the last page? Do you have additional news to give me?"

"A little bit more. But I am winding down. You can't expect me to accomplish each point in one day."

"I'll revise a report on the misses next week."

"No. You won't. Try again in six months when I'll be more prepared to branch further out."

"Please continue," Mark finally said.

"You wrote a book and not a report. Joking," she said when he scowled at her. "Moving on ... Mellie and Mom are officially off bake detail. But Mellie will manage the fundraisers from her home. During the renovations, I approached several people about working at Timeless Pastries. Today your cousins accepted jobs as part-time cashiers. A single mom at our church will be the full-time baker. My cousin will decorate pastries and make candy. My old neighbor is a social media whiz and will manage the website, plus event planning and execution for Saturday celebrations in the banquet hall. Four teenagers that attend our church will assist her on Saturdays."

"You've made progress. How did you slip on a human resources cap today along with the other hats you wear?"

"Mom took over my office at eight thirty. By noon, employees were hired, papers were signed, and Mom left the building. Except for the teens, everyone starts work on Monday. Mom will manage my employees free of charge."

"A fitting end to a busy morning. I'm pleased you read the report. Lavine thought it required too much mental exertion for an overworked body."

"You and your administrative assistant share a special bond. When will I meet this unique lady?"

"That's her favorite question since we got engaged. Any further Timeless

Pastries news?"

"Not yet. But I will give you weekly updates."

* * *

One week later, Pamela closed her book when Mark walked into the family room. She left her reading chair and headed to the couch.

"How did it go at work today?" she asked.

"The same as usual." He paused, grinning. "It's been one week since the last Timeless Pastries update."

Pamela laughed. "Can't believe you waited for me to tell you."

"It wasn't easy. Now, how did the first week with having employees go?"

"Great. I feel like I can breathe again. I actually have time to think during the day." She touched his arm. "I did notice something I had missed. People are bringing in their own lunch food and then they buy our dessert."

Mark double blinked, staring off in space. He nodded his head. "The décor is inviting. The dessert tastes great. The little waterfalls you insisted on installing are relaxing. The shop is probably a tranquil haven in their hectic day. Did you provide tables you didn't expect people to use, even if they could only buy dessert?"

"I wanted to set the proper atmosphere for when we began serving lunch, but until then, I expected people to purchase their goodies and leave the shop. Like Skylar does each morning. But each day a few parents bring in their children with takeout bags from other restaurants. Even from places where they could have bought dessert."

Mark double blinked again. "Really? Customers buy food from other establishments, then buy their dessert from Timeless Pastries, and eat all of their meal in the dine-in area?"

Her head bowed. Directives nine through thirteen came to mind.

Here comes another detailed report on how to open the café side in less than six months.

* * *

The following morning, Mark opened the door at Timeless Pastries for two men who left the shop one behind the other. Several customers were scattered at separate tables inside the dine-in area. Some people read paperbacks, a few used e-readers, while others worked on laptops. Students? In the industrial center? Then Mark remembered that the community college and technological college were both less than a mile away. The lure of Wi-Fi worked its magic on students every time.

He searched the room for the perfect research spot and selected the table closest to the amber waterfall.

At the counter, an older woman studied a showcase before his cousin reached her.

When the door opened, a male jogger walked in, and two casually dressed females followed in behind him.

Mark reached the counter first but waited behind the lady paying for her purchase.

"Lemon drop cookies taste best with natural flavors," the woman said. "Eating one of yours is like drinking a lightly sweetened glass of lemonade."

Emily smiled. "I agree. We only use natural flavors in our baking."

"Glad you work here now. The owner was running herself ragged. In the kitchen, selling goods, and wiping tables."

"I'll be late for work if you talk much longer," a man standing behind Mark said.

The woman's eyes formed perfect circles once she spun around. "Goodness gracious. A line has formed. You guys are so quiet. Someone should've spoken up before now."

Picking up her bag, the woman hurriedly left the counter.

Mark left his place in line and opened the door for her.

The worried expression left her face. "Thank you. Some young people are still polite. I didn't mean to take up every one's time."

"No problem. The homey atmosphere makes you forget you're not at home. Do you like the lemon drop cookies best?"

"It's a tie between those and the almond crunch." Waving the bag at him, she ambled to her car.

The line had cleared when Mark reached the showcase. "Hey, Emily. Six lemon drop and six almond crunch cookies. How do you like the job so far?"

"Love it. I see you brought your briefcase. Are you staying awhile?"

"I am," he said, biting into a lemon drop cookie.

* * *

Later that morning, his head rose from the spreadsheet he pored over. A familiar hand placed a steaming cup of tea before Mark. He'd spotted Pamela replenishing showcases and wiping down tables several times that morning.

How had his enterprising wife managed alone? No wonder she had fallen asleep in his arms each night.

"How's the kitchen staff and Emily and Tina working out? Any problems?"

"Nada. We have a freezer filled with prepped items. I whip up a fresh batch every other day. Some items sell better than others. I'm learning which desserts are bestsellers."

"This morning a lady favorably compared your lemon drop cookies to a lightly sweetened glass of lemonade."

"Was she short, sweet, and very talkative?" Pamela sat beside Mark when he nodded. "Mrs. Patterson enjoys conversations sprinkled with lemon drop and almond crunch cookies. She comes in every morning. And I expected you to come today."

"I'm sure you did." He sipped the brew in the cup. "Green tea? You know, some folks enjoy drinking coffee even if the proprietor doesn't."

"Get off the coffee kick. I stand by my decision to only serve green, ginger root, and Thai tea. Although hot-chocolate thoughts are making their presence known."

Mark took another swig of tea. "Winning businesses please their customers and not themselves."

"Somehow I knew you would say that. So, what's the strategy going forward?"

"Serving lunch and catering Saturday events in the banquet hall and at off-site locations. Heidi Hampton booked a fundraiser for nursing homes at the end of this month. A Mrs. Cathey requested one for the animal shelter in early June."

"We hired a dedicated Saturday crew for banquet-room events. We're booked solid for the next two months."

"We're talking real money. Heidi plans to one-up Valerie. Geraldine Cathey won't be left behind. Their one-upmanship will gift Timeless Pastries with free advertisement."

"They both plan to serve food and treats in the banquet hall?"

"Off-site. Heidi requested the same menu we provided Valerie."

"Everyone will get a different meal if we cater the food. I want to test various lunch menus."

Mark scooted his chair closer. "That remark offered promise. Are we through with your twelve-month plan?"

"Concerning lunch, I think … yes. I will tell my family my decision tomorrow. *But,* I won't cater off-site fundraisers. We catered the medical center's fundraiser thank you lunch as a favor for Dad and Valerie."

"That gracious gesture benefited Timeless Pastries big time. Good deeds still bless the folks who do them."

"We'll handle off-site fundraisers for Mrs. Hampton and Mrs. Cathey but no one else. A part-time lunch staff may want to work additional hours or Saturdays by catering events in the banquet hall. In-house." She rose and picked up his empty cookie plate. "Leaving soon?"

"Yes, I'll see you at home this evening."

* * *

The next afternoon, Mark left Shiatown and headed toward the Ellis Bridge.

While driving on the bridge to South Town, he remembered a conversation he'd had with an old high school pal. Mark headed to the auto parts store where the man worked, but he slowed the car while crossing a busy intersection. He circled the vehicle around the block, then parked on a side street across from the Bianchi's parking lot.

His wife leaned on her car while chatting with Hodges.

He eyed the clock on the dashboard and continued his vigil.

Five minutes later Ace walked up, hugged his sister, and tucked her safely into her car. Ace watched her make a successful left turn into oncoming traffic. The show of affection allowed him to see Mark's stakeout across the street.

Without an observable reaction, Ace followed Hodges to Bianchi's front door.

"Whew! A narrow escape. Ace didn't see me spying on my wife."

While holding onto the door, Ace turned around and gazed at Mark before he entered the restaurant.

"So he saw me. Eh ... who cares?"

If Pamela and Hodges met by chance, then what Mark saw didn't matter.

Would the brother tell his sister what he had witnessed?

Mark had the right to confront Pamela if he chose to.

He started the car. The assurance he had offered his wife yesterday struck him today.

He'd said that good deeds still bless the folks who do them. Evidently not today, not with what he'd seen at Bianchi's when he had returned to South Town after supporting his wife's business in Shiatown.

Now Mark was blindsided by the baking football star for the second time

That afternoon Pamela met Anna in the Timeless Pastries parking lot. She waited to talk until her mother stood beside her. "I have great news. Oh, I see Mellie's SUV is here. Let's go on in and I'll tell you both together."

"I abhor waiting," Anna said. "Give me a hint."

"And ruin your surprise? Never!"

They headed toward the kitchen and waved at the cashier who waved back and met them at the kitchen door. "We've had a steady stream of customers all afternoon." She pointed to customers who sat alone. "Mark credits Wi-Fi for the long visits. I think customers like the homey atmosphere."

Anna grinned. "This place is soothing. Sometimes I sit by one of the waterfalls and eat dessert."

"I sit by the rainbow waterfall and think about the day," Pamela said.

"I think that's true of lots of folks who stay awhile," Tina agreed.

Pamela quirked an eyebrow at Anna as the women entered the kitchen. She always breathed easier once she reached the shop. The staff was busy as usual. Sally loaded a tray filled with cookie dough into an oven, and Tracy decorated tartlets.

"Hello, ladies. Did any problems arise while I was gone?"

Sally closed the oven door before she turned around. "Smooth sailing back here."

Tracy nodded. "The kitchen is always on schedule. And Pam, Tina said a man left you his business card. Look on the right edge of the box and container table."

"Melinda's inside the office," Sally added.

Melinda was crunching numbers on a computer spreadsheet when they walked into the room.

"Hi, Mellie," said Anna. "Are my grandchildren with your folks?"

Melinda swiveled the chair around. "Yes. They're spending the night. Mother's taking them to Vacation Bible School in the morning."

Anna drug a chair to the desk. "I'm waiting on Pam to tell us some big news. She wanted to tell us together."

Pamela sat on the desk's edge. "Today I ate lunch at Bianchi's with a couple who will open a convenience store in a singles community next month. They're installing a fresh food cooler today. And they want Timeless Pastries to provide desserts and light meals. Also, I ran into K.C. in the parking lot after lunch. In early August, Gibson High's football team will launch our fundraisers until after school starts."

"Yay, K.C.!" Melinda said.

"There's more good news. Earlier Mark texted that we have another breakthrough. I'll have the specifics later." She faced Anna. "Mom, I know you recommended I set up a twelve-month business plan before serving meals. But last night, I decided Timeless Pastries will start serving lunch in two weeks. We might supply food for Saturday banquet hall events next month. We're catering two off-site fundraisers for Valerie's friends."

Silence enveloped the room. Melinda and Anna glanced at each other.

"Who overturned your twelve-month plan?" Anna asked.

Pamela sighed while staring at them.

Her good news had fallen on fallow ground. She knew that somehow the people closest to her blamed Mark for her decision.

She rounded the desk, took her seat, and smiled. "Let me give you some more details. The medical center's fundraiser was a success story for Timeless Pastries. As you know, some customers bring in their lunch but buy our sweets, while others eat their lunch elsewhere but come here for dessert." Pamela hesitated. "Are we on the same page so far?"

"Don't be condescending," Anna said. "Continue your speech."

Pamela glanced at her sister-in-law when Melinda laughed. "Did you hear something funny?"

"Mom wants you to get to the gist of it. As I do," Melinda responded.

Pamela's cell phone rang. "Hi, Skylar. ... Yes. He texted me earlier. .. What? ... If that's what he thought, seeing you proved he was wrong. He could've just come over. ... Yes. I am upset. I don't cheat on my spouse. ... No. Mom and Mellie are here. We were discussing Timeless Pastries' future. .. I believe that too. Thanks for calling."

Pamela rested her elbows on the desk with her face on her palms. "I trust Mark even though he hasn't earned my confidence, yet he won't trust me. And we've been friends a long time."

Melinda scooted her chair beside Pamela. "Whatever my husband said requires prayer before reaction."

"What happened?" Anna asked.

"Skylar showed up for his lunch with K.C. before I left Bianchi's. After I drove off the parking lot, he saw Mark parked on a side street. He'd been watching me and K.C. talk. We chatted about ten minutes before Skylar came.

I don't know how long Mark spied on me or why he had driven across town."

Anna sighed. "Don't jump to conclusions. You're making progress in your relationship."

"We were until today." Pamela raised her hands then dropped them on the desk.

Anna stood beside her. "Years of low self-esteem can't be quickly eradicated. Mark battled against absentee-parents syndrome and did an incredible job raising himself. Living a confident life is a war he hasn't yet won."

"I know. But it's difficult to deal with his mood swings," said Pamela. "His fuse burns slow and will ignite this evening. But thanks to Skylar's call and your sound advice, I won't pour gasoline on Mark's fire."

Father, let Your Holy Spirit strengthen me to weather storms. Against all hope, Abraham in hope believed.

Chapter Thirteen

Mark jiggled change in his pocket as he entered the front door. He had waited an entire afternoon to confront his wife. His gaze went to where she sat on the sofa. His defenses broke. Pamela always sat in the living room if she wanted to talk to him as soon as he arrived home. The life he craved stood at an obvious crossroads. Fight left Mark as he focused on the woman who loved him. Never again would he allow negative thoughts to undermine his confidence in his wife.

He sat beside her. "Ace told you that he saw me parked on a side street across from Bianchi's."

Her lips quivered as she tried to smile. "My brother called me."

"Let me explain my actions. Lavine called me on the drive to work. Her sorority sisters were meeting in Shiatown at nine o'clock. The group is seeking means to subsidize an October Caribbean cruise reunion for their members. I left the meeting with consecutive fundraiser orders until a week before the trip. On the drive back to South Town another potential fundraiser opportunity hit me. I had thought about a previous conversation with an old high school friend. Do you remember Dempsey Collins from Gibson High?"

"No. I don't recall him," Pamela said.

"He remembers you. Dempsey graduated with Ace and Melinda. He aims to champion underprivileged kids who live in his neighborhood. I passed by Bianchi's while headed to the auto parts store where Dempsey works."

Pamela smiled. "I'm happy to know you weren't following me. Sorry," she said, shrugging. "I couldn't come up with a reasonable explanation why you were across town at the same time I was."

Words escaped Mark. He could only look at her, so he nodded, clearing his throat. "I ..." he finally said. "I suggested Dempsey partner with area churches and provide an after-school and weekend alternative for junior high students."

Pamela glanced away and then back at him. "Sports? Tutoring? What program did you suggest?"

"Free tutoring and creative writing labs along with music and dance lessons. Confidence gained in junior high will give them a leg up in high school."

"That was thoughtful of you. Do you want Timeless Pastries fundraisers to offset their costs?"

"I do. We'll figure out the fine points later."

"Okay. Keep me posted."

Thank God for a supportive wife. Pamela had always backed him up even when he hadn't returned the favor. Even when upset, she still wanted to work beside him.

He clasped her hands in his. "You won't cheat on me. I finally recognize the fact."

"Why did you doubt me?"

"I can't explain my overreaction. You're better than the thoughts I had about you."

"Rule ten on our marriage agreement states, 'Pray and read scripture together weekly. Nurture His presence within our home.' Well, we are way behind schedule, and I think we could use some prayer and scripture."

Tension left his shoulders. His wife was on point as always. She brought God into the mix. He wanted to live a God-centered life but didn't know how to begin.

"I think we should start tonight before we go to bed. Agree?"

She released a long sigh. "I do. We'll end our workweek on a high note."

The couple stood up together.

Mark drew her into his arms, burying his nose in her hair. "I love your fresh-scrubbed scent. You smell like home."

He noted tears in her eyes. But he was relieved when she accepted his outstretched hand.

Pamela sighed. "I have big news to tell you over dinner. It's time to eat."

* * *

She buttered a breadstick after saying grace. "I ate lunch with a couple opening a convenience store in a singles community next month. A fresh food cooler was installed this afternoon. They want Timeless Pastries to provide daily desserts and light meals."

"Congratulations, love. Now I really feel bad that I suspected you had secretly met Hodges."

136

Pamela smiled. "It's already been forgiven."

"But not forgotten. It takes time to get over the hurt of being misjudged." His hand reached out as he hesitated in thought. "You're good for me, Pam. I aim to be good for you as well." When tears filled his eyes, Mark dropped his hand and cleared his throat. "Uhm ... what menu did your new clients request?"

"I will select the food. But they'll let me know what items end up selling best."

"You do like to micromanage. I should have known you would choose the menu without my asking you."

"No, sir. You are the control freak," Pamela said.

Mark's eye's narrowed slightly as he chuckled. "What terms did you quote?"

"I told them my business manager husband will call them this weekend."

He nodded when she laughed. "Perfect. I can hardly wait to get their information. This will be Timeless Pastries' first time to provide meals to a store."

Mark suggested various scenarios while they ate dinner.

Pamela slumped in her chair. "We need a money tree to expand the business. Look at the cost involved."

She ticked the list off her fingers.

"Don't give up," Mark said. "Each service you named is doable."

"How? Our families have extended a tremendous amount of goodwill. For now, maybe we should stick with what we know: baked goods."

"The convenience store requested food items. We might lose their business if we wait longer to supply meals. We have another resource."

"What is it?"

"My savings will prop us up for a while. I can spot us three months."

"Thank God for miracles." She briefly closed her eyes. "I am exhausted. Bedtime for me." She hesitated.

Hmm ... might as well jump in.

"I almost forgot my other good news. K.C. said Gibson High's football team will launch our fundraisers from early August until after school begins."

She braced herself for the explosion.

"That *is* good news. I hope Hodges keeps promoting your business." Mark followed her from the kitchen. "We can pray and read scripture before you fall asleep. It won't take me long to close down the house and join you."

A week later, a finger tapped Mark's shoulder in the checkout line. His stomach clenched on contact. He knew Jessica stood behind him. Until today he had avoided talking to her. He parked his car inside the garage each time he saw her watering the lawn.

He glanced over his shoulder as he loaded items onto the conveyor belt.

Jessica wore a tiger-print bodysuit and black mini skirt to grocery shop. She pressed close to his side.

Mark inserted his bank card into the payment terminal. "When did you take up grocery shopping?"

"I see you still remember my habits. But some of those things have changed." Lines crinkled around her eyes. "You used to look around while driving. Now the married man stares straight ahead."

"You're right. I'm more careful these days. Family men usually are."

"Prove that claim. Spend time alone with me."

Mark couldn't contain the chuckle. He was becoming more and more like his wife.

"Prove I'm a family man by hanging out with an old girlfriend? You can't be serious."

The wide-eyed teenaged cashier snickered as she handed him the receipt.

He accepted it from her hand and exited the store.

At home he relayed the incident to his wife over dinner.

* * *

In a short time, Timeless Pastries opened for lunch from ten to two. The initial response to the new service was more than Pamela had expected. The shop was flooded with steady diners. Customers queued at the door. The eleven to one onslaught of customers had so many people they had to open up the banquet hall to have room for everyone. Children-friendly programs streamed on the television. Kids adored eating inside the makeshift family room.

Numerous changes had taken place in Pamela's life since getting married. These days Pamela spent time with her girlfriends who didn't play spades. And Mark had surprised Pamela when he gave up his Saturday afternoons to teach violin to students that attended Dempsey Collins's afterschool and weekend initiative.

Now her honeymoon offered fond memories and a glimpse of future family vacations.

Jessica was the puzzle in Pamela's busy life. The woman who took pride in causing scenes had remained out of sight. Sometimes Pamela saw Victor arrive home on early mornings. On each occasion, he waved a hand and moved along. Mark no longer saw either of their neighbors, and he hadn't altered his schedule. Not that he wanted any reminders of their neighbors.

Was Jessica purposely laying low to spring a trap?

* * *

One evening, Pamela parked inside the garage, changed her shoes, and headed back outside. Something she had eaten had upset her stomach, so she hoped her after-work walk through the neighborhood might dislodge her digestive system from her mind.

She locked the front door, then turned around when someone called her name. Pamela glanced across the road. The senior Prentises were sitting on their front porch.

Pamela waved and trekked down the steps. "Hello, neighbors. It's a beautiful day."

"We're finally getting a cool breeze," the woman said. "May we bother you a moment?"

Curiosity overcame her queasiness. She headed across the street.

Pamela alighted the stairs and sat on the top step. "I'm always glad to meet our neighbors. To what do I owe this honor?"

Mr. Prentis grinned at her. "I'm Lester, and this is my wife, Simone. We both wanted to thank you in person for your thoughtful gift."

Simone nodded. "You gave a couple with green thumbs the best present. Thanks for the Shasta daisies. Lester planted them in our backyard that same evening."

"Ah, they were too lovely to resist. I wanted to buy you guys a present. The daisies seemed perfect. Glad you liked them."

"We told our Sunday school class about our gracious neighbor. And then we discovered your grandparents are longtime church members."

"I didn't hear about that. My grandparents are wonderful people."

"That they are," said Lester.

"I like hearing their stories about life in general," Pamela added.

Lester glanced at this wife. "We oldsters love to pass on wise advice."

"Do you have grandchildren?"

Mrs. Prentis smiled all over herself. "Our daughter has four children. Her family lives in Texas. Our fall and winter months are spent in Houston. Our son, Victor, and his wife, Jessica, are your next-door neighbors. They don't have any children." The woman's avid gaze pierced Pamela. "Your grandparents told us you and your husband are longtime friends who fell in love after dating the wrong people."

Time to continue her walk around the block.

Pamela stretched her limbs and stood. "We met in high school," she said.

Lester rose with her. "Your grandfather said you're the best baker in South Town. The first week your shop opened exceeded expectations. And he said your husband heads the IT department at Techno Plus. He's Ed Simon's only child and loves sports."

Her grandparents had laid the buildup on thick.

"Thanks for calling me over for a visit," Pamela said. "I'll tell Mark I met our neighbors. Bye-bye."

Pamela waved and then continued her stroll down the street. Why did the couple introduce themselves now after three months of spying on them? She glanced at the other Prentis house when she passed by.

Why hadn't she and Mark seen the junior Prentises lately?

* * *

A week later, Pamela put down her book and picked up her cell phone, peering at the caller ID. Mrs. Simon. Was Mark ignoring his mother's calls again? She wanted to invite Celeste and Ed over for dinner, but her husband had warned her not to interfere between him and his parents.

She answered the cell phone seconds before the call went to voicemail. "Hello, Mrs. Simon. How are you and Mr. Simon doing?"

"Just fine. But please don't be so formal. Call me Mother or Celeste. The choice is yours."

"Then I choose to call you Mother, like my husband does."

"An excellent pick. I spoke to my son earlier, but my subsequent calls went to voicemail. Are you guys free for dinner this evening?"

Oh no. Mark will throw a hissy fit if I accept. My goodness. She has put me on the spot.

Her finger tapped on her forehead. *What to do? Hmm.*

She'd rather err on her established family values than on her husband's splintered home life.

"I'm thinking about Mark's work schedule. He should've been home by now. He splits his time between Techno Plus and Timeless Pastries."

"He said that earlier. Is Saturday a better day for you both?"

Pamela nibbled her thumbnail. "My schedule is free this Saturday. Mark will call you once he comes home."

"I'll tell Ed you guys are coming to dinner Saturday."

I didn't say Mark was free. Here comes that hissy fit.

"Thanks for the invitation. What's your favorite dessert?"

"Both Ed and I love your classic yellow cake with chocolate frosting."

"That's the one we'll bring." She heard the door creak. "Ah, the door just opened. Hold on."

Pamela hurried into the living room and pointed to the cell phone.

Mark stopped in front of her and shook his head.

She mouthed, "It's your mother," and held out the cell phone.

Mark ignored her hand. "No," he said louder than was necessary.

"No hurry," Celeste said as if she'd heard him. "Tell him to relax and call me later."

His mother must not have heard her son's reply. Her tone of voice never changed.

Pamela rolled her eyes at him. "Will do. Goodbye ... Mother."

"Your mom?" Mark asked. "I thought you were talking to my mother."

"I was. She called me and wants you to call her later."

He skirted around her. "I spoke with her this afternoon."

Pamela followed him into the den, where he placed his briefcase and laptop on the desk.

She leaned on the built-in bookshelf, staring at him.

"Is dinner ready?" He grinned when Pamela nodded. Winking at her, he brushed a kiss across her forehead as he passed by her. "You and Mother sounded cozy. What's up?"

Pamela walked behind him into the bedroom. She sat on the bed, wiggling her toes.

Mark discarded his keys onto the nightstand, undid his tie, and stepped into the closet. He re-entered the room carrying grey cut-off jeans and a chalk-blue T-shirt.

"I'm still waiting on your answer. Mother didn't call on the landline. Why did she call you?"

141

How to break the news. Might as well jump right in. "Ahem. Mother. Yours. Not mine ..."

Pamela laughed when Mark looked perplexed. "I had two choices. Mother or Celeste."

The couple laughed together as Mark stripped off his shirt.

"I'm used to saying Mrs. Simon," she said with a shrug. "Calling her Mother feels weird." She snapped her fingers. "Oh, yeah. By the way, you should call my mother, Mom."

"I didn't receive permission from Mrs. Hayes."

"You did from me."

Mark sat on the bed beside her. "I hope *Mom* agrees with your logic. Now give me the lowdown on the call. What did you commit us to?"

"Ouch. Why would you think I would do that after you told me not to?"

"Pam ... you might as well fess up."

"Dinner. But I got you a four-day reprieve."

"What?" Mark stood and stuffed his hands into his pockets. "You promised not to run interference between me and my folks."

"You had to be there. I didn't accept your mother's invitation. She just assumed that I had. I told her you would call her." She hesitated. "Am I forgiven?" She almost bit her tongue after asking.

"I'll forgive you if you give me a back rub."

I don't waste energy on sullen men. Forgive your folks then ask me nicely for a massage.

"Dinner's cooking. You need an office chair with back support. Like the chair in our den."

"So, you refuse to help me. Anyway, whatever is cooking smells delicious. I skipped lunch." Mark headed toward the bathroom. He swiftly turned around at the door. "Is something wrong?"

Pamela stood in the same spot where Mark had left her. "What are you talking about?"

"Your facial expression. You look confused. Tell me your thoughts."

You were willing to take your father's help to renovate my commercial kitchen, but you refuse to repay his kindness by visiting them. You can't use people then throw them away. What happens when my usefulness runs out? Will you dump me as well?

Don't think negative thoughts. She tried to smile. "Pray about how you treat your parents."

"I treat them fine. We talk. And I visit the shops twice a week."

"Perhaps they need to spend actual time with you. Will you at least think about it? Please?"

"I love my parents. Don't act as if I don't."

"Your ... mother ... called ... my cell phone. Show them that you love them. Don't make them guess."

"I look forward to eating dinner there. Beatrice is a terrific cook. Look," he added when she turned away. "I'm joking. Our visit is overdue."

Pamela headed toward the door. "I'll call you when dinner is ready."

* * *

After dinner, Mark cleared off the table while Pamela watched him.

"I saw your dad at the pharmacy," he said. "He almost walked past me. He acted distracted the entire time and left his car keys on the counter. I spotted the keyring before he reached the door, and I ran to give them to him."

If hearts could skip a beat, Pamela's did. She loved her father despite the callous way he had treated her mother, and she was worried about why he would be so distracted.

She called him and twisted her wedding rings while she waited. "No answer on the landline or the cell phone. Valerie is next." Pamela thumbed through her contacts, then placed the call. Moments later, she glanced at Mark. "The call went to voicemail."

Her phone pinged as she laid the cell phone on the counter. Pamela read the message. She studied her shoes, sighing.

"What's wrong? Who texted you?"

"My friend Lizzie. I'll deal with her latest crisis after I contact Dad."

Moments later Pamela jumped to her feet and rushed from the kitchen.

* * *

Mark pursued her into the bedroom and watched her from the doorway.

She grabbed her purse from the shelf, looked around the room, then brushed past him.

He knew she was headed to the garage before she veered right into the laundry room.

Mark bolted behind her. "Where are you going? I thought we were staying in tonight."

Pamela placed a foot inside the car. "Something is wrong. My single-focus father is never distracted. I'll call Mom in the car and head their way."

"Your father and Valerie most likely went out for dinner. They're fine."

"More than likely they did, but I don't know for sure. Valerie could be sick again. You seeing Dad at the pharmacy could be significant. Maybe she had a relapse. Or Dad is ill. I love my father, no matter what he's done."

"Your father and Valerie are fine. But check on them if it will make you feel better. Drive carefully. Call me when you reach their house."

Her solemn nod almost prompted Mark to go with her, but he believed she wanted to settle her emotions alone. Pamela had sat at the kitchen table twisting her wedding rings after he had told her about seeing her father. She normally didn't resort to nervous tics.

He stood in the laundry room doorway until the garage door lowered. Should he have gone with his wife?

* * *

Mark grinned as he read the text message twenty minutes later. All was fine, and his wife was on her way home.

Chapter Fourteen

Later that week, Mark scrolled through his inbox, deleting useless emails. He removed any alerts that didn't pertain exclusively to IT.

As he sorted, he realized that while he was talented in numerous arenas, he'd missed the mark in many others. One sad fact remained in the background of his marriage: His wife held private reservations about his judgment, even though she accepted most of his suggestions without debate.

Claims that she'd forgiven his Jessica blunder floated from her lips whenever Mark asked her, but deep down he knew she hadn't. Her perplexed expression in unguarded moments revealed her negative inner thoughts. Still, his life grew sweeter as he devoted quality time to Pamela. He no longer looked for his identity in other people but encouraged appropriate relationships when needed.

Lavine knocked on his open office door and stepped into the room. "I've noticed you've changed your dress since getting married. Have you adopted a more laid-back style thanks to Pamela? The dress policy here at Techno Plus has always been business casual."

"Yes, Pam lives in jeans and T-shirts, so I've gone more casual lately."

"She's balancing you out. I like that."

Mark chuckled. "One day you must meet my wife."

"When? You made that promise four months ago." Lavine grinned. "Mind if I grab a seat?" She sat in the chair opposite Mark before he answered. "Few people are wise enough to marry a friend. Deep bonds precede the best marriages. Age and maturity will alter our habits, ideas, and dreams, so that basic bond is important."

Mark leaned on the chair's back cushion. "That's one of the truths I've learned since getting married. In many ways Pamela and I are growing up together."

"Friendship defines my marriage with Stan," Lavine said. "He consults with me before making decisions. I agreed for him to open a skydiving school to teach his hobby after he retired. We celebrate our fortieth wedding anniversary next year."

"Accept my advance congratulations. Care to pass on a few secrets?"

"Gladly." She clasped her hands on the desk. "Communication is the main ingredient in a successful marriage. Compromise unlocks longevity in relationships. No one gets their own way on any issue."

Teamwork required engaged listeners. Mark hadn't listened to anything Pamela had said that didn't involve him until the couple arrived home from their honeymoon.

"You just went deep in thought," Lavine surmised. "I hope something I said clicked."

"It did." He puttered with papers on his desk. "Tell me about Stan's skydiving classes."

Lavine described the skydiving school and invited him and Pamela to visit a jump session.

Mark circled a date on his calendar in early September. "Can't wait to watch the trainees hit the bull's-eye. I will surprise my wife with the outing, otherwise she may not come."

"She wouldn't want you to get ideas to start jumping?"

"Pam's a daredevil who isn't fond of heights."

Lavine pushed back her chair. "Stan's probably outside waiting for me. We eat dinner out and take in a movie on Thursdays."

"Leaving right behind you. Playing doubles racquetball with friends while Pam takes an easy night. I'll make a quick stop by home."

* * *

A little while later, Mark bumped into Pamela in the bedroom doorway. His outstretched hands saved her from tripping over his feet.

"Whoa!" Her cell phone and key ring hit the floor when she clutched her chest. "I thought you were going straight to racquetball?"

Mark spoke through clenched teeth. "I came home to kiss my wife goodbye and caught her here before *she* left the house. Where are you going? I thought you planned to stay in tonight."

"Me too." Pamela retrieved her cell phone and key ring off the floor. "Lizzie called. She was craving Italian food. Josh is working the late shift this month."

"Let's try this again. Where ... are ... you ... going? Evidently it's not to bed."

Pamela's nostrils flared. "Don't shout at me. I'm meeting friends at Rolando's in Shiatown."

"Friends? I thought Lizzie called you."

"I read the latest text as you collided into me. A few more people decided to tag along. I don't know who all is going. So don't ask."

Mark refused to downplay his wife's thoughtlessness. "You know I'm playing doubles at six with Brett, Turner, and Danny at the racquetball club. What happened to you staying home tonight?"

"Really, Mark? Itineraries change, as mine did. Deal with it like an adult should."

"You don't get what happened, do you? I would've thought you were at home if I hadn't stopped by to kiss you."

Pamela went into the bedroom and grabbed a note off his nightstand.

I should have texted, but Mark would've called and asked me to stay at home.

"Here you go. I left a note." She shoved the paper into his hand and skirted around him. "You're running late. Your friends are waiting."

Mark scanned the note and put it on the dresser.

"You missed the point. Why didn't you text me? Or call? I wouldn't have known my wife left the house until I came home tonight."

Pamela spun around and faced him. She sighed. "I should have called or sent a text. And, said no when you asked me to stay home. Don't deny that you would have," she said as his mouth opened. Her lips puckered. "Kiss me and make up. I will keep you better informed."

Mark accepted the kiss his wife brushed across his lips and watched her head to the door that led to their garage. He left the house and sat in his car until Pamela backed her car out the garage. He didn't know how to make amends.

She tooted the horn before she drove away.

* * *

On Friday, Pamela dimmed the light over the "open for lunch" sign in the front window. This was her normal practice at the halfway point of lunch. The lobby and dine-in areas were crowded. She nodded at the busy cashiers. Emily now worked from eight to two. Tina worked from ten to four. Inside the kitchen, Charlotte worked meal orders and Mia chopped vegetables and cheese for tomorrow's meals. Whereas the food side bustled with activity, the pastry area was quiet and squeaky clean. Time to start another bake round.

Minutes later, Melinda arrived at the shop with the children. She entered the kitchen carrying four-year-old Maeve in her arms. Eight-year-old Myles and six-year-old McKinley instantly spread throughout the room. The boys pulled out cabinet drawers, opened lower cabinet doors, and peeked inside pantries.

Her sister-in-law stopped beside the salad prep table. "Hello, ladies. Customers are loving the food options."

"Pam penned the menu before Mia and I came," Charlotte said.

Mia looked up from slicing tomatoes. "She won't let us tweak the menu. I keep pushing for my mother's baked potato soup. The recipe tastes scrumptious."

Melinda set Maeve down. "Keep trying. One day we may serve soup."

The pantry that held the baking tins door closed. A woman wearing a chef's hat walked into the room.

"Hey, Sally," Melinda said. "The kids gobbled up your coconut pie for dessert yesterday." Then she spoke to the woman removing unfrosted cupcakes from the cooler. "Hi, Tracy. We'll be out of your way in a minute."

Pamela monitored the boys' explorations. "Guys, the ovens are hot. Peer through the glass from a distance."

Maeve tapped Pamela's thigh and pointed to her leg.

Pamela stooped beside her niece. "Did you hurt your leg, Maevey? Is it starting to feel better?"

Maeve squeezed her eyelids together. Nonexistent teardrops refused to fall. "Um-hum. I fall down. And I cried a lot too."

Pamela tweaked both cheeks. "Were they crocodile tears?"

That comment caught her nephews' attention. The boys beelined to their aunt.

"Crocodiles don't cry," Myles said.

"Alligators might," McKinley added.

Myles spread his hands apart. "They don't cry either. No one has ever seen them cry."

McKinley kicked at his brother. "You don't know. You don't go everywhere."

"Neither do you," Myles said.

"Settle down, boys." Melinda pointed toward the breakroom. "I'll set out our lunch in the breakroom so customers don't have to listen to your debates."

"Why can't we eat lunch with the other children?" Myles asked.

"*Color by Me* is playing in the breakroom, not in the banquet hall."

Melinda set filled plates on a cart that she rolled into the breakroom. The boys ran ahead while Maeve hopped behind her mother into the room. So much for achy legs, Pamela thought.

* * *

Mark pulled into the fill-up station with his mind occupied by an IT campaign. A black Mercedes was beside him. Hodges' car. Ace occupied the passenger seat. Deep in conversation, neither man noticed him at the gas pump. Should he greet them? The brothers-in-law hardly spoke to one another these days.

Ace and Melinda had befriended Mark after Mark and Pamela got engaged. Ace attended the bachelor party, took Mark out to lunch, and served as a groomsman in their wedding. Mark's Jessica blunder had eroded their relationship. Someone had to halt hostilities before bitterness became entrenched.

Mark swallowed hard. Heat infused his back and neck. He rounded his car and tapped the passenger window. "What's going on?"

Ace exited the car wearing a wide grin. The man still moved with an understated grace. Watching him run the football had been a joy. Those days had long passed, yet his presence overpowered people when he entered a room.

With a wide-legged stance, Ace stood between both vehicles. "I got engrossed in K.C.'s debatable tale. I didn't notice your car pull up. Heading home for the night?"

Mark nodded and made small talk.

K.C. finished pumping gas first. He closed the gap between the men with long strides. "We got off on the wrong foot. How about we start over. Handshake?" He extended his hand to Mark.

Mark couldn't ignore Hodge' outstretched hand again.

He shook his hand. "My wife never told me you and she had dated. Someone else did after our honeymoon."

Ace laughed. "Stale gossip travels faster than fresh news. Pam and K.C. are firm friends."

"My wife is loyal. I recognized her awesome qualities the moment I met her."

"Then it's me you mistrust. Relax, Simon. I don't break up families."

"He's a good guy," Ace said. "He once helped an elderly lady cross the street. I caught him in the act."

K.C. laughed. "Don't spread that tale around. Some naïve person might believe you."

Ace glanced at Mark. "Maybe our families can get together this weekend. I would like that. Check with your wife."

"I will," Mark said, bewildered by Ace's behavior.

On the drive home, Mark thought about Ace's friendliness in front of his best friend. His actions indicated Ace valued his sister's marriage.

Yet somehow Mark felt uneasy about the encounter.

Why did his brother-in-law choose this day to mend their relationship? Then again, why wouldn't he? Mark had chosen that day to mend the relationship, too.

* * *

Pamela locked the shop's door once the last worker left the building. Turning off lights along the way, she sauntered into the breakroom and sat beside Melinda on the couch. The kids' attention switched between watching an animated show on television and working individual jigsaw puzzles on the floor.

"All done," Pamela said. "Everyone's gone home. We have enough food left over to cover both of our families for dinner. Mom's eating out tonight."

The women eyed each other.

"Speaking of Mom, I still think she has a significant other stashed away somewhere," Melinda said.

"It appears so. She won't answer direct questions about it."

"She does the same thing to Ace. Mom met him at the front door when he dropped by the house last week. An unknown car was parked at the curb. Although, it could have been a neighbor's car. But—"

"Mom should tell us if she's dating someone."

"And receive the third degree from her children? I don't blame Mom for blocking you guys. Both you and Ace lead your own lives. Leave Mom's love life alone."

"That's easier said than done. I would accept the man in a heartbeat if she introduced him to us."

"Remember those words. I guarantee I won't forget them." She leaned against the cushion and crossed her ankles. "Is Mark behaving himself at home?"

Pamela twisted her wedding rings. Tough questions never allowed for easy answers.

"It depends on how you look at it," she finally said. "Mark hardly saw me while he dated Jessica. Now he requires continual contact night and day. He sends me text messages at the grocery store and calls me on the drive home whenever I go out."

"Why do you suppose he does that?"

"Who knows? He gave Jessica and the other women he dated space. Way make me the lone exception? I don't require constant Mark updates."

"He's jealous of K.C. Maybe he thinks other men might hit on you."

Glancing at the children, Pamela scooted closer. "I went twenty-six years without acting like a floozy. Does he think I waited until getting married to behave like one?"

Melinda shrugged. "You know your husband better than I do."

"Maybe I don't know him well enough. I can go anywhere I please with my family, just not with my friends." She sighed. "I love my husband even when he acts unreasonable. I suppose some behaviors can't be identified until you get married."

Melinda nodded. "I figured that out two weeks after I married your brother. Ace's controlling behavior caught me off guard."

"Skylar has always been bossy." She hesitated. "I do have good news to report."

"Good. Let's hear it."

"The K.C. controversy has finally died. Mark hasn't mentioned 'the baker' in weeks."

Melinda laughed. "That *is* good news. How about the ridiculous woman who lives next door?"

"I haven't seen her. She hasn't targeted Mark and me."

"Yet. Keep up the guard. The showdown will come your way soon."

"It's so nice to live in peace. Sometimes I forget Jessica lives next door."

"She'll approach you when you least suppose she will."

The women rose together when the TV show ended. Pamela switched off the television.

"*Glory Trails* is over," Melinda said. "Put the puzzle pieces back inside the box. It's time to go home."

The women hugged each other outside the building.

"Thanks for saving me from cooking lunch and dinner," Melinda said.

"No problem." Pamela opened the SUV door for the children. "Auntie's looking forward to taking a bubble bath. How about you guys?"

"I like the bubbles," Maeve said.

Myles and McKinley shook their heads.

* * *

Thirty minutes later a knock hammered the garage door Pamela had just lowered.

She hesitated inside the laundry room. Jessica. She just knew her neighbor waited on the other side.

Is she stalking our house? Or was she outside when I pulled into the driveway?

Either way, the outcome remained the same. This was a handpicked confrontation moment. Melinda had nailed it. Should she ignore the pesky woman or see what she wanted?

Pamela decided to talk to her on Pamela's terms. She didn't want to let an enemy dictate conditions.

I won't raise the garage door again. I'll go to the front porch.

Pamela walked through the house and opened the front door. Then she closed the door behind her and sat on the glider. Jessica's in-laws could receive a picture-perfect view if they watched.

Dressed in Bermuda shorts, a tank top, and tennis shoes, Jessica pounded on the garage door. The noise was almost muted on the outside of the house. After a long minute, she headed home.

How ironic. The ex-girlfriend had retained her tunnel vision. Either her way or no play. Well, not this day.

Pamela cleared her throat. May as well make this skirmish count. "May I help you?"

Jessica swung around with her fist clenched. She strolled to the Simons' porch and climbed the steps until she stood over Pamela. "We need to have a conversation that is long overdue."

Stretching her legs, Pamela lounged on a cushion and gestured toward a chair.

"Please take a seat. Stay and visit awhile."

Cold laughter spewed through Jessica's pinched lips.

"Anytime," Pamela said. "The floor is yours."

"I think I tagged you wrong before. You're not the mealy mouthed helpless little girl that you pretend. You usually act like a clueless female who needs

Mark's help. Which part are you playing today?"

"The one I'm destined to win. I don't play fatalistic roles."

Jessica stared at Pamela's ring finger.

Pamela flashed her ring assemble in an arc. "Do you like my rings?"

Jessica studied Pamela's rings again. Her lips drooped once she looked up. "You took advantage of my mistake quick enough. I'm paying better attention these days. Did you and Mark discuss me before you got engaged?"

"Mark and I never kept secrets from each other. We compared notes biweekly."

Jessica's laugh sounded like a snort. "Don't pretend you had an upper hand on me. I called the shots in Mark's and my relationship."

"You truly believe that nonsense, don't you? Did you ever wonder why we still met twice a week, even though you demanded that Mark ditch me?"

Wrinkles formed on Jessica's forehead. "Give me your version of the story."

Wow. The woman actually had demanded Mark drop me. He never mentioned that before.

"Version? Only my perspective counts."

Jessica's body shook when she rose. "Mark is on loan. Enjoy my leftovers until I'm ready to take him back."

Pamela glanced at the car turning into the Prentises' driveway. "I wonder how your husband will take those threats." Laughing, Pamela stood beside Jessica. "Oh, good. Your husband is home. I'll ask him for his viewpoint."

Jessica's chest caved as she studied the man staring at them from beside his car. She did Mark's twiddle-fingers wave. "You're home early," Jessica called. "I was just talking to our neighbor. I'm on my way." She glared at Pamela. "Round one goes to you."

"Round one?" Pamela flashed her rings in Jessica's face. "Mark and I are married. I flunked Toy Sharing 101 at age two."

Pamela opened her front door and stepped inside her house.

Chapter Fifteen

Mark noticed two people standing on his porch as he rounded the corner into the subdivision. He recognized his wife a half block away from the cul-de-sac. Movement in the neighbor's driveway caught his attention. Victor stood beside his car, eyeing the women with his hands inside his pockets.

Mark sped up the car. Pamela strolled into the house before he reached the driveway.

He decreased the speed as Jessica beat a hasty track across the lawn. Victor clamped a hand on her upper arm. They walked together to their house. Jessica broke the hold and flipped her hand at him before she went inside. Victor appeared to chuckle before he closed the door.

Mark could tell his neighbors were angry. It appeared that Jessica had violated an agreement and Victor demanded retribution for the offense.

Too bad Pamela had gone inside the house and missed the grand finale.

Mark checked the other houses from his vantage point in the driveway. Victor's mother watched the drama from a downstairs window.

Their neighbors were at odds with each other.

Pamela had floated into the house.

She didn't tolerate being abused, so he wondered what she had encountered.

Mark entered the house torn between two issues he wanted to discuss. Should he start off the conversation with Jessica's visit or with his latest Hodges theory? Jessica's senseless diatribes meant nothing. Either Hodges still had feelings for Pamela or Ace's unusual behavior didn't deliver a cryptic message.

In the kitchen, sautéed onions, garlic, and green peppers wafted from the slow cooker. He laid the Toomey's bags on the island and lifted the slow cooker's top. Potato and beef stew. It smelled fantastic.

He found his wife curled up on the loveseat reading a book in the family room. He kissed her cheek and sat beside her.

"The potato and beef stew smells delicious. But I stopped by Toomey's on the drive home."

Pamela dragged her gaze from the page. "We can eat today's dinner on Sunday. Your Toomey's surprise provided me with a cookless weekend." She set the book facedown on her lap.

"I cancelled my handball game tonight. A relaxing evening should build up my stamina for dinner at my folks' house tomorrow. Spending the evening reading?"

"I'm too pooped for any activity other than turning pages."

"Give me fifteen minutes to shower and change before we eat dinner."

* * *

The doorbell rang ten minutes later. Mark was changing clothes in the bedroom.

Pamela hurried down the hallway. "I'll get it. Are you expecting anyone?"

"No," a muffled voice replied.

When she reached the door, two of Mark's friends grinned at her from on the porch.

"Sorry for the spur-of-the-moment visit," Ron said. "We have a few details to discuss with your husband."

"We won't take long," Gabe added.

"Hello. Take a seat in the living room. I'll tell Mark you're here."

Ron resembled a sturdy and hairy mountain man, while Gabe had a medium height and wiry build. The two men and her husband had become fast friends in college. Ron married his childhood sweetheart five years ago Gabe proposed to his business partner last month. Pamela got along well with both women.

Mark was leaving the bedroom as she passed by. "Gabe and Ron are waiting for you in the living room."

His eyes lit up. "We have irons in the fire to increase business for Timeless Pastries. I'll fill you in later."

How like her husband to exclude the business owner from the discussion.

Pamela worked on a jigsaw puzzle in the family room while the men discussed her bakery.

Thirty minutes later, Mark breezed into the family room rolling a small serving cart. He'd transferred their food boxes to dinner plates and had included cutlery and folded napkins. Plus, he had poured their fountain.

drinks into glasses.

"Does my plate presentation compensate for ruining a marvelous meal?"

"Yes, sir. Thank you much." Pamela sat down on the sofa next to Mark. Grabbing a plate off the cart, she snuggled beside him. "Explain your friends' drop-by visit."

"Okay," Mark said when she set her sandwich on the plate. "I commissioned Gabe and Tracy to promote Timeless Pastries' catering service to their seminar clients. Rob and Elaine will feature your baked goods and candy at their mini-mart location."

"Thank you. Invite them to a private meal at the shop."

"Great idea. We can include a few other individuals as well."

"Set up something next month. But enough business talk. Your old girlfriend came calling."

Mark chuckled. "I saw you stroll into the house as she scurried across the lawn. Victor appeared displeased. What happened?"

In between bites Pamela told her story from beginning to end.

Mark filled in the parts she missed by going inside the house.

"They don't seem to be happy. What do you think?"

He piled their empty glasses and used utensils onto the cart. "Who knows. But enough about our neighbors. I can work on the puzzle while you read."

Pamela munched on the last french fry, then patted her tummy. "I'm stuffed and may be gaining weight. We need a scale."

"You look the same to me. I'll clean this mess up."

He pushed the serving cart out of the room.

Pamela picked up the book she'd been reading from the end table. She smiled when she heard him load the dishwater.

Minutes later he sat beside her. "I saw your brother and Hodges at a fill-up station. They didn't notice me at first, but once they did, Ace treated me like a long-lost friend."

A bright smile stretched across her face. "He likes his brother-in-law."

"I wouldn't go that far. Yet I sensed he wants us to have a successful marriage. He's conveyed that hope to his friend."

"Why would he bother? That expectation goes without question."

"Hodges may want a different outcome. The baker might pursue you if Ace agreed. But after seeing them both today, I know he won't."

If parallel universes existed, Pamela had just entered one. Melinda had told her to keep watch for Jessica. The woman sprang an attack within the hour.

In the same conversation, Pamela had told Melinda that Mark had stopped his rant against K.C. Now he just started the same nonsense again.

One step forward. Fifty steps backward. This back and forth made her dizzy.

"That's a dead topic. We can sabotage our relationship without anyone else's help."

She left the family room and leaned on the wall beside the door.

Her patience had been vexed beyond belief. She understood his concerns to a certain point. Beyond that grace period he should keep his ruminations private. His K.C. conjectures needed her cooperation to wreck their marriage, so she would keep quiet. How could he mistrust her when he was the one who'd been dishonest?

I listened to your speculations. Now let the topic rest.

Pamela retrieved her book from the sofa and curled up on an armchair. "You haven't started the jigsaw puzzle."

"You lashed out at me and left the room. Can we have a candid discussion?"

She lowered the book onto her lap. "After today's conversation, do not link his name with mine."

His head shook. "We don't have 'no discussion zones' where our marriage is concerned. Get used to hearing my concerns voiced out loud."

"I love you. You don't have a valid worry. This topic isn't close to being real."

"Here we go. What are you accusing me of?"

Pamela headed toward the door. "Sometimes I do not like you."

A cooking program played on the television before she exited the room.

Insufferable man.

She went into the guest bedroom and called her brother.

Her foot tapped the floor until Skylar answered his phone.

"Hey, sis. Thanks for sending Mellie home with dinner."

"Anytime." Pausing, she took a deep breath. "What happened at the gas station? Mark claims K.C. likes me."

"He loves you as a friend. After Mark proposed, K.C. wondered if somehow you and he could have made it work. But that wasn't mentioned at the gas station."

"That's because he hasn't settled down. Is he dating anyone?"

Skylar laughed. "That's part of the problem. Too many women and not serious about any of them."

"Classic K.C. Hodges. Mark and I will find him a wife."

"I'm sure your husband will agree with your plan. Tell him I said hello."

"See you Sunday."

"Bye, sis. Enjoy the rest of your evening."

Pamela slid onto her knees and buried her face into the quilt.

"I need wisdom, Lord. It's hard to chart a straight course. Please help me."

* * *

Mark switched off the television when Pamela sat beside him.

"I love you," he said. "Overlook our last discussion." He tilted his head and stroked her cheek.

Tears filled her eyes. "I called my brother to ask him about your theory. He said K.C. loves me as a friend."

"Well, Ace knows the man better than I do. Perhaps Hodges sees you two as kindred spirits. After all, you both love to bake and enjoy family life."

"Then finding K.C. a wife will be our top priority."

"I can agree to that," Mark said. "Let's call it a night."

Pamela stood up and headed to the door.

Mark turned off the television and followed behind her. "Hey, before I forget again. I planned a surprise outing for us on the first Saturday in September. And do not ask where to," he added when Pamela turned around to face him.

* * *

Saturday evening, Celeste opened the front door, dressed to the nines.

"Come in. I've been waiting for you guys."

The couple stepped inside the door. Pamela held out the dessert box. "Thanks for inviting us to dinner."

Celeste removed the box from her hands. "Mmm. Chocolate always smells delicious. Go into the living room. I'll take the cake into the kitchen, and then I'll join you."

Mark hugged his mother before she left. "My stomach just growled. Beatrice still has the magic touch. Tell her whatever she's cooking smells fantastic. Can't wait to eat."

"That'll make her happy. You'll probably receive an extra portion."

Tucked away from sight, Ed barked orders over the phone. Some poor worker was receiving a blasting. Intimidation, pure and simple. Pamela would have quit the job on the spot. What nerve.

"See that it gets done. Tonight!"

The disgruntled man crashed the phone in the person's ear. The employee should have done the honors first.

Celeste shook her head when she entered the living room. She sat on a chair that faced the couch. "Ed's having a rough evening. Ignore him."

Ed seemed more composed as he strutted into the family room. "I suppose coming over five months after getting married is better than not coming at all." Ed sat on a recliner. He pointed to his wife as he glanced at Mark. "Your mother got here thirty minutes before you did."

Celeste's broad smile took in their guests. "We haven't seen you guys since Martha Frierson's luncheon. Your grandmother is a gracious hostess, Pamela."

Pamela beamed. "Grandmother is a marvelous person."

"I wouldn't go that far," Ed said.

Celeste glared at him. "How are you guys settling in? Have you had any unexpected surprises?" She laughed when Ed grunted. "Every couple faces challenges in the first year of being married. How are you guys coping?"

"Very well," Pamela said. "I enjoy being married to your son."

"No surprises? I had a few when Ed and I married. No. Make that a tremendous number of shockers and bombshells."

Ed's lip curled as he glared at his wife.

No wonder Mark hadn't visited his parents. Maybe dealing with them was too depressing.

Quick, a diversion. "I discovered Jessica and her husband live next door," Pamela said. "And Mark learned I dated K.C. for six months more than three years ago."

Their shocked faces proved priceless. At least Ed appeared less vindictive.

"I heard that rumor and dismissed it," Celeste said. "You and my son were made for each other." She smiled when her son nodded.

Pamela relayed what had happened once the couple arrived home from their honeymoon.

Celeste glowered at her son. "Did you know Jessica lived next door?"

"I only knew they lived somewhere in the neighborhood."

"Some women would have filed for a divorce the same day."

Ed's scowl included everyone. "People who file for divorce after one mistake should've remained single. Married couples should support each other through difficulties."

"Only if the support is warranted," his wife said. "A person can't misbehave and then shrug off the offense. The concept is simple, men. Remain single if you want to fool around."

Ed's second grunt surpassed the first one. "Name the female's responsibility in marriage."

Celeste focused on the couple. "Total commitment is the key to having a successful marriage. You love each other. The future will bode well for your family."

Walking across the room, Celeste slid open the barn door to the kitchen. "I'll check on Beatrice's progress."

Ed grunted a third time. "People have a right to live their life without another person's interference."

"I humbly disagree with your opinion," Pamela said. "You can't get married and keep a self-serving attitude. Two becoming one is a lifelong commitment."

"I don't buy that nonsense." When Ed stood, he jingled change in his pockets. "Numbskulls let others chart their course. Strength comes through exercise and precision."

"And grows with perseverance to do the right thing," said Mark.

"Don't buy that garbage, son. Each person must determine what the right move is for themselves."

"No, sir," Pamela insisted. "You must esteem others higher than yourself. You can only trust godly standards. Of course, you must read the Bible to know what they are. Most people never seek God's will for their life."

"Who died and left you judge, missy?" Ed turned toward the kitchen. "Hey, in there, is dinner ready?"

Celeste's head poked inside the room. "I will call you when it is. Do not upset Beatrice."

Ed sneered at her. "Right. And then you will have to learn how to cook."

"Or hire someone who'll demand more money to fix your favorite foods." She slid the barn door across the entrance to the kitchen.

Taking a deep breath, Pamela massaged her wrist, wishing she could leave.

Over dinner, Pamela watched her husband set the tone for the evening. She was surprised to see both Simons fell in line.

After dinner the couples played her favorite card game.

Her husband winked at her after each game he and his mother won.

She should've chosen to play hearts instead of letting him learn how to play spades.

Chapter Sixteen

At church the next morning, Pamela abruptly stopped as she walked through the sanctuary doors. Anna sat in their pew beside a man who had his arm wrapped around her shoulder.

Mark whispered in her ear. "You knew this day was coming. Behave yourself."

"I don't know him, nor do I like his body language. It's too possessive."

"Their relationship is serious, love. Mom brought him here to meet the family." He leaned closer. "People are watching us."

True enough. Steven and Valerie had spotlighted them from their seats across the sanctuary.

The dutiful daughter commanded herself to smile and went to sit beside her mother. She studied the stranger's friendly expression. "Hi, Mom. Introduce your friend."

Anna kissed her daughter's cheek. "Behave yourself," she whispered, then she turned to Mark. "Hello, Mark." She glanced over her shoulder as noise erupted beyond the stranger.

Skylar and his family entered the row from the other aisle. Now her brother could sit next to their mother's friend.

Perfect. Pamela breathed easier with backup present.

Mark's lips touched her ear. "Ace needs to behave himself as well. Your proprietary attitude regarding your mother's love life is wrong."

Pamela nudged his chest with her head. "Oh, shush."

Across the sanctuary Steven's and Valerie's interest piqued. Her father now sat at the end of his and Valerie's row.

Anna spoke when the latest arrivals reached them. "Nathan, this is my family. Pam and Mark. And Skylar, Mellie, and my three grandchildren: Myles, McKinley, and Maeve."

"Nathan Hendrix and I dated throughout high school. Yesterday this wonderful man proposed, and I accepted. We set a wedding date in September." Laughter bubbled from her lips. "Now, don't everyone fall over yourselves congratulating us."

Melinda slid in front of her children. "Excuse me. I'll sit next to your father." She linked her arm through Skylar's arm. "Hello, Nathan. We're all pleased to meet you. However, September is two weeks away. We need more time to plan the second wedding of the year."

Nathan grinned at Anna. "We both want an intimate ceremony. A true family affair is doable on short notice."

"It's about time you made your intentions known." Mark reached out his hand. "We're all astounded at the short notice but not surprised by the engagement."

Nathan laughed and shook Mark's hand. "I respected Anna's wishes and disregarded my own preferences. She met my children this morning." He pointed across the room, where several heads were turned their way. "I reserved the banquet room at a restaurant in Shiatown for lunch after church service. Let's have our first official family get-together. My children and parents are free today. How about you guys?"

Melinda's cheek brushed Skylar's shoulder.

"We wouldn't miss your celebration," Skylar said. "Thanks for the invite."

Mark nudged Pamela's side.

She beamed a bright smile. "Thanks for including Mark and me."

Nathan gazed at Skylar. "Anna and some of your family call you Skylar. Everyone else I know calls you Ace. Which name do you prefer?"

Skylar chuckled. "Whatever is your preference. I answer to both names."

Anna's eyes twinkled as she smiled. "Pam, will you and Mark pick up your grandmother after church and bring her to the restaurant?"

"Yes, ma'am," Pamela replied. "So, Mom, Grandmother will meet your fiancé today too."

"Not quite," Nathan said. "I met Martha Frierson before I learned to crawl. Our parents are old childhood friends."

"Nathan and I have eaten dinner with our parents every Saturday for almost two years."

Pamela remembered her mom used to talk about a man she'd dated throughout high school. Their relationship hit the skids when he attended a college in a different state. Was Nathan divorced like her mom?

Pamela sighed. Anna Hayes was an engaged woman. Pamela felt better knowing the couple had known each other longer than two years.

She hugged her mother. "Two secret-ridden years. Glad Grandmother kept tabs on you."

"Martha Frierson will always have her say." Nathan squeezed his fiancée's hand.

Anna's love-filled eyes smiled up at him. "Your grandmother gave our engagement two thumbs up."

After the church service ended, Pamela and Mark drove across the Ellis Bridge to Shiatown. Pamela's grandmother lived close to the restaurant and drove her car daily. She could've easily made the trip on her own.

Martha was waiting on the porch when Mark pulled up at the curb. Grandmother had dressed for the occasion. She wore white leggings and a pink, white, and black tunic. A black rectangular scarf draped over one shoulder. Nude ballet pumps completed the ensemble.

Pamela met her grandmother on the landing, escorted her to the car, and tucked Martha into the front seat. Pamela sat in the seat behind her.

"Thanks for picking me up, Mark. It was this old lady's prerogative not to drive."

Pamela released the seatbelt and leaned closer. "Are you feeling okay? Should I spend the night?"

"No, no. My health is fine. Just having a lazy day." Turning to the side, she faced her granddaughter. "Did you like Nathan?"

"It's too soon to tell. He seemed nice enough. Why did Mom hide Nathan from us?"

"You should ask your mother."

"She's getting married in September. Mom would blast me if I had done something like that."

"I'll fill in the blanks," Martha said.

Grandmother supplied background history on the short drive to the restaurant. Anna and Nathan had played together as children. They dated in high school. Then the couple broke up their first year in college. The relationship sputtered long distance. Nathan got a girl pregnant his freshman year. Anna married Steven nine months later. Nathan married the child's mother the following year. The Hendrixes had a happy marriage, but his wife suffered an aneurysm that claimed her life ten years ago. Anna and Nathan had talked off and on since Anna's divorce. She refused to date Nathan when he initially asked her out. The couple had their first date two years ago.

Nathan's son and daughter met Anna this morning, but they knew about the relationship before the first date. Nathan and his family lived in Shiatown. His family came to South Town that morning to meet their father's fiancée and to support him. Anna planned to sell her house and relocate to her hometown after the wedding.

"Why didn't Mom tell me and Skylar before today?" Pamela asked when her grandmother paused.

"Have that discussion with Anna," Martha said. She sang Nathan's praises until they reached their destination. That one action made Pamela a captive audience. Her grandmother's constant chatter lightened Pamela's heart with each spoken word.

Reaching the parking lot, Mark parked behind Skylar's car. As they entered the restaurant, Pamela searched for her mother inside the spacious room and saw Anna talking to an older couple dressed in bohemian-style clothes.

She pointed across the banquet room. "I know those people."

Mark hugged his wife's body to his side. "Ace is looking at them too. Who are they?"

"Grandmother's friends. Caleb and Nancy ... Hendrix," she glanced at Mark, frowning. "They always attended my grandparents' special celebrations. Nathan was never there."

"Perhaps he and his wife didn't receive invitations. Let's mingle." Mark tried to move the couple forward.

Pamela anchored her feet to the floor. "Do I have to?"

"Yes." He chuckled. "And did you see your father's face in the church parking lot?"

Pamela giggled then touched her lips. "Sure did. He looked like he'd sucked on a sour pickle."

"He can't imagine seeing your mother happy without him. Although he should have known this day was coming. Mom is an exceptional woman. She suffered his garbage to keep the family intact."

Her eyes opened wide. "I thought you liked my dad."

"Your father lost my respect years ago. Now, go mingle so your mother can stop watching you."

My husband doesn't like my father? "Might as well jump in," she said.

She smiled at him when he squeezed her hand as she worked her way around the room. Nathan's parents, Caleb and Nancy, were as lovable and unconventional as ever. Nathan's daughter, Rhea, was a single mother who worked in retail. Her seven-year-old son, Timmy, was in the second grade. Nathan's son, Gary, was three years younger than his sister and was a clerk at city hall. His wife, Penny, was a joyful homemaker. The couple had two daughters, five-year-old Karrie and two-year-old Gracie, who sucked both thumbs.

People mingled together like they had known each other all their lives. Both families appeared determined to cement a familial bond.

That Anna didn't tell her children about her relationship with Nathan for almost two years still bothered Pamela. She spotted the bubbly woman selecting fruit from the dessert bar and sped across the space. She had waited an entire hour to catch her mother alone.

Picking up a dessert plate, she stopped behind her mother. "We need to talk. Before you ask, I like Nathan. Sorry his wife died young."

"Her sudden death shocked everyone. Michelle appeared to be a healthy person just before she collapsed. Live your life to the fullest, babe. Don't wait for favorable conditions. No one lives a trouble-free existence. Remember that."

"Listening as always." Mother and daughter laughed together. "I will act on your advice. Happy?"

"Surrender wins me over every time. Did you catch me alone on purpose?"

"Uh-huh. His staying single for ten years proves Nathan waited for the right woman. Grandmother likes him too. Tell me about the new romance."

Anna placed grapes and diced pineapple into a bowl and moved around the banquet table. "We eat lunch together on most weekdays and take in an occasional movie in the evenings. We spend weekends together and eat dinner with our parents on Saturdays. Nathan and I share a bona fide connection."

"Why didn't you tell me and Skylar?"

"Because I ..." she hesitated, and then she smiled. "You and Skylar knowing I was dating someone I truly liked might have pushed me faster than I wanted to go. I don't want another failed marriage. Three lives suffered needless hurt and pain because I refused to admit my bad decision before the wedding."

Pamela twisted her wedding rings. "What happened, Mom?"

"I drove myself to church on my wedding day, but I pulled off on a side road and cried. I arrived at church twenty minutes before the ceremony began. I panicked when I saw the cars streaming onto the parking lot and went along with the wedding."

Her focus seemed far away until she smiled again. "Your grandmother pulled me aside in the dressing room. She said, 'If you're having second thoughts, end the engagement this minute.' "

"I almost did until I considered the embarrassment factor and huge expense. Yet my fear at nineteen culminated into twenty-one miserable married years. Only you and your brother made it worthwhile."

Anna set her plate on a nearby table and hugged her daughter. "I never regretted raising my adorable cheeky children one second."

Pamela batted her tear-filled eyes. "I love you so much. You infused love and stability inside a war zone. Thank you for not giving up on us even though you lived a horrible life."

"I don't mention Steven much because I refuse to trash talk your father to his kids. Even though our family life failed, your father loves you and Skylar. Selfish love is a lesser caliber of the genuine emotion, but it can't be ignored. The way the Father loves us is incomparable."

"I feel closer to you now than I ever have before," Pamela said. "You faced the giant and won the war. God gave you a remarkable achievement."

The women hugged as tears freely flowed between them.

Anna dotted her face with napkins she grabbed off the utensil table. "I love hearing accolades from my daughter. My children still fill my life with meaning."

She dried her eyes as Nathan approached the dessert table.

He hugged her and winked at Pamela. "Sorry to intrude. I miss my fiancée."

"Your fiancée misses you. Is it time to wind down our celebration?"

"Not yet. The staff will push us out the door in one hour." He gazed at Pamela. "Thank you for making Anna's day."

"Thanks for making Mom happy," Pamela said. Then her gaze sought the man who watched her from a few steps away. Proverbs 14:1 instantly came to mind: "Every wise woman builds up her home, but a foolish one tears it down with her own hands."

Pamela had married the man she loved. The couple would fine-tune all their problems together.

She hurried to his side. "My love for you continues to grow." Fighting back tears caused her lips to tremble. "We will make our marriage work," Pamela said.

Mark pulled her into his arms as he hummed an old tune.

She melted against him as the couple slow danced throughout the banquet hall.

Martha and Melinda clapped while husband and wife danced minus music. Caleb and Nancy circled around the room behind the couple.

Skylar winked and held up two thumbs.

The festivities ended an hour later. The get-together had united two families.

* * *

Pamela slid into the car, closing the door behind her. "I think Rhea and K.C. will make a good match. Do you see any possibilities there?"

Mark gazed at her. "I heard her say she and her son had met Hodges. What makes you think those two might work?"

"The wonderful comments she made about him. K.C. visited the children's wing while Timmy was recuperating from a tonsillectomy. He entertained Timmy when she came late to the evening visit. Eight months later, K.C. sent Timmy a promised football, pads, and helmet on Timmy's birthday."

"Rhea sang the man's praises due to his good memory and one good deed. I would say she's ripe for picking."

"Be nice." Her fingers tapped her lip. "Should I bounce my idea off Skylar?"

"No one knows K.C. better than your brother."

She buckled her seatbelt. "A ready-made family is just what he needs."

"You think so? Little bakers probably run around in ten states."

"Shame on you. He doesn't play fast and loose."

Mark glanced at her. "Get Ace's opinion first."

Steven called Pamela on the drive home and grilled her about Anna. She giggled when he called Nathan Anna's church guest. Why not say Mom's boyfriend or date? Denial. Pure and simple.

She listened some more then glanced at Mark. "Dad's upset. Head over to their house."

"Not today. Hold his hand tomorrow."

Her jaw dropped. "Please."

"Listen to me," Steven yelled.

"I am. I liked Nathan and his family. Skylar and I met his parents at Grandmother's house before today. You've met them too. His parents are my grandparents' lifelong friends."

She listened as her father continued his rant, then she tugged Mark's sleeve. "Please. Drive over to Dad's house."

Mark sighed and checked his mirrors.

"Thank you," she said when he turned the car around. "We're on our way, Dad. See you soon."

The couple stayed silent on the drive across town.

When they reached the house, Steven stepped outside, closing the door behind him. He focused on his daughter. "What else do you know about this man?"

Mark draped an arm around Pamela's shoulder as he said, "Mom's marrying Nathan in September."

Steven snorted then glared at his house. "Mom. You don't call me Dad. Neither does Mellie. She never calls me by any name. She just talks." He studied his daughter. "Why would you and Ace turn your spouses against me?"

"Come on, Dad. Please. Go inside."

Valerie stood on the other side of the door Steven opened. "Anna's engaged. Pam will fill us in."

Right. Pamela coughed into her hand.

"We can talk in here." Grasping her elbow, Mark led her to the living room.

Her father and stepmother followed into the room behind them.

Peacemaker. Last night he played a similar role with his folks.

"Let's hear it, Pam." Steven demanded answers before she sat down.

Pamela twisted her wedding band several times.

Here we go. Umm ... I still don't know what to say.

She cleared her throat. "Mom's engagement ring is gorgeous."

Steven glared at her. "Stop talking nonsense."

"I'm injecting a little lightness."

"Cut to the chase. How long has Anna known ... what's his name?"

"Nathan. Hendrix," she added when Steven glowered.

Valerie and Steven listened as Pamela and Mark described the engagement lunch.

"A civics professor at Shiatown University," Steven said. "I'll have him checked out this evening. I do have some responsibility regarding your mother."

"How so? Wait ... don't answer that," Pamela said. "I prefer not knowing your reasoning."

Chapter Seventeen

Ninety minutes later, Mark drove into their driveway. The couple had spent an hour pacifying Steven. Today marked the first time Pamela had witnessed a remorseful father. The man who had callously divorced his wife had regrets nine years too late. The entire situation highlighted his self-absorption.

Pamela headed toward the bedroom. "Think I'll take a nap. Wake me up if you need me."

"I'll follow your example. Between my folks and your father and step-mother, I need some rest before work tomorrow."

"Me too. I'm exhausted."

The visit with her father had turned her happy day upside down. He had praised the woman he divorced in front of the wife he divorced her for.

She realized he might have built his second marriage on a flimsy foundation. The relationship appeared to tank before her eyes. Had Valerie's usefulness reached its ultimate limit? Pamela wondered if she should interact with her father and step-mother more?

Fortunately, there was a high point in the day. Anna and Nathan cherished each other. The couple interacted with sincere friendship. Genuine love and warmth bolstered their relationship.

She scooted over when Mark lay beside her.

He pulled her closer. "Don't forget we're headed to Dallas in October. Healthy Headway's CEO emailed a four-point agenda last Friday. Their plan combined precision and enthusiasm in equal measure. I will set up their program on the trip."

"That's high praise coming from a policy wonk." She laughed at Mark's surprised expression. "I recognize your aptitude for technical details." Pamela hesitated when he grinned. "Still leaving Techno Plus at the year's end?"

"If not sooner. Did you prepare for your absence at the shop?"

"Sure did. The place will run smoothly without me. Hiring helpers freed up my days. I'm wide awake each evening. I observe sunsets along with sunrises. They both are equally beautiful."

"Welcome to the land of the living. Let's get out and about more often."

"Lizzie and I are going to the movies on Thursday with Luci, Arlise, and Chris."

"I meant us two, not you and your buddies. How long will Josh work the evening shift?"

"He works three months off and three months on. One more month and he's officially off evenings for a while. I chose Thursday because the pawn shop will hold a midnight madness sale."

"You can always stand beside me while I work."

"Or I can think about you during the movie."

"You enjoy spending time away from home."

Pamela kissed his cheek. "Only because absence makes the heart grow fonder. If you miss me, you'll welcome me back home."

"My wife doesn't subscribe to twisted logic unless it works on her behalf."

Pamela laughed and snuggled against Mark's side.

* * *

One Tuesday, Pamela assembled her husband's favorite Timeless Pastries foods and dessert on the breakroom table. She packed a wicker picnic basket with food and tools necessary for a cozy luncheon. A sudden desire to share a quiet meal with Mark had surfaced after the mid-morning break. Over the weeks, both their minds had been preoccupied with other people. The couple had already encountered enough negative twists and turns to last a lifetime.

Her husband had readily agreed to her proposal to slip away for peace and solitude.

He stood at the curb in front of Techno Plus when she pulled the car up.

Sliding into the car, he kissed her upturned lips. "Where to, love? Your invitation provided an unexpected pleasure."

"The Amazing Facts Trail holds cherished memories for me about you. And I hope, vice versa."

Mark nodded. "I truly opened up to you for the first time there. I've wanted to go back."

"Our private alcove at the halfway mark is the perfect spot to eat lunch alone. I enjoyed watching butterflies play."

Mark loosened his tie and unbuttoned the top two buttons on his shirt.

Pamela loved the way her husband paired ties and casual shirts with denim. Mark had made three significant changes since getting married. He bought a business casual wardrobe, attended his extended family's special occasions, and maintained a low-key lifestyle.

When they arrived at the alcove, Pamela spread a lilac linen tablecloth on the alabaster table. Then she placed chicken club wraps and southwest avocado salad onto silver plates. Apple cinnamon dumplings occupied saucers. Sterling utensils sat atop white linen napkins. Fresh-squeezed lemonade filled wine goblets.

Mark buried his face into her hair when she smiled at him. "Your love makes me feel more alive than ever. I could cuddle you in my arms all day."

"Did you have a busy morning? How has Techno Plus treated my husband?"

"The company operates on well-structured inefficiency."

Pamela checked her watch. "We'd better eat so you can return to the fray."

Only a few people hiked the trail that day. Several folks waved as they passed by the couple. The private alcove provided the tranquility they both needed to regroup. The cathartic atmosphere helped Pamela clear her thinking. Wading through their obstacles as a couple was hard enough without tackling family members' problems too.

She cleared the table once Mark ate the last bite of apple cinnamon dumplings.

He pulled her onto his lap after she repacked every item into the picnic basket.

Mark gazed into her eyes. "Thank you for thinking about us. I'm surprised you left work and ate lunch with me. How's business going?"

"Booming. But you're very quiet today. Care to share your thoughts with your favorite fan?"

"Thinking about our marriage. In the past, yakking filled an unnamed void. There's nothing to prove to anyone, including myself." Pausing, he kissed her lips. "You're good for me. Our marriage began my destiny."

Pamela rubbed her nose against his. "Bliss is sharing a peaceful lunch with my dream man." She hesitated, smiling. "What else is bothering you?"

Mark fiddled with the picnic basket handle. "IT is a time-consuming job. I prefer working beside my wife in our restaurant."

Pamela squirmed in his lap. "You are kidding!"

"Nope. Planning our future."

"The pawn shops. One day you'll run both locations."

" 'One day' is a long trek down the road. Those stores are Father's babies until he hands them over to me—even if I do stop by both locations each week."

Pamela blinked as Mark held up two fingers. His lopsided grin was engaging.

"A full-scale restaurant is possible within two months," he said.

"I thank God for Timeless Pastries' success. In twelve months, I'll know if I want to take on a full-scale restaurant."

"OK. Until then, we can tweak Timeless Pastries' current status."

She relaxed against him. "Mom suggested we add a location in Shiatown that is only a retail bakery. Rhea could manage the shop. But Dad won't financially assist me this time."

Mark's head bobbed while Pamela laid out the scenario. "I like the idea."

"Mom and Nathan discussed several options for when Timeless Pastries opened the shop to customers. The current bakery will supply baked goods for both locations." Eyes closed, she tapped her lips. "I'm stumped on the timeframe."

"We renovated our current shop in less than thirty days. After finding the best locale, expenses will be our biggest hurdle."

Pamela gnawed her knuckle until she faced Mark, wearing a huge grin. "A partnership, perhaps? Mellie appreciates the business as much as I do. I think she and Skylar will come partner with us."

"Your father said he'll give you the building. Do you know when?"

Pamela remembered her dad's negative comments about her husband when Steven mentioned deeding her the building.

"I guess when he decides to do it. He will. Sooner or later. I hope Mellie will partner with me."

She pulled in front of Techno Plus thirty minutes later.

Their gazes met as Mark leaned in for a kiss his wife accepted.

"I enjoyed our lunch date. Next week?"

"Same day, same place, same time," Pamela said, laughing. "But I will bring a different lunch."

* * *

At the shop, she stepped into the office and closed the door behind her. "Let's talk business," she told her sister-in-law.

172

Melinda swiveled the chair around from the computer screen. "How was lunch?"

"Perfect. I enjoyed our quiet afternoon alone." She hesitated, searching for the right words. "Mom had suggested we open up a shop in Shiatown. Mark agreed with Mom's suggestion. I called her on the way here."

Pamela glided across the floor and stood beside her sister-in-law. "I understand you'll need to talk to Skylar first, but will you partner with me and Timeless Pastries?"

Melinda's eyes opened wide as she grabbed her cheeks. "Oh, my goodness! Yes. I will!" Her bear hug knocked Pamela off balance when she let her go. "Oops. Sorry," she said when Pamela hit the floor. She quickly helped her sister-in-law stand. "Wait until I tell Ace. I prayed that you would ask me."

Pamela massaged her hip as she stood. "Why didn't you say so? I wanted to partner with you at the beginning. Look at the time we wasted. Don't ever hold back."

"I almost blabbed after your father set up the commercial kitchen. Ace recommended I wait to be asked. He said we both must be equally invested. I'm all in. What's our next step?"

"Mark is probably scouting the answers now. We're thinking Rhea will manage the Shiatown shop. But Dad won't help us finance it. He hasn't given me the deed to this building."

"Ace said your father bought the building for you as a gift, but now he's waiting for Mark to settle in before he signs it over."

"Which is unnecessary," Pamela said. "My husband wouldn't steal the business from me."

"It's the Jessica-living-next-door thing. But we aren't the ones Mark has to prove himself to. Let Ace broach the subject with your father."

"Good idea. Dad ignores my opinions unless they perfectly sync with his."

* * *

One Friday, an uneasiness perplexed Pamela throughout the morning. She kept fighting urges to visit Mark's parents. Rule number eight came to mind. *Remember both sets of relatives. Keep familial ties alive.*

She had dismissed the idea once, and then twice, but not for the third time. She stepped inside her office and called her husband.

Mark answered his cell phone on the first ring. "Hey, love. I told some of the guys I might join them to watch Washington Tech play the Razorbacks tonight. We can pray and read scripture after I come home."

"Glad you didn't totally commit. Your parents were on my mind all morning. What do they do for fun?"

"Besides making their son's life miserable? Can't think of anything else they both enjoy doing."

"Stop teasing. I can't squash the feeling that we must rally around your parents. This evening, if possible."

Mark took a deep breath and exhaled it in short, breathy puffs.

Pamela sat on the desk's edge. She had tried to convey an urgency and not trepidation.

"You're spending the night at your mother's house tonight," he said. "Her pre-wedding celebration was planned last week." He continued when Pam remained silent. "I will cancel with the guys and call the folks if you think visiting with my parents is important enough to arrive late at your mother's house."

Pamela released the breath she held. "Perfect answer. Let's take your parents for a hike on our favorite trail. Around six?"

"I'll tell them to wear walking shoes."

"Sounds good. Hope they join us."

"If they don't, we'll drop by their house unannounced. Do you have their favorite yellow cake on hand?"

"I'll stash one in the cooler. See you at home."

Pamela grabbed her wallet and strolled to the classic cake showcase. Minutes later, the cooler held a dessert box with the Simons' favorite dessert.

* * *

That evening, Pamela ambled into the kitchen from the laundry room. She lay her clutch on the counter.

Mark walked into the kitchen, searched the counter and island, then he opened the refrigerator door and peered inside. "Where's the cake? Did you leave the box inside the car? I'll bring it inside. The garage gets too hot."

"I left the cake on the breakroom table at work. We'll give them the grand tour and eat dessert there."

When he jiggled coins in his pockets, she stood behind him. She finally recognized the coin-jingling habit was anxiety-driven. His father did that same thing.

Pamela touched his shoulder. "Want a back massage?"

When Mark nodded, her hands massaged his neck and shoulders. She kissed his shirtless back. "Are those tight muscles loosening up?"

"Yes. Much better."

"Maybe you should get a lumbar support chair for work."

"It isn't needed." He leaned into her embrace. "Look. I plan to leave Techno Plus at year's end."

"Mark ... don't make hasty decisions about our livelihood."

Mark turned around and wrapped her in his arms. "Don't fret over finances. I can work full time at the pawn shops."

Pamela's mind flitted between her husband stuck in a job he disliked and the couple filing bankruptcy. Their forever home came with high mortgage payments. Too bad she had already encouraged her mother to scout out a potential Timeless Pastries Shiatown location.

Mark touched her forehead with his forehead. "Pam, your earlier warning—"

"It wasn't a warning. I didn't sound an alarm but communicated my scattered thoughts."

"I understood the message. We'll get on our way after you shower and change." He looked at his sockless feet. "It's been a long day. I'm ready for it to end."

"I can soak in a bubble bath at Mom's house tonight. Last night I packed everything I will need for tomorrow. Will you drop me off at Mom's after we visit with your parents?"

Mark's lips brushed her cheek. "Yes. And I can't believe I'm saying this, but thanks for making quality time for my parents even though your mother is getting married in the morning. Your plans were made last week, but you considered my folks important enough to rearrange them." He paused, then grinned. "I already miss you not being here tonight."

"Missing you too. Though I must say I am excited about Mellie's idea for her, Grandmother, and me to stay overnight with Mom. We don't get such opportunities often. Mellie will ask Skylar to drive us to church for the wedding tomorrow."

Chapter Eighteen

Pamela gasped when Mark turned into a double lane that led to the nature trail.

"They didn't drive over together! Your father parked at the end of the lot. Your mother parked her car beside his truck. I prayed that they would come together."

Mark turned off the engine then captured her hands. "My parents have lived separate lives for many years. I wonder where those two hang out these days." His love-infused eyes captured hers. "Don't worry. I will know more information before the evening ends."

* * *

Mark and Ed lagged behind the women, who wandered off the trail turning over rocks. Whatever the pair discussed kept his mother laughing. Even his father commented on Celeste's carefree spirit. The women giggled together like teenagers.

"I can't recall the last time I heard Mother laugh. I would love to eavesdrop on their conversation." He bumped his father's shoulder. "You're looking more easy-going yourself. What did you get into today?"

Ed eyed him. "Work. Businesses don't run themselves. My son couldn't care less about his inheritance."

Mark steeled himself against his father's bully tactics. "I left the pawn shop at midnight last month. I work eight-hour days at Techno Plus." He hesitated when a thought hit him. *Don't blow the reason why you came.* He cleared his throat. "Enough about me. Where did you head once you left the pawn shop?"

"Stop fishing for answers concerning my personal life." Ed jabbed the air with his finger. "Be direct with your criticisms, but tread lightly. I approve my own lifestyle."

Mark chuckled. "Humor me for once. I dare you, Father. You might discover we play ball on the same team."

"I drove around downtown wondering about your invitation. We've only seen you two times in six months. Why did you invite us here?"

"My wife and I wanted to spend quality time with my folks."

"Hogwash." Ed nudged Mark's side with his elbow. "Did you forget we have a family business?"

"How can you ask me that question when I worked the midnight madness sale? Also, I drop by both locations twice a week."

"One night of work out of six months is nothing. Weekly drop-ins when you knew I had already left the building don't count. We need to have regular face-to-face meetings."

"Look—"

"Secondhand reports mean squat to me. Discuss changes you want to implement with the decision-maker."

Mark stopped his teeth from grinding. The information dump he had unloaded on the managers was targeted to that specific store. He provided details that were concise and objective.

"Did you read the reports I left?"

Ed's voice lowered. "Several times. The ball is in your court."

* * *

Celeste stood on her tiptoes, inhaling the sweet fragrance that wafted from honeysuckle shrubs and vines. She bent over to pick up three multicolored rocks.

Pamela gazed around her. Time stood still in their tranquil oasis. Running brooks and chirping birds supplied peace.

She sighed out loud and grasped her beltloops with her thumbs. "Who could be burdened in an atmosphere like this?"

Out of nowhere Ed's gruff voice barked through the stillness.

Celeste's head jerked toward the irate man stopping beside them. "Him. That's who." She glared at her husband. "Don't make our son and daughter sorry they invited us out."

"Then instruct your son to attend to business."

"Listen," Mark said. "I drop by both pawn shops twice a week. Sorry I missed you."

"Do you want Mark to come at a certain time?" Pamela asked.

"Yeah. When I'm not transitioning between two stores. Coordination goes a long way."

Ed's pain-riddled eyes tugged at Pamela's heartstrings. Mr. Simon thought his son was rebuffing him on purpose. He tormented everyone around him to hide his hurt feelings.

She clutched her husband's arm before he spoke. "I'm a creature of habit, Mr. Simon. I call Mrs. Simon Mother. May I call you Father? I will understand if you say no."

Ed's stature rose like a load lifted off his shoulders. "Thanks for the honor, daughter." A stern gaze censured his wife and son. "Humble individuals put other people first. Pam and I are on the same page."

"That's rich," Celeste said. "Humble? You? Since when?"

"Since my daughter-in-law asked to call me Father." He studied his son. "Can you top our compassionate spirit?"

"I'll meet you at the South Town office on Monday at five thirty. How about that?" Mark asked.

Celeste grinned when Ed glanced at her. "Don't expect any concessions from me," she said. "I refuse to stay home and talk to you." Laughing, she faced her daughter-in-law. "May we continue our walk?"

Linking arms, Celeste spurred Pamela along.

"My friends and I play cards on the second Saturday of each month." Pamela glanced at Celeste. "Would you like to join us? I could pick you up and drop you off at home."

Dabbing her eyes with her fingers, Celeste nodded. "Like mother, like daughter. The Hayes women are kind people. Please pick me up."

* * *

An hour later Celeste wiped her mouth with a napkin. "What a marvelous way to spend an evening. Eating my favorite dessert with my loved ones and touring my daughter's shop."

Ed sneered, touched Mark's arm, then pointed at his wife. "Am I one of the loved ones, darling?"

Celeste glanced at Mark when he chuckled. "Don't encourage his antics, son." She stowed the half-eaten cake into the box. "The food menu is brilliant. Can't wait to sample lunch. I'll tell everyone I know how great this place is."

"We both will toot this fantastic shop's horn." Ed cut another slice of cake from within the box. "I spread the word before, but now I will give a firsthand report."

Pamela looked at Mark. She realized that his parents hadn't come to her shop because they hadn't been officially invited. She blasted herself for the oversight.

A short time later, Mark drove his car behind his parents' vehicles from the parking lot.

"I believe we made a valiant start," Pamela said. "What do you think?"

"That I'm glad I listened to my wife's better judgment. You received the message I refused to hear. I want you and me to help them get their marriage on track." Sighing, he made a left turn at the corner.

* * *

Saturday ushered joy mingled with sadness into an otherwise glorious morning. Pamela peered out the window of her old bedroom. Yesterday, Pamela, Melinda, and Grandmother had spent a tranquil evening reminiscing about Anna's life and showering love on the bride-to-be.

This morning, Pamela's mother had woken up in the South Town family house Pamela grew up in. She would go to sleep in Nathan's Shiatown home. A lifetime of Pamela living close to Anna would end this day.

Last night, Mark had enfolded Pamela in his arms as they waited for her mother to open the door. As footsteps sounded inside the house, he said, "Cheer up, love. You still have me. I will miss my wife lying beside me tonight."

Pamela left the window when a knock sounded on the bedroom door.

Anna and Skylar entered the bedroom.

Pamela took a deep breath. "You're early. What's wrong?"

Skylar hugged her. "Do you think of problems whenever you see me? What if I brought good news?"

"Hope you did," Pamela said.

"I asked your brother to stop by for a quick visit," Anna said. "The children are waiting with Mellie downstairs." Anna smoothed bedcovers with her hands. The mattress dipped when she sat on the bed.

"After the divorce, I received this house and half of our shared assets. Stocks and nonmonetary possessions were liquidated and placed into bank certificates. You guys were added as joint owners on all my accounts when the divorce decree became final. Once this house sells, I will equally split the proceeds between you. Both of your names are on the deed."

She hesitated. "Nathan and I signed waivers exempting ourselves from each other's personal assets. Mother, along with Nancy and Caleb, made their grandchildren their sole beneficiaries. Our stepchildren will not inherit our personal property." She shrugged, smiling. "Sorry for the information dump, but I wanted to let you know before the ceremony, and there hasn't been a good time. Do either of you have questions?"

"No," Skylar said. "You only confirmed what I had suspected."

"This is the last thing," Anna continued. "My children are my sole beneficiaries."

Pamela jumped off the bed. "Mom, this is your wedding day. Don't talk about dying."

"This is a reality-check day for all of us. Business matters are important, especially since I'm getting married." Anna rose, studying her children. "If no one has questions, Mother and I will spend this time together."

"Mom," Pamela said before Anna reached the door, "thanks for teaching us valuable lessons about life in general. Especially stress-free living."

Skylar hugged his mother before following her out of the room.

* * *

The wedding procession began when Myles and Timmy escorted their great-grandmothers into the chapel. Then the flower girls, Maeve and Karrie, walked down the aisle carrying flowers and holding on to Gracie's hands. McKinley followed on their heels with an ivory lace pillow that held two miniature gold rings.

The guests faced the door after the children reached the altar, where Nathan stood beside his best man and brother, Philip.

His son, Gary, tucked Penny's hand around his elbow. Husband and wife walked down the aisle. Skylar and Melinda kept in step behind them. Mark and Rhea brought up the rear that led to the matron of honor's entrance.

Pamela fought back tears, and then she winked at the bride.

She reached the altar as breath intakes reverberated throughout the place.

Escorted by her favorite uncle, Dan, Anna stepped into the chapel.

This time Anna's wedding ceremony began without her crying on a side road before reaching the church. On this day, her mother blended her life with an attentive man.

The reception began thirty minutes after the ceremony ended. Sixty-plus cars filled Timeless Pastries' parking lot.

Mark turned the vehicle into the subdivision and stroked a finger over Pamela's cheek.

"Wake up, sleeping beauty. Almost home."

Pamela sat up straight. "Can't believe I nodded off. Mom was a lovely bride."

"Only one bride was lovelier than your mom. I woke up several times last night. I missed my wife."

"Ah! Then you must be bone-weary tired like me. How about an early evening?"

"I plan to stay home the rest of the day."

"Me too. Curled within your arms and fast asleep."

His cell phone vibrated as the couple stepped onto the porch. He read the text message in the living room.

"Mother sent a lengthy text." He passed Pamela the cell phone. "Read the message for yourself."

She read the message then passed the cell phone back to him. "A cryptic message. What do you think it means?"

"It's anyone's guess. I'll change clothes and head right over. Our rest will have to wait until tonight."

"You're a devoted son. I'm praying for you all."

* * *

Celeste was waiting on the porch when Mark parked the car and jogged up the steps, jiggling nonexistent change in his pocket.

Her red-tinged eyes betrayed the brave smile. Clutched hands wrung together on her lap. Teardrops rolled down her splotchy red cheeks.

Moisture beaded above his upper lip. He sat beside her on the loveseat.

What had happened to make her cry in front of him?

He rolled his shoulders in circles and cleared his throat.

Celeste's hopeful gaze robbed his speech. He didn't know what to say

"Forgive me for taking you away from Pam. I ..." She bit her lips when they trembled. "This afternoon, reminiscing about your childhood brought me unbearable pain, even though I deserve it. Because of my selfishness, I treated you horribly while you were growing up."

"I admit I was angry with both of you for awhile, but I've had a change of heart. I don't want you to beg for forgiveness."

"There is no defense for my hideous performance. I failed my only child." Brushing away tears, she lay her face on the cushion.

Mark knelt in front of his mother on one knee, just looking at her.

"I hated my life when I was growing up," she said with a sigh, "but I treated you the same way I had been treated. It's hard to believe it now, but your grandparents were once very selfish people. Instead of shaping the family life I had craved, I followed my parents' poor example."

Mark understood exactly what his mother meant. Learning from past experiences hadn't been a strong point in his life. His wife's phone call had reminded him how much he loved his parents. While growing up he had hated being treated as an afterthought but had given his best friend the same treatment. Mark didn't accept his love for Pamela until he almost lost her. Needing mercy from his wife helped him to understand forgiveness. Otherwise, he might have died an unforgiving man.

"There aren't any perfect people," Mark replied. "I rejected Pam's unselfish love but accepted scraps from a narcissist. Only my ego suffered when Jessica rejected me. I wouldn't survive a divorce from Pam."

"You would. But that outcome will never happen." She wiped tears off her cheek. "I love Anna's gift of laughter. Wish I had it. Watching her marry her childhood sweetheart finally woke me up."

He nodded. "I think it did the same for a lot of us."

Celeste patted his cheek.

Mark froze. It was the first spontaneous, affectionate act his mother had ever shown him.

"I don't have anything else to add." Fresh tears filled her eyes. "I want to improve our relationship, not destroy what little respect for me you may have left."

"Mother—"

She shook her head. "Please believe I loved my baby boy the moment I saw you. Forgive me. Let me be a part of your present and future."

"You and Father already are. I love you and that stubborn man inside the house." He stared at her. "Father is home, right?"

"Ed's in there. And that's why I waited for you outside."

"Will you and Father put your relationship onto the right track?"

"Rushing water runs under our bridge. We are negotiating a truce of sorts." Tears welled in her eyes again. "One day you will fully comprehend our fractured family life."

"It won't matter when I do. God forgives our sins and forgets about them. I'll save two seats for you and Father at church tomorrow."

"It would be the first time either of us has attended an actual service as adults. We might surprise you and come."

"Please do. I will expect you both."

"Go home to your adorable wife. Tell her Anna and Nathan make a delightful duo."

Mark held her hand as he rose.

Celeste's eyes lost their bleakness. Her fingers lingered on his cheek.

He welcomed the long-overdue affection.

"Tell Father not to stand me up for our Monday meeting."

"That won't happen. Last night, Ed rescheduled a prior commitment. He will attend every meeting his favorite son sets up."

"How long will that attitude last?" He backed up, and then he stood still. His head tilted to the side. "Favorite son?"

"Just making sure you were paying attention. You are the only child for either of us. I promise."

"I'd better be. All right. I am out of here. See you guys tomorrow at church."

Mark reassessed the day as he drove home. Since remorse lay behind his mother's partial confession, she should get a peaceful night's sleep. What secrets had she left out? He didn't require a full confession for each offense. For the first time ever, one of his parents had acted out of character. He'd always considered himself shock-proof. But today his mother apologized and might attend church tomorrow.

He knew what his wife would say when told: "Forward movement. Pure and simple. I'm pleased."

Yesterday she rallied around his folks.

Today his parents drove to Anna's wedding together.

His wife helped people wherever possible.

Mark loved her.

Pamela loved him back.

Yet there was a rift in their relationship that he couldn't define. She watched him with a perplexed expression in unguarded moments. He wanted her to accept his love without reservation.

183

Mark unlocked the front door and froze inside the living room. The stillness inside the house rocked him. Pamela was gone.

He checked his cell phone. Not one message had been left.

A card was on a chair in the family room. A new jigsaw puzzle box lay beside the note.

Rhea mentioned K.C. at the reception. He's dropping by Skylar's house. On my way over there to test my theory. Don't cook our dinner. Skylar's grilling salmon fillets & veggies. I'll bring some home for us. Start the puzzle without me, but do not eat. I did not want to interrupt your conversation with your mother. Love you much!!!!

His wife had jaunted off to another people mission.

Chapter Nineteen

"Okay. Pumped and ready. Mellie, you tell K.C. I'll back you up."

Skylar laughed. "You can't bring a football on the field and refuse to play. Women can't come to term and then refuse to deliver the baby."

My goodness. Quit with the football and medical jargon.

"Your wife is a superb organizer. What if I fumble the ball?" Pamela asked.

"Regroup and finish the play."

Clichés from the man with an extensive vocabulary. He even had her using football terms.

"Last month, you agreed that K.C. and Rhea might be a good match. Thank you. Your part is done." She crossed her fingers over her lips and faced his wife. "Will you help me?"

"Yes. This should end the Pam and K.C. saga for good. Ace's tolerance for the nonsense has evaporated."

Skylar removed sweet potato rounds from the grill. He jerked his head toward Pamela. "Patience was a requirement with that one as a sister. She befriended undeserving people."

Pamela wrinkled her nose at him. "My husband considers me a good character judge."

"Mark received the biggest benefits of my doubts."

K.C. opened the side gate and walked into the yard. "I'm late but made it here," he said, waving at the playing children.

"You came alone," Melinda said. "I'd hoped you would bring the woman you took to dinner last night."

"We didn't click. Consider her out of the running." He sat in the chair beside Pamela.

Mellie leaned closer to K.C. "That's fine. We found you another woman to date."

"We?" K.C. laughed. "Did Ace endorse your choice?"

185

"He did," Pamela said.

Melinda nodded. "Your football game kept you from reuniting with your future wife at Mom's wedding. Mom married Rhea's father today."

K.C.'s eyebrows wrinkled. "Rhea Hendrix? Does she have a son named Timmy?"

"Aw. You remember them," Pamela said. "How sweet is that."

"The little tyke had a tonsillectomy when he was three. I'm surprised she's still single. Rhea and I clicked, but she came with baggage. Timmy's father is a jerk."

Mellie shook her head. "An ex-boyfriend wouldn't stop you from dating a woman you liked. Why didn't you ask her out?"

"She was looking for marriage and I wasn't."

"You're ready now. Pam has her number. Will you call her?"

"Settling down looks better than ever. My heart never left South Town. Ace can confirm that fact, can't you, buddy."

Skylar lifted his fish kabobs off the grill and carried them to the table. "I verify, validate, and endorse that statement." He sat beside his wife. "When you need answers, just ask me. I'm open for business."

His wife and sister each punched one of his arms.

Pamela studied the man thinking private thoughts. "Timmy would make a great son. He outgrew the football gear you gave him on his fourth birthday but won't pass them on. Get this: Your poster hangs on his bedroom wall."

"Now I'm nervous," K.C. said. "But text me her phone number. Hope she remembers me and doesn't reject me."

"Haven't you been rejected before?" Pamela asked.

"No. I would hate to break my winning streak." He paused, grinning. "I will call her. She can only say yes or no."

"Who's Timmy's father?" Skylar asked.

"Paul Hagen." K.C. stared at him.

Skylar grunted. "Overlook Rhea's prior bad judgment."

"Oh please," Melinda said. "We just hope she overlooks K.C.'s."

Pamela pulled out her cell phone when it pinged. "Gotta run. My hubby's home."

Melinda rose with her. "I'll fix your food to take home. Then I'll walk you to the car."

Pamela hugged the children before the women left the backyard.

* * *

Pamela opened the laundry room door to a solo rendition of Vivaldi's Violin Concerto in A Minor that lured her into the den. Mark's back faced the door as he played the timeless piece. The last time she'd heard her husband play violin was when he won the tri-state championship his senior year in college.

She reclined on the settee with her eyes closed. The melodious tone reignited delightful long-forgotten memories. With tear-filled eyes, she gazed at Mark's back when the instrument lowered.

He stared into space, still facing the opposite direction. Time had ceased to exist as if contentment had nourished a depleted soul.

He swiveled the chair around when she clapped her hands.

"Bravo. Will you play Mozart's Violin Concerto No. 3 in G Major? You won an award playing that too."

His eyes widened with amazement. "I can't believe you remember that. I'd almost forgotten those special occasions."

"You remembered the composition. Do you regret forsaking a music career for a technological job?"

"I only regret discontinuing playing violin altogether. I've made too many either/or decisions. Choosing a different career path didn't have to negate making music."

"I applaud your insight. You learned a well-earned lesson."

"These days I set my focus on making good decisions."

"For a rusty old man you performed an excellent solo without a printed sheet."

He grinned all over himself. "I quit playing after meeting Jessica. Playing violin seemed pretentious while dating her."

Mark placed the instrument inside the case then sauntered toward his wife.

Pamela flowed into his open arms.

"Will the baker call Rhea?"

"Yes. Though he's nervous. He liked Rhea and Timmy. It sounds like the only hiccup is that Timmy's father is a jerk."

"That won't stop Hodges. Why didn't he pursue her before?"

"She was tired of just dating. Now K.C. is on the same page. Don't you love happy beginnings?"

"As long as they end in a satisfactory manner."

"This relationship will. Watch and see."

"I love you and your optimism." He interlaced their fingers and led her to the kitchen. "What goodies did you bring home?"

"Fish kabobs and grilled sweet potatoes. What happened at your parents' house? Can you share information?"

Pamela spread out the food she'd brought home from her brother's house. They sat on stools at the island while Mark relayed the conversation with Celeste.

"Mother ended the conversation with hints that a bombshell exists. She said the revelation might destroy any respect for her that I may have left."

"Did you tell your mother how much you love her?"

"I did. Whatever she left out is big, love. I invited her and Father to church tomorrow. She claimed they might surprise me and come."

Pamela beamed. "Forward movement. Pure and simple. I'm pleased."

An unmistakable look of pleasure appeared on Mark's face.

"What made you happy?" She paused when his eyes twinkled. "Why are you smiling?"

"I know you better than you know yourself." He laughed when her eyebrows rose. "I predicted you would say, 'Forward movement. Pure and simple. I'm pleased.' See there. I keep learning more about my fascinating wife."

"I like that compliment. Thank you. Let's eat so we can cuddle while I sleep."

"We're in perfect agreement once again." Mark bit into his fish kabob. "This tastes delicious. Tell your brother we'll take seconds." He stared at her. "Just kidding. Do not leave this house."

Pamela's laughter floated around them.

* * *

In the parking lot at church the next morning, Mark joked about every person they passed. He didn't say anything negative or harsh, but he had honed his people-watching critique skills.

After they entered the sanctuary, he escorted her to the side and whispered in her ear, "Visitors are sitting in our pew."

Pamela's eyes sparkled. "Your folks came!"

"As did Rhea and Timmy. There they sit next to Hodges." Mark glanced around them. "Look at the women's faces. I recommend Hodges attend Rhea's church in Shiatown."

"Why? K.C. never dated any woman who attends our church. And I don't count."

"From their expressions, it wasn't because the women didn't try."

"Oh. You're worried about territorial stalking incidents."

Mark chuckled. "Territorial stalking. Did you just coin that phrase?"

"Uh-hum. Creative of me, huh?" Pamela thumped him. "Stop laughing because I congratulated myself. Someone has to do it."

"Careful, love. Self-justification is worse than praising yourself."

Pamela's lips drooped until she saw Anna. Grabbing Mark's hand, she hurried to their favorite row.

"I thought you and Nathan weren't coming to church this morning." She hugged her in-laws. "Hello, family. So glad you came to worship with us."

She waved at Mellie and Rhea. "Okay. Where are we all going for lunch?"

"Home," Mark said while the others laughed.

"Spoilsport." She sat beside him, still surprised the newlyweds were there. She whispered in Mark's ear. "Why do you think Mom and Nathan came?"

Mark looked past her down the row. "Rhea. Timmy. And Hodges. Need I say more?"

She shook her head and glanced down the row again.

I suppose not.

The choir came in while Pamela studied her father and stepmother. She almost waved. They both watched Pamela's row from across the room. She looked up front when Pastor Paul delivered highlights for the upcoming week. Then he introduced the guest speaker.

A middle-aged woman took the microphone and began her text.

"How do we live in God's presence? Ask, seek, and knock. Whenever scriptures on ask, seek, and knock are taught, they usually reference prayer. Even though a wide gap exists between prayer and worry, the gulf isn't so great when you consider most Christians worry while we pray. God's children must pray without ceasing and thank the Father for answered prayers. The Holy Spirit's truths thrive within submissive Christian hearts."

Pamela retrieved a notepad from her purse, but she listened too hard to take notes. The speaker seemed to speak directly to her.

She began writing when the speaker said, "These are my final points. Please write them down. Don't rely on your memory."

"Our transformation begins once we accept Jesus as our strength. God's power works within our weaknesses. Jesus is our:

Redemption – He gave His life so we can live eternally with the Father.

Righteousness – Through His sacrifice, we can come boldly into the Father's presence.

Sanctification – Because He is a holy God, we must live pure lives.

Wisdom – In the name of Jesus, we have the mind of Christ.

Purity of heart and mind belong to God's children."

Pamela stuffed the notepad in her purse. Having a relationship with God and living in His presence required persistence. Her only quiet time had been on Friday evenings when she read scripture with Mark while falling asleep. Those dynamics will change this day.

The guest speaker had brought the exact message Pamela required to live an abundant life.

* * *

Mark knocked on the guest bedroom door then peered inside the room. "Still praying? I miss you. You spent the afternoon without me."

Pamela closed the Bible and patted the space beside her. "Come join me."

The soft tone drew him near.

"This morning's message hit me where I live," she said. "I need to pursue a consistent relationship with God. I offered the Holy Spirit complete access. He accepted."

"The message touched me and my folks. They took Pastor Paul and Joyce out to lunch. Both of my parents accepted Jesus as their Savior in the restaurant's parking lot."

"Thank God! I tried to arrange a group lunch, but God had an ultimate plan." Her fingers tapped her lips. "Hmm. Should they join a Bible study? Mark ..."

"No, ma'am. Let them enjoy their journey without us. Time to eat a light meal."

"Glad it isn't a full dinner. Lunch filled me up."

"That's because you fixed a feast," he said. "I can't wait to see what else happens in our families."

She scooted off the bed and patted her belly. "Speaking of families, on Friday I set up a doctor's appointment with Mellie's obstetrician for Wednesday morning."

Mark jumped up beside her. He squeezed her body against his so tight she couldn't breathe. "Are you serious?"

Her body relaxed when he loosened the hold. "I was nauseated two months ago for several days. The nausea passed and I haven't skipped any months. Besides gaining weight, there are no obvious signs that I'm pregnant, but I might be."

"Just think. I could become a father next year."

"I have mixed feelings. Especially since you may bail on our only guaranteed paycheck."

"Don't stress over money. I can always earn a decent salary at the pawn shops."

"People deserve to be happy with their job. You will always be a great provider."

"I try hard. The CEO set up a very important meeting with me for the same day as your appointment. We'll see what happens."

* * *

Mark stepped inside Enough for Everyone's South Town location. The showroom was unusually full for early evening.

"Hello, Bertie," he called to the gray-haired lady behind the cashier's booth. She waved and pointed to his father's office.

Bertie Townsend had worked at the pawn shop for over thirty years. She was more like a favorite aunt than a long-term employee. A spectacular retirement package waited for her whenever she retired.

Ed met him at the office door. The weary expression and attentive gaze surprised Mark.

Ed sat behind his desk.

Mark chose a spot on the desk's edge.

"Do you remember my plans regarding Bertie's retirement?"

"Of course," Ed said. "It's the one item concerning business we agree on."

"How can you make that assertion? We never discuss the pawn shops."

"Your silence on the subject says it all." The direct gaze pierced his son. "You're either indifferent or ignorant about running this business."

"You read the reports I gave your managers. A pro taught me."

"Timeless Pastries' success attests to that fact."

A grin broke across Mark's face. Ed's reluctant compliment meant more to him than anyone else's accolades could.

"What did you and Celeste discuss? Decency demanded I let you two speak in private."

"Why? You don't bow to politeness."

Ed speared Mark with steely eyes. "Being twenty-eight and married doesn't give you the right to disrespect your old man."

Mark sighed and looked away. "No offense was intended. Mother and I have had limited personal conversations over the years."

"Don't blame me for your mother's faults. I answer for my own negligence, no one else's. What did you discuss?"

Mark finally understood that his father's blusters were due to insecurities, not aggression. He thought about the conversation with his mother on Saturday. Another frank discourse about his childhood loomed ahead. It wasn't necessary to explain their former relationship. Old doubts and hurts regarding his father had been buried during their Friday walk. No one needed to regurgitate their past sins. Mark was dealing with his childhood disappointments.

"While you grew up, I followed my father's example with my family," Ed said. "My father was seldom home and relegated child-rearing to my mother. He was a good provider, and I adopted his outlook on family relationships. But providing financial support shouldn't have ended my family obligations. Give me an opportunity to correct those blatant errors." He hesitated as if to collect his thoughts. "Nothing would satisfy me more than knowing that the son I love more than this life has forgiven me."

Haze evaporated in an instant. Mark viewed his early years without painful memories.

Nothing could change his parents' lack of interest in Mark during his childhood. The Simon family must move beyond the deadlock.

He stopped himself from grinding his teeth. "I love you more in this moment than I ever thought possible. My childhood wasn't a complete bust. And now our future awaits us."

Ed nodded and pointed to the space beside his desk. "Pull up a seat."

During their discussion the men agreed Mark would play an active role in setting policy at the pawn shops.

Ed slid a folder across the desk.

"I added you as a joint owner on my business and personal accounts. You just need to sign the signature cards."

Mark read the material, then held them in his hands.

Ed passed him a sealed manila envelope. "Celeste signed an affidavit five years ago that relinquished claim to my personal and business assets. I signed

192

one that said you would always be my sole beneficiary. The documents and a copy of our wills are inside."

Mark couldn't think straight. His parents' actions didn't make sense.

The documents appeared to be legal and in order even though the logic behind them failed. He read each signature card twice before he signed his name.

Ed replaced the signed signature cards into the folder before putting the packet into a briefcase.

"Neither of your actions add up," Mark said. "You were married almost twenty-five years by then. Why would Mother accept a pittance and then sign away what's rightfully hers? Why stipulate that you will leave everything you own to me?"

Ed's features turned complacent. "Have that discussion with Celeste. I'd hoped she had told you Saturday. She knows we're meeting this evening. Expect a call."

What could make his mother relinquish her livelihood?

"Vague statements don't help me understand what's going on."

"It's not my place to tell you her thoughts. Talk to Celeste."

Mark's brows lowered. "How does Mother support herself?"

"She has my full support while I'm alive. It's up to you not to kick her out when I go. She trusts her son won't leave his mother destitute." Even though Ed gave Mark a half grin, his eyes looked sad. "Enough about me and your mother. Where are you headed?"

"Toomey's for takeout. Pam's eating dinner with friends."

Ed's placid gaze studied his son. "Spot you dinner."

"Let's head that way," Mark said. Perhaps he could discover vital answers.

Father and son left the building after Ed locked the office door.

Mark couldn't stop thinking about his mother. She and Father lived together. Why would she sign away her marital claim? Nothing made sense.

Ed stopped beside his car. "Both your outlook and disposition have matured since getting married. You and Pam are a matched set."

Mark nodded as he chuckled. "We are. I just missed turning into a total wreck."

"Love shared with the right person will secure a sound marriage."

"This may be a big leap, but are you saying you and Mother shouldn't have married?"

"Ask Celeste if you want answers."

Ed slid inside the car and closed the door.

Mark got into his vehicle and tailed his father out of the parking lot.

* * *

"See what I mean?" Mark asked as Pamela spread the affidavits on the cocktail table.

He picked up his cell phone when it rang. "It's her. Father said to expect her call."

Pamela scooted closer and lay her head on his shoulder. "It will be okay. Don't let the call go to voicemail."

He took a deep breath and pushed the talk button. "Hello, Mother."

"Were you busy?" Celeste asked.

"Talking to Pam about my meeting and dinner with Father. We ate at Toomey's."

"Then you must be tired. Go ahead and finish your conversation with your wife. I won't keep you. Just wanted to make sure you weren't mad and would talk to me."

His brows drew together while Mark focused on a lit, scented candle. "I signed Father's signature cards and reread your wills and affidavits. He legally bound himself to leave everything to me while you forfeited claims to his assets and settled for a paltry sum. Father is worth more than the fraction you accepted. Why, Mother?"

"Ed told me he didn't tell you. Good. You and I will have a private talk."

"Expect me in fifteen minutes."

"Not tonight. We'll talk at a later time. Goodnight, son."

He glanced at the cell phone and then at his wife. "Guess our talk will wait. She said goodnight and hung up."

"The buildup must be worse than what occurred. Guilt makes people do foolish things. Your father caught her at a low moment."

"It's bad. Mother gave up her rights to her home. She loves that place."

"She didn't walk away penniless. Your father bought her out and still supports her everyday expenses. She knows you wouldn't make her move."

Mark stood. "Mother told me not to come by tonight, but I'm heading over there. My visit will take her by surprise."

Pamela tucked her arm through his. "It's scripture-reading time. We should pray and go to bed."

He studied her features then stroked her cheek. "Right as ever. Can't crowd them. Perhaps the outcome proved worse than the original offense."

"Uh-hum. It looks like two people jumped the gun to me. They will regret their actions once they become closer. A course change is coming soon. Your parents accepted Jesus into their hearts. Let's pray."

Chapter Twenty

Pamela read a tempting slow cooker recipe while she waited for her doctor's appointment. She snapped a picture of the recipe with her camera phone. She already had almost all of the needed ingredients in the pantry.

She looked across the room when a door opened. A younger woman dressed in scrubs smiled at her. "Pamela Simon?" she asked.

Standing to her feet, Pamela couldn't stop beaming. Even without the obvious sign of skipping her monthly period, she hoped to hear positive news.

* * *

"I'm pregnant," she told the receptionist before she left the doctor's office. "You're going to see a lot of me."

"Congratulations," several voices behind the partition rang out.

Inside her car, Pamela drove to the grocery store. The couple would celebrate her pregnancy with a scrumptious new meal. She had just enough time to shop for ingredients and run by the house to set up the slow cooker before Timeless Pastries stopped serving lunch.

An hour later, she turned the corner into the subdivision and spotted Mark and Jessica talking in the Simons' driveway. The curtains were drawn at the house across the road.

How long had they been chatting before she saw them? They talked for ten minutes while Pamela stewed in private. Crazy thoughts entered her mind. Don't go there. Imbeciles met their girlfriends in front of their house. Her husband wasn't stupid. He'd simply stopped by their house for something, and Jessica had approached him in their driveway as he left.

Their conversation ended when Jessica flounced across her lawn.

Mark watched her progress then entered his car.

Moments later, he stopped his vehicle beside Pamela's. His fish-mouth expression proved priceless.

She couldn't resist driving off.

Pamela parked in the driveway, then carried her bundle into the house. She was unpacking groceries when Mark stood in the doorway.

"Step inside the family room before you ask for an explanation," Mark said. He left the spot.

She followed behind him but stopped before she reached the room.

"I don't suspect you of having an affair with Jessica," she blurted out. "You came home and she accosted you at the car. I parked down the street to avoid a confrontation."

He clasped her hands and kissed her fingers.

She rubbed her face on his chest. "Now, why did you want to meet me in the family room?"

Mark led her into the family room and turned on the laptop propped on the coffee table. "This is a preview of my surprise for tonight. We'll view slides ranging from nursery designs to children-friendly vacation spots and more." He hesitated. "Should I have waited until the doctor confirmed you're pregnant? Are we having a baby?"

He grinned when her head nodded. "Perfect timing."

She held up four fingers. "I'm four months. Either I'm super busy or super unobservant. And I've gained four pounds. Dr. Yeardley said I should gain twenty-five to thirty five pounds during pregnancy."

"I'm ecstatic, love. Wait until I tell my folks another Simon is on the way. That will make them happy."

Pamela beamed. "How did your important meeting go?"

Mark checked his watch. "I changed the time to two o'clock so I could work on your surprise. I'll drop you off at work to guarantee I'll leave work on time today. I won't make my wife wait for me."

"Will you give me twenty minutes? I came home to set up your surprise slow cooker meal."

"Tell me what the doctor said while I watch you cook. I'll give you a Jessica update."

"Why bother? Her repertoire is surprisingly limited."

* * *

Pamela floated through a hassle-free afternoon. No crises could diminish Mark's tribute to his wife and unborn child. She was amazed that her husband had postponed an important meeting to set up her surprise. His family's well-being stayed uppermost in his mind. Thank God she had married a like-minded man. Sometimes they were like identical peas within the same pod.

And then at other times, well ...

* * *

Mark locked the Timeless Pastries door at four thirty sharp, bustling Pamela into the car. "Can't wait to eat my turmeric chicken dinner. I don't recall eating that particular spice."

Pamela yawned as the vehicle turned into the subdivision. Her gaze went straight to Jessica's red Jeep parked in the Prentises' driveway.

"This is the first time I've seen Jessica's Jeep parked in the driveway. Hmm ... wonder when we will officially meet the mister. Do you know anyone who knows him?"

"That reminds me," Mark said. "My ex issued fresh threats against our marriage."

"The repetitive warning gets stale after six months. What's her goal?"

"To torment us, which means she doesn't know my wife."

Mind games. Jessica planned to live inside their heads. Perhaps they missed a larger plot. *Maybe she realized her initial mistake of confronting us and laid a long-term strategy.*

"My grandparents know his parents," Pamela said. "Valerie knows his sister. Do you know anyone who knows him?"

"Father does. He said Victor is a hard-driving man who demands loyalty from business associates."

"Really? And he accepts crumbs from his wife?"

Mark pulled into the driveway. "The man my father described wouldn't tolerate her antics. His parents' sentry post across the street confirms Victor covered bases."

"Hmm ... nothing adds up about the Prentises' relationship." She looked over her shoulder, laughing. "Perfect timing once again. He just pulled into their driveway. Let's see what he knows." She opened the car door.

"No, ma'am. We don't need their drama. Between our families we have enough."

Determination won out over prudence. She twiddled her fingers at her husband and exited the car.

Mark reached her side as the hawk-featured man observed their progress.

Victor executed the perfect half grin. "To what do I owe the pleasure?"

"No need to be formal," Pamela said. "Mark and I have waited six months to meet our neighbor. Now we have a voice to go with the hand waves."

"Victor Prentis. Thanks for the lovely blooms you gave my parents. I am pleased to meet you both."

"The flowers reminded me of them. Pam Simon. This is my husband, Mark."

Victor eyed Mark. "My wife told me you two dated for three years before we married. My proposal broke up your relationship."

Pamela snapped her lips together. What just happened? Did Victor somehow challenge Mark?

An astute gaze replaced her husband's quizzical expression. "Your wife accepted your proposal and rejected mine. Congratulations."

A peculiar brotherhood had surfaced between the men. Victor's loaded remark and Mark's frank admission de-escalated tension.

Victor turned to Pamela. "I hear you're Steven Hayes' daughter and Ace's sister."

Pamela laughed. "Yes. We're stuck with each other. At least I have Mom."

A crooked smile teased his lips. "I cheered your brother's athletic prowess for eight years straight. I hear he's a brilliant physician."

"It's what Skylar has always wanted to do. Thank God football didn't redirect his dreams."

He turned to Mark. "Ed Simon said your wife is a wonderful baker."

Mark chuckled. "South Town is a small city. You know my father?"

"And Celeste. Ed won't do business with me. Yet!"

"Then I'll tell my parents we met," Mark said.

"Perhaps both families will join us for dinner one weekend. I wanted you to settle in first."

The front door slammed shut.

Dressed in a side-slit, strapless, floral midi-dress and white ballet flats, Jessica sauntered across the driveway and offered a cheek for her husband's kiss.

"Did you forget to invite me to the gathering?"

Amusement lit Victor's eyes then quickly vanished. "You saved me a trip inside. I invited the Simon and Hayes families over for dinner one weekend."

Jessica glanced at Pamela and Mark, then she eyed her husband. "Which Saturday?"

Victor smiled at Pamela. "How about in two weeks? The invitation certainly includes your mother, Pam."

"Mom is honeymooning. Two weeks sounds fine for the rest of us. I'll check with everyone."

Victor nodded. "Two weeks it is."

"Six o'clock," Jessica added. "Let me know if we need a date change."

"Sure will. We'll bring dessert. Do either of you have favorites?"

"Surprise us." Victor caught Jessica by the arm when she headed toward her Jeep.

She glanced at his hand, then shook it off. "Just a quick run. My mother requires my help with a problem."

"Come inside. We need to talk before you leave." He studied his neighbors. "I enjoyed meeting you both. Good day."

Victor ushered an obviously reluctant Jessica inside the house.

Pamela and Mark hooked arms and headed home.

"Wow!" Pamela said. "Someone declared war. But Victor struck first. I think our Jessica is outmatched."

"That was Father's deduction when someone told him who she married. He said, 'Few people will test Victor Prentis.' "

Once they reached the house, Pamela lounged on the living room sofa. "I thought Victor was friendly, although the spur-of-the-moment dinner invitation seems bizarre. What do you think?"

"He's looking out for his business. However, he spoke as if he and my folks are more than associates." Mark reached out his hand. "We wasted fifteen minutes next door."

Pamela let him pull her off the couch. "Her husband seemed, um, somewhat like a gangster."

Laughing, Mark led them toward the master suite. "Stick with reading romances. No more delving into murder mysteries. He's a straightforward guy who cuts to the chase. He doesn't make you guess his intentions."

She sat on the bed and kicked off both shoes. "So, he knows his proposal broke up your relationship with Jessica. Why did he tell us?"

"The warning shot across the bow. He laid his cards on the table. Now, can we celebrate our baby?"

"Of course," Pamela said, following him across the room.

During dinner, Pamela set down her glass filled with apple cider. "I thought of baby names."

"Me too. Sasha and Kennedy."

"I like those names. But how about Sierra and Tanner?" She winked at him. "Maybe we'll have quadruplets and use all four."

He stared at her with weary eyes until he chuckled. "Going with Sierra or Tanner works better than using all four names in February."

"I agree. Sierra or Tanner it is. I'm glad we are in agreement on the big things."

"Most times we agree. And we do share a similar taste in food. The turmeric chicken tastes even better than it smells. Would you consider serving dinner during the week and on Saturdays?"

Mark's father owned two pawn shops his son could manage. Mark should revamp Enough for Everyone and leave her bakeries alone.

"Mellie and I like Timeless Pastries as it is. We have plenty to handle with two locations. I am serious, Mark," she added when his head tilted sideways. "Don't try to weaken my resolve."

Mark grinned. "Your happiness means everything to me. I won't try to change your mind."

Yeah. Right.

Mark turned off the laptop when the presentation ended.

"What do you think? Did I bombard you with too much information?"

Her husband had provided details that would appeal to both their personalities in multiple areas, from the baby's birth until college graduation. She had viewed daycares, preschools, and after-school programs. Plus different types of furniture, yard equipment, and vacation choices.

She blinked at Mark. "Well ..."

"Don't let the wide-ranging information intimidate you. We have six months before definite selections become necessary regarding the child's first year."

Say something nice. Quick.

"Each slide was under thirty minutes," Pamela said. "You gave an in-depth report. I liked the multiple examples and the reasons behind each one."

"Repeat that comment." He chuckled when Pamela told him he did an excellent job. "I purposely put one topic on each slide. We won't have to search for answers."

Pamela cleared her throat. "We shouldn't set up a nursery and then change it out with juvenile furniture a year later. We can buy a baby bed and regular bedroom furniture that will last until they move out."

"You mean buy a baby bed that matches the single bed's style?" Mark continued when she nodded. "What about a toddler bed? The child can't transition from a baby bed into a single bed."

"We can teach him or her not to roll onto the floor," Pamela said.

She fell over herself laughing when Mark frowned.

"Thanks for laughing. I thought you were serious. Now, to the crux. When will we find out our baby's gender?"

Pamela gasped. "We won't know until he or she is born. Wouldn't you rather be surprised like in the olden days?"

"No. I wouldn't. We might purchase the wrong color clothes. I don't want to wrap our son inside a pink blanket."

"After I have an ultrasound, I will ask about the baby's sex, if you insist."

"Good. Learn to respect science."

"Yes, sir."

"Glad you agree. Did you keep Saturday free for our surprise trip? Don't ask where we're going," he said when her mouth opened. "Be surprised."

* * *

On Friday morning, Mark leaned against the chair cushion with his hands behind his head.

Lavine knocked on the door, then poked her head inside the office, pointing to the printer. "Do you have a large print job? I came in to see if the start button got stuck."

Mark waved her inside the room. "What can I say other than that I'm a busy man."

"And mighty relaxed for someone on the hot seat. I just read the latest email from the second floor. They're in an uproar upstairs because The Last Stop's CEO sprung a surprise visit. We don't have time to unroll a detailed conversion package for a Fortune 500 company."

"Not receiving a concise report is the usual outcome when people drop in uninvited."

Lavine's gaze switched to the printer. "Did my astute boss customize a design because Techno Plus is a top contender?" She smiled when Mark nodded. "What's the plan to win the contract before they leave?"

"Jenkins and company flew into Tulsa yesterday and met with All Things IT. Their driving to South Town that afternoon means All Things IT failed to clinch the deal." He pointed to the chair beside his desk. "Close the door and take a seat. We have five hours to win the contract."

* * *

A school bus pulled into the Timeless Pastries parking lot. Forty hungry teenagers swarmed the lobby within seconds. An entire showcase vanished in less than twenty minutes. Before the bus pulled off the parking lot, a haggard espresso bar owner bustled into the bakery, barking orders at Emily. His only oven had malfunctioned that morning. Now neither of his three locations could offer fresh baked goods.

Wringing her hands, Pamela slumped against a showcase as the man purchased half their cookies, cakes, and apple cinnamon pies.

He called over his shoulder on his way out of the door, "Making another run by here later this afternoon and tomorrow morning. Stock up on your caramel brownies, cheesecakes, and fruit pies."

Ten minutes later, an older lady dressed in business attire strolled into the shop. Salt-and-pepper hair flattered her fashionable bold colors. The woman perused the showcases while whipping out a bank card. Her appearance and actions alternated between a power broker and a lovable granny. Even though she ran Emily around in circles, Pamela liked the woman on the spot.

Emily beckoned Pamela to the counter and pointed to their customer.

Pamela walked right over. "Hi. May I help you with anything?"

"Mrs. Tibbs just requested two hundred pecan tart cupcakes. For today," she added when Pamela smiled.

"I hate being a bother, but our company's CEO requested that very item." The woman's keen gaze studied Pamela's face as if sketching Pamela's features onto her brain. "Unexpected visitors dropped in. Our CEO specifically requested pecan tart cupcakes. Yesterday one of our guests ate that particular item here."

Pamela sought a way to redo the order. The remaining stock in the cooler wouldn't last until closing. The baking staff was busy filling fundraisers and established client orders. What could she do to keep the company as a satisfied customer? Most people who requested so many of one item would place the order in advance.

"We never bake large quantities of any item without prior notice. However, I can put together a sampler package your boss will love."

The woman's eyes sparkled as she gazed at Pamela. "My boss will praise whatever you bake. But our company's CEO placed the order." She hesitated, glancing over showcases. "Make me a believer. I'll also buy a half-dozen jalapeño cornbread muffins for my husband's dinner."

Twenty minutes later, Pamela loaded assorted baked goods and candies into the woman's small SUV.

She handed Mrs. Tibbs a bag filled with six plain cornbread and six jalapeño cornbread muffins. "Hope you enjoy our house samples."

"My husband will inhale all twelve tonight. His mother had a similar item he loved. Thanks again. You saved this old lady's hide."

"You are very welcome. Please stop by for lunch on the house soon."

Mrs. Tibbs nodded. "I would stay for lunch today, but our company has a contract to win this afternoon."

"Then I'll pray for your company's success."

"Thank you. We plan to make a grand impression in one afternoon." Mrs. Tibbs slid inside the car. "That's a stratagem of my enterprising boss. He's trying to win big for our company and CEO."

She waved as the woman drove off. "I bet Mrs. Tibbs is a lovable granny."

Pamela walked inside the door behind a man she'd seen in the shop before.

"How may I help you?" Emily asked him when he reached the counter.

"Give me three dozen cupcakes. My daughter loves strawberry cheesecake."

Pamela forestalled Emily's apology. "We just sent the last of those cupcakes out the door. Might I interest you in our sampler pack?"

The man surveyed the showcases. "Do you give free samples?"

"We will for you," Pamela said. "I'll give you three to try: lemon drop, caramel chocolate chip, and banana supreme."

"Thank you. My little girl is celebrating her ninth birthday. I'm taking cupcakes to her school."

Emily placed a plate filled with the three cupcakes onto the counter.

The man took a bite of all three. "These are good. Hook me up. I may return later this afternoon."

He gobbled the three cupcakes while Emily packed his order. He grabbed the packages off the counter.

"Thanks for accepting the substitute cupcakes," said Pamela. "Bring your family over this afternoon for an after-school snack. We'll give your daughter her favorite cupcake on the house. And we'll supply balloons."

His eyes bucked open. "No kidding? What an excellent birthday surprise for my little girl." He waved at Emily and Pamela as the door closed behind him.

Pamela slumped on the counter and wiped her brow. Sampler packages saved the day again.

"It's only eleven thirty and we're running out of baked goods. When Tina gets back I'll tell her we're celebrating a special birthday later today."

"I like that man's family," Emily said. "Sometimes the mother brings her children in for lunch."

* * *

That evening, thankful it was Friday, Pamela spent ten minutes soaking in an aloe vera bubble bath. Belting a robe around her waist, she opened the Bible and lay across the bed, muttering her favorite Psalms. During her parents' divorce, three Psalms had comforted her like nothing else had. Even today Psalms 62, 91, and 145 were her go-to scriptures whenever she felt overwhelmed.

Laying her Bible on the nightstand, she closed her eyes and fell asleep, cradling her baby bump.

* * *

Mark placed chilled blueberries and diced pineapple into the refrigerator. He sampled the turkey and potato hash simmering in the slow cooker. Nine thirty was too late to eat a full meal. The table set for two meant his wife had waited on him to eat dinner.

The quiet house meant nothing. Mark knew his wife was at home.

On his way to the bathroom he found her fast asleep inside the master bedroom. Her open Bible lay on the nightstand. She had followed through with the couple's Friday Bible study without him. He stared at her restful body. Pamela cradled her baby bump in her sleep. He'd seen her doing that a lot lately.

He removed his tie and studied his face in the mirror as he pulled off his shirt. His life had changed forever in less than twelve months. God had given him a new beginning. He was a happy man.

Mark leaned on the vanity with his head bowed. Anxious thoughts assaulted his mind. He couldn't forget his wife's perplexed expressions in unguarded moments. He'd witnessed confusion on her face whenever she thought he wasn't looking. The easy comradery the couple had shared before coming home from their honeymoon was still missing from their relationship. Now a chasm of uncertainty existed between them.

Mistrust? Familiarity? What had caused the shift in their relationship?

Everything appeared to be fine on the surface. Anyone who looked at their relationship would tell Mark he was crazy. That his wife loved him more than she ever had. Yes, his wife loved him. But she also didn't believe in divorce and wanted to make her marriage work.

Taking a shower failed to dislodge the concerns from his mind. He put on a robe when he stepped out of the shower and sat beside his wife on the bed. His finger stroked her upper arm. He chuckled when she sat up, rubbing her eyes. A bedraggled state suited her to perfection. She wore a bedspread-patterned face quite well.

"You finally came home to me. I can't believe I fell asleep." She covered her mouth when she yawned. "What time is it?"

"Ten o'clock. Let's eat some fruit salad and call it a night."

"Works for me. Turkey and potato hash for dinner tomorrow."

* * *

The next morning Mark left the den, stuffing his wallet into his back pocket. He'd just finished an illuminating discussion with Ed. Pamela's persistence had cemented his and his father's tattered relationship. Ed accepted his son as an adult. Until last month, his father had treated Mark like Ed's father had treated Ed. Mark would not let that continue into the next generation. None of his children would battle low self-esteem, especially within the family business.

Business ownership pumped through Simon blood. Had Mark carved out a career in technology just to escape his father's thumb?

One hint that something bad might happen to either of his parents had cleared his vision. Life was too short to hold grudges, especially toward loved ones.

He paused in the bedroom doorway. Pamela had returned to bed after eating breakfast. His wife lay on her back and patted her stomach. Mark sat beside her, covering her hand with his. He sought the same affinity his wife and baby shared. Sometimes she woke up during the night humming lullabies.

"It's hard to believe we stood at the altar just six months ago," Mark said. "Hard-learned lessons have been crammed into each day."

Delighted eyes robbed his speech. She captured his hand with hers.

"Life throws unforeseen curveballs," Pamela said. "I now have a stepfamily."

"Speaking of the Hendrixes, how goes the romance between Hodges and Rhea? We haven't seen them at church."

"Their romance is off to a good start. You told me K.C. and Rhea should attend her church the first time they came to our church. And they did just that. My husband possesses brilliant counsel he hates giving—unless his wife is the victim. Or should I say 'pupil'?"

Mark checked his watch then kissed her lips. "How about you're the recipient of wise guidance?"

"I accept your accurate description without rebuttal," Pamela said.

"Good. Rise and shine. You can't loll in bed this morning. We're leaving at ten."

She rolled on her side in the queen-sized bed, staring at him. "To go where and do what? This is the first Saturday I've had when I can rest all day."

"Last month I asked you to mark this date on your calendar. I reminded you again last week."

Pamela grabbed his hand. "You didn't tell me where we're going. How could I log a blank destination? I enjoy being well prepared."

"Enter my name instead of the destination for our next surprise excursion." He released her hand and stood beside the bed. "Get up, love. Meet me at the front door in twenty minutes."

* * *

An hour later, Mark exited the highway at the Tulsa International Airport exit.

The airport? Are we making an out-of-town trip? His Dallas meeting is next month.

"Why are we at the airport? Are we taking a short jaunt somewhere?"

"No. We are not," Mark said. "Relax. The location is nearby."

Her mind calmed when he passed by the airport entrance.

His speed decreased once they reached a corrugated steel building that resembled a warehouse. A black sign with gold lettering snagged her notice.

"Jump Town America. I can't read the smaller words in white paint." Eyes squinting, Pamela leaned forward. "The small print says, uh, sky diving instructions." She gazed at Mark. "As in free-falling from an airplane?"

"Pam—"

"Forget about risking our lives. I won't take lessons, and neither will you."

"Are you telling a grown man he can't choose his leisure activities?"

"When my husband decides to risk his life, yes. As Grandmother used to say when Skylar and I were school age, 'my foot is on top of my word.'"

Laughter rocked Mark's body. "Both of my grandmothers made the same quip. Guess pithy remarks are a grandma's prerogative. Don't worry. We won't be skydiving."

He led her to the building. "On this trip we dropped by to watch my co-workers hit the bull's-eye."

Pamela pointed to a black and red mat lying northwest of the parking lot. "No wonder someone placed a target inside the square. I hope their parachutes open up."

"We all do. Come inside and meet my staff."

In a sea of strangers, her gaze lit upon a known face. "Mrs. Tibbs is here. Yesterday she bought baked goods from Timeless Pastries. Plus, she left a generous tip."

"Right. I forgot to mention my administrative assistant's last name is Tibbs."

"Lavine Tibbs. Why didn't she introduce herself at the shop? I would have recognized her first name."

"She probably wanted to communicate with you without you knowing who she was. You did us proud, love. Techno Plus employees will flock to your shop. And they've only eaten your desserts. Wait until they taste your food."

When Pamela turned around, Lavine stood beside them. Pamela hugged her.

"Mark talks about you all the time. Thanks for supporting my bake shop."

"It's all in the family, dear. Techno Plus will alert sweets lovers everywhere that Timeless Pastries supplies fantastic treats."

Pamela touched Lavine's sleeve. "Ah. Thank you."

"Today you meet the real me. Yesterday you met the scatterbrain. The CEO demanded a specific dessert on the serving trays before lunch." She removed imaginary lint from a spotless denim jacket. "Mark is so proud of you and your accomplishments. He's a walking advert for your business."

Pamela clutched Mark's arm and smiled at him. "My husband is my biggest supporter. He expanded Timeless Pastries from a commercial kitchen into a retail bakery, slash café."

"Then he did a fantastic job all around." Lavine turned away when a gray-haired man flanked by six young adults called her name.

"On my way, honey." She touched Pamela's arm. "That's my husband, Stan. We'll talk later."

"Do you hear that sound?" Mark craned his neck toward the window. "An airplane's approaching fast. The daredevils will make their first jump. Four of my co-workers are headed outside the building to watch the action. Let's mingle with my team."

A thin man with curly, sandy hair pointed an accusing finger at the couple once they joined the group. "Mark brought the pastry lady to mock us eating doughnut holes."

A protruding belly overflowed a middle-aged man's pants. "Your treats taste better than this morning's pasty snack. I'm eating lunch at Timeless Pastries on Monday."

Pamela beamed. "Thanks. We look forward to seeing you."

As an airplane hovered overhead, a yellow spotlight highlighted a black and red circular bull's-eye.

One by one, six daredevils took the plunge. Two of the men worked at Techno Plus. A tall woman used a megaphone and called each jumper by name. None of the risk-takers hit their target. Trailing parachutes behind them, each skydiver high-fived the other jumpers as they landed.

One of the jumpers approached Mark. "Do you think you'll take the plunge?" he asked.

Mark shook his head. "My wife already told me that I can't."

"That's rough," the man said, shaking his head. "Come on inside. We are about to celebrate. The skydiving school supplies food for friends and families of those skydiving."

Lavine laughed when Mark glanced at her. "Stan's contract with the caterer ends in December."

* * *

"My team raved about how down to earth my wife is," Mark told Pamela on the drive home.

"Down to earth. I've heard the saying before without knowing what it means."

"Realistic and unpretentious. They congratulated me for having a well-grounded entrepreneur for my wife."

"So your co-workers think I'm a realistic, unpretentious, knowledgeable, and rational person?"

Mark laughed. "I see you know what well-grounded means."

"Tell them I said thank you very much."

She faced the passenger window. "I think I'll take a nap until we reach home."

He touched her knee. "Is everything okay? You became very quiet after the jump."

That was because their lives had flashed before her eyes. She was unhappy with the couple's relationship and didn't see significant changes in their future. Anna had told her to deal with the Jessica incident. Pamela had thought she had. Now she realized Mark hadn't apologized. He'd explained his actions and asked her to overlook them. No wonder it was difficult to forget what he had done.

She wanted her baby born into a home imbued with trust and love.

Could she trust God and distrust Mark's self-serving disposition?

He exited the highway. "In January Timeless pastries will receive the skydiving school's catering contract. Who knows where that project might lead us." His fingers drummed the steering wheel when Pamela didn't respond. "All we do is work and more work. Let's steer this train onto a social track before our baby arrives."

"Agreed. No more business discussions today. Opening the Shiatown branch clipped Timeless Pastries' wings. My innovation hat is off. Mellie and I will keep the business steady."

Mark looked at Pamela longer than was appropriate for prudent driving. "Timeless Pastries waving a white flag never entered my mind. I want one exclusive weekday for us. You choose the day."

"Wednesday. Will we go out or stay at home?" she asked.

"Let's take turns doing both."

Chapter Twenty-One

Two weeks later, Pamela kept vigil at the front window, nitpicking their preplanned evening. Her uncertainty about going to the Prentises' house for dinner contrasted with Mark's indifference. Their folks had readily agreed to come. Only Melinda and Skylar had refused the invitation.

"Our folks are pulling into the Prentises' driveway one car behind the other. We can join them in ten minutes."

"Why wait ten minutes? The sooner we eat dinner, the quicker we can leave."

"Too bad guest protocol doesn't work that way. Okay. Make it five." She counted to three hundred out loud.

Mark chuckled. "Sometimes I worry about you."

Pamela wrinkled her nose at him and picked up the items on the sofa. "Purse. Shades. Cherry crumb cake. Okay. Ready."

She made her way to Mark and laughed when he shook his head.

He opened the front door wider. "This visit will put the charade behind us. This is my first and only visit next door."

The couple strolled across the walkway to their neighbors' house.

Pamela glanced at the empty house across the road. Her other neighbor had said the senior Prentises had left South Town early for their yearly Houston hibernation. No wonder their son was at home more often during the evening. Why did Victor marry a woman who required a short leash to behave herself?

Mark held her hand and rang the doorbell. "Hello," he said when their host opened the door, dressed in gray chinos and a peach polo shirt.

"Good evening," Victor said. "Come inside. Your parents are on the back deck."

Mark grinned. "Are we late? Or did our parents arrive early?"

Victor ushered the couple into the house. "From where I stand, all our guests are right on time."

While he led the couple through the house, Pamela checked out the design.

The décor proved too ornate for her taste. She did like the Mediterranean-style kitchen's earthy tones.

Victor kept up a steady stream of chatter as they headed outside.

Lively conversations greeted the couple when they reached the back deck.

Victor sat on a bronze chaise and talked business with their fathers. Valerie and Celeste exclusively chatted with Jessica. They skillfully alternated between asking questions and issuing compliments while the younger woman cheerily played along.

A different woman presented herself at dinner that day. Jessica had perfected the elegant hostess role. Mark's old girlfriend displayed an eloquence Pamela had doubted Jessica possessed. Victor Prentis appeared to have coached his wife in appropriate social etiquette.

A jittery stomach alerted Pamela someone was watching her. She looked up to see seven pairs of eyes staring at her. What suddenly made the only silent person sitting on the deck the center of everyone's attention?

Celeste's gaze fastened upon their hostess. "Ed and I are pleased Mark and Pam finally got it right."

"Their little detours didn't faze us," Ed said. "Foolish behavior does reach its limits with intelligent people."

Jessica's glittery eyes contradicted her gracefully curved lips. "I'm surprised Timeless Pastries receives such raves. Pam never struck me as a businesswoman or a baker."

Steven's eyebrow quirked. "My daughter has diverse interests. She is proficient in each one."

"Yes," Valerie said. "My stepdaughter and son-in-law turned a commercial kitchen into a charming café and retail bakery."

"In less than six weeks," Celeste added.

Pamela breathed easier knowing their folks were on guard tonight. All slights to her were dutifully recognized. She stole a quick peek at Victor, who appeared to relish the performance. He had intentionally placed his wife in the hot seat and sat on the sidelines, but only to a certain degree. Was he teaching his wife how to fend for herself in social settings?

For dinner, Jessica served a wonderful Mexican meal al fresco. After the group finished eating, everyone except for Pamela headed to the conversation area.

Pamela rose from her chair. "You all finish your conversation. I'll tidy up."

She cleared off the table and threw napkins into the slate-gray trash can. Next she piled plates, glasses, and eating utensils onto a rattan serving tray and headed across the deck.

Jessica called her before she reached the door. "Let me help you. We can make one trip count."

Celeste reached in front of Jessica and picked up the cake plate. "Entertain your guests. We'll just be a minute."

Jessica thanked Celeste, then accepted her husband's outstretched hand. She sat next to Victor on the glider.

Within thirty minutes everyone went home.

Victor and Jessica escorted their guests outside.

"Tonight's outcome is more than I expected," Victor said.

Steven nodded as he opened the passenger door for Valerie. "How about a follow-up lunch at Timeless Pastries? Ed. Victor. Will this week work for you?"

"I'm free on Thursday at noon," Ed said.

"My schedule is free that afternoon," Victor added with a crisp nod.

Steven hugged Pamela on his way to the driver's side of his car. "I'll run the date by the medical center's procurer Monday."

"I look forward to your call," Victor said. "Jessica and I briefly met Jorgenson and his wife at a dinner party last year."

Ed steadied Celeste when she tripped over loose pebbles. "Keep me in the loop. Jessica, thank you for the delicious meal."

Jessica glanced at her neighbors before replying. "I enjoyed the company more than eating the food."

Mark spoke under his breath, "Right."

"Goodnight, everyone," Pamela broke in, hoping no one had heard him.

"Great night," Mark added.

Pamela and Mark waved at everyone then trooped across the lawn.

* * *

One late September evening, Pamela trekked down the street wearing a lightweight silver jogging suit. She loved to reflect on her life as she walked around the neighborhood.

Her business was doing fine, but her marriage still caused Pamela problems.

The couple didn't mesh in significant areas. Her friends had recently invited her on a canoe trip for summer's end. Mark railed when Pamela accepted the invitation, saying her pregnancy was too far along to take a canoe trip. Dr. Yeardley had said a canoe trip on gentle water provided maximum mind and body relief. She had only voiced one restriction, not lifting the canoe, which was a no-brainer.

The standoff clearly displayed his obstinate attitude. Her husband didn't know when to back down. She ended up reneging on the canoe excursion. The couple attended a cookout at the park with his friends that day instead.

Mark's determination to know their baby's gender prevailed. The couple expected their baby boy in five months.

Cementing a love-centered relationship remained her top priority.

Victor greeted Pamela on her fourth trip by his house on her walk.

Busy thinking about her issues with Mark, she hadn't noticed him standing beside his open car door.

She stopped beside him. "Hello, neighbor. Is work keeping you busy?"

Victor gave her a wide grin. He appeared more lighthearted than ever. What a welcome change.

The wide grin broadened. "Home and work often conflict. I deal with life as situations present themselves."

Pamela laughed. "Somehow I thought you might say that."

A light gleamed in his eyes. "I ate lunch with your father last week. My company might strike a spectacular deal with the medical center."

"Dad doesn't manage the business side. Mr. Jorgenson handles procurement."

"Steven's influence reaches farther than you may think. He's an astute businessman. Speaking of business, my company is a few blocks away from your Shiatown location. I go there often and met the lovely Anna Hendrix. I hear your South Town location offers catering. My secretary will contact her for the information."

"Perfect. I will tell her that we're neighbors."

Victor laughed. "Be sure to mention my wife waved a white flag."

That would help, Pamela thought.

Victor squinted through sunrays that beamed directly at them. "I live by my convictions. Only a few of us brave hearts buck decorum."

"Are those your personal beliefs? Or the prevalent popular view?"

"I never put stock in other people's opinions. My words validate themselves."

Even with the odd word choices, Pamela knew Victor rebelled against the status quo. Was this a lead-in to talk about his wife?

"How do you defy standard principles?" she asked.

"By going against the grain. For instance, I am a family man who won t have children. I remedied that hindrance years ago."

Pamela's feet wobbled under her legs. Their conversation had veered off course. His baffling personality became more inscrutable by the moment.

"Our dinner verified that you're the type of woman I thought I'd married."

She tried not to react to his comment. "No, sir. You're an excellent character judge. Victor Prentis married a woman like himself."

A full-throated laugh bellowed through the air. "Not quite. Although Jessica did steal my heart. Such as it is."

Pamela's shoulder muscles relaxed. She found herself back on solid ground.

"I understand how thieves of the heart function. Mark stole mine the first day we met. He hooked me and I never jumped off."

Keen eyes peered through her. "You are delightful."

The screen door hit a planter on the porch when the Prentises' front door flung open. Jessica stood in the doorway dressed in black jeans and a ruby-red tank top. Her two-inch-heeled foot tapped the doorstep.

"The pot roast you requested for dinner is getting cold."

Victor turned to Pamela. "I'm pleased we had a chance to talk. I see your husband coming toward your driveway."

Jessica stepped onto the porch. "I prefer eating hot food."

"So do I," he called to her. "It was a pleasure, Pam. Give your husband my regards. I hope our chat didn't keep you from cooking dinner."

"Mom dropped off some barbecue for us. Enjoy your dinner and evening."

"Those are my exact plans. Enjoy yours."

Victor waved to Mark on the stride to his wife.

Pamela strolled across the lawn as her husband watched her.

"I spent too much time chatting with Victor. I won't take my last lap around the block today. We're eating a picnic meal this evening. Mom and Nathan grilled us a barbecue dinner."

"Your married mother is still providing her children with food. She should let her grown kids fend for themselves."

"She's also cooking meals for two extra families. I hope Nathan pulls half of the weight."

Mark wrapped an arm around her waist, leading her toward the house. "Don't form opinions about their relationship. Let them discover what works best for them." He gave an uneven smile. "Hey, what's new at the Prentis house?"

"Victor unloaded a significant amount of random facts." Pamela unlocked the door and stepped inside. "He said he loves Jessica, but he said I am the type of woman he thought he married."

Spontaneous laughter shook her body when Mark's mouth hung open. "I understand why you're shocked. Listen to the other things he said." She ticked another finger. "He never puts stock in other people's opinions. His words validate themselves. And, Jessica stole his heart. Such as it is. Oh. He had a vasectomy too."

Mark rubbed his chin, chuckling. "I'm at a loss as to Victor's motive. This time he supplied personal information for an unknown reason."

Following Pamela into the kitchen, he leaned against the counter while she removed a platter from the counter and a salad and sliced kiwis from the refrigerator, setting the food on the table. "All done," she said. "Sit down and bless the food."

She bowed her head and prayed behind Mark.

The couple chatted some more about their neighbors while they ate dinner.

"Mmm," Pamela said. "This homemade barbecue sauce is full of flavor. I bet Mom made this spicy masterpiece."

"Do you ever side with anyone other than your mother?" Mark asked.

"No."

"Just remember to side with me sometimes," her husband said.

* * *

A week later, Mark finished a two-thousand-piece Nova Scotia jigsaw puzzle after dinner. Working at the pawn shops three evenings this week had left him little time to finish it. He leaned on his left elbow. "This wonderful picture is worthy of framing. I see why people shellac and frame their finished puzzles," he said. "Can you imagine this tranquil scene on our living room wall?"

Pamela lay her book facedown on her lap. "No. I can't." Her eyes twinkled. "But I do admire your determination and drive in everything you do."

"You're becoming quite the flatterer," Mark said. He pulled open a cabinet drawer filled with unopened puzzle boxes. "I'll downsize to five hundred pieces on this go-round."

She crawled next to him. "Choose a puzzle with flowers and I'll help you finish in two days."

216

"Okay. Thanks for the promise, love."

Mark sorted through various boxes until finding the correct one. The hothouse orchid blooms drew him in. Placing the box on the cabinet top, he pushed the unchosen puzzle boxes back inside the cabinet and wagged a finger at his wife. "You will pay a penalty if you don't help me."

Pamela laughed. "Keep the penalty in line with leaving an unfinished jigsaw puzzle."

"You pledged assistance, supplied the deadline, and requested a specific category."

Pamela returned to the couch. "Do you ever give in graciously?"

Mark sat on the couch beside her. "I didn't ask for a notarized statement, but a promise is a promise."

"Name your pound of flesh," Pamela said.

"You will work daily on five consecutive puzzles of my choice." Grinning, he stuck out his hand. "Deal?"

"No. Forget about our working a puzzle together. I prefer reading a book and watching you complete each one. Unless I go out with friends. Everyone complains I don't hang out with them enough."

"Suggest they acquire new friendships. Speaking of being away from home, don't forget our trip to Dallas this Friday. Healthy Headways's IT staff will set up Tuesday's rollout over the weekend while I assist them."

"Every detail is prepared at the shop for an easy transition. Mellie will hang around the kitchen during the week I'm gone."

"Can you freeze enough products to carry both shop locations through the week?"

"We can try. It's a blessing having Sally bake full time. Don't forget Mom and Mellie can pitch in if they're needed." She kissed his lips. "I'm looking forward to our trip."

Mark smothered her face with kisses, then he sat at the low table. "I expect you to keep your promise to help me compete this puzzle before Thursday."

Why? You don't always keep your promises.

She rose from her seat and said, "I'm coming."

A quiet Pamela watched her husband mechanically line puzzle pieces on the table. Despite his busy hands, Mark seemed to wrestle with hidden problems. Was he devising tasks to keep her at home in the evenings? He hung out with friends after work if they called him while she had her pajamas on. He only declined to leave home if his wife hadn't settled in for the evening.

Mark grinned when Pamela fitted the first two puzzle pieces together. "I appreciate spending evenings alone." He hugged her.

Pamela returned the embrace. Yeah. Unless she had her pajamas on. Mark didn't mind leaving the house if he thought his wife would stay at home.

* * *

On Saturday morning, the couple held hands as they stepped out of the hotel elevator and headed to the front desk. The couple arrived at the hotel the day before. "My wife is sightseeing this morning. Do you provide guide maps of Uptown attractions?"

"And shopping locations," Pamela added.

The tall, reed-thin man behind the desk had red curls that bobbed with his head. He extracted a color brochure and a black and white pamphlet from underneath the counter. "You can't go wrong in Dallas's West Village. One day isn't long enough to view attractions."

Pamela reached for the information Mark accepted. "Thank you. Good thing we're here for a week."

She scanned the highlights when the couple left the building. "Since we ate dinner in the hotel restaurant last night, I'll scout a new place for our dinner this evening." She glanced at Mark. "Are you excited?"

"Yes. I haven't worked hands-on at an off-site location since the year I started at Techno Plus. One of our team members normally makes these trips. They contact me if there's a problem. The company will go live at eight on Tuesday morning."

Her gaze searched his face. "Do you foresee problems?"

"None. I handpicked two of our top people to fly down if necessary."

"I'm sure they won't need to," Pamela said. "My husband is always on the business ball. Enjoy your day."

"Always, love. Keep in touch."

The couple kissed on the corner, then parted ways.

Chapter Twenty-Two

Uptown Dallas outdid South Town's four-mile strip. Pamela skipped visits to large attractions and busied herself with McKinley street boutiques. Finding a pair of cowboy boots she thought Mark might like, she whipped out her cell phone but couldn't enter her passcode. The screen remained dark. How could her cell phone be out of charge? It had charged all night.

Hopefully Mark won't try contacting me and won't worry if he does.

She forged ahead with her planned shopping expedition. Trendy local boutiques filled the immediate area. For lunch she stopped at a promising-looking outdoor café. She knew trying new eateries could uncover a goldmine of valuable information as a food-service owner.

While eating lunch in a breezy gazebo, Pamela chatted with three generations who sat at the next table. She told the women about Timeless Pastries and dined on a flavor-filled meal. A tangy lime vinaigrette dressing added a punch to the salmon and spinach salad.

Setting her fork aside, she signaled the server.

"I'm truly stuffed," she told the women as she waited on the server. "The spicy salad hit the spot. Although the food is terrific, the lively conversation proved better. Glad we met, ladies."

"We're glad we met you," the younger woman said, while the other women agreed.

As she went to pay, Pamela realized her bank card was missing. Staring into space, she twisted her wedding rings. Her last stop had been at a specialty bookstore. She had purchased several books and kept up a running conversation with the owner. Another valuable lesson was learned. Pay attention. Talk less.

Did I lose my bank card? No way. That card must be here.

She searched through each compartment of her purse several times. As her spirit plummeted, she noticed the three women who sat at the next table stood beside her.

"Is there a problem?" the younger lady asked.

"Can't find her credit card," the cashier quipped. The doubt on his face filled his voice.

The woman who wore a floral pantsuit stepped forward. "Don't panic, young lady. Slow down and go through your purse again."

Pamela searched her purse again. Nothing. She had lost her bank card somewhere. Her shoulders drooped as her heartbeat accelerated.

I'm stranded in a strange city and can't contact Mark.

Blinking back tears, she zipped her purse. Her nails clicked together.

The oldest lady came closer. "Try taking everything out and look through each item one at a time."

She started by pulling out her black business card case. Eureka! She had placed the bank card into that case and not inside her wallet. Thank God the women had encouraged her to check each item in her purse carefully.

"Thank you all so much. I'd almost lost hope. Please let me buy your meals."

"That's not necessary," they said together.

"Where are you headed next?" one of the women asked.

"More shopping. Then I'll meet my husband at the hotel. Thanks again. I appreciate your concern."

Pamela waved as the women drove off the parking lot, and then she crossed the street.

* * *

Mark stored his cell phone in his jacket pocket. Pamela hadn't answered or returned any of his six calls. She always responded to his messages within an hour. He felt sure some mishap prevented her from calling him. He retrieved the cell phone then shoved it back into his pocket. Calling the police at this point was overkill.

"Okay, guys. It's four o'clock. I'll see you all bright and early in the morning. Eight o'clock."

The computer and information system manager walked Mark to the lobby. "We're looking forward to the rollout in the morning," the grinning man said.

"Likewise. Your excellent team is well prepared. Two Techno Plus specialists are on call if needed."

Mark prayed for his wife's safety the entire trip to the hotel.

He entered an empty suite twenty minutes later.

Within ten minutes Pamela limped into the hotel room, laden with multiple bags.

Mark quickly met her inside the door. He removed the bags from her hands and plonked them onto the nearest chair.

"You're hurt. What happened? I called you six times in the last two hours."

Pamela shut the door with a snap. Heat suffused her face and arms.

"My cell phone lost its charge. I'm having difficulty walking after a little fall. But at least I made it back here."

He helped her to the couch and knelt before her. "Tell me what happened."

"I was walking to the hotel and a man in front of me almost fell. As I moved to help him, I tripped over his cane and stumbled over scattered rocks near the curb."

She lightly rubbed her wrist. "I broke my fall with my right hand. My knees hit the ground and I might have twisted my right ankle."

"The fact that you're walking means the ankle isn't broken." Mark manipulated her ankle while Pamela grimaced. "There's minimal swelling. You'll have a nasty bruise by tomorrow."

He sat beside her on the couch. "How are you and our little one really doing?"

"The baby moved earlier. He and I are fine," Pamela said.

"Is your cell phone in your pocket or in your purse?"

As she removed the cell phone from her purse, each movement caused her excruciating pain.

Her husband fiddled with her cell phone until the logo appeared on the screen. He placed the cell phone on the table.

"You had a full charge. Next time, try removing the battery and then restarting it." Mark glanced at her. "How about wearing walking shoes to shop tomorrow instead of heels?"

Pamela grabbed her cell phone off the table and then rethought flouncing off. Hobblers couldn't make haughty exits.

"One-inch heels don't impede my walking."

"Evidently they do in emergencies. Please wear sensible walking shoes if you're able to go out tomorrow."

"Leave ... me ... alone. I'm in a lot of pain. I can live without your snide remarks."

"Protect yourself and our unborn child. I care about what happens to my family."

Mark removed his cell phone from his pocket when it rang. He listened for a while, then he sat up straighter. He studied his wife with startled eyes.

"Okay, Mother. I'll book us the first flight out."

Pamela's heart sank. Her peculiar unease last month, when she and Mark had taken his parents for a walk on the Amazing Facts Trail, had come to pass. Rubbing the area around her knee, she waited for Mark to lower the cell phone.

"What happened?"

"The paramedics are at the pawn shop. Father is unconscious. They believe he suffered a heart attack." Mark hesitated, shaking his head. "Mother's picking up my grandparents then heading to the hospital."

He opened two suitcases on the bed. "Pack as quickly as you can."

New bouts of pain erupted as she shifted positions. She closed her eyes to keep from crying.

Easing off the cushion, Pamela hobbled toward the bathroom, moaning silently to herself. Multiple aches and pains had escalated since she had entered the hotel room.

"You should stay in Dallas, Mark. Pack my luggage for me. I'll stay overnight at the hospital until they discharge your father."

Mark stared at her. "Earlier, you fell in the street. You have a bruised and swollen wrist. That ankle looks nasty. You're in obvious discomfort. You and the baby—"

"Are fine. Take care of my flight arrangements while I tidy up."

Once inside the bathroom, she closed the door and balanced her body on the tub's edge. Her kneecaps moved when she touched them. Her heart raced. Pamela immediately called her mother. It was hard keeping the pain out of her voice while she talked to Anna. But she did, and she never mentioned falling, or that her kneecaps had moved when she touched them—although her mother repeatedly asked if Pamela was all right.

* * *

Mark met her at the door with her overnight bag and a small suitcase. "A Tulsa flight will leave Love Field in ninety minutes. Your cab is waiting out front."

Barely able to walk, she hobbled to the elevator, trying not to cry.

The cab driver pulled up to the lobby door when he saw them. Pamela slid into the back seat but couldn't slide over. Unable to lift her head without her entire body aching, her chin rested on her chest. "What are you doing?" she asked when Mark entered the backseat from the other side.

"Riding to the airport with my wife. You're traveling alone against my better judgment."

Her eyes closed. Nothing erased the pain from her mind. Exhaling, she cleared her throat.

"Why? God is here now. He'll travel with me. And He'll be there when I arrive. Stop worrying. Nathan is picking me up from the airport."

"I'm glad someone in the family will pick you up." He smiled down at her. "Pam, thanks for insisting I repair the breach with my parents. And for the warning the evening we took them walking on the trail. You saw this unfortunate day coming," Mark said. "I'm happy I didn't blow off your concern and cancelled my plans with friends to walk with them. Thank God I listened to you. How do you stay focused on our families?"

Pamela hoped her shrug was an adequate response.

At the airport, she sniffled quietly to herself but rested her body on Mark at the security checkpoint.

She hadn't had time to buy a pain reliver or check her bags, and the pain was growing more intense. She pushed her body away from Mark's support. "Now both sides of my body ache."

"Don't go alone. We can both fly out on a later flight."

"I'm sorry. I shouldn't complain."

"The severe pain is speaking for you."

Her lips curved into a lopsided grin. "Love you much. Do not fret about your father or anyone. Pray. Finish your assignment and come home."

* * *

Pamela disappeared, inching along the concourse, carrying her overnight case and a weekend bag. She had to stop several times because of the pain.

Mark glared at the security personnel. He understood rigorous airport safety, but if he could've helped his wife to the plane, it might've lessened his guilt.

His legs buckled underneath him. Cads let their injured wives cover their spouse's responsibilities. Techno Plus's new campaign would survive with the proper backup. He had already preselected a qualified team. He had been selfish to let his wife fly home alone.

He whipped out his cell phone. Each call went to voicemail. Unanswered calls to Pamela meant she had boarded the flight. Mark called his mother-in-law.

* * *

An hour later, Pamela inched her way off the plane. Every part of her hurt at this point. Even her earlobes had surrendered to an unrelenting throb. At least her baby moved again right before the plane took off. Throughout the flight she cuddled her belly, thanking God for protecting her baby.

As she made her way toward the airport exit, the overnight case and small suitcase slid from her grip. People rushing behind her practically ran Pamela over. A young man wearing a backpack retrieved the cases.

"Let me carry your luggage. Is someone picking you up?"

Pamela gasped at the searing wrist ache. "My stepfather should be waiting outside. Do you have more luggage you need to carry?"

"I travel light," the man said. "Your limp is worse than it was when you boarded the plane in Dallas. Your wrist is bruised. That right ankle looks ghastly. I noticed you rubbing your abdomen on the plane."

"I'm trusting God my baby is fine."

"God, huh? Think he'll listen?" He held out an arm. "Hold on to me. It won't take long."

She glanced at him, but her lips refused to smile. "I quoted scripture throughout the flight. I knew I would safely reach my destination. Jesus will never leave nor forsake me. My God is always with me," she said through tears. "Disasters always work out for His glory and my good. The difficult part is remembering those truths within the trial." She brushed tears from her cheek with the hand that held her purse. "Thanks for helping me. I'm Pamela Simon. What's your name?"

"Kirby. Dennison. You can share my cab if your ride isn't here."

"Ow!" Standing still, she closed her eyes and took a breath. "Okay. Let's go. Sorry I keep stopping."

"It's amazing you've progressed so well this far. You need a wheelchair. Seriously," Kirby added when her head shook.

Pamela scanned the lobby once they reached the baggage claim area. No sign of her stepfather. Anna had said that Nathan would pick her up at the airport. Her mother had repeated the same promise in her last text message.

A khaki-clad man pushing a wheelchair headed their way.

"My stepfather brought a wheelchair. I didn't tell anyone at home that I had fallen."

Kirby stood still, and Pamela waited beside him.

Her stepfather quickly reached them.

Studying Pamela, he spoke to Kirby. "Nathan Hendrix. Thanks for helping Pam."

"Her encouraging words helped me more."

Nathan secured his stepdaughter in the chair, then he reached for her luggage.

"I'll carry the cases to your car," Kirby said.

Nathan's gray sedan proved a welcome sight. Pamela felt better just looking at the vehicle.

Kirby stowed the suitcases onto the back seat. Nathan placed the aching Pamela into the front passenger side.

Her sitting down unleashed another bout of pain. "I'm achy all over. Could you secure my seatbelt?"

Nathan complied, reclining the seat as far back as possible. He touched her forehead. "No fever."

Nathan held out a hand that Kirby shook. "Her mother and I appreciate your compassion and concern."

Kirby nodded at Pamela. "Hey, for the record, your promoting Jesus during a personal crisis is worth remembering. Your witness reminded me of conversations with a cherished aunt. So long, Pamela Simon."

"Thanks, Kirby Dennison." She tried to smile through the pain. "God loves you."

"Perhaps He does," Kirby said. Waving, he crossed the street to a vacant cab.

Nathan faced his stepdaughter after he slid into the driver's seat. "I called Anna when I saw you shuffle down the concourse in obvious distress. Your mother wants you to go to the emergency room in Tulsa if necessary. I believe you should see your doctor or a physician your father approves. Think you can make the trip to South Town?"

"Yes. To visit my father-in-law in the hospital."

Pulling off from the curb, he glanced at Pamela when she whimpered. "I commend your courage, but I also hear misery in your voice. Your face is filled with pain."

"Is Mom still at the hospital with my mother-in-law?"

"She is. Along with Ed's parents."

"Do you have good news to tell me?" Pamela asked.

"Your father-in-law is conscious, though he's still in the emergency room. Things are looking better for Ed than before you left Dallas."

"Thank God. What's the prognosis?"

"They don't think Ed suffered a heart attack. His EKG and echocardiogram came out normal. They keep running lab work because certain cardiac enzymes are slightly elevated."

Pamela gave a loud sigh and closed her eyes. "We'll take Father home after they read the latest test results."

"Ed isn't going home tonight. They're waiting on a room to admit him into the hospital."

She opened one eye. "Why are they admitting him if he didn't have a heart attack?"

"Something caused Ed to lose consciousness. They're eliminating the usual culprits. The scope will widen after those test results register normal readings. Have patience. The trauma team is first rate."

Pamela maneuvered her purse closer to her left hand. "I'll text Mark the good news. I'm trying to keep my husband on the job in Dallas. It broke his heart not to come with me to see his folks."

Nathan glanced at her. "Mark's mother keeps Mark updated regarding Ed's condition." He hesitated. "Should you be texting? We heard an account of your accident. Your husband is anxious about your safety."

"The baby and I are fine. Ouch! Please unzip the side pocket on my purse."

Nathan retrieved the cell phone and laid it on her lap. "Your joints are swollen, and you have multiple bruises on your hand and foot."

"Mark overdramatized the fall."

"I don't think he did based on the look of those bruises. Your family has a right to show concern. A five-month pregnant woman falling is a big deal."

"Mom always overreacts whenever she thinks I'm injured. Mark will probably call me before the message is barely sent." She pushed the send button.

Her cell phone immediately pinged.

Pamela grimaced at her stepfather before taking the call.

Finished mumbling to Mark, she lay the cell phone on her lap. The tiniest movement caused severe pain.

"Don't mind me. I'll close my eyes for a while. Talk if you want to."

Anna shook Pamela awake forty minutes later. Nathan had parked the car in the cardiology wing of the parking lot. The hospital had already transferred her father-in-law into a room.

"How are you, babe?" Anna moved aside when someone walked up behind her.

Steven appeared behind his ex-wife, pushing a transport chair. "Let's get you inside the building."

"I won't go to the emergency room for any reason."

"No one asked you to go there," Steven said sternly. "Cassie Yeardley is waiting to examine you in a vacant room inside the cardiology wing."

"Mom! Who called my doctor?"

Anna placed an arm under Pamela's elbow to help her out of the car. "Skylar. We've interrupted your doctor's weekend off. Don't make her wait longer than is necessary."

Chapter Twenty-Three

Dr. Brinkman, an orthopedic surgeon, walked beside Pamela while Dr. Yeardley pushed the transport chair that carried their pain-ridden patient down the hallway. They stopped outside Ed's room. Anna and Steven waited beside the door.

"Steven, your lovely daughter schooled me on my job performance," Dr. Brinkman said.

Pamela remained silent. Her throbbing body consumed all of her attention.

Steven opened a door across the hall. "In here. We can talk privately inside."

Inside the room, Dr. Yeardley touched Pamela's left shoulder as she spoke to Steven. "I ran a complete battery of tests. Fetal heart tones are normal. Pam should call me if she experiences vaginal bleeding, embryonic fluid discharge, or uterine tenderness." She squeezed Pamela's shoulder when Pamela glanced at her. "You're a healthy young woman. None of the mentioned scenarios will occur. Don't take pain medication stronger than acetaminophen."

"However, Pam has a sprained wrist, a grade-three ankle sprain, and patellar contusions on both knees," said Dr. Brinkman. "She needs the stirrup brace on her ankle for two to three weeks. I don't know how she managed to walk at all. As we discussed earlier, her wrist and both ankles will require a brace." He studied his patient then gave detailed instructions for her recovery, physical therapy, and office visit.

"Cassie, Clyde, thank you both for taking time from your families to treat Pam," Steven said.

"Yes. Thank you, Cassie, Dr. Brinkman," Anna added. "We appreciate you both giving your time."

Dr. Yeardley squeezed Pamela's shoulders again. "I believe Pam will be fine, even though trauma can have untold consequences on pregnancies. From an OB-GYN standpoint, both mother and baby are doing well."

Both doctors retreated down the hall while Anna and Steven glared at their daughter.

"The orthopedic surgeon cut my new jeans to the knee. Who called him?"

Anna studied Pamela's bruised and swollen legs, knees, and arm. "You're experiencing tremendous discomfort whether you admit it or not. The pain is evident in your whiny voice."

"Rational adults don't make foolish decisions," Steven said. "You should have gone to urgent care before flying home. Grade-three ankle sprain. The torn ligament is the result of your carelessness. It should've been attended to before you left Dallas."

Anna kissed her cheek. "Celeste and Ed's mother will stay with Ed until he gets released."

Changing positions bathed Pamela's forehead and upper lip in sweat. "I'm glad my father-in-law is doing better. Since Mark's grandmother is staying with his mother, I'll catch a flight back out to Dallas tomorrow."

"Mark is on a job assignment, not a vacation," Anna said. "You look ready to pass out. Those injuries require constant care that I'll provide."

Steven held Pamela's wrist in his fingers, studying his watch. "Pain has elevated your heart rate. Have you taken pain medication since the fall?"

"No. I didn't have time to buy medication."

Steven removed a medicine bottle and three packages from his jacket pocket. He passed the items to Anna and looked back at Pamela. "The crutches will be delivered soon, but you can't use them until your wrist heals. Let Ed know you're doing well, and then go home with your mother." He looked at Anna. "Do you have a blood pressure monitor and thermometer at the house?"

"We'll pick up those items on the drive home."

"Take her blood pressure an hour before you give the second dose. Only two capsules every six hours. I'll come check on her in the morning."

"A visit isn't necessary. Sleep and rest will facilitate Pam's healing."

Steven froze. "You have a problem with me checking on my daughter? If so, Pamela's going home with me."

"Pam's restricted to forty-eight hours of bed rest. Four areas require ice packs for twenty minutes every four hours."

"Look—"

"I will call you if her condition changes."

"See that you do. My daughter's health is vital to me." Steven's flinty eyes stared at Anna.

Skylar walked into the room. "Dad, I'll drop by Mom's house in the morning."

He took the braces from Anna and wrapped one around his sister's wrist and knees.

"Well, sis, you banged up yourself pretty good," he said.

Tears rolled down her cheeks even with her eyelids squeezed tight.

"Are you okay?" Anna asked once Skylar completed the task.

"Pressure from the braces has eased the pain somewhat." She took multiple deep breaths. "I'm breathing easier too. I think I hyperventilated a few times on the airplane." She glanced at the man who had turned his scowl from Anna to her. "And no, Dad. I didn't request a paper bag." She sighed and looked at Skylar. "How's my father-in-law doing?"

Skylar stuffed the empty packages inside his jacket pocket. "They're still running tests, but he's stable and wondering how his daughter-in-law is faring. Your color has improved since you got here."

"How would you know? You haven't seen me since I came."

"I have, you've just been in too much pain to notice."

Wincing when her head bobbed, Pamela refocused on Anna. "Mom, will you check available flights out of Tulsa for tomorrow? Make one for the afternoon. I should be feeling better by then."

Steven swung around at the door. "What part of bed rest for at least forty-eight hours and no travel until your doctor's visit didn't you understand? It takes torn ligaments eight to twelve months to heal. You will probably start physical therapy after the doctor visit."

Her head hung. Pamela felt like she was fifteen again. She turned to Skylar, who viewed his sister through half-closed eyes.

"Look," he began, "don't turn a painful inconvenience into an avoidable complication—which you have already accomplished with the ankle."

"Oh, please. Can't you ever support my decisions? Mark is all alone in Dallas while his father is hospitalized for the first time in Mark's life."

Skylar leaned closer to her. "Help your husband by taking care of yourself and the baby."

Pamela lifted her hand. "Ow!" Glaring at him, she lightly touched her wrist. "See there; you made me move."

Her brother chuckled. "Thanks for proving my point. The kids want to see you. Are you up for youthful visitors tomorrow?"

"I will be by then. Maybe my aim for selflessness centered on fear of Mark being alone. I don't want anyone to worry about me."

"Thank you for thinking about us." Anna pushed the transport chair across the hall. "Let's make a quick visit to Ed so we can get you home."

Her father-in-law looked better than Pamela imagined a person who had passed out would. Many gadgets were attached to his body. Multiple monitors pinged and blinked on and off. Irene hovered over her son's bed. Ed's father, Fred, lounged on a recliner. Celeste perched on a chair by the window.

Ed gestured to his visitors. "Pass out cold and people will fall over themselves behaving civil."

Fred's head jerked toward his son. "Ed got his second wind. My son is feeling better."

"You look good," Pamela said. "Mark is worried about you."

Ed suddenly looked tired. "I was concerned about you. Thanks for coming home."

"I would've seen you sooner, but people wearing white coats interfered. Glad you're feeling better, though. Mark hated not coming with me."

"My boy cares about his old man." He eyed Celeste's bland expression then turned away. "Don't try to visit me tomorrow. Get yourself some rest."

Pamela beamed through the pain. "Yes, sir. See you real soon."

"Pam's restricted to bed rest for at least forty-eight hours." Anna pulled the transport chair backwards. "I'm bringing lunch tomorrow at noon. You look tired, Fred. We'll drop you off at home, and I'll bring you back tomorrow."

Fred eased out of the seat. "Thanks for the ride home. I'll drive myself back here in the morning."

Celeste met them at the door. "I'll walk you all to the parking lot."

* * *

Mark secured the cell phone between his ear and shoulder. Removing a pair of white denim jeans, black slacks, and two shirts from the closet, he packed casual clothes for his overnight trip.

"Thanks, Lavine. Your help is invaluable. ... It hasn't been easy, but circumstances might've been worse. ... AFib. His heart returned to normal rhythm without their intervention. They're running tests. ... He will remain in the hospital another day. Father hasn't had a physical since he was in his twenties."

Mark set the packed suitcase by the door. "A lifestyle change is important. ... Right. Slowing him down will take a miracle. God has more than one reserved per family. ... My wife's a real trooper. She's staying at her mother's house in Shiatown. ... Sure. I'll text you Anna's address. Pam will welcome your visit."

He sat on the bed as he gazed around the room. "Lavine, may I be candid? I trust you and your wise counsel. ... I made a brash mistake during my engagement to Pam. Pam became aware of the problem after the honeymoon. ... Forgetting my misstep isn't easy for either of us. Pray that God will strengthen our marriage. ... I won't give up. Tell Stan I will take him up on the offer. Goodnight."

Laying his cell phone on the desk, Mark checked the last item off his list.

His busy evening was paying off. Two hours after his first conversation with Lavine, his prepicked workforce was on a Dallas flight. They checked into the hotel at ten thirty. An early breakfast conference would jumpstart the morning.

Mark booked a flight to Tulsa for the morning and a return flight to Dallas on Monday evening.

After today's unsettling events, Mark admitted to himself that the Simon family required an overhaul. His father's health issues demanded family, business, and personal changes. The doctor had emphasized to Mark that stress overload had proved to be the culprit. Unless his father modified his work and personal routines, his physical decline would accelerate.

Countless fronts required wise decisions. No person remained exempt from Mark's inspection. Talks with Celeste tested Mark's personal resolve. Over their last telephone conversation, he requested facts regarding his parents' marriage. After an eerie silence, she had promised to provide him a full account.

Pamela's hobbling down the concourse carrying luggage recaptured his mind. So did his last talk with Anna when she confirmed his wife had fallen asleep for the night. Mark shook his head. His self-interest had endangered his wife's health.

He'd noticed the ugly bruises and swelling during the cab ride. Besides, his wife could hardly walk. A compassionate person would've instructed the driver to go to the emergency room. But not the man who lived to please himself. He had again let down the most important person in his life. Mark handed her the lead in Simon family matters that required his immediate attention. His self-centeredness had caused his wife agony and severe complications.

His hand scrubbed over his face as his body refused to relax. His character had received the final rebuke when Pamela put his welfare above her own

Mark had always detested changes that didn't personally benefit him. Her unexpected injury and Ed's sudden illness thrust him into survival mode. Once again, his wife endured hardship from another of his mismanaged problems.

Would Pamela forgive misguidance that affected her health?

Turning off the light, he stretched fully clothed across the bed.

Once again, only time would tell.

* * *

A light touch shook Pamela awake. Dim lighting infused the room.

Unlike earlier, only one side of her body throbbed.

She squinted her eyes to peer at Anna. "Mom, you're up again. I hate interrupting your rest."

"Delighted to help. It feels like old times. Remember when you sprained your wrist in-line skating? Or the time a softball beaned you on second base? Or the time you backflipped off the sliding board?" Anna laughed. "Need I continue?"

"No. I see the pattern. Those injuries didn't hurt as much as these do."

"Age. You whimpered in your sleep. It's time for more pain relievers. And then I'll ice you down. Let's take your blood pressure first."

Anna wrapped the blood pressure cuff around Pamela's upper arm.

When the monitor pinged, her mother unwrapped the cuff, then wrote the reading on a writing pad.

"Sit up, babe. The meds will lessen the pain."

Anna helped Pamela into a sitting position and then gave her medication and a glass of water.

Pamela swallowed the capsules then handed her mother the glass.

Anna placed the glass on a tray and removed the wrist and knee braces before she touched Pamela's ankle.

"Ow! Ooh! Searing pain. Please leave the brace on."

"I'll ice your wrist and knees first. We'll skip the ankle until the pills kick in."

Forty-five minutes later, Anna replaced the brace on Pamela's knees.

"Three down. One to go. Are you ready?"

Tense fingers gripped the sheets when her mother touched the brace. "Oh, my goodness. Ice me down later. Okay?"

"Concentrate on our conversation," Anna said. "Twenty minutes will pass fast enough."

Pamela covered her eyes, moaning. Moisture beaded on her face. Her ankle throbbed more than her wrist and knees had. Her hand had broken the fall. Her knees had hit the ground. She didn't remember her ankle being involved at all.

"I bet Nathan's ready to say goodbye to me," she said through clenched teeth. "I'm surprised he doesn't drive me to Dallas himself."

Anna shushed her. "He was happy to help and pick you up. Although the war wounds from the fall and the complications from the travel caused us worry."

"I shouldn't have traveled. But how could I remain in Dallas? My in-laws required personal care their son couldn't provide."

"You called me because you knew I would go to the hospital. You should've gone to urgent care and then come home."

"I didn't expect you to stay overnight like I would have, just long enough to keep his mother company until I arrived."

"Your presence overnight wasn't needed. Irene had decided to stay with her son and Celeste during the night. And by the way, four pairs of eyes lit up when you rolled into the room. Your husband's family truly likes you."

Thank God they do.

Pamela gazed at her mother, trying to find the words to convey her true feelings. Unpleasant memories had tortured her throughout the night. Distasteful thoughts chipped away at her kindhearted act of telling Mark to remain in Dallas. Even though Mark had made the on-site visit for a lucrative contract, he could have turned the assignment over to his handpicked team and returned to South Town with her.

Pamela had recognized her grave error while she changed clothes in the hotel bathroom. She called her mother when her kneecaps moved, but she failed to tell Anna what had happened. Plus, the pain throughout her body had intensified. But backing out on her promise to go back to South Town at the last minute would have disappointed her husband.

Despite his denials, Pamela could tell that Mark had wanted her to travel alone. Pure and simple. He remained in Dallas with scant resistance. Did he miss her obvious injuries? Several people at the airport voiced concern about her traveling. But not her husband. After she insisted on taking his place, the man who had hated her to go anywhere without him had instantly caved

Anna's palm touched Pamela's forehead until she sat back and stared at her daughter.

"No comment? Feeling okay?"

Pamela's eyes briefly closed. She had picked an awkward time for retrospection.

"The Simons aren't a thoughtful family," she finally said. "But I do love Mark's folks, although I never imagined I would feel that way." A loud sigh escaped her lips. "Too bad each Simon is strong-willed and opinionated. No wonder Mark fights to have his way in every instance. They probably buried him under their ideas and expectations when he was younger."

"Could be. But the boy grew into a man. As we stake our independence, we experience sorrow. We learn. We grow. As your grandmother often says ..."

"I know. Toughen up the rump. Life goes on."

Anna laughed. "I see you're catching on."

"Mark lives and breathes business. Pursuing an IT career thwarted his family's wishes."

"He admitted to making a major judgment error? His owning the mistake surprises me."

"He didn't make a confession. I just comprehend my husband better these days. I thought I knew every detail about Mark. Likes. Dislikes. Character. Sad to say, I had only scratched the surface regarding a complicated man. I'm grasping his personality better now." Her hand grasped Anna's. "Remember the day you rescued me?"

"On the day you arrived home from your honeymoon?"

Pamela nodded. "Your opinion at Bianchi's was accurate. My husband projected a confidence he hadn't felt. The world saw an extrovert scaling the heights unafraid, yet fear directed Mark's steps more than bravery ever had."

"Which shouldn't have surprised you, when you had seen the real Mark. His weakness brought out your protective spirit in full force. I think you finally understand why he dated Jessica."

"Maybe he recognized that fear drove her narcistic behavior, even though he had failed to identify the fear within himself." She paused. "I still love my husband in spite of our difficulties."

"Which means my daughter has matured since getting married. You both have. I enjoy watching you guys grow together. Anticipate bright days for your future."

"Hopefully with stability and peace. Our little one will soon be here. Can you imagine me as a mother?"

"Absolutely. Pamela Simon will cultivate a loving family." Anna removed the ice pack and replaced the stirrup ankle brace. "The bruises look worse, but the swelling hasn't increased. You, my dear, are on the mend."

"My eyes opened to less pain. Only one side of my body throbbed. I'm exhausted but feeling better."

"Traveling with intense pain depleted your energy reserves. Proper rest will replenish everything lost. Sleepy?"

"Um. A little bit." She hesitated, searching for the right words. "My mother-in-law's walking us to the car got me thinking. Mom, do you know anything about Celeste and Ed's relationship?"

"Not much. I believe they kept separate lives. Why do you ask?"

"Mark suspected they didn't enjoy a real bond. I guess he nailed the problem. They gave up on each other instead of working on their marriage."

"Life is messy," Anna said. "People are complicated."

"Living to please yourself after getting married is selfishness. Pure and simple. What about their son?"

"Both parents loved Mark even though they lived separate lives."

"My husband's family poses a dilemma for us. Maybe Mark misinterpreted their relationship. They could get along better now. He doesn't know for sure if there's a rift between them."

Anna laughed. "Unacceptance and avoidance are first cousins."

Pamela thought about the affidavit and wills. She tried to change position. "Ouch! I can't roll over without pain." Her eyes closed. "Father, why are you making Mark and me conquer this problem without each other's direct support? We work better when we're together."

Anna tucked a sheet underneath her daughter's chin. She smoothed the cover with both hands. "I'll supply an answer without you asking me. God demands your dependence on Him and not on other people."

"But I like the way we strengthen each other through our problems."

"Two people who become one are still each an individual child of God." Anna picked up the tray she had set on the nightstand, switching off the light when she reached the bedroom door. "Goodnight, babe. Get some sleep."

Tears slid over Pamela's cheeks. Her eyes adjusted to the moonlit room.

236

"Father, will Mark always need my compassion? His neediness makes it impossible to deal with his selfish behavior. Especially since I brought each challenge on myself by making the wrong decision." She sniffled several times, then tried to laugh. "I'm too drained of energy to think straight. Please strengthen my trust in Your constant love. Teach me how to cling to You."

Chapter Twenty-Four

The front door opened to Anna's smiling face. She hugged her son-in-law and beckoned him inside.

"So sorry to drop by this early," he said. "I wanted to check on Pam before heading to the hospital."

Anna closed the door behind them. "Surprise my daughter whenever you like. She took another dose of painkillers at four. Her sleep is more restful now. Another medication round begins in two hours."

"Then I won't wake her up to pain she can't relieve. A quick peek is all I need."

"Down the hall. First door on the right. Are you staying overnight or flying out today?"

"I booked a flight for tomorrow evening. I'll divide my time between here and the hospital."

Anna stood in the archway then followed behind him. "Can you eat breakfast with us?"

Mark turned around at the unexpected question.

His mother-in-law was a caring person.

He had been anxious about dropping by her house unannounced. Especially since she only answered one of his calls after Pamela arrived in Tulsa. She had probably cooled off overnight.

"I appreciate the kind offer, but Granddad arrived at the hospital minutes ago. He ate breakfast at home and took Mother and Gran breakfast sandwiches. I plan to take Mother and Gran out somewhere to stretch their legs when I get there."

"A great idea. They probably need the exercise after sleeping in a recliner and a cushioned window seat."

Mark nodded. "Their absence will give Father and Granddad privacy to reach an agreement about who will oversee both pawn shops going forward.

Something tells me Father will require a strong hand. I'll weigh in my opinion with him later."

Anna's hand covered her yawn. "Excuse me."

"You're tired," Mark said. "Pam probably slept more soundly than you did last night."

Her eyes twinkled. "Perhaps. Her sleep deepened after the second round of pills."

Nathan appeared in the kitchen doorway sipping coffee.

"I peeked in at Pam. She's looking more like her usual self today. Her appearance at the airport was shocking."

Mark's hands flexed at his side. "I saw the bruises and swelling on her wrist and ankle. Pam shouldn't have traveled alone."

"You married a capable woman." Nathan paused, staring at him. "On Friday, we invited the family over for grilled burgers and veggies today, so plan to eat with us since you'll be in town."

"Spend the night here," Anna said. "Give my daughter a longer visit."

I do not deserve this nice treatment. No wonder my wife has a forgiving heart.

"Thanks for accepting my unspoken request to spend the night." Swallowing hard, Mark hesitated. "Mom, don't bother taking lunch to the hospital. We've intruded on your time too much." He nodded at Nathan. "I'll check on Pam and then head out."

"Just let yourself out when you're ready to leave," Nathan said. He wrapped an arm around Anna's shoulder and ushered her down the hallway in the opposite direction.

Mark scrubbed a hand over his face before he grasped the doorknob. While taking deep breaths, he walked into the bedroom.

Pamela lay on the edge of the queen-sized bed. Maybe the pain was too intense to move farther onto the mattress. Scooting her over would wake her up and cause her needless pain.

As he studied his sleeping wife, their life together flashed before Mark's eyes. For eleven years he had paraded women in front of a friend who loved him. And wearing a bright smile, Pamela listened while Mark had broken her heart.

Then he tricked her into buying their house. Next, he let her travel alone while she was severely injured. Did Pamela view him as a man who used her when the situation benefitted him?

He had striven for seven months to earn her trust. Would her love survive his latest selfish act?

Mark knelt beside the bed. Moisture pooled in both eyes.

Why had he dated other women with an amazing lady available? He had cast his soulmate aside and dated women he hardly liked. Mark had never completely discarded Pamela. But he felt like he had held her captive.

One day his grandmother, who lived in Tacoma, had told Mark that the perfect girlfriend lived closer to his home.

Mark had thought she'd meant nearness in location. He learned at his wedding she had been referring to his sharing family values with a cherished friend.

He rested a hand on his wife's stomach, praying to keep her trust and love. Maybe she had undergone too much pain to reciprocate his endearments on their last phone call. He had told Pamela that he loved her and regretted letting her travel to Tulsa alone. She had said, "Goodnight. I'll talk to you tomorrow."

Pamela's pain-tinged voice had condemned Mark's miserable response to his family's crisis.

He lightly tapped her on the shoulder several times. The exhausted woman never moved a muscle. He felt tempted to wake her up. Instead, he stroked her cheek and prayed softly. Then he kissed her abdomen before he backed toward the door.

Grasping the doorknob, Mark sighed, shook his head, and left.

* * *

Celeste and Mark sat across the table from each other at a coffee shop. Neither one pretended they were eating. The tempting warm apple strudel remained untouched. Irene had stayed at the hospital, eating the breakfast sandwich her husband had brought her.

Mark required answers his mother withheld. Stall tactics at a crucial moment wouldn't make telling the story easier. She may as well tell him now.

Five more silent minutes passed before Mark had had enough.

"Waiting won't make the explanation clearer." He leaned on the chair cushion.

Celeste looked everywhere except at him. "A difficult discussion to have with friends is heartbreaking to have with my son."

"Yesterday our family reached the point of no return," Mark responded.

240

"We can't tread water or backtrack. I love you guys and want to make life easier for you both." He paused until she looked at him. "I have a wife. Our baby will be born in four months. I must make decisions regarding my family and my folks. The truth will help me chart the proper course."

Celeste studied her hands. Her body shifted in the seat.

"You and Father appear closer than ever," Mark prodded. "Are you restoring your relationship?"

"Ed and I were in love with love, and not with each other. People can't recapture emotions they never held."

The bomb drops and retreat tactics irritated Mark.

"Then why did you two bother with marriage? Neither of you care about traditional values." His lips compressed.

Her haughty gaze met his. "Remember who you're speaking with. You asked for this discussion. I did not."

Mark sighed. "Any disrespect is unintentional. Mother, you signed an affidavit renouncing rightful claims to Father's assets. You both will leave me everything you own. You relinquished future claims on his assets and accepted a fraction of his worth. Why?"

Celeste's forehead rested on her hand. "You might hate me, but you won't leave me destitute."

"Give me the full story," Mark said. "Father said the story wasn't his to tell."

"That's rich. At least he could've revealed his past sins." Her gaze darted around the room until she got up and sat beside her son. Celeste held his hand, hung her head, then released the grasp. "Ed and I stopped kidding ourselves when you moved out. You were the reason we got married and stayed together."

She hesitated. Her lips visibly trembled. "I began a four-year affair three weeks after you left the house. Johnny died two years ago. One year into the relationship, Ed threatened to tell you about Johnny unless I preserved your future."

"By giving up your marital rights? You had been married for almost twenty-five years by then."

"Ed wanted to insure no one but you would inherit Simon property. I opted to take the settlement."

"But you settled for pennies." Mark massaged his neck. "Earlier, you implied that Father wasn't faithful to you. Why did you forfeit what was rightfully yours?"

"Guilt. Your father played loose but not for keeps. He chose women living in Tulsa or Oklahoma City. He conducted his affairs away from South Town and Creek County."

Conducted? Have they stopped?

"Past tense? He's faithful to you now?"

"Ed has concentrated on business since I signed the affidavit."

Mark leaned forward. Faithfulness was a good foundation to rebuild their relationship.

"Right now, you both are faithful. Retract the agreement."

"Your father said we can't retract a legal document."

"Did you seek legal counsel from an attorney better than the one you had?"

"No need to. I won't fight Ed in court."

"Father wouldn't go that far," Mark said. "Mother? Did you seek legal advice to rescind the affidavit?"

Celeste shook her head and glanced away.

"Why not?" Asking difficult questions was necessary. Mark braced himself for the reply.

"Was Johnny the only affair you had?" he probed. "Do I know him?"

"No. He lived in Wagoner County. There wasn't anyone else. Ed believes me." She paused. "Loneliness overwhelmed me after you left. Even though you were hardly at home even when you lived there, I always knew you were coming back."

Mark could barely sit still. He cleared his throat as his mind roved. Somehow, his parents must resolve their differences today.

"How do you see your and Father's future?"

"We will stay together. Our salvation is real to us both. When I saw Ed unconscious in the emergency room … my place is with your father. Last night, Ed promised we'll live inside a home and not on a battlefield. You just smiled. What made you happy?"

"My parents are on the same page for once. From your disclosure, I'm surprised Father didn't suggest Pam sign a prenup."

"The first day Pam visited our house, Ed said, 'That girl's a keeper. I hope Mark appreciates his good luck.' "

Mark chuckled. "At fourteen? A mere freshman?"

"Ed charted her growth. When she turned eighteen, he said you might lose her if you failed to act. We knew Pam truly loved our son."

"I had no idea about either of your wishes. Or hers. Go figure."

Celeste surveyed her cold pastry and lukewarm drink. "Would you mind getting me a fresh apple strudel and coffee?"

Mark scooted back the chair. "Be right back." He initiated their hug for the first time in his life.

Celeste cried on her son's shoulder before he walked away.

He wiped his eyes before he reached the counter.

Mother and son had finally bonded. One month before his twenty-ninth birthday.

* * *

Pamela glanced across the room when the bedroom door opened. Struggling to sit up in bed, she moaned, falling flat on her back. She fingered her wrist, gazing at Anna. "I had vivid dreams and one ... oh well. Dreams aren't real."

On the nightstand Anna set down a tray holding a small tub filled with ice cubes, a glass of water, Pamela's meds, and a blood pressure monitor.

"I thought Skylar planned to drop by this morning," Pamela said.

"Your brother has come and gone. He checked your blood pressure readings and left. He refused to interrupt your snoring."

Her eyes widened. "I never snore."

"You did this morning. You performed quite a symphony."

Pamela's lips formed what she thought to be the perfect pout. "How long will you take my blood pressure? I don't need to have that done."

"The doctor thinks you do." Anna held up the blood pressure cuff. "Your arm, please."

Pamela pursed her lips and stretched out her arm.

Anna returned the blood pressure monitor to the tray. "One hundred over sixty. We are done with that. Happy?"

"Ecstatic. If I can hobble to the bathroom, then I can hobble to the living room and settle on the sofa."

"Or you can follow the doctor's instructions and go back to bed after using the bathroom."

"I suppose so," Pamela muttered. "Just wanted to keep you company."

"Don't worry about me. You get well."

Anna sat on the bed. "Here you go." She handed her daughter two caplets and a water-filled glass.

Pamela downed the pills and returned the glass to the tray. Her right side still throbbed. Dr. Brinkman had said pain and swelling would subside in five to six days. Too bad she could not take stronger medication.

"I know it's difficult maneuvering in bed, especially when you need to get up," Anna said. "Nathan's bringing a backrest home. That should make sitting up more comfortable." Anna gently unwrapped Pamela's wrist. "Tell me about the dreams."

Pamela smiled. "I had several consecutive dreams but will save my favorite one for last." She recounted the dreams while Anna iced her bruises and asked questions.

"All done. Now tell me your favorite dream." Anna replaced the final brace and grinned. "You just smiled for the first time since coming home."

"With good reason. I dreamed my husband came by here to see me. He stroked my face and prayed, and then he kissed my belly."

Her mother laughed. "Mark flew in this morning. He stopped by to see you before he went to the hospital to see Ed."

Pamela's head felt like it had exploded. "What! I went through that agonizing trip for nothing. He showed up anyway?"

"Or you can say, 'Although my husband flew to Tulsa late, he did arrive.' And I would've preferred Mark had taken my daughter to urgent care after her fall and then brought her home. But adults deal with facts instead of their wishes."

"Doing the right thing after the fact is okay? You didn't raise me with false values."

"You were there and didn't stop the madness. Last night, you admitted your kneecaps had moved when you touched your knees while at the hotel, but still you traveled alone—and without receiving medical attention. So, here we are. Your husband is spending the night here. Decide where you go from here."

"I don't intend to behave—" Pamela looked away. "Oh, forget I said anything. Maybe pain is talking for me."

Anna brushed the hair off Pamela's face. "You offered to come back without Mark, and he let you. Spread the blame evenly, if at all. No one is exempt from making bad decisions. Good or bad, we must take responsibility for our choices."

The ringing doorbell grabbed their attention. Anna rose, still staring at Pamela. "Mellie and the kids are here. They were coming straight over after church. Your niece and nephews will keep you occupied for now." Her eyes glittered as she studied Pamela. "Ed's going home this afternoon. Mark's flying back out tomorrow evening."

She left the door open as she exited the bedroom.

Pamela's left fist shook at the ceiling.

Mark is here, and his father is recovering. I guess Mark's dream team flew in after all. My pain-filled trip was for nothing. Mom said unacceptance and avoidance were first cousins. Does that make selflessness and foolishness related?

"Auntie Pam, may we come in?" Maeve shyly asked from the doorway.

Five pairs of eyes stared at Pamela. Their affectionate gazes overtook her bitterness. Words failed. Copious tears freely flowed down her cheeks. Many people loved her.

Anna hovered in the background. "Your aunt is mending. Just be careful of her injuries—and don't jump on the bed."

Mellie ushered the children into the room. "Give your aunt a hug, then work your puzzles in the family room."

The three children rushed into the room and spread around the bed.

McKinley reached the bed first. "Wow! Four braces. Can we see your bruises?"

"Parts of her leg and arm are purple," Myles said.

"They're black and blue too. No wonder she's crying," Maeve added.

Maeve pulled Pamela's toes. Thank God she had chosen the left side.

Pamela smiled through teardrops. "Sorry, guys. I hurt all over when anyone touches the braces."

Anna beckoned the children. "Give her a hug and head into the kitchen. Your mom said you can have a treat. Watermelon slices are on the table. Play with your puzzles in the family room after you finish eating."

The children hugged their aunt before stampeding out of the bedroom.

Melinda closed the door behind them. "Do you still think flying home without treatment was a wise move?"

Pamela shook her head.

"Happy your husband came home?" Melinda pressed.

"I'm upset with Mark for coming home. Everyone knows his itinerary except me. The one person who has a right to know."

Melinda pulled a chair beside the bed. "Maybe he reached a decision while you were airborne."

"We talked on the car ride home from the airport, while I waited to get X-rays, and before I fell asleep. Filling me in on any of those occasions would've worked."

"You were safe in Oklahoma. Why should he torment you further?"

"You mean, why should he admit I made an unnecessary hasty trip home? That's what happened."

Melinda leaned forward. "You both dropped the ball. You did not go to urgent care. And Mark didn't escort you home."

"Going to urgent care would've delayed my arrival. I wanted to reach South Town ASAP."

"Your bad decision caused you unnecessary complications. You should have received proper medical treatment before going home. A wheelchair should have waited for you when you disembarked the airplane. Doctors in South Town would've rechecked you at the hospital, and then you could've visited with Ed before Mom brought you here."

"Well, yeah. I know that now."

"You should have known it then," Melinda said. "After Mark brought you home, you would have stayed with Mom and Nathan. Ed's going home today would've allowed Mark to fly back to Dallas tomorrow. Which is what he plans to do."

"Hindsight. Pure and simple." Pamela felt her eyes tear up. "My father-in-law is going home today. Do you know anything about his condition?"

"Ace called Mark after we left church. Ed has constant adrenaline rushes. He needs to alter his lifestyle if he wants to avoid a death sentence." Pausing, Melinda leaned on the chair cushion. "Here's the deal. Ed must cut his workload and adopt a healthy lifestyle."

Pamela nibbled a fingernail. "Mark might quit Techno Plus. He's ready to leave, but we have my business and our personal bills to pay. I asked him not to quit his job."

Pamela felt like a selfish boor. She would give up Timeless Pastries in a heartbeat for her mother. Why would she expect Mark not to leave Techno Plus if it prolonged his father's life?

A loud sigh escaped Pamela's lips. "My father-in-law's health is more important than our house. Mark needs to take over the pawn shops and lessen his father's load. My husband will resign from Techno Plus, as he should."

"I'm sure Mark will discuss his options with you first."

Skepticism rose. Mark lacked a credible track record regarding honest and open communication.

"You think so, huh? We will see."

Melinda smiled. "For him, talking to you is a courtesy. He already knows you will agree with him, because it is the right thing to do. Ed can't eliminate work stress without his son's full-time help at the shops."

"Understood. However, I need my husband to really talk to me. I refuse to go any further with the way things are now."

"During the first year Ace and I were married, my mother bought me a scripture bookmark. Proverbs 14:1 is my lifesaver. I still refer to it. 'Every wise woman builds up her home, but a foolish one tears it down with her own hands.' Ace began compromising after I stopped fighting him. Until then, he saw my opposition as a winnable contest."

"I thought of that scripture at Mom's and Nathan's engagement brunch on the Sunday we met him," Pamela said. "It's significant that you're repeating it to me." Pamela twisted her wedding rings. "I've worked hard on this marriage. I overlooked the Jessica debacle and every negative thing Mark has done."

"Not dealing with your problems was a key mistake," Melinda said. "Because you swept over Mark's deceit, you couldn't forgive him nor forget the offense. You think about what happened whenever your husband makes any type of mistake."

Pamela rolled her eyes and then stared at Melinda. "I think I hear the children calling."

"Mom will answer her grandchildren if they do." Melinda shifted position. "When Jessica dropped Mark, you changed your life around to accommodate his freedom. Two things changed for Mark: He no longer saw Jessica, and he saw more of you."

Pamela's shoulders drooped as if an elephant hung around her neck.

She felt helpless for the first time ever. She felt useless while trapped in bed.

Had she volunteered to come home without Mark to help him or herself? Over the years, accommodating him had verified her usefulness. Did she still operate in "please need me" mode? Making herself indispensable had never earned his love. He discovered he loved her after he thought he might lose her.

The backside of her hand covered her eyes. "I blamed Jessica when Mark didn't show interest in my business. A year after she dumped him, he still didn't care. He learned Timeless Pastries' name by default the day after we came home from our honeymoon. I got his undivided attention after discovering his deception. And then he held my simple business concept hostage to his ideas."

"That's because you let him do it. An only child who jockeyed for attention became a selfish person. But he's working on himself." Melinda rose. "But now, you should rest. Ace is dropping by for dinner. Think about our discussion. See you later."

Melinda smiled at Pamela when she reached the door, then she left the bedroom.

Pamela muttered prayers for several minutes.

Brushing aside tears, she texted Mark.

Chapter Twenty-Five

Mark's cell phone pinged as he tailed Celeste across town while he drove his father home from the hospital. He debated pulling over to read the message. *The text isn't news about my wife. The person would have called me if something had happened to Pam. My wife is fine. Better deal with my folks.*

He aimed to solidify plans for his parents' future before reaching their house. His grandfather had insisted that Ed had agreed to adopt a lighter workload. Granddad knew his combustible-temper son better than Mark.

Yet the solid assurance of Fred Simon did not satisfy Mark. Doubts remained about his father being reasonable concerning business.

He glanced at Ed's solemn expression. "The doctor said you're sidelined from work this week. Granddad said you agreed to work four-hour weekdays and one store per day going forward." He paused, then he continued when Ed didn't speak. "He and I will oversee both store locations until I take over. Are you on board with that scenario?"

"You deserve a say in your future business," Ed said. "Consider me the board chairman and yourself the CEO. I will establish policies and make decisions on major issues. Agreed?"

Mark chuckled. "Driving. Can't shake hands."

"A verbal 'yes sir' will suffice. When will you resign from Techno Plus?"

"Today I will turn in my two week notice." He felt his father's gaze boring through him.

"You're quitting your job in two weeks? Is Pam in agreement with your timetable?"

"My wife loves you guys." Slowing down, Mark turned on the street where the Simons lived. "She will tweak my plans to her satisfaction, but she will agree. Family is her life. Your daughter-in-law would give up Timeless Pastries for her mother if she needed to."

"No doubt she would. I am glad you'll be in agreement. Every marriage requires a firm foundation to succeed."

Mark chuckled to himself. *Thanks for breaking the ice on my next topic. Now to get the desired response from father without making him angry.*

"I agree that marriages need a durable base. And speaking of firm foundations, what about Mother? I know the full story regarding the marital lapses of you both. What changes will you make?"

Ed gazed straight ahead. "Celeste grows on you. She stays. Your mother and I talked during the night." He paused, leaning on the seat cushion. Laughter filled his voice when he continued. "Your grandma snores."

Mark laughed. "I might pass that tidbit on." He glanced at Ed, carefully choosing his words. "You and Mother?"

"We will give our marriage a real chance. Our son and daughter, plus their future family, are worth the effort. Besides, obedience is a God command. Need I say more?"

"No, sir. I hear you."

Mark pulled up to the curb, exited the car, and hurried to the passenger side. He opened the car door for Ed, holding his father's upper arm.

The disgruntled man shook off his hand. "I'm not an invalid. Back off."

"Then you will walk the Amazing Facts Trail with me four days per week, beginning this Saturday?"

Mumbling to himself, Ed hobbled over cobblestones to the steps, while Mark glided beside him, ready to catch him if he slipped.

Celeste had reached the house first and waited for them on the front porch.

Ed glared at his wife. "I survived. Call off the watchdog."

"Are we walking four days per week?" Mark repeated.

"Yes. We will walk the trail. Go see about your wife. I don't require tucking into bed."

Celeste unlocked the front door. "Come inside, Ed. Mark, he's feeling better. Leave us in peace."

Ed scowled at her and then at his son. He stomped into the house. "See you Saturday morning."

Mark followed his mother inside and closed the door. "I planned to discuss menus with Beatrice before going."

Ed mumbled under his breath, although Mark caught a few adjectives.

"You had better be joking," Ed said. "Hire a cook if you want to talk to one. Goodbye. Take care of your wife."

His father retreated down the hallway.

Mark winked at his mother. "Granddad will visit both shops daily. I'll divide my after-work time between both locations until I take over operations in two weeks."

Celeste's eyebrows drew together. "You're leaving Techno Plus in two weeks?"

Mark nodded. "Here's the scenario."

He explained his conversations with his grandfather and father while Celeste asked questions.

"Please join us on our walks," he said after he answered the last question.

His mother stared at him. "I am speechless. That man has never behaved this reasonably." Celeste studied Ed, who had circled back to the foyer. "You accepted a reasonable work and exercise schedule?"

"Try waking up attached to tubes and with medical equipment alarms going off." He turned Mark toward the door. "Goodbye, son. Take care of your wife."

"I'll drop by again tonight," Mark said as he stepped onto the porch.

He waved as his father shut the door.

Reading the text message on the walk to his car, he replied before driving off.

* * *

Three hours later, Mark parked his car in front of Flowers for Every Occasion. He left the store carrying a yellow rose bouquet. The short detour fortified his confidence. Earlier he had conferenced with Techno Plus's founder and board chairman, and the CEO. Now, only one task remained unchecked on his lengthy to-do list for that day. Tomorrow morning, Mark would talk with both pawn shop managers, and the pawn shop's longest employee, Bertie Townsend.

For the first time in his life, he walked a straight pathway on solid ground.

* * *

Resting all day relaxed more than Pamela's body. Her spirit rejuvenated, and her mind came alive. She reread the text message she had sent to Mark.

My weaknesses are your strengths and vice versa.
Father and Mother need our help.
Find a way to resign before you leave South Town.

Eyes squinting, she read his noncommittal reply.

No more self-pity. I am a blessed man.
God, my wife, my family, and her family love me.

* * *

Laughter outside his mother-in-law's house drew Mark to the backyard. Cheerful people dotted the landscape. A steady breeze set the perfect ambiance for the get-together. Three young girls jumped on a trampoline. Three boys swung on a wooden swing set. In two years, Mark's son would join the fun.

Pamela lay alone shut inside a bedroom. Time for his wife to join the fun. Well, at least for five minutes.

Mark waved at the group. Scaling the steps onto the deck, he sailed inside the house.

The doorbell rang when he reached the kitchen. Gift in hand, he headed that way.

* * *

Outside noise drifted through the open window. The children's laughter fascinated Pamela. This time next year, little Tanner Kennedy would join the fun in a baby swing. Her thoughts drifted to her husband. Where was Mark? She had hoped he would drop by for lunch. They needed to talk sooner rather than later.

Where are you? Melinda said your father was released from the hospital at eleven. Don't you feel the need to talk to me?

The doorbell rang as she was in mid-thought. Pamela heard muffled voices talking in the foyer.

* * *

Mark opened the front door and stepped aside.

"Hi Lavine, Stan. Come in, friends. I just arrived."

The smiling couple stepped inside the foyer.

Mark closed the door behind them.

"Lavine, thanks for setting up the meeting with Carl and Les on short notice," Mark said. "I passed on your suggestion for my replacement."

Lavine smiled. "Thank you for agreeing with my selection."

"For the next two weeks I'll act as a consultant and let her handle the job. Stan, I can upgrade the skydiving school's computer system next month."

"No rush. I understand you've got a few things on your plate."

Mark nodded. "Is that exquisite potted orchid for my wife?"

Lavine pointed to the yellow rose bouquet he held. "Like-minded twice in one day. We're on a roll, boss."

Anna appeared in the living room doorway. "Hello, everyone. I'm Anna Hendrix, Mark's mother-in-law."

Mark moved closer to Anna. "Mom, this is my remarkable administrative assistant and her husband, Lavine and Stan Tibbs."

Lavine offered the flowerpot to Anna. "We came to cheer up Pam. Hope she's up for visitors today."

"What a lovely bloom. It's beautiful." Anna placed the pot on a hall table. "Pam will love the gift and your visit. Join us for dinner. Then you can say hello to Pam."

"We'd love to join your dinner," Lavine said.

"Then follow me." Anna ushered their guests to the deck. She called over her shoulder to Mark, "Pam had her meds two hours ago. She's due for another icing in an hour."

"Thanks for all you do," Mark told her retreating back. He listened as Anna introduced their guests.

Taking a deep breath, he turned away. His steps slowed as he neared the guest bedroom. Exhausted, he hesitated outside the door, then he grabbed the doorknob. Last night, Mark had accepted responsibility for his marriage. He owed Pamela the same constancy she had always provided him. It was time to brave the lion's den.

* * *

The sound of footsteps had padded down the hallway and stopped outside the bedroom door.

Pamela knew Mark was on the other side.

Lord, let us have a heartfelt discussion.

Pamela licked her lips and finger combed her hair.

The door opened. Her husband's head poked inside the room. He entered and set on the nightstand a beautiful peach vase filled with yellow roses.

The gorgeous bouquet brought back happy and sad memories.

Pamela sniffed the air, smiling. "These flowers are beautiful."

"Lavine and Stan just came by to say hello. They're staying for dinner. Mom suggested they visit with you later."

She cleared her throat as tears filled her eyes. "Glad they came over."

"Feeling better?" Mark asked. "You look more rested than you did this morning."

"I feel like a dream compared to yesterday." She patted the bed beside her. "You should've woken me up when you stopped by."

"The lady I observed required sleep." He brushed his lips across her mouth. Pulling back an inch, he studied her expression. "I will always love you as you love me. We will build our family on our love."

She could feel teardrops overflowing her eyes.

Mark rounded the bed and slowly stretched out on it beside her.

"Straight talk?"

Pamela nodded through tears. "I can't think of a better way to have a discussion."

"Your compassion has always encouraged me." He paused, sighed, then brushed a finger across her cheek. "I survived eleven years of dating the wrong women while limiting my soul mate to biweekly lunches. You are my past, present, and future."

He hesitated as her shoulders heaved. "I endured an unhappy lifestyle and never realized love had met me twice a week."

Rapid blinking couldn't contain the tear avalanche. Had she finally reached a breakthrough with Mark?

Lord, please let it be so.

"People assumed I was a trailblazer who charted his own course. My only thought was of survival."

Her body trembled as she listened. Pamela lost total control over her emotions.

"My wife supplied hope, clearer thoughts, and a relationship with God. I failed myself. Success follows His pathway. Teenage Pam never mentioned Jesus, yet she lived according to His word."

"I had good examples," she said through tears. "Mom and both sets of grandparents practiced godly principles. They weather life's storms with Bible study and prayer. I plan to follow their example."

Mark's thumb stroked her cheek. "For eleven years I basked in your love but never reciprocated real affection. Last night, I understood why."

Her heart seized. Knowledge was good if acted upon.

254

Raising on his elbow, Mark kissed her mouth and both cheeks. "I trusted your affection soon after we met. You liked me. I'd sought love since childhood and found acceptance in you. But I failed to appreciate the depths of your feelings for me."

He kissed tears off her damp cheeks then cupped her face in his hands. "Thank you for loving me without question. Please forgive my deception about where Jessica lived. And my lack of apology until now. I'm sorry, love. You have always deserved much better than I provided." He hesitated. "And I don't dislike your friends. They know you better than I do even though I've known you longer than most of them have. I hate playing catch up with your life."

Words escaped Pamela. Her husband had issued a genuine apology with an explanation. She was amazed. But she also realized Mark hadn't explained why he had come home from Dallas and what's next on his agenda.

He stared at the ceiling. "I let you travel home alone without seeing a doctor. Please forgive my selfish attitude. I requested backup in Dallas before I reached the hotel so I could come home." He turned toward her. "I've had a hard time looking at your family."

She closed her eyes to control her response. "They blame me far more than they blame you. I felt like a teenage numbskull."

"You mother didn't say a word, but Ace and your father expressed their true feelings."

"Well, they usually do." Pamela paused. "Um, do you have any more news to share? How are your parents?"

Mark gave detailed information about his father's health, his parents' relationship, Techno Plus, and the pawn shops.

He stroked her arm when the conversation waned. "Any more questions?"

"None that I can think of now. How do you feel about these sudden changes?"

Mark turned onto his back. "Good question. I will deal with each one. In two weeks, Techno Plus will become a fond memory." He slid from the bed and looked down at her. "Someone gussied you up. Your mom?"

"My hair and I are squeaky clean. Forget about a medal, that woman deserves a crown."

"Tonight she can sleep straight through. I will take care of my wife. Are you up to visiting in the backyard for five minutes?"

Her cheeks dimpled when she laughed. "Yes! I get to go outside ahead of schedule. Just ignore Skylar when he butts in."

Mark chuckled. "I'm sure he will. Ready?"

"Sure am. Though I can't use my crutches until my wrist heals, so I'm not sure how I'll get there."

"Perfect. I'll carry you—and steal kisses while I do."

"Ooh. Please be gentle. I should stamp 'fragile' across my forehead."

Mark scooped her into his arms when she tried to sit upright.

"Against all hope, Abraham in hope believed," Mark whispered. "You quoted that scripture to me when I got the Techno Plus job."

"That verse helped me more that day than it did you." She brushed her forehead against his cheek. "I love you, Mark Simon. Thank God He answers prayers with a yes, no, or wait." She smiled when he looked confused. "Throughout the years I kept the confident hope you were a wait and not a no."

Mark smothered his wife's face with kisses. "God delayed your answer long enough to grow me up. There's still more to learn."

"For us both." Pamela lay her cheek on his chest.

Thank you, Lord, for growing us up together.

Chapter Twenty-Six

November. One month later.

Pamela hung up the phone with Bertie and sat on her desk. Enough for Everyone s longest-working employee had come through for her once again. Bertie had advanced Celeste and Ed's party strategies according to plans. She produced a problem Mark must solve before he left work. His surprise birthday party remained on target. Her husband expected a quiet dinner at After Hours, not the large affair the Simons had planned in the Timeless Pastries banquet hall.

Pamela had taken a balloon bouquet to his job that morning. At noon, a courier delivered fifty Timeless Pastries lemon custard cupcakes to both pawn shop locations. The gifts were her peace offering for being abrupt with Mark yesterday evening when he kicked against her helping a friend move to Texas this weekend. Although his reaction was over the top, his opposition seemed reasonable on second thought. She was doing physical therapy and still had a slight limp from last month's accident in Dallas.

Still, Pamela had lost it when Mark followed her through the house, blasting what he had termed as her careless behavior. As if a six-month-pregnant woman had to be told not to lift heavy items. And, of course, she would take her cane with her.

Pamela had accepted the invitation because she wanted to spend time with her friends before the baby arrived. But at work this morning, she had realized that the idea of her going on a trip had probably stirred up Mark's memories of her disastrous Dallas trip.

Both spouses were learning to compromise in their positions. Pamela agreed not to go and stay home.

Now Pamela carried the proverbial ball to further the Simons' party plans. A manufactured problem would force her husband to pick her up at Timeless Pastries after work.

Considering her options, she reached for her cell phone and smiled when Mark answered the call on the first ring.

"Hello, hon. Am I forgiven for my obstinate attitude last night?"

"I accepted your apology before you gave it this morning."

"Good. I need a huge favor."

"What do you need, love?"

She could almost see his grin. "A lift. My car's acting spotty. I don't want to get stuck somewhere other than home. Could you please pick me up at six thirty? Remember our date at After Hours is at eight o'clock sharp."

"That doesn't give us enough time to get ready. Why are you working late? What happened?"

"Actually, everything is going well. I'll fill you in later. What time are you leaving the store?"

"In enough time to pick up my wife from work at six thirty. We're swamped here. The ever-efficient, never-put-a-foot-wrong Bertie handed me a mind-blowing problem this afternoon. What's going on with your car?"

She smiled to herself. *Love that Bertie.* "The engine's acting a little funny."

"Don't drive the car even if the engine starts. Wait until I get there. Promise?"

"Yes, sir." She paused, smiling. "Thanks for loving me even when I kick against your concern. Love you, hubby."

"I love you back," he said before hanging up.

Limited time remained to pull off a birthday celebration for a much-loved man.

* * *

Only Pamela's car was parked outside the shop when Mark pulled into the lot.

The shop door sprung open before he reached the building. He drew Pamela into his arms. Cuddling her closer, his lips brushed her cheek. He couldn't resist patting her belly. She was rounding out nicely. Her fresh-scrubbed scent tickled his nose in a pleasing way. He squeezed her body against his as close as possible before he loosened the hold.

Mark had found his way home and had found peace within himself.

Pamela wriggled in his arms, kissed his chest, then smiled at him.

"Sometimes I pinch myself to ensure I'm awake. I enjoy being cherished by you."

258

Mark gazed into the eyes of a smitten woman. Double blinking, he captured the image to view for a lifetime. This moment engraved itself onto his heart forever.

She clasped his hand. "Come inside and see my surprise."

Pamela led him toward the darkened banquet hall.

Lights came on when he entered the room.

"Surprise!!! Happy Birthday, Mark!!!"

Mark froze. At least sixty joyous people were cheering at once. His gaze settled on both sets of grandparents standing with Celeste and Ed. Also, his aunt and uncle, along with his cousins and their children, made the trip from Tacoma. He smiled when Bertie waved at him.

He wrapped an arm around Pamela's waist, urging her closer. He was grateful that she still adored Mark despite their clumsy beginning.

"Spotty car?" he said with a smirk. "I know you hate lying. Thanks for caring enough to throw red herrings."

"I don't deserve your praise," she said. "I preferred a quiet family affair at home. Your parents preempted those plans. They arranged what they termed as their son's first authentic birthday tribute from his doting parents."

Mark glanced at his folks. Celeste dotted her eyes with tissues. Ed gleamed with pride. His parents' partially contained exuberance undid Mark's composure. They organized an event that included his family, friends, and co-workers. Their priorities had truly soared higher.

Standing on her tiptoes, Pamela wrapped her arms around his neck, whispering in his ear, "Happy birthday, Mark. Affairs of the heart will win the prize every time."

The End

A Note From E. C. Jackson

"The Write Way: A Real Slice of Life" is the slogan on my website and Facebook author page. If every person reading my book feels connected to the characters, my job is done.

The Confident Hope is the fourth book in the hope-themed series. And in some ways, it was the most difficult one to write. This time I fell short of my goal to publish one book per year. Life happens, as it did to me on this go-round.

Book five, the final book in the standalone stories, is coming soon. *Hopefully, it will be published in 2021.*

If you liked reading this novel, please check out my other books and leave a review on the site of the retailer of your choice.

Thank you for your time!

Listed below are descriptions of my previous hope-themed books.

Book One: *A Gateway to Hope*
Nikhol "Neka" Lacey and James Copley
Twenty-one-year-old Neka is a bit of an introvert, she also happens to be stunningly beautiful. When she discovers her friend James is about to be dumped, she sees the perfect opportunity to escape from her quiet life. Can she summon the courage to leave it all behind?

James Copley comes from a ruthless family. It's rubbed off. Years ago, he disengaged from his brother's smear campaign, but now his father has offered him an ultimatum, "Get married or lose your seat at the table." Plotting to stamp his design on the family business, he proposes to a woman, even though he doesn't love her. But his carefully laid plans start to unravel when she leaves him on the day she's due to meet his family. Could years of planning his comeback vanish with her departure?

A possible solution comes in an unexpected form: Neka. She's not only a friend, but the daughter of his benefactor. And she's right there, offering to support him. But will her support stretch to marriage? He attempts to win her over to his plan but collides with her powerful father who wants to leverage the situation for his own gain.

In their fight for survival and love, they are forced to face some uncomfortable truths. Can they overcome thwarted dreams and missed chances to find true love, or does forcing destiny's hand only lead to misery?

Book Two: *A Living Hope*
Sadie Cummings and Kyle Franklin

It was a match made in heaven. Or so everyone thought. Sadie Mae Cummings is all set to marry her childhood sweetheart, Kyle, when she is assigned to tutor Lincoln, the new college football running back. This sophomore phenomenon has all the girls on campus knocking on his door. But Sadie isn't interested in his advances.

Lincoln's overblown ego doesn't take well to being shunned, and he resolves to make Sadie his own. He pursues her relentlessly, until finally Kyle finds himself shut out of Sadie's life, with their shared future crumbling around him.

After two years, Sadie's relationship with Lincoln ends, and she is left having to put the pieces of her life back together. She desires nothing more than to recapture her relationship with Kyle. He has stayed true to the dreams they had planned together, living the vision even without Sadie by his side.

When she moves back to her hometown, she labors to rekindle their love. But things have changed, and Kyle has moved on. Sadie quickly discovers how hard it is to rebuild burned bridges.

Follow Sadie's story as she fights for a chance to restore broken dreams. Will love endure?

Book Three: *The Certain Hope*
Tara Simpkins and Luke Cassidy

Love at first sight. It's every girl's dream. But Tara Simpkins is finding out it's not as easy as it seems. Is this truly the man God sent to be her husband, or is she just desperate to escape her loneliness? The recent loss of both parents has left her reeling, and close friends don't think she's in any position to make major life decisions. She and her new-found love are convinced they can live happily ever after in the home of their dreams. His family thinks he's moving way too fast and might disappoint the kind-hearted woman he's fallen head over heels for. And then there's Leah. Leah is supposed to be part of his past, but what if she decides she's his future? Tara's match made in Heaven may be over before it truly begins.

Pajama Party: The Story
Companion book to *A Living Hope*

Pajama Party: The Story is adapted from a play I wrote many years ago.

Most sleepovers are simple. Food, fun, and pillow fights. But sixteen-year-old Karen Duncan has bigger plans for her slumber party. Family troubles have changed her over the past year, and she's no longer the petty, selfish girl she used to be. Now she's ready to shake things up with her friends. The guest list comes as a surprise to some and a slap in the face to others. This popular girl has invited some not-so-popular guests. Even more shocking, she's left out some of the girls she's hung out with since middle school.

Diane and Evette are outsiders, nervous about being stuck in a house with the same girls who tease them at school. Kathy, Lisa, and Joann come to the party with the confidence of the in-crowd, but they're masking inner turmoil that is bound to surface. Sandy and Angela are usually the voices of reason … usually. And then there's Linda, the friend that got away. She may not ever forgive the girls who abandoned her years ago. Karen hopes to change her mind.

Her agenda is ambitious, and it could spell disaster. But Karen is convinced God will use this party to spark a new beginning for everyone involved. This companion book to *A Living Hope* gives us the inspired story Sadie Cummings wrote for the girls of Shiatown.

About the Author

E. C. Jackson began her writing career with the full-length play *Pajama Party*. For three and a half years she published the *Confidence in Life* newsletter for Alpha Production Ministries, in addition to writing tracts and devotionals. Teaching a women's Bible study at her church for eleven years led naturally to her current endeavor of writing inspirational romance novels and teen and young adult fiction. Her mission: spiritual maturity in the body of Christ through fiction.